Hope Toler Dougherty

Rescued Hearts

For Sheila!
Blessings!
Hope Toler Dougherty
Jeremiah 29:11

MANTLE ROCK
PUBLISHING LLC
MantleRockPublishingLLC.com

©2017 Hope Toler Dougherty

Published by Mantle Rock Publishing LLC
2879 Palma Road
Benton, KY 42025
http://mantlerockpublishing.com

Printed in the United States of America

ISBN 978-1-945094-23-1 Print Book
       978-1-945094-24-8 EBook

Library of Congress Control Number: 2017912933
Mantle Rock Publishing, Benton, KY

Cover by Diane Turpin, dianeturpindesigns.com

Published in association with Jim Hart of Hartline Literary Agency, Pittsburgh, PA

Dedication

To the men and women in all the different uniforms who stand in the gap between good and evil. Thank you for your sacrifice. I appreciate your service.

Acknowledgements

Writing is a solitary pursuit much of the time. Growing a story from an idea to a published book, however, takes many people.

For this first attempt at Romantic Suspense, I attended the Writers' Police Academy and interviewed law enforcement officers in Johnston County, North Carolina. Many, many thanks to Sheriff Steve Bizzell, Detective Charlotte Fournier, Captain-Narcotics (Retired) Craig Fish, and Sergeant Jordan Haddock. These people discussed their jobs and guns and criminals. They patiently and generously shared their expertise without making me feel stupid. I am grateful. Any errors concerning the suspense part of the story are wholly mine.

Others who contributed to *Rescued Hearts* include the following:

Lane Dougherty—He and his college ROTC buddies allowed me to experience guns firsthand at some of their target practices. He also proved that a heavy chair, when resting on a strong, young man's palm, could keep the young man pinned to the floor. Thanks for humoring your mom, buddy.

Early readers—Kevin and Hattie Dougherty, Danielle Haddock, and Krista Reisdorf Berns found grammar and storyline problems. Fresh eyes are always good.

Friends—Ideas come from everywhere. Sometimes a conversation at a YMCA family camp, or a book club, or a Bible study, or choir practice inspires a scene. I may not speak, but I'm listening.

Prayer warriors—Many people pray for me, and I covet those prayers. One special lady, ninety-six-year-old WWII ARMY nurse, Barbara Duffy, is one of those people. I hope to visit and bring some chocolate ice cream soon, Ms. Barbara!

Family—A sweet group of people claim me. Although they call me out on whatever I need to be called out on, they give solid support with a hefty dose of cheerleading. Most of all, they accept my particular brand of crazy and pray for me every day. I am blessed.

Jim Hart of Hartline Literary Agency—Thank you for continuing to believe in my writing. I appreciate your hard work.

Mantle Rock Publishing—Thank you to Kathy Cretsinger for being excited about the story, Diane Turpin for the beautiful cover, and Pam Watts Harris who broke the news to me that Chicago Manual of Style now recommends no comma before "too" at the end of a sentence. I'm still recovering from the disappointment.

Finally, I'm forever in awe of the God Who allows me to walk on this writing journey. He saw the desire of my heart and granted it. My cup runs over with blessings.

Chapter 1

The air changed, rustling a cool breeze that ruffled wisps of hair escaping from under Mary Wade Kimball's bike helmet. She relished the drop in temperature as she detoured from the paved road onto a sandy path. Enjoying fresh air and nature was the perfect antidote to the four-hour drive from Charlotte in her little Honda.

She smiled to herself. The quick bike ride should smooth any remaining cricks her time in the spa chair had failed to erase. Glancing at the pedals, she wiggled her toes, tipped with a new hot pink color, Feelin' Cheeky.

Thank you, Agnes, for the pedicure. Just what I needed today.

Clouds formed on the horizon to her right. "I see you, clouds. I'll be back to Agnes' in a few minutes. Plenty of time before the storm."

A hurricane churned several miles off the coast, but forecasters warned that although the projected path fell safely north of the local area, the weather could be affected with wind and rain as soon as tonight or tomorrow morning. The cooler temperatures signaled stormy weather might arrive sooner rather than later.

Pushing the pedals, she slogged the wheels through the sand, feeling a burn in her thighs. A puff of air tainted by a nearby cow pasture assaulted her nose. She pedaled harder to leave the sharp odor behind and noticed an abandoned farmhouse nestled into the edge of trees at the end of an overgrown path.

A movement caught her eye.

Tangled in a honeysuckle vine threading through a hydrangea bush mewed a tuxedo kitten. Prickles on the back of her neck rose, similar to when a stranger had held open the grocery store door for her earlier in the afternoon. She'd smiled and thanked him, but he remained silent, assessing her with the most unusual eyes she'd ever seen.

Although her memory colored them silver, they must have been light blue. Right? A shiver shimmied up her spine at the recollection. Who was he? Agnes had never mentioned a newcomer in town, and if anybody would know, Agnes would.

Someone like that guy sticks in a mind. A few locks of sandy brown hair hooked behind his ears. An elastic captured the rest in a three- or four-inch ponytail. In his worn, wrinkled clothes, he stood well over six feet tall with the girth of a wide receiver. The beginnings of a scruffy beard, overtaking what was once a goatee, covered his face. Formidable. Unyielding. No-nonsense.

Maybe a little scary.

She shook her head to clear the unsettling image and turned her bike toward the stranded kitty. Black and white kittens had always been her favorite. When she freed it—and no mother could be found—should she adopt it and take it home? Could she?

One more thing on her plate. One more expense when, truth be told, she didn't have room or money for one more magazine purchase, much less a live thing with vet bills.

She dismounted the bike and dropped the kickstand. Time to revisit her budget. Again. But first…rescue the kitten. "Hey, sweetie. Can't you get free? Let me help you." She pulled on the vine, and the kitten cried louder.

"You won't scratch me, will you?"

"Easy, little kitty. I want to help, okay?" She tugged at another vine, but it tightened around the left back paw. The kitten's movements ramped from frustrated to panicked. Front claws slashed the skin of her left hand. "Ow." She paused to flex her fingers and draw in the sweet honeysuckle scent. Intent on the rescue, she leaned in again. "Come on. I'm trying to help. Let me—"

A hand closed around her mouth and her waist, yanking her away from the hydrangea, the kitten, and one of her flip-flops. Rough fingers shoved up against her nose. The pungent stench of tobacco, grime, and sweat smothered her frantic gasps for breath.

෨)෨)ᘓᘖ

Legs and arms flailing, Mary Wade fought against the brawny form dragging her up the front porch stairs. A hard shove landed her on gritty linoleum. She scrambled to stand, but a fist caught her jaw, knocking her back to the floor. The sharp taste of blood trickled into her mouth. She stayed on the floor but rose to sitting. Breathing took effort with the panic blooming in her chest.

"Looky what I found, Skeet." A cackle froze her insides.

She spread her hands against the gritty floor, begged her mind to work. What is happening? Got to get out. Get out. She inched toward the door.

"What've you done, boy? We don't need nothing else to worry about." The second man, older than the one who'd grabbed her, stood with his hands on his hips, shaking his head. "You crazy?"

"Yeah. Goin' stir crazy in this dump. Phone don't work half the time. No TV. Missy here'll be just the ticket for some fun." Another cackle.

Heart pounding so hard her chest hurt, she slid another inch.

"Why'd you hit her for?"

"She needs to know who's in charge." He stretched his arms over his head.

"You ain't in charge. Just wait till Doc gets back. Wonder what he'll do when he sees what you've done?" The man shook his head. "You ain't thinking, boy."

"Am too. I'm sick of waitin' and twiddlin' my thumbs with y'all. I want some fun, and she's the one to give it." He turned his attention back to Mary Wade. "Hey. Get away from that door."

The younger man grabbed her again, dragging her back to the center of the room. "She's feisty. My shins got the bruises to prove it. Already trying to escape. No problem. We'll take care of that. Don't move." He rummaged through a duffel bag near a canvas camp chair.

Think. Think. How to get out of here? Her gaze darted from wall to wall. A door off the little kitchen in the back. Three camp chairs. Dirty, limp curtains hung on two windows. A duffel bag. Two back packs. A row of empty, crushed beer cans. Nothing to help her. She squeezed her arms around her waist.

He returned to Mary Wade with plastic zip ties in his hands. "Put your hands behind your back."

The words knocked around her dazed brain. She hesitated.

He growled. "I said, 'put your hands back,' woman."

Twisting one arm behind her, he caught her wrist against her spine and crushed the other on top. The zip tie sliced into her flesh as he tightened it, locking it in place. She cried out at the searing sensation ripping through her shoulder.

He squatted in front of her. "Don't like it rough, huh?" He stretched closer and grinned, revealing a gap where an incisor once stood. Plaque bordered the gums on his remaining crooked teeth. Rancid breath rushed her nose. "Well, I do." He reared his palm back, slapped her across her face, and howled.

Dear God in Heaven, help me.

ဢၢ၁ၢၢ

"Dusty, quit being so rough. She's scared to death." Skeet rubbed the back of his neck.

The man called Dusty hiked up the waistband of his faded jeans. "She shouldn't be scared. Naw." He cracked his knuckles. "She ought to be excited. She'll have the time of her life."

Skeet sniggered. "I can't believe you kidnapped a girl. Doc is going to be royally—"

"He's gonna be thankful for something to do besides staring at your goofy face and carving them stupid pieces of wood. In fact, he'll be so delighted, he'll probably promote me. Let me go to town for supper next time." Dusty laughed, rummaging through the duffel bag again. He drew out a wadded-up bandanna.

He crouched beside her, flicked the bandanna beside her ear. She flinched at the popping sound. A ripe odor from the cloth clouded her nose. "Ha. Nice. You're learning." He grabbed her shoulder. "Be still." He unsnapped the strap under her chin, freeing the helmet to bounce off the floor. "That's better. Look at that red hair, Skeet. Not half bad. She'll do in a pinch. And we're in a pinch, for sure."

She closed her eyes and pulled in ragged streams of stale air. Physical abuse. Emotional abuse. Promised sexual abuse. A surreal, nightmarish ending to the beginning of her week's vacation.

Fabric violated her mouth, stinging her busted lip and intensifying the ache of the earlier slap. Her stomach roiled against the filthy gag. Dusty snatched the ends into a knot, distorting her jaw.

Tires crunched in the gravel driveway, and an engine silenced behind the house. A car door slammed.

Skeet folded his arms across his chest. "Doc's back. You better get ready to talk quick, Dusty."

Another one? Her heartbeat kicked into half-time.

The back door screeched opened. A man burst through carrying a handful of plastic grocery bags and tossed them onto the kitchen counter. "Where'd that bike come—?" He swung his gaze to the center of the room. "What the—?"

The same man who'd held the door for her. The same silver eyes assessed the situation now but without one indication of recognition.

He turned those eyes on Skeet. "Explain. And it'd better be good."

Skeet shook his head. "No, siree. It's Dusty's story."

Dusty puffed out his chest. "She was snooping around the front porch, and I got her. I got her for us."

The new man scrubbed a hand across his chin. "Are you crazy? Do you realize what you've done?" Frustration or anger strained against the cords in his neck. Although his voice remained calm, a muscle in the side of his cheek twitched. He ran his hand through his hair and pulled out the elastic from the ponytail.

Dusty slapped his hands on his hips. "Yeah. I'm about crazy staying in this cracker box twenty-four seven with you two. God sent this present for us right to our doorsteps." His mouth stretched into a wicked grin. "If Skeet don't want to, you and me can share."

The man they called Doc crossed the room and knelt on one knee in front of her. His eyes searched her face, holding her stare for several seconds. He reached toward the gag, and she butted her head into his chest, knocking him backward on the floor.

"Uh huh. I told you she was feisty." Dusty hooted and clapped beside Skeet.

Her stomach tightened. *Dear God. What now?*

Gritting his teeth, Doc righted himself and made eye contact with her again. He lunged toward her, grabbing under her arm and jerking her to stand. "That's how you want to play it, huh?"

She shivered at the promised threat and closed her eyes.

He dragged her across the floor and shoved her into the side room. She stumbled and hit the floor, a thin sleeping bag the only thing to break her fall.

At the threshold, he turned back to the men. "Get that bike. Hide it in the shed out back. And find her other shoe. I assume she came with two."

Dusty shuffled across the room. "Don't take too long, man. I want my turn. I'm ready for some fun too."

"I'll take as long as I want." The gruff words, laced with steel, compounded the dread pressing on her racing heart.

"But—"

"You got a problem, Dusty?"

"No, but I found her."

"And I have her now."

Chapter 2

Closing the door, Brett Davis pressed the lock and rested his head against the wood. What a mess. What was he supposed to do now? Anger churned in his chest and threatened to commandeer his fist. Instead of succumbing to the quick but useless release a punch would bring, he sucked in a long, slow breath. Anger wouldn't lead him to the next step. Anger was a luxury he couldn't afford. Not with somebody's life on the line.

How in the world did she come to be at this house? On a bike. In flipflops? He already had to deal with two people who weren't the brightest bulbs in the chandelier. Now this woman. He turned to face her.

She'd struggled to a sitting position on the sleeping bag. She pinned him with her eyes, and he stared back. He noted the blood at the corner of her mouth and redness on her cheek, hinting of a future bruise. Thank God he'd come back when he did. No telling what Dusty would've done if he'd tarried in town.

No, he knew exactly what Dusty would've done. What Dusty was waiting for right now.

Laughter in the other room spurred him to cross toward her. Kneeling, he reached for her, but she flinched. He dropped his hand.

Slow down. She's petrified.

He caught her eyes with his. No tears just wide, scared-to-death green eyes. The greenest he'd ever seen. No flecks of gold just pure, mossy green with a lighter circle—

13

Focus, man. You've got a situation here.

Keeping his hands down, he gentled his voice. "I'm going to untie the gag if you'll let me. I'm not going to hurt you."

He raised his right hand. "Okay?"

She blinked and inclined her head a quarter of an inch.

He reached behind her, untied the bandanna, and tossed it away from her. She worked her mouth, wincing at the movement.

Rifling through his back pack, he pulled out a water bottle and a Swiss Army knife. He opened the new water bottle and set it beside her. Palming the knife, he waited for her to lift her eyes. "I'm going to cut the zip tie, okay?" After a slight nod, he slid behind her.

Her wrists were jammed together, angled in an awkward way. The tie strangled her wrists and gnawed into the soft skin. Cutting the tie without nicking her would be tricky. He swallowed his frustration and leaned in. Bracing himself on his knees, he caught a whiff of coconuts.

She smelled like the beach?

She smelled like the beach.

He wiggled his finger under the tie and heard the first sound from her, a whimper. "Sorry. Just about got it." He angled the knife beside his finger and sliced the plastic strip. The tie popped against her back, her hands dropping to the floor.

Swinging around to face her again, he folded the blade back into place. She rolled her arms forward, grimacing with the effort. He tossed the knife into the backpack. "Sorry. Didn't mean to add to the hurt, but the zip tie—"

"Rape always hurts."

"What?"

"You heard me." Her husky, low voice, cracked.

Didn't pull punches, this one. "I'm not going to rape you."

"Calling it something different doesn't change what it is." She sat with her knees drawn up to her chest.

For protection?

"'It' isn't going to happen."

The confusion and mistrust mingling in her eyes niggled at him.

"I promise you—I'm not going to rape you, and I'm not going to let those yahoos," he nodded to the other room, "rape you either."

Tears welled around those green irises, then she worked her jaw and blinked them away. Tough, huh? Good, because you'll need to be, lady. "Here." He handed her the bottle of water. "You can rinse out your mouth and spit into this bag. The only bathroom is back out there."

She shuddered as she followed his glance at the door with her eyes. He snapped open a plastic grocery bag. "It's not cold, but it's wet and it'll help."

As she accepted the bottle, he noticed the blood on her hand. "Did he—"

She flexed her hand. "The kitten."

How much more bizarre would this day get? "The kitten?"

"It was tangled. It scratched me when I tried . . .when I tried . . ."

Her chin trembled, but she swallowed some water. Determination flickered in her gaze.

"You saw a helpless kitten, tried to save it, and Dusty got you instead."

She nodded.

"Let me clean your hand. I've got some first aid stuff in my pack." He slid the black bag closer to grab what he needed.

❧❧❧❧

Mary Wade swirled more water around her mouth, but she couldn't wash away the lingering rancid taste. Her shoulders ached. Her arms tingled back to life. Thank goodness she didn't break anything when she hit the floor. The zip tie track on her wrists burned. The kitten's scratches stung. Her cheek felt swollen. The pink on her toes caught her eye. The pedicure seemed like a lifetime ago. What was she going to do?

God, I am scared. Petrified, actually. I need help. Now. Please.

Pings on the tin roof signaled the early arrival of raindrops.

Doc offered his hand, flat and palm side up, nonthreatening. "Can I see those scratches? We need to take care of them. You don't want to get cat scratch fever."

She laid her hand on top of his. "Like the song?"

He studied the marks. "Yeah, but it's a real thing too." He set her hand on her knee and motioned to the water bottle. "Mind if I use some?" He poured a bit of water onto what looked like a clean handkerchief—infinitely cleaner than the bandanna—and offered his flat hand again. "They call it something different now, but it's a real thing. My sister got it when she was about ten."

She tugged at her hand with the first sting. He held for an instant, then let go. "Sorry about the sting. We need to clean it, then we can put on antibiotic cream."

Mary Wade stretched her hand back toward him. "You have a sister?"

"Just one. You sound surprised." He glanced at her. "Don't I look like somebody with a sister?"

"Sorry. I didn't mean . . . I don't know . . ." She blew out a breath, lifting tangled tresses from her face. "I'm not sure of the conversation a situation like this calls for. I've never been in a situation like this before." She bit her lip. How was she going to get out of it?

His mouth twitched. "No. I apologize. I was making small talk to take your mind off your stinging hand, and see? All done except for the bandage."

She studied the gel glistening on top of the jagged lines crisscrossing her hand. "You're going to have to find a brilliant topic to take my mind off the bigger problem."

"Yeah, well. I'm working on that." He affixed a bandage,

then turned her wrists. "These are going to be black and blue before too long. Take some of these." He broke the seal on a white, plastic bottle retrieved from his pack, opened it, and shook out three capsules.

At her quirked eyebrow, he showed her the label. "Ibuprofen. You've been banged up pretty good. These might help." He ducked his head. "Sorry about the shove in the room. I had to convince them."

"You convinced me too." She popped all three capsules into her mouth and swallowed a big gulp of water.

He locked eyes with her. What would he see? A feeble attempt at humor? Simple honesty? Unadulterated terror? She dropped her gaze.

"I hope I've convinced you that I'm not going to hurt you. Do you understand that?"

She shut her eyes against images of the men in the other room. "I want to believe—"

Thunderous whacks vibrated the door. She bolted upright and clutched his arm, searching the room for a hiding place.

He stilled her with a hand on her elbow, then rested an index finger against his mouth. His eyes commanded her to be silent.

"You 'bout done? Hey. Matt. Can you hear me? I got her stupid shoe. It's my turn now."

"Get away from that door." His words, quiet but threatening and spoken to Dusty, shook her soul.

"Come on. Time to share." Dusty whined on the other side of the door.

"Did you not hear me the first time?" Icicles shimmered from every word.

Muted footsteps scuffed the linoleum.

She let out a breath she'd been holding since the beats sounded on the door, grateful that this man appeared to be on her side.

"Hey. Look at me." He dropped his hands from her elbow and waited for her to focus on him. "I promise. I'll keep you safe."

Nice sentiment. But what good is a promise from a criminal?

ℰℰ)ℰℰ)(ℛ)(ℛ

How am I going to fulfill that promise? How am I going to keep Dusty's paws off her? Skeet? No problem. He followed rules without questions, but Dusty. Dusty was just the right amount of twenty-something bravado, ignorance, hormones, and emotion. He thought of something. He said it. Something angered him. He hit it. He always strained against the reins, questioned every order, pushed against every boundary.

Think of something, Brett, and think of it quick. The assignment was only days from completion. He'd almost begun counting the hours until he'd be through with Skeet and Dusty.

Growing in volume and intensity, raindrops slammed against the window. Thunder crashed seconds before a lightning bolt exploded nearby.

She startled, wincing and rubbing her wrist. "That was close."

He gritted his molars and rubbed his jaw. Pouring rain and testy criminals. He caught the woman staring at him. Could she read his mind? Did she realize what she'd walked into? Correction. Ridden her bike into apparently. What had she been thinking? One crazy afternoon and months of undercover work could be jeopardized.

Not her fault. Not really. She was the innocent in the situation, and now it'd be on him to get her out of it unscathed.

He sighed. "I'm going to have to go out there, try to appease them. Buy some more time. Those men aren't nice. Dusty especially. We got a storm raging on top of us. You've got one," he raised an eyebrow at her feet, "shoe. I wouldn't advise going

18

out that window. I promise to keep you safe and get you out of this. I can't keep you safe if you leave out that window."

She lifted her chin, lowered her eyes.

"I know it's hard to trust me, but please listen. I can protect you if I'm with you. I can't protect you out there." He tipped his head to the window. The storm had hastened a premature twilight, hinting of an early evening.

"You won't let them in here."

"Absolutely not." He rose from beside her. "Sit tight. I'll be right back."

Chapter 3

Mary Wade listened to the door click behind him, counted to nine, and pushed herself from the floor. Halfway up, she crouched, arms outstretched as she waited for a wave of wooziness to subside. She closed her eyes and forced her backbone to straighten to her full height.

Furious voices rose in the next room. She glanced at the door before tiptoeing toward the window. Another backward glance and she touched the windowsill with the pad of her middle finger. A fresh sting panged from the top of her hand.

Sorry, Doc or Matt or whoever you are. Thanks for the bandage and for saving me from Dusty, but I won't depend on a criminal. No thanks for your plan. I'll try my own.

Reaching the lock, she tugged on the stubborn lever, moving it shy of half an inch. Her sore shoulder complained, summoning a wince. Ignoring the pain, she wedged her hand behind the lever and pushed against it with her palm. The lever resisted. She regrouped, repositioning her feet for better leverage, and tried again. Her palm ached with the pressure, but she refused to give up. With one more push, the rusty lock released.

Her shoulders sagged with relief, but she had more work to do. Open the window.

She strained up against the window lock.

Nothing.

She pushed against the middle slat.

Nothing. The window was as tight as a size eight shoe on a

size nine foot. She hit the window's middle slat with the heel of her hand. Her wrists buzzed in protest, and her cheek throbbed.

Let go, window. Let. Me. Out.

She hit it again as another lightning strike lit up the field beside the house. She jumped back, swallowing a scream.

"What're you doing?" Doc slammed the door.

She whirled to face him, but he'd sprinted across the room, standing inches in front of her. His silver eyes flashed ice.

"You're trying to escape?"

She frowned. "Do I really need to answer that?"

He worked his jaw. "I told you not to. I told you to sit tight. That I'd protect you."

Raising her chin, she met his chilling stare. "You may be Dusty and Skeet's boss, but you're not mine." Her attempt at bravado fell flat, like her escape attempt.

"Are you kidding me? I just spent ten minutes calming those two. Buying us more time. You're supposed to switch partners first thing tomorrow, by the way."

She blanched, bile rising in her throat. "And you wonder why I was trying to get out?"

He blew a frustrated breath through his nostrils. "Just so you know, that window is sticky. Takes more than skinny arms to open it."

Anger widened her eyes. "Threats and insults. That's how you roll, huh?"

His mouth flattened into a straight line. A muscle twitched in his jaw. He breathed in a slow stream of air before speaking. "I didn't mean to insult you. Sorry I mentioned the switching-partner thing."

She folded her arms gingerly in front of her. "That was mean."

A corner of his mouth twitched. "Agreed. But I thought we were agreed on you not escaping without me."

"Why do I want to escape with a criminal?" As soon as the

words were out, guilt assailed her. Except for the initial shove, this man had helped her. Been kind to her.

He worked his jaw and blinked. "I believe we're even now. To answer your question, because I can keep you safe."

The silver eyes bored into her with the intensity of a hundred-watt bulb. She dropped her attention to his chest. "Says you."

"Stubborn—" He tightened his mouth and snatched his ponytail loose. Sandy brown ends brushed scruffy whiskers. "There's more to this situation than you can see right now. We'll come up with a plan that'll save you, but you have to trust me." He shifted his feet. "Can you do that?"

Could she trust him? What made him different than the two on the other side of that door? What made him trustworthy?

She didn't have many options at this point. She lifted her face and encountered a softening expression, one that hinted of trustworthiness. She nodded.

He raked his hands through his hair, held it off the back of his neck. "I brought in some food and your flip-flop. We'll eat and make a plan. Sound good?"

"Do I have a choice?"

A sigh preceded a curt shake of his head. "You don't have to eat, but I'll need your input to succeed in freeing you."

The handful of Cheez-its she ate before the bike ride was history, but thinking of food churned her stomach. Her mouth still tasted the filthy bandanna.

"I don't know if I can eat."

"Try."

₧₧₨₨

Brett retrieved the bag of food he'd flung to the floor when he caught her standing in front of the window. What was she thinking? Leaving in this storm? He couldn't blame her though. He'd do the same, but he knew how to get away. This woman. She rode her bike with flip-flops.

Flip-flops.

She painted her toes hot pink.

Wait. That information wasn't pertinent. Delete and forget. Think about the important facts.

She got herself kidnapped and put a wrinkle in months of work. Yeah. Stick with that kind of information.

He lowered himself to the sleeping bag and motioned for her to join him. "I wasn't expecting guests, so I bought only three chicken dinners." He raised the bag. "I'll share."

"No. Thank you. I'm not really hungry." She sat at the far edge of the shabby material.

Legs crisscrossed in front of him, he opened the wax paper covering, took one half of a chicken sandwich, and handed her the half with the paper. "You need to eat something."

"If I try to eat some of that greasy fried chicken, I think I'd need another grocery bag."

"Refusing fried chicken? I thought everybody in Grafton County ate fried chicken." She needed to eat something, although he understood her queasiness. "I went the healthy route and chose apple slices instead of fries. Think you could try one of those?" He offered a plastic baggie of green wedges.

She accepted the bag and wrestled with the stubborn pouch. She frowned and rotated her left wrist.

"Let me." He ripped it open with one flick of his fingers. "Nibble on one and see how it goes."

She put the apple to her tongue, tasted it but didn't bite it. "That crack about Grafton County people eating fried chicken is kind of an insult." She bit off the very end but didn't chew, instead held it in her mouth.

He realized he hadn't answered her when she tipped her head to the side. "Sorry. I was thinking." About her mouth. Another idea to delete and forget. "Ah, I didn't mean to insult exactly. Just wanted you to eat."

She swallowed and took another bite of apple. He took two out of his sandwich, concentrating on his food, not her.

"What's your plan?"

He popped his head up and encountered a steady, green-eyed gaze. Swallowed. "Direct. I like that. How far'd you ride your bike? Are we close to your house?"

She nodded. "Not far."

He wiped the corner of his mouth with a logo-imprinted napkin. "Close enough to walk?" He gestured toward her feet. "In those shoes?"

"Yes. I can walk." She tossed the last bit of apple into her mouth, wiped her hand on her shorts.

"In flip-flops? In the rain?" He jutted his chin toward the window. "'Cause it sounds like the rain's here to stay."

She pursed her lips. "I said, 'Yes.' It's just up on the paved road, not even a mile probably."

"Probably." He shook his head. "In flip-flops."

She curled her toes and slid her legs back to sit on them. "Again with the flip-flops. What do you have against flip-flops?"

"Nothing. In the shower. On the beach, maybe, but you rode a bike with them. What were you thinking?"

With the tips of her fingers, she traced the bandage on the back of her hand. "I was thinking I didn't want to ruin my brand new pedicure."

Those toes again. He searched for her feet, tucked away and partially hidden. A few pink tips peeked out.

The bandage held her attention. "I was thinking I'd be back in ten minutes or so. I just wanted to get some fresh air. I didn't think—"

"Exactly. You didn't think." He chomped on the last apple slice.

She shifted a second time, pulling her knees to her chest, burying her forehead against them.

Congratulations. You've hurt her again.

"I'm sorry. It's just that you need to wear solid shoes on a bike. You could do some real damage." He shrugged. "Course, in light of the bigger problem . . ."

She rested her chin on her knees and raised wary but unwavering eyes. "What are we going to do about the bigger problem?"

"You've got to get out of here. I'm taking care of it." He lifted the other half of the sandwich, tipping it toward her. "You sure you can't eat this?"

She shook her head.

"You can find your house in the dark?" He started in on the chicken.

"Of course. You think I'm that dumb?"

He sighed through his nose, pushed the bite of chicken to the side of his mouth. "I don't think you're dumb. I think you're in a tough situation, and it's up to me to get you out."

"If you open that window for me, I can get out myself."

He swallowed. "I'm sure, but I'm also sure about those men in there. They might look like dumb and dumber, but don't fool yourself. Dusty is determined and ruthless. You got just a little taste of his charming personality."

She dropped her eyes.

He balled up the wax paper and tossed it into the fast food bag. "So. Let's talk about getting out of here."

ജ്ഞോജ്ഞാരുൽ

Ignoring her protesting wrists, Mary Wade squeezed her legs closer to her chest, felt her racing heart against her thigh. Thank goodness he ate the sandwich. Maybe the faint aroma of dead chicken and dill pickles warring with her stomach would fade in a while. The apple slice surprised her by staying down, but she didn't want to risk anything else.

"How 'bout we start with introductions." He offered his hand. "Call me Matt."

A real name or an alias? She clasped his hand. Long, thin fingers. Short, clean nails. Nice hands.

For a criminal.

But his handshake was warm and firm, promised strength and dependability.

"Why do they call you 'Doc'?"

He smirked. "Teasing me because I don't say 'ain't' or 'he don't.' They say I sound smart, like a doctor or teacher or something."

"Are you? Smart?"

His eyes held her gaze. "I'm smart enough to get you away from them."

God, is he trustworthy? He's kept me safe so far, but . . . Please, help us.

He wiggled her hand. "And you are?"

"Mary Wade." She pulled her hand out of his grasp.

"Mary." He nodded. "Sorry we had to meet like this."

"You're not the only one. And it's Mary Wade. Two names."

"Sorry. Interesting name."

She ignored the question in his statement. Sharing the origins of her name landed at the bottom of her priority list right now.

"Okay, Mary Wade, this is what's going to happen. When the rain stops or at least subsides, we're going to climb out that window and run like crazy to your house. We are not going to scream. We are not looking back. We are not saying a word until we're safe inside, got it?"

She loosened her arms around her knees, flattened her hands against the tops of her feet. "When we get there, then what?"

He rubbed the side of his jaw. "We'll cross that bridge when we get to it. Any other questions?"

"No."

"Good." He studied her cheek, glanced at her wrists. "I need to take your picture."

She caught her breath. "What?"

"For evidence. Just a few of your wrists and face."

She frowned. Evidence? Why did he care about evidence?

"Don't get creeped out. The pictures will help in kidnapping charges. I'll take the bare minimum." He palmed his cell phone. "Please. I wouldn't ask you to do this if I didn't think it'd be important later."

She stretched her arms in front of her. He knelt beside her, took a picture of the top and bottom side of her wrists.

"I'll just take your profile. I can get the cut and swelling now. The bruises will take a while to show up." He reached toward her chin, then dropped his hand. "Could you turn just a tad toward the right?" Two more pictures, and he slid the phone into his pocket. "Thank you." He rose and stretched, then moved in front of the door. "Do they have anything of yours? Cell phone? Your wallet with your ID maybe?"

"No. Just my helmet."

His jaw dropped. "You wore a helmet but—"

"Don't say it."

"Okay. I won't. Why don't you try to get some rest. Lie down on the sleeping bag if you want. I'll sit over here just in case." He moved to the door.

"Just in case what?"

He raised an eyebrow. "Just in case."

She had no intention of sleeping. Not until she was miles and miles away from here and safe. That's right. She wouldn't sleep till she was in her own bed in her own house back in Charlotte. She'd just stretch out her legs and maybe lean against the wall. She'd have to have every bit of the energy she could muster to keep up with Matt.

He had the body of an athlete. Not a used-to-be high school athlete. The toned muscles bunching at the edge of the T-shirt sleeves advertised a strenuous, daily workout. If she couldn't keep up with him, he'd probably drag her behind him.

No. That was unfair.

He'd been mostly kind and patient with her. Especially when he dressed the wound on her hand. True, he'd insulted her a couple of times when he was exasperated, but no doubt she'd thrown a wrench into whatever was going on here.

What was going on here?

Matt looked every inch the criminal. Maybe not criminal, but at least a tough guy. Scruffy beard, unkempt, shoulder-length hair, muscles for days. People considered her tall at five foot seven, but he had at least five or six inches on her. He posed a solid, intimidating presence in a room.

Except he'd been gentle with her, after the first shove. He didn't grab her. He waited for her to allow him to touch her. His speech patterns weren't rough either.

"Mary Wade."

She jolted back to reality.

"Try to rest. I'll wake you when it's time."

"I'm not going to sleep."

He shook his head. "Rest then."

She scooted up to the wall beside the window and leaned her head on the faded roses in the wallpaper.

The sound of the relentless rain could have been soothing, but sporadic cackles from the other room tensed her shoulder muscles. What were they doing? How long would they take orders from Matt?

God, I'm out of my league here. What am I supposed to do?

Chapter 4

A hand clamped over Mary Wade's mouth. Her eyes flapped open, rolling to focus on something, anything, but pitch black suffocated the room. Adrenaline pumped in her veins, racing her heart to galloping speed.

"Don't scream. It's time. Promise me you won't scream." The voice, quiet and urgent, murmured in her ear.

Whimpering, she scraped at the steel bands thwarting her movements, kicked her feet to get traction to stand, but they tangled with the sleeping bag.

"Mary Wade. Relax. It's me, Matt. Remember? Calm down. We need to leave now. We're running to your house." His other hand spanned the back of her neck with gentle pressure. His thumb stroked below her ear.

Scenes from the afternoon crashed into her fuddled mind. It was real. Really real. Another whimper escaped from her throat.

"Listen to me." Warm breath brushed her ear. "I'll move my hand, but you can't scream. Do you promise not to?"

She nodded.

"Good girl." The hand covering her mouth loosened before leaving completely. His other one slid to her shoulder, his thumb trailing to her shoulder blade. He kept his voice low. "Sorry I scared you, but we can't afford a scream right now. Ready to go?"

As her eyes adjusted to the darkness, his face appeared inches from her own.

He kept his voice low. "Give me your hand. I'll help you up."

She wanted to tell him she could stand by herself, but she swallowed her stubbornness and let him help her. Smart idea. Her bottom felt numb. She swayed on wobbly legs.

He steadied her, gripping her shoulders in a firm hold. Comforting, not threatening. "Take a minute to get your bearings."

Strength and determination emanated from him. The thought to lean into his solid chest and fall apart, give in to the tears scratching at the back of her throat, was almost as powerful as her desperate need to quit this nightmare. She angled away from him. "Let's go."

"Hold up." His grip tightened. "We've got time for you to clear your head."

She glanced over his shoulder.

"They're asleep. I've listened to their snores for the last half hour. The rain's slowed. Not pouring but not exactly sprinkling either."

Darkness shadowed most of his face, but silver eyes showed through the dimness. "Time to make our move." He released her arms. Her legs surprised her by supporting her weight. But would they keep up with him on their flight away from here?

He shrugged the backpack onto his shoulders. "So. We go back up the path to the road. Then which way?"

"Left on the dirt road then right on the paved one." She donned the flip-flops waiting by the window.

"Could you get to your house as the crow flies so to speak? Not by the roads?"

She lifted her shoulders. "Ahm. I guess so, but there's a wide creek to cross."

"Got it. The road'll have to do. Maybe nobody'll be out in the middle of the night in the storm. If a car does come by, we'll drop to the ground, capiche?" He thwacked his palm against the window twice and pushed upward. The window rose without a protest.

Stupid window. Why didn't it cooperate with her earlier efforts?

He peered through the opening. "About how far is it?"

"I don't know. Not far."

Leaning on the windowsill, he glanced back at her. "A mile? Two miles?"

"I don't know. Not more than a mile, I guess."

"You probably notice cars by color, not make."

"Another dig. Also sexist."

He straightened and hiked up his backpack. "Didn't mean it to be. I meant it to be teasing." He sloughed her arm. "Loosen up. The run'll be easier. It's going to be tough enough in the rain and mud." His gaze flicked to her feet. "In those shoes."

Loosen up? Seriously? "Quit with the shoes already. Let's go." She stepped toward the window.

He held her back. "Here's the deal. I'll go out first. Then you crawl out. The drop's not but three or four feet tops. I'll take the lead, and we'll hold hands. We are not getting separated out there. Not an option."

Of course, he's leading. No idea where he's going, but he's going to lead.

He bent and swung his leg over the windowsill. He swiveled his other leg through and landed with a splash. "Ugh."

"Are you okay?"

"Landed in a puddle. Caught my arm on a nail. It's on your right, so be careful."

She straddled the sill, gripping the dangling flip-flop with her toes.

"Give me your hand. Try to jump clear. I'll help."

As she brought her second foot through the window, he jerked her hand, knocking her tender cheek straight into his chest. His rock-hard chest. Raindrops had already dampened his T-shirt. "Ow." She clutched her smarting cheek. One foot tangled with his, connected with his arch.

He endured like a stoic soldier, then set her to the side. Clear of the water. Clear of him. "Sorry about that. I thought you were ready."

"Because my leg was completely through? Because I said, 'Okay,'?"

He ignored her. "We don't have to run at full throttle, but I want to make tracks. Keep up."

To answer him, she lunged toward the path. He passed her with a stride and a half, his hand clamped around hers.

❧❧❧❧❧❧

Brett wiped the rain from his face, but the wind slapped more water into his eyes. *Because my leg was completely through? Sarcasm? At a time like this? We'll see how far sarcasm gets you on this mad dash to freedom, lady.*

And jumping ahead of him back there. Did she really think she'd lead him? Of course, she'd have to tell him which house was hers, but he'd lead till then. He heard her deep breaths behind him.

He could run a six and a half-minute mile when pressed, but that was in perfect conditions, not leading a woman through mud and rain and who knows what else. Not to mention—don't think it.

The hurricane remnants had transformed the dirt path into a mud slide, turning the run into a slow jog. Dusty or Skeet wouldn't come after them just yet. They'd sleep till eight or so, but getting her to her house sooner rather than later was imperative.

He glanced back. Her head tipped toward the road. Impressive. No complaints. No trips and falls. Maybe they could pick up speed on the paved road. Sprinkles grew into full-fledged rain as they approached it. Out of habit, he checked his left before turning to the right. No cars. So far so good.

A tug on his hand and a gasp behind him signaled trouble. He tightened his grip and grabbed another look over his shoulder. Still upright. Great. Keep moving.

He barked a question behind him. "How far on this road?"

"Not too far." Her words were breathy but clear.

Great. Explicit directions. "I need to know something."

"Or I could lead."

The rain was almost as annoying as her silly suggestion. He ignored both. "Are we close? Do we turn to another road?"

Her panting increased. "No."

"How many houses? Right or left side?"

"Left side. Fourth house. A ways up. This is country, not a neighborhood."

"No kidding." Still enough breath for sarcasm.

A dog barked to his right. A neighbor joined the first. Perfect. Just what we need. A chorus of dogs to wake the whole community.

The second mailbox appeared and receded. He had the third in his sights, but after that, dark. "Are you sure it's the fourth one? Are we close?"

"Yes. Keep going." More panting. "A white fence. There."

Pale streaks parallel to the road came into his view. "Cut into the yard. Forget the driveway."

"Oh—"

His arm wrenched backward but didn't stop his forward motion "Come on. I see it. The white two-story, right?"

"Let go. You're dragging me."

He slowed his stride and stopped at the fence. Bending to crawl between the railings, he reached to help her. Managing some sort of weird lurch and hop, she favored her right foot. Her right, naked foot. "You lost—?"

She slipped through the fence. "Come on. We're here. Go to the side door under the garage. It's open."

"You didn't—" Of course she didn't lock it. Who knew what they'd find inside? He scooped her up, picking up speed now that he could run like he wanted to.

"Put me down. I can run."

"Stop wiggling." He squeezed her tighter and sloshed past a young tree. Rounding the far corner of the house, he spotted their goal, the garage open, a compact car waiting. Unlocked, too, no doubt.

The shelter of the garage offered welcome relief from the wind and rain. He slipped as he stepped onto the soaked concrete but righted himself. Spotting the back door, he lit up the steps two at a time and stomped across the welcome mat. He pushed open the door, but before he could cross the threshold, two arms forbade it.

She gripped the doorjamb with a stranglehold. "Put me down. I can walk inside."

He moved forward.

She resisted, surprising him with her strength.

"Don't be stubborn. We made it. I'll set you down inside."

"No, I said."

In her eyes, he saw determination that rivaled his and a flash of something else before she lowered her lashes. She struggled against him without releasing the doorjamb. He let her slide to the landing the size of a small porch.

She flicked her remaining flip-flop to the side and limped through the doorway.

Chapter 5

Mary Wade stepped on the ball of her foot, keeping her heel from touching the floor. It ached worse than her cheek, her wrists, and her shoulder that caught the floor when Matt threw her into the room yesterday.

Yesterday.

Eons ago.

Thank You, God. Thank You, God.

Agnes' house at last.

A prickle grabbed her spine and ran the length of it. She flipped on the light switch.

"You're soaked. You need a shower before you catch pneumonia."

At the click of the door lock, she faced him, both of them squinting in the light. "So are you." His drenched T-shirt revealed a six-pack it had hinted at earlier. His feet were bare, shoes left behind the closed back door. He palmed dripping, long hair back from his face. Mud splotched his forearms.

Twisting to observe her calves, she found a film of mud spread over them.

"We both need to get cleaned up, I guess."

Now what? She hadn't really thought about after the escape. They faced each other in Agnes' laundry room. Brett breathing hard and she, shivering. She'd lead him to a shower, let him begin, and hightail it out of here before the mud swirled around the drain.

No way would she wait to find out what his plan was. She'd grab her keys and point her blue Honda west, not stopping till she reached her Charlotte driveway. No matter that her luggage rested in the room at the top of the stairs or that she was freezing. The car had heat.

But wait. He and his friends could rob Agnes blind. Except that her small, flat-screen TV was at least ten years old. Agnes hadn't bought a laptop yet. The house showcased beautiful antiques, but Dusty and Skeet didn't strike her as knowing good furniture lines. She bit her lip.

Did Matt?

"Mary Wade."

She jumped.

He studied her with his hands on his hips. "You're shivering. You need a shower."

Feigning nonchalance, she opened a cabinet, found two towels. "You go first." She handed him one. "I'll make some tea."

"Thank you." He wiped his face. "I don't drink tea. You're going first."

She mirrored his hands-on-hips stance. "No."

"Yes." He looped the towel around his neck, scrubbed over his face again. "You always this stubborn?"

"I've never been in this situation before, leaving a criminal alone in a house."

He flinched. "A criminal who just rescued you, carried you partway, remember?"

Folding her arms in front of her chest, she winced at the pang from her wrists. "I told you I could—"

He flattened his hand in front of her like a shield. "Enough. I'm not a criminal. I'm an undercover deputy. I'm not going to rob you while you shower. And my real name is Brett Davis, by the way."

She blinked. Her mouth rounded. A policeman? Not a

criminal? Shouldn't he flash a badge about now? But undercover cops don't wear badges, do they? How could she believe him? She buried her face in the towel, breathed in the scent of fabric softener.

"Trust me, Mary Wade. You're safe now. Go shower. Then we'll talk."

ഇരുഇരുഇരു

Brett connected with her searching gaze, peeking over the towel. I'm telling the truth. You can trust me.

Her eyes flicked to his chest. Was she looking for a badge? Sorry. Won't be able to deliver on that one. Yet.

"Let's get cleaned up, then I'll explain as much as I can. I promise."

Her shoulders sagged. "I have to wipe off my feet first. I can't track mud upstairs." She fluffed the towel to its full length and bent to wipe the mud from her feet. Scratched pink toes peeped through dark splatters.

She straightened, narrowed her eyes. "I won't be long." She tossed the soiled towel on top of the washing machine.

He flipped the light switch. Darkness descended again. "Don't turn on a lot of lights."

"I've got to see. Define 'a lot.'"

"Turn on what you need. Then turn it off. I don't want to broadcast we're here and awake. When the sun comes up, it won't matter. In the meantime, be prudent with the lights."

She exited the laundry room without a word.

No sarcastic comeback. Good. Was she beginning to trust him? Maybe.

But he didn't completely trust her.

Extracting a pen light from his soaked backpack, he checked all the keys hanging on the wooden rack by the door. Not one Honda key. Where could hers be? He moved into the adjoining room. Storm clouds hid any helpful light from the moon and stars. He flicked the light switch. The kitchen. A grocery bag sat on the counter by the sink. Imperishables not put away yet. A breakfast table nestled in a bay window.

Bingo.

A purse hung on one of the slat-back chairs. Had to be hers.

Dousing the light, he waited to become accustomed to the darkness. Moving with care across the room, he found the chair and purse. He slipped out the wallet and spied the driver's license with the penlight. He studied the card.

Mary Wade Kimball. Two first names. Right.

1073 Stony Creek Way. Charlotte.

Charlotte? If she lived in Charlotte, who's house . . .? She'd have some explaining to do.

5' 7" Yep.

Green eyes. Absolutely.

Organ donor. Stand-up citizen.

He replaced the wallet and dug around the bottom of the purse for keys. Cell phone. A devotional. A believer? Mecklenburg County Library ink pen. Keys. Sweet. He checked for a Honda key, found it, and pocketed the set.

Sufficiently hobbled the lady upstairs. Check. Time for a quick shower. And a phone call. Collecting his backpack that maybe had protected his extra set of clothes, he anticipated the hot water on the way to the stairs.

ಐಐಐಐ

The caressing water beckoned Mary Wade to stay under the waterfall shower and ignore the mysterious man downstairs, but she refused to succumb to the tantalizing sensations soothing her battered body. She hopped out of the tub within minutes of entering. Having lived with wells as a water source most of her life, she knew how to take a quick shower.

Her wet hair in a turban, she swiped the mirror with a wad of bathroom tissue to examine her face. Not much improvement after the soap, but it was at least clean now. Her left cheek, already showing a hint of black and blue, puffed slightly more than the right. She worried the cut in her lip with her tongue. How long would it take to heal?

Dark circles underscored her eyes, traces of sleep deprivation and stress. Oh, those wretched freckles. Without thinking, she grabbed the sunscreen tube from her cosmetic case and slathered it across her nose, being careful with her cheek. Although vanity forced her to apply a quick coat of mascara, she zipped the case before other makeup could tempt an application. Her light brown eyelashes looked nonexistent without some help, but she didn't have enough time to cover up the bruises and dark circles.

She raked a wide-toothed comb through most of the tangles in her hair, then swirled it into a messy, damp bun. No time to dry and style. She needed to check on Brett, if that was his real name. She switched off the light.

Opening the bathroom door, she peered through the darkness. No lights in the kitchen. He meant what he said about keeping the lights out. Sounds down the hallway caught her attention. Running water. Not rain. A faucet. He was in Agnes' shower.

Bold for him. Perfect for her.

After snagging a pair of sandals, she limped down the stairs, favoring her right heel as much as she could, and slapped the light switch as she passed the kitchen's doorway. Grabbing her pocketbook, she thrust in her hand and stirred the contents. No keys. Shook the bag and stirred again. No keys. What did she do with them? Nothing on the counter but the groceries she would've put away after her bike ride.

She bounded into the laundry room. Agnes' keys hogged the key rack. Where were hers? She stomped her foot and yelped at the pain shooting from her heel. Standing on her left foot, her sore heel raised behind her, she spied the towel she'd tossed earlier. Maybe . . . she seized it to check underneath.

"Freeze!"

The towel slipped out of rigid fingers. She peeked toward the kitchen. Brett crouched in the doorway, pointing a gun at her. A big, black gun.

"What happened? Why'd you scream?" His breathing came in quick pants, heavier than after the run. "Are you crazy? I thought they were here."

"I . . . I . . ." What could she say? The back of her throat scratched, and a tiny prickle stung in the tip of her nose. She knew what was coming and didn't try to stop it.

For the first time since the horrible dream began, a tsunami of tears boiled up from her insides like an angry wave on an ocean. She couldn't check them even if she wanted to. She'd been kidnapped, beaten, half dragged across the countryside, and had a gun pointed at her. If anybody deserved to cry, she did. She sobbed into her hands. Her nose would turn as red as Agnes' geraniums under the backyard pergola, but she didn't care. She didn't care what Brett thought either. She'd tried to get away by herself twice and failed twice.

She'd cry as hard and as long as she needed.

ఠఠ౧౩౧౩

Sticking his nine-millimeter in the back of his waist band, Brett reached her in two steps. She was already shaking. He wrapped his arms around her and pulled her in tight. An image of another woman crying in his arms floated through his mind. Lacy. He knew better now. He'd offer compassion, support, but then he'd draw the line. He'd learned his lesson hard.

Mary Wade had had a tough twelve hours or so. She'd been stoic and resilient. If she needed a cry, he'd grit his teeth and let her. By the intensity of her sobs, he might be letting her for a solid few minutes.

He stroked her hair and positioned his mouth near her ear, wispy tendrils of drying hair silky against his freshly shaved face. "It's okay now. You're safe. I'm not going to hurt you. Nobody else will either. I promise." She still smelled like coconuts and sun. Why did she smell like the beach?

Shampoo? He sniffed. No. Her hair smelled like flowers, but she had a definite beach scent going on. Another image, an impression really, of pink toes, white sand, and long, tanned legs formed in his brain. He shook his head. Focus, buddy.

Quieting his voice, he hoped the subdued sound of it, or his words, or just his presence would help calm her. "Sorry about the gun. Didn't mean to scare you."

Still sobbing, she flattened her palms against his T-shirt, ramming her forehead into his chest, and cried more.

Minutes passed with nothing but the sound of her sobs until a grandfather clock chimed the half hour from deep within the house. She shuddered and sucked in an unsteady breath. "I'm s-s-sorry. I c-can't stop sh-shaking."

"You're probably in shock and chilled too. You need something warm to drink. You mentioned tea. Got anything herbal like chamomile or some sort?"

"I'm sure."

"Too bad we don't have what would really do the trick." He loosened his hold on her. "A little scotch mixed in would help you relax."

She clung to his arms, burrowing her face into his chest. "Alcohol? This early in the day?"

Chuckling, he tightened his arm around her waist. "I'm talking about a tablespoonful, not a snoot full. Strictly medicinal."

Her breath hitched. "There's some in the kitchen. In the broom closet."

Interesting. He arched an eyebrow. "Alcohol? In the broom closet?"

She nodded. "For recipes."

"Mmm. Whatever you say." He shifted to step back from her, but she fisted the fabric of his T-shirt into tight wads. "Mary

Wade." He smoothed soft curls from her temple, tipped her head back. Puffy lids combined with a red nose, but he focused on the spiked lashes framing the jade green eyes. Mistake. "Listen to me. I'm not going to let anything happen to you. You've been through a lot, but you're safe now." Fresh tears threatened to join the trails streaking her cheeks. "I keep telling you that. I want you to believe it."

He massaged the back of her neck. "We're going to make some tea. Maybe some coffee if you've got it. And we'll talk. Okay? Ready to sit in the kitchen?"

She loosened her death grip on his shirt but didn't step back.

With gentle hands, he turned her toward the kitchen, keeping one arm around her shoulders, turning off the light with the other.

Chapter 6

Mary Wade reached for the cabinet door, but Brett stopped her. "You sit down. I'll make the tea."

"Sorry I lost it, but I'm fine now."

He drew a chair from the breakfast table. "Sit. From here you can direct me to where everything is. I got this." He folded his arms across his chest. "But first, why did you scream in there?"

"I stomped my foot. I stepped on a rock on the way here." She ducked her head. "After I lost my flip-flop."

"Uh huh. Why'd you stomp your foot?" He grabbed the teakettle from the stove and leaned his hip against the counter, waiting.

She dabbed at her eyes and nose with a napkin out of the wooden holder in the center of the table. She'd shellacked the wooden teapot cutouts in Girl Scouts years ago, embellished the sides with violet bouquet stickers, and given the artwork to Agnes at Christmas. After more than fifteen years, Agnes still used the gift. Her heart pinged with gratitude for her godmother.

"Mary Wade."

She dragged her attention to the present.

"Why'd you stomp your foot?"

She took a deep breath and let it out with a burst of words. "Because I couldn't find my keys."

With a slow grin, he delved into the pocket of his black jeans. "You mean these?"

Gasping, she dropped her jaw. "You went through my pocketbook. Why?"

"Because I thought you'd cut and run as soon as you knew I was in the shower. Looks like I was right."

She held her palm out. "I'd like my property back, please."

He pocketed the keys again and turned to the sink. "All in good time. I can't have you leave me here. We're in this together for a while."

She'd love to wipe that smug smile from his lips, but she fiddled with the napkin instead. She'd bide her time. "You shaved."

Filling the kettle with water, he grinned over his shoulder. A dimple dotted the center of his chin. "Yeah. I borrowed a disposable razor. Never shaved with a pink one before."

An attempt at a smile hurt her cheek. "First time for everything. Hey. You changed clothes."

"Had an extra set in my backpack." He swiveled from the sink, and evidence of her tears splotched the front of his black Harley Davidson T-shirt.

She nodded to his damp chest. "Now you need another one. Sorry about that."

"Just one backup set of clothes, but don't worry about it. It'll dry in no time. Where're the tea bags?"

"In the tall cabinet at the end of the counter. There's also a French press and some coffee. Alcohol too."

He examined the cabinet, brought out a box of tea, the press, and a bag of ground coffee. "Now for the good stuff. Hmm. Let's see. Kahlua. Vodka. Peach Schnapps. Must make a lot of recipes. No scotch." He pulled out a bottle and set it on the counter. "But Jack Daniels'll work. Where're the mugs?"

She pointed to the cabinet next to the sink. He poured a good drop of whiskey into one of the mugs and measured a substantial amount of coffee grounds into the press.

"You didn't put any in yours."

"I don't drink on duty."

On duty. Was he really a policeman? Could she trust him? She rolled the damp napkin into a ball with trembling fingers. Although she sat, safe in Agnes' house, fear continued to reign in her body. A stranger prepared tea for her. A stranger who'd rescued her at the risk of his own life. Who was he really? She crushed the napkin to quell the shaking.

"How do you take it?"

She shoved the chair back. "With sugar."

"And it's where?"

She pointed to a cabinet.

The teakettle began to whistle as he set the sugar bowl on the counter. "Sit tight. I got it." He filled her mug and the press with the boiling water.

Gathering both mugs in one hand and the French press in the other, he joined her at the table. As he reached for the chair opposite hers, she flattened her palm on the space beside her. Across the table seemed so far away. "Will you sit here, please?" At his hesitation, she bit her lip. "I'm sorry I'm being timid and silly. It's . . . I . . . ." She gave up and focused on the sinking bag of chamomile tea.

He capitulated, taking the chair beside her. "You're not timid. You've been through a trauma. You're going on fumes. No sleep, no food, a midnight dash through what was probably part of the hurricane people were talking about in town. You're holding up pretty well."

She squeezed the mug, melting into the warmth seeping through the stoneware. "But you think I'm incompetent." New tears surfaced. She blinked to keep them from falling.

Pouring the coffee from the press, he made a face. "Not following."

"Because of the flip-flop thing. Not locking the door. Getting into this mess because of a kitten. But believe me. Nothing like this has ever happened to me before. I'm responsible. I'm independent. I . . ." She clamped her mouth tight. Why did she want to explain herself to him?

He clasped both hands around his mug, studying her with full attention. His skin looked fresh and soft without the beard. He'd slicked his hair into a damp ponytail.

"You what?" He sipped his coffee.

She didn't have to explain herself to him. It didn't matter what he thought of her. Did it?

Yes. Unfortunately, it did. But without evidence, her assertions of responsibility and independence sounded like a child's whiny, "I can do it myself." Why was his good opinion of her important?

He set the mug in front of him, hooked his thumbs over the rim. "You what?"

The sharp tang of the alcohol rose in the steam as she played with the tea bag, pulling it to the surface then dunking it as she contemplated answering his question. What could it hurt? "I own my own business. And my house." She wrapped the string around her spoon and let the bag drip into her mug. "Well, working on that part. But I'm not a ditz."

"Never said you were." He leaned against the chair slats and scanned the kitchen. "Nice house."

She rubbed her forehead, aching from the crying. "Thanks, but this isn't mine."

߷߷߷߷

Points for being honest. Brett tipped his head. "Not yours? Then why are we here?"

"I'm house-sitting for my godmother, Agnes."

Sounded like more honesty. "I think that gig's over."

Concern darkened her green eyes. "I just got here yesterday. I'm supposed to stay till Sunday morning."

He leaned forward. "Mary Wade, the men who kidnapped

you are a mile from here. We've got to get you back home." He took another swallow. "Where do you live?"

She traced the rim of the mug with trembling fingers. "Charlotte."

He pointed to her cup. "Have some tea."

She wrinkled her nose. "The warm mug is helping me relax."

"Go ahead. I didn't put in much. You won't even taste the alcohol."

She sipped it and grimaced. "If you want me to trust you, start by not lying to me. I don't taste anything but alcohol."

Emphasizing the truth of his statement, he pinned her with his gaze. "You can trust me."

"I haven't seen a badge. Aren't you supposed to flash one when you say you're police?" With an arched brow, she shoved his easy words back in his face.

"Not when you're undercover."

She slapped her hands on the wooden table top. "Well, how am I supposed to believe you? You could pretend to be an undercover cop to me and an astronaut to someone else. A pilot to the next girl and an Army Ranger to the next. Stories like that are all over TV. How can I—"

Closing his hand over her forearm, he silenced her. "Whoa. Slow down and take another sip." He pushed her mug closer. "You could start by looking at the facts. Number one," he extended his index finger. "I protected you back there. Kept you out of their paws." His second finger joined the first. "Number two, I rescued you from that mess and got you back to your house. Without a thank you, I might add."

She blinked. Her face paled, highlighting freckles peppered across the bridge of her nose and cheeks. "Oh. Right. I never... How could I forget—"

Lowering his eyes to the coffee, he hid his frustration about the aborted assignment. She didn't need more guilt. "Don't worry about it. It's my job."

She rested her unharmed cheek in her hand. "Thank you... Brett."

His ears perked at the way his name sounded with her husky voice. Nice. Focus. "I was teasing you. So, please, don't mention it."

"About your job. What was going on back there anyway?" She tried to conceal a yawn with the back of her other hand.

Her adrenalin was ebbing. Drooping lids half shielded her green eyes. She needed to rest if they were going to finish what they started, but if recent history revealed anything about her, she wouldn't go down without some pushback.

"Why don't we talk about that after you get some sleep?"

She jutted her chin. "Why don't we talk about it now?"

With a chuckle, he rubbed his jaw. "I knew you'd say something like that."

She sipped the tea again.

"Fine. But it might be tough to hear. You could rest first. Be a little stronger to hear what I have to say."

"I won't faint. I can hear it." She released the mug, threading her fingers in front of her, waiting.

"Started out with drugs."

"Okay."

"Then gambling, then guns."

She nodded.

"You peel back a layer and find something else." He drained the cooling coffee. "The last layer revealed human trafficking."

She drew in a sharp breath. What little color that had returned to her face receded at his words. "Human—"

"Yeah. It's hard to hear, I'm sure."

"And you were part of it."

"Undercover. Yes."

"For how long?"

"The investigation's been going on for at least a year." He rubbed the back of his neck. "I joined a few months ago."

Her knuckles, stacked together, whitened with the strained pressure. "You lived with those guys for months?"

"No. I've known them that long. We moved in a couple days ago."

"And you ruined your cover, the investigation, to rescue me?"

He studied the inside of his mug. "Ruined's a harsh word." Although, admittedly, he wondered if the word might fit.

"But it fits, doesn't it?"

He slid the mug to the side of the table. "We have a lot of evidence. We're closing in on the operation. Made a bust a couple months ago. Found some women and girls. A local shelter took them in. A few underlings were arrested. The top boys are going down next."

She glanced at her wrists. "That's why you took the pictures. To help put them in prison?"

"Every bit will help."

A shudder racked her body, shaking a solitary tear off her eyelash and marking a glistening trail over her bruise. He wanted to gather her up into his arms again, make her feel safe, but he restrained himself. He'd already crossed the professional line back in the laundry room. As much as he wanted to comfort her, he knew professionalism won cases.

To be honest, though, he wanted more than to reassure her. He wanted to smell her beach scent again, feel her molded up against him. Smooth back those waves of auburn hair from her temple and find the soft place near her ear...

Concentrate, man. On the conversation, not on her. Don't think like a high school boy. Think like a seasoned deputy. He tamped down the images of her scent and touch before he spent too much time enjoying them. He'd been down that road before. An interest in someone who had the in-love-with-the-rescuer syndrome might be in his past but would not be in his future.

But did she have that syndrome? Maybe she wasn't drawn

to her knight in shining armor at all. Maybe she tracked every move he made making the tea to figure out if she could trust him. Maybe she wanted him sitting right beside her because she was simply scared out of her gourd.

He rested his chin on his clasped hands. She'd dried her face with a new napkin. Good. What did his sister call it when his niece found her thumb, quit crying on her own? Self-comforting? Yeah. Mary Wade, a self-comforter. She didn't need him to sweep her up into his arms. She sucked it up by herself.

One less thing for him to worry about.

Why, then, did something uncomfortable, feeling a lot like disappointment, knock in the middle of his chest?

 ഇ ഇ ഇ ഇ

Mary Wade crumpled the fresh napkin in her fist. Don't think about what you left behind. What could have happened. Think about here and now. Think about getting back home. Getting back to normal.

Normal being a relative word, of course. Would she ever be able to feel as free as she did before yesterday's bike ride?

Thank You, God, for sending Brett to rescue me. Please help him do his job, and please let the undercover job not be ruined. Please help bring those missing people home.

He'd moved his hand toward her arm after his revelation about human trafficking. She thought he was about to touch her, but she must have been mistaken. He drank his coffee instead. A prudent thing, really. A second embrace in those strong arms, a second chance to burrow into that buff chest, could move into a habit. One she didn't need. At all. She had too much on her plate already. The house, the store, creating her designs, sewing her designs, finding new customers. No wonder Robert had complained about her lack of interest and found someone else to watch NCIS reruns with.

So Brett had done her two favors, rescuing her and not

feeding fantasies about more hugs. She'd get plenty of hugs from Daphne and Tess when she returned home.

Glancing from her wad of napkin, she caught Brett staring at her. Her heart fluttered. "So . . .ahmm. When will you give me my keys back? When can I go home?"

"You don't have any other questions?"

"I thought with situations like this, the fewer questions the better."

"You watch crime shows?"

"NCIS. Sometimes." More like every day and a couple of times all Saturday if a station played an NCIS marathon. A great show to sew by. "I don't recall one where someone broke a cover like this."

"Yeah, well. I need to make a phone call about that. Check out this storm, too. Why don't you try to rest for a couple of hours? Maybe the storm will pass, and we can get going by then."

"We?"

"Yes, we. I need to get to Charlotte, or at least I'll know for sure after I make that phone call, and so do you. Problem settled."

Going back together? "I thought you'd need to wrap up stuff here. Why do you have to go to Charlotte?"

"I usually work there. I got sent down here because no one would recognize me."

"Then this assignment must be a huge deal. Pulling people from other counties. Drugs, gambling, guns . . ."

He nodded. "All investigations are important, but, yes. This one could have a lot of ramifications."

An undercover investigation here in Bandon, in Grafton County. Did she know people involved in it? She was almost a part of it. She closed her eyes. Her stomach churned. Was it the alcohol or the shock of what she'd just learned? Maybe a little of both.

"You look all tapped out."

She frowned as she smoothed annoying strands from her forehead. "Thanks so much."

"I meant, why don't you sleep for a while? Then we'll talk some more. You need some rest, Mary Wade."

"So do you." She glanced toward the stairs. Going all the way upstairs didn't appeal to her. Staying close to Brett, even if it did make her look fragile, did. He'd told her to trust him. Could she really?

Yes, he'd been involved in something illegal, but had he told her the whole truth? He'd protected her, rescued her, been kind to her when she fell apart in the laundry room. Strong evidence to trust him.

But still . . .

"I'll catch a few winks after I make this call and check the weather."

If she reclined in Agnes' Lazy Boy in the family room, she could keep tabs on what he did. As long as she stayed awake. The scratchy feeling behind her eyes reminded her she hadn't slept, except for the fitful dozing back at the abandoned house, in over twenty-four hours. A headache pounded behind her eyes. Her bruised body longed for sleep.

"A quick nap sounds like a pretty good idea." As she rose, her legs threatened to give way. She grabbed the table for support. Brett jumped to his feet, ready to help but relaxed when she steadied herself. She headed toward the family room. "Maybe when I wake up, all of this will have been a nightmare.

Chapter 7

Good luck with that wish coming true.

Brett quirked an eyebrow as she moved into the next room, bypassing the stairs to the bedrooms. A "quick nap?" Still not completely trusting, eh? He didn't blame her. Not really.

He punched in the numbers to call his captain. Not a call he looked forward to. Especially in the middle of the night.

Tony Nolan answered on the second ring. "Nolan here." A door clicked closed in the background.

In clipped tones, Brett brought Tony up to speed as he listened without comment. Scratches from pen strokes against the perpetual legal pad, as much a part of the man as his badge, filled the silences when Brett paused.

"So she's safe now?"

"Yes."

"Good. And you cleared out all your belongings?"

"Yes, sir."

"Weather reports indicate the storm is slow-moving but should be out of your area in a coupla hours." The older man sighed, an indication of his frustration? His fatigue? "Be safe, but get back here, and we'll discuss. Sort it all out."

"Yes, sir." The line disconnected.

Brett scrubbed his face. Sort it all out. That'd take some doing. He might be looking at a mandatory vacation for breaking his cover. Or not. What happened when you broke cover instead of finishing the mission?

He joined Mary Wade in the family room. She reclined in a floral chair. She'd removed the elastic that held her hair in place, and the drying locks fell in soft waves around her relaxed face. Good. She'd fallen asleep.

Stretching out on the navy blue couch, he set his cell phone alarm to wake him in three hours. Not exactly a full night's sleep, but he'd learned to manage on a few hours here and there. He placed the phone on the coffee table, folded his arms over his chest, and was asleep before the cell light faded to black.

ℰ�ℰℛℛ

The black and white kitten gazed at Mary Wade and showed its tiny white teeth, but an annoying ringing came out of its mouth instead of a mewing. Why was the kitten ringing? Crazy kitten.

She opened her eyes erasing the kitten, but the ringing persisted. Where was she? Where was the kitten? In a flash, her brain kicked in. Agnes' family room. Agnes' recliner. Another ring. She focused on her lap and grabbed her cell. Most of her body protested with dull aches or sharp pains.

The screen shone with her parents' number.

Wonderful.

As she placed the phone to her ear, a movement to her right caught her attention. A man stretched out on Agnes' couch. A strapping man.

The events of yesterday flooded her mind. Not a nightmare. Reality.

"Hello, Mary Wade? Mary Wade. Are you there? Hello?" Her mother's voice shot through the phone.

"Yes, Mother, I'm here." As she spoke, she gathered her hair, let down to dry while she slept, and chanced a peek at Brett. Sitting upright now, he pressed his fingertips into his eyes, his elbows on his knees. Trying to tame the unruly curls, she twisted them, one-handed, into a knot at the side of her neck.

"I'm just calling to let you know we're okay. We have a tree down, but it missed the house. Did Charlotte get any rain?"

Mary Wade frowned. "A tree's down? What're you talking about?"

"The storm. The hurricane? You're so far inland you probably didn't get any rain. We don't have power. Your father is hooking up the generator right now. I ought to go help him, but I didn't want you to worry."

Mary Wade pumped the recliner to its straight position, forcing herself to concentrate over the pounding in her head. Brett fastened his gaze on her, blatantly eavesdropping. She slanted her shoulders away from him. "Wait. So you had a hurricane?"

"Are you all right? You sound off. Maybe I should speak to Daphne."

"I was asleep." She checked her watch. Not even six o'clock. "She isn't here."

"Where is she? Did she go visit her parents?"

A not-so-subtle dig about her own sporadic visits. She rubbed her forehead with the back of her hand, wincing when her wrist protested. "No. I mean, I'm not at home. I'm at Agnes'."

"What? Then you had the hurricane, too, or at least the side of it. Gary Franks on Channel Five talked about it all day yesterday."

Mary Wade massaged her temple. "I didn't watch TV yesterday."

A screened door slammed in the background.

"Why? What are you doing at Agnes'? Why aren't you at the shop?"

"She's on a cruise. I'm here till she gets back." She had to end this conversation. "Mother, I need—"

Her father's voice interrupted the line. "You're not at the shop? Why? What's wrong?"

Mary Wade pursed her lips. Everything, but not what you think. Not what you hope.

"Nothing, Daddy. Nothing's wrong. Everything's under control. Tess's watching the shop while I house-sit for Agnes."

"You left Tess watching the shop? Not leaving the shop is always your excuse for not coming to visit us. What's the matter?"

"Nothing." She took a quick breath. "Listen, I'm glad you don't have any damage. I hope you get the generator started. I'll call back soon, okay? Love you both. Bye." She pressed the end button and raised her gaze to find silver eyes zeroed in on her. Now what? Could he hear her parents' side of the conversation? Sometimes their voices carried as if she'd engaged the speaker button.

The surreal quality of yesterday and last night had given way to an awkward silence this morning. Hard for her mind to compute.

Both his eyebrows stretched toward his hairline. "'Nothing's wrong? Everything's under control?' Is that you being positive or delusional?"

"With my parents . . ." She lifted a shoulder and sighed. "Good morning. I slept about like you'd expect in a recliner. Thanks for asking. And you were eavesdropping, by the way."

"Hmm mm." He swiped his eyes. "Sorry. I haven't exactly needed good manners in the last few months. Except to open doors for nice ladies carrying too many packages."

Her eyes flew to his. He did remember her from the grocery store.

"Plus, you learn a lot from listening to conversations. It's a habit I need in my job. Can't shake it." He rose from the couch and reached for the ceiling, leaning to the left then to the right. "Why don't I scramble some eggs for a quick breakfast, and we'll talk about what happens next. Okay?"

ഇഇഇ

He grinned to himself as he considered her surprise that he'd noticed, and remembered, her from the grocery store. How could he not remember her? He'd noticed her eyes even in the glance she'd given him before her quiet, "Thank you." Yeah, he wished he could have met her looking his best, not head deep in his unshaven, long-haired, undercover look.

Offering his hand, he helped her out of the recliner. She closed her eyes and groaned.

"Sore?"

"Only every muscle in my body. What the knocks and shoves didn't batter, the full-throttle run over hill and dale covered."

He scowled, remembering shoving her away from Dusty yesterday. At least she had a sense of humor. "You'll need more ibuprofen."

The knot of hair she'd twisted during that interesting conversation with her parents tumbled in ripples and wafted a floral scent in his direction. He rubbed the back of his neck to keep from wrapping a curl around his finger. Concentrate on eggs for breakfast, not other, more interesting things.

As they entered the kitchen, she flipped the light switch. Nothing. The kitchen remained the same early morning gray. He checked the digital clocks on the microwave and oven. Black. "Power's out." He flipped the switch to the OFF position. "Unless she's got gas, no eggs. We'll need a plan B."

"Electric stove. I bought cereal and milk, granola bars. Or you could have a peanut butter and jelly sandwich." She leaned against the sink beside him.

Although the impulse was powerful, he vetoed the idea to bend closer and catch a whiff of sunscreen or more of her flower smell. Instead, he studied the hazy view out the window. "I can make out a tree pushed to a forty-five-degree angle. Probably from the saturated ground. Can't see any other wind damage so far." He half turned toward her. "According to reports I saw, Bandon was on the perimeter of the storm. Sounds like your parents got hit? They're east of here?"

She nodded. "On the coast. They lost a tree. My dad hooked up the generator."

He studied her, weighing whether or not to dig for more information. Why not? "From the sound of things, not much visiting between there and Charlotte."

"Yeah." She hugged her arms around herself, lost in thought.

Adding the body language and the parts of the conversation he overheard, something definitely was going on with her and her parents. An interesting development. He'd enjoy unraveling the mystery, especially since he and Mary Wade would be spending the next few hours together. Plenty of time for questions to be asked and answered.

"How about some breakfast?"

ⅆⅆⅆⅆⅆ

Thank goodness frying eggs was no longer an option. Thinking about the smell of sizzling eggs in butter was enough to roll Mary Wade's stomach. She'd humiliated herself enough in the past few hours. She didn't want to include tossing her cookies to the list of indignities.

Guilt added to her queasy stomach. She hadn't planned on her parents finding out about her visit to Agnes'. Of course they'd be hurt and disappointed. When was the last time she'd seen them? Christmas? For exactly a day and a half. She'd begged off Easter because of commitments at church, which were acceptable as excuses and never induced frowns or resigned sighs from her parents.

How would they take the idea of her staying at Agnes' for a whole week? Not very well.

Mary Wade swirled the squares of wheat in her skimmed milk. Although her stomach felt empty, the act of eating seemed monumental. She scooped up one square and laid it on her tongue. So far so good.

She should have known her parents would call. She should have expected it and let it go to voicemail. Of course she was glad they were fine, but she didn't need the questions, the ever-present disappointment, the guilt. Not today. She had decisions to make, bills to pay, designs to draw, outfits to sew, yet here she was recovering after a kidnapping.

A kidnapping.

Brett swallowed the milk from his second bowl of granola and reached for the peanut butter. "Something's got your brain going. What's up?"

"You mean besides being kidnapped, running through a hurricane, having breakfast with a stranger?"

He grinned. "You forgot spending the night with a stranger."

Warmth climbed up her neck. "Yeah. That too."

"I'm a good listener. Wanna talk about it?"

She moved her bowl to the side, folded her hands. "Why don't we talk about what happens next?"

"Eat first. And don't say you're not hungry. You had an apple slice—one slice—for dinner." He slathered peanut butter on a slice of bread, folded it in half, and bit it.

"No jelly? Agnes has scuppernong grape in the refrigerator. We made it last fall."

He swallowed. "We don't need to open the refrigerator more than we have to." He grinned. "And I'm sweet enough. Thanks."

"Ha. Ha." She fished out another wheat square, considered it in the puddle of milk on her spoon. Her stomach accepted a second square.

"I just need some protein." He pointed the sandwich toward her. "This is fine. All right. Listen up. We'll talk about our plan."

"Our plan?"

"Fine. It's my plan that we're gonna carry out."

"Why does it have to be 'we?' I can drive you somewhere, and you can get on with your life. I can finish my house-sitting and go back home."

"Do you really want to spend the rest of the week in the same neighborhood as Dusty and Skeet?"

When he put it like that . . . "Do you think—"

"I don't think. I know what kind of people they are. They're going to be ticked this morning when they knock down that door and find an empty bedroom. They're going to seethe when they realize I left with the keys to the truck."

The spoon splashed into the cereal bowl. "They'll be furious."

Brett nodded. "Makes their lives a little tougher. For a while at least."

Her life was spinning out of control. Caught in the middle of human trafficking, drugs, criminals, and who knew what else, she needed to get home.

Get back to normal. Get away from this man with silver eyes who made her catch her breath. Try to forget about the cleft in his chin and the way his arms felt around her when he comforted her last night. No, this morning. Her head hurt from the churning thoughts of Brett and her parents, the bruises, and the lack of sleep.

She needed to go home.

Home.

She closed her eyes. That word sounded so good.

Brett tapped her fingers. "Mary Wade, here's what we're doing, okay?"

Chapter 8

Brett popped the rest of the sandwich into his mouth. He wished he could read her thoughts. Something was troubling her. Something more than the events of yesterday. He'd bet a pizza and a frosty drink on it, but at the moment, he had to focus on relaying the plan to her. Maybe he'd get her to open up on the drive to Charlotte.

He hooked his arms over the back of his chair, grabbed the side spindles. "We need to get out of here. Soon."

She shook her head. "I'm supposed to stay. Agnes' yard . . ."

"Right. I know that, but you're not staying here. We'll put the house back in order, lock it up real tight." He surveyed the kitchen. "Does she have pets?"

"No."

"Excellent. We'll collect our things and head for Charlotte in," he glanced at his watch, "ten minutes."

She knitted her brow. "Ten minutes?"

"People'll be waking up, if they aren't already. They'll be out clearing brush, sawing downed trees, checking in with the neighbors. You don't want them to see me, do you? You don't want Agnes having to answer a lot of questions when she comes home." He changed his voice to a falsetto. "Who did Mary Wade have staying with her in your house, Agnes?" He grinned and returned to his normal voice. "We'll get out of Dodge before people start wondering. And before our other friends come looking for us."

She dropped her gaze, the hair on her neck standing at attention. "What will you do in Charlotte?"

"Check in with the captain. Give my report. Help with the arrests from there."

"Because your disguise was ruined."

He shrugged and shook his head. "Not your problem." He pushed back his chair. "Come on. Let's get this show on the road."

℠℠ℙℙ

Mary Wade hadn't thought of what people might say about a strange man coming out of the house with her. Agnes would understand because she'd get the full story. But her neighbors. Nosy Nan, the little old lady who lived across the road and down from Agnes spent most of her time watching out the front and side windows of her home. She spent the rest of her time reporting what she'd seen, enhanced with her own opinions, to anyone who'd listen. Nosy Nan would enjoy spinning tales about the house-sitter and her handsome companion.

"Fine. I'll be ready. Just have to grab my stuff from upstairs."

"That was easy. What changed your mind?"

She lifted her shoulder. "Agnes will understand. She wanted to do me a favor by getting me out of Charlotte. I'll do her a favor by not stirring up gossip." She left him for the stairs before he could ask for an explanation.

Eight minutes later, after a quick freshening up and corralling her hair, she dragged her suitcase down the stairs. Brett met her halfway. "I'll get this one to the car and then come back for the others."

"This one's it."

He glanced over his shoulder. "You packed for a week in one suitcase? I'm impressed."

A warm glow spiraled through her midsection. "I thought you'd be harder to impress."

With a grin, he pushed through the back door. "So you think I'm easy."

"Your words, not mine."

He opened the trunk with her key and gaped. "It's full of boxes." He lifted a cardboard flap. "What've you got in here?"

She joined him at the back of the car. "Unused yarn. Whenever I visit, a friend of mine who owns a yarn shop gives me extra yarn for my crochet ladies."

"You've got crochet ladies?"

"I coordinate a group of women in various stages of cancer fights. We crochet a couple of times a month at the hospital. Ellen donates yarn to us."

"Cool." He banged the trunk closed and moved to the back door of her Honda. "The backseat is full of stuff."

"It's fabric. I stopped at a vintage fabric store on the way here yesterday. I found some sweet prints I couldn't pass up. Just move them to one side. Or put my bag on the floor."

He wedged the luggage between the front and back seats and tossed his backpack in the other side. "All right. Let's lock up and get moving."

After one last look at the secured house, Mary Wade reached for the driver's side handle.

Brett's hand beat hers to the door. "Uh uh. I'm driving."

"Are you kidding me? It's my car." She tugged his arm, but his clasp stayed firm.

"You're still recovering."

"I know where we're going."

He raised his eyebrows. "We're east of Raleigh. We're going to Charlotte. I know how to go west. Hop in."

"You're such a bossy boss." She mimicked him. "I'm driving. Get in the car." She plopped her hands on her hips. "You act like you're in charge of the world."

The corner of his mouth twitched. "'Bossy boss?'" He wiped his palm over his face, clasped his chin. "You're right. I apologize." He inclined his head, caught her eyes with his. "I'm not sure the kind of conditions we'll be driving through. You're still banged up dealing with aching bruises. You're sleep-deprived. So am I, but I'm used to operating on less than a full eight hours. For all those reasons, I thought I'd be the better choice for driving." Crossing his arms over his chest, he leaned back against the door and waited.

She didn't want to back down. Brett probably always got his way, but when he explained it, his idea seemed more like a gift than a mandate. More like a help than a restriction. More caring than bossy. Her bruises did still hurt. The phone call with her parents had unsettled her. The idea of resting in the passenger side and letting Brett deal with traffic appealed much more than being in the driver's seat herself. She relaxed her shoulders, softened her features. "Okay. Thank you."

He blinked. "That was easier than I thought too. You must be warming up to my charms." He met her on the opposite side of the car, holding the door for her.

"I'm immune to your so-called charms, so don't get used to winning every argument. I just know a good deal when I hear one." She gritted her teeth as he laughed to himself on his way to the driver's side.

කාකාශ්‍රශ්‍ර

Brett settled in beside her and let the seat back as far as it would go. She struggled with her bandaged hand and the seat belt. When he clasped the buckle to help, she snatched her hand away.

Immune to my charms, huh? Famous last words, maybe. He'd like to pursue that discussion, see where he could take it, but they'd already lost several minutes negotiating the packed car and the driver's seat. They needed to make tracks.

"Here's what we're going to do. We'll take highway 70 to I-40, then take that to I-85 all the way in to Charlotte. We'll stop when we need gas." He checked the gas gauge. "Looks like that'll be a ways down the road. Good job for not leaving the car on empty."

She glared at him.

He ducked his head. "I meant that as a compliment." He backed out of the carport and down the drive. She shielded the side of her face with her hand. "It's still early. Not many people will be out yet."

"Don't bet on it. Nosy Nan will probably be scanning the neighborhood for all she's worth. She's the unofficial neighborhood watch." She leaned into her lap, fiddled with her sandal.

In the corner of his eye, he caught a flutter in the front window. Somebody watched them leave. "You can sit up now. We're past the neighbor's house."

She grabbed her phone from her purse, punched in numbers. "I hate leaving Agnes' yard with limbs and leaves all over it. Plus, that dogwood tree needs to be righted."

"We need to get down the road. We can't take the chance of Dusty and Skeet seeing us."

"I know." She lifted a finger to pause the conversation. "Hello, Ellen? I figured you'd be awake. I know. How'd you fare in the storm?" She nodded with the phone against her ear. "That's great. Agnes has a few limbs in her yard. The backyard dogwood needs some attention. Listen, I've had a little emergency," she crossed her fingers, "and I need to get back to Charlotte. No, nothing bad. Just need to get back. I hate leaving without cleaning up her yard. Do you think you could ask Tommy to bring the youth group by to set things right? I'll make a donation to the summer mission trip. Great, thanks. No, I'm fine. Call you soon. Bye."

"A little emergency?"

"I couldn't very well say that I'd been kidnapped, now could I?" She punched more numbers into the phone. "Hello, Agnes. I hope your cruise was great. Listen, a hurricane came through—well, just the edge of it, really, but your house is fine. You had some debris in the yard, but don't worry about that. I'm sorry, but I couldn't stay the whole week. Keep the thank-you present I'm sure you bought me since I didn't earn it." She gave a throaty giggle. "Call me when you get back, and we'll swap stories. Love you. Bye."

They drove for several minutes in silence, skirting around a tree partially covering the road before turning onto Highway 70. Water filled ditches to overflowing. Fields looked like ponds.

He eyed her. "You gonna call your parents?"

She dropped her phone into her purse. "Maybe later."

More awkward silence. He could think about the case, but he'd grappled with it before they ran away. He discussed it briefly with Tony over the phone this morning. Nothing he could do from here. He squeezed the steering wheel in frustration and glanced at Mary Wade.

Angled away from him, she kept her focus on the window. The passenger side view must be fascinating. What was she thinking about? What was the deal with her parents? Why did Agnes want to give her a break from Charlotte? So many questions. And about four hours to find the answers.

Setting the cruise control button, he adjusted the seat belt strap lower on his shoulder. "So. Why did Agnes think you needed to get out of Charlotte?"

Her head whipped toward him, eyes flashing emerald sparks. "What? Why do you think that? And anyway, it's none of your business."

"You're right. It's not my business, but we've got four hours. Unless you want to listen to four hours of hurricane reports, I thought we could talk. You said she did you a favor."

She pushed the latch on the glove compartment. "I have some CDs in here." She dug out a few and spread five like a fan in her hands. "You can choose."

He gave a quick scan of the choices. "Good taste. Classic Van Morrison sounds good."

She placed the disc in the player and *Brown-eyed Girl* filled the car.

He mentally changed the lyrics to "my green-eyed girl." Lowering the volume, he met her gaze. "Great background music. So why did she do you a favor?"

Chapter 9

Mary Wade blew a bothersome tendril away from her forehead. Why did she care if he knew about a failed relationship? She'd never see him again after they parted in Charlotte.

"I'd been working a lot and then stopped seeing someone. Agnes thought a change of scenery would be excellent medicine." Her exact words, in fact. "So I came to keep her house. She's supposed to come home on Friday, and we were going to spend the weekend together." She flipped her hands in an end-of-story gesture.

"That's it? Working too much and a breakup?"

"Yeah. Pretty much."

He shook his head. "I smell more to this story. Why'd you break up? Did you break up with him?"

Nosy Nan had nothing on Brett, but maybe if she shared about what had happened with Robert, she'd understand more about the relationship, more about herself. What did she have to lose? Her dignity had dissolved in that abandoned house.

"Robert . . . started seeing someone else. I saw them entering a movie theater." She turned back toward her window.

Brett shifted in his seat. "So he cheated on you. Bummer."

She fiddled with her seat belt strap. "According to him, he didn't consider it cheating. He didn't think we were serious."

"Did you think you were serious?"

"We saw each other three or four times a week. I think most people would consider that serious."

He stroked his chin. "What did you do when you were together?"

Scenes of their dates filtered through her mind. She'd sit at her table poring over designs while he sat on the couch watching NCIS reruns or old movies. Or she'd sit with him and hand sew garments. At the time, their evenings together felt comfortable, easy. From this vantage point, however, those times sounded a bit dull, not exactly something she wanted to put forth for judgment. "We just hung out. Watched TV. Whatever. He's in grad school studying psychology. He likes programs with well-developed characters."

"So you watched TV together three nights a week. I guess you cuddled together on the couch during the shows."

Her stomach constricted. Embarrass much? Licking her lips, she tasted salty perspiration. "No. Not really."

"You just sat and watched the program?"

She crossed her arms in front of her. "He graded papers. He has a fellowship and teaches two classes while he takes his own. I had work to do too."

"What kind of work? Something with all that fabric maybe?" He nodded to the backseat.

"I design children's clothes and sell them in my shop and online."

"Cool. So let's get this straight." He pointed his index finger toward the windshield. "He graded papers," and added a second finger, "and you sewed little dresses?"

Obviously, he wasn't going to let this go. Fine. Admit the whole thing and be done with it. Who cared what Brett thought of her or her love life? A few more hours, and he'd be out of her life too. She capitulated, sliding her clammy palms down her capris. "This is the way it was. He'd sit on the couch with tests or essays. I'd sit at my table with my designs, either sketching ideas or cutting out patterns. Real exciting stuff."

"Did you ever do anything else? Go out to dinner? Go to a concert? Ride bikes through the park?"

"He took me to a Thai restaurant for my birthday."

"So he paid for it?"

"Yes."

He checked his rearview mirror. "What did he give you?"

This man was relentless. How could she stop this interrogation?

"Did he give you a present?"

She gritted her teeth. "No."

"Did you give him one for his birthday?"

"Yes."

"Uh huh."

"What does that mean?"

"Look. I'm no dating expert by any stretch, but if I was serious about a beautiful woman, I'd do more than watch TV with her."

Heat swirled in the pit of her stomach. Did he think she was beautiful?

"Is he a good kisser?"

Her mouth fell open. "Are you seriously asking me that question?"

"That's your answer then?"

She turned away from him to hide her burning face. Brett had enough information about her love life. He didn't need to know she'd never kissed Robert. They usually ended their nights with a quick hug. They'd pecked each other on the cheek a couple of times after birthdays and special events. "You're not supposed to ask questions like that."

"There goes my lack of manners again."

She could hear the grin in his voice. "You know, you don't have to be so smug. We had a nice relationship."

"Relationship or friendship?"

"A friendship can grow into a relationship."

He changed lanes to pass a pickup with furniture crowding the truck bed. "I've heard people say that."

"You don't believe it?"

"Friendship is important, I'll give you that, but a relationship needs a spark. An attraction. Something to get excited about."

"You believe in love at first sight?"

He lifted a shoulder. "Maybe not love, but definitely interest. You have to have interest to move forward. No offense, but what you described sounded like a brother and sister, not Elizabeth Bennett and Mr. Darcy."

Surprise widened her eyes. "You know *Pride and Prejudice?*"

"Hey. I've got some depth. I had to read it for school and survived the experience. Figured you'd be a fan. My sister reads it once a year. Watches the movie more than that if she can. I'm talking the PBS version." He checked his side mirror and merged onto I-40.

Brett was right. Her dates with Robert sounded like a get-together with a brother. Robert was like a pair of fuzzy bedroom slippers. Warm and comfortable. Not exciting like a pair of strappy black heels.

Strappy black heels. Where would she wear those? More importantly, where would she get the money to buy them?

Mary Wade conceded the boring point about the relationship. But why did catching him with someone else still sting? Humiliation swelled again in her chest at the memory of seeing the two of them, his arm around her shoulder, gliding into the theater. A new question niggled her mind. If they were friends as Robert suggested, why didn't he tell her about the date? Tears pricked at the back of her eyes. She chewed the side of her cheek and willed them to stay in place.

She knew she didn't love Robert, not like Elizabeth loved Mr. Darcy, for sure, but he was her plus one for weddings and church events. He understood the dynamics between her and her parents. He was comfortable, yes.

But definitely not exciting.

She glanced at the man beside her. A lock of sandy brown hair had worked its way out of his pony tail and grazed his cheek.

Definitely not fuzzy slipper material.

ജ്ഞൊഌൕ൧

Hooking an annoying strand of hair behind his ear, Brett checked the rearview mirror, then his speed. He dropped his hand to his thigh, keeping one on the steering wheel.

Why did he mention his sister? He never talked about Carly to other people. He never talked about a lot of stuff to other people. He smiled at the memory of shocking Mary Wade with the *Pride and Prejudice* reference.

Her phone buzzed. After reading the number on the screen, she closed her eyes, letting it ring a second time before answering.

"What's up, Mother?"

Her mother's voice crackled in the car. "Mary Wade, you practically hung up on us a while ago. I would've called right back, but your father needed help with the generator. Now tell me again. Agnes is on a cruise, and you're at her house?"

"I was. Now I'm heading back home."

"Mary Wade. What is going on? You're there. The storm comes. Now you're leaving? Did Tess call about the shop? Is something wrong at the shop?"

"No, Mother. Agnes' power was out, but everything's fine. I decided to go home. She'll understand. Listen, I'm on I-40. I'll call later, okay? Love you. Bye." She ended the call with a click, dropped the phone into her purse, and sighed.

He chanced a sidelong glance at this passenger. "Your voice changes when you talk to your parents."

Her head whipped toward him. "No, it doesn't."

"Yes, it does. Your voice is soft and husky in a regular conversation. When you talk to your parents, it gets a little firmer, a little edgy. Like you're guarding something. Of course, there's the obvious. You haven't mentioned the last twenty-four hours in either call, but I think there's something else going on."

She hugged her arms to herself. "You got all that in a two-minute, one-sided conversation?"

"Your mom's voice carries. I heard almost every word. Sorry."

The opening measures of *Ro Ro Rosie* began, but Mary Wade punched the forward arrow.

"You don't like Ro Ro Ro Ro Rosie?"

She scrunched her nose. "Not my favorite." She pulled the elastic from her bun, smoothed her hair, and re-coiled a new one.

"Do you ever leave it down during the day?"

"What?"

"Nothing." Thinking out loud. Not smart, man. Get back to safer questions. "So you didn't tell them about the kidnapping or the strange man who's driving your car. What other topic is off limits?"

One eyebrow rose. "Does meddling in my life help you drive?"

He grinned. "I like figuring things out. Let's see. They asked about your shop both times. I think it's something to do with that."

She smoothed the edge of the bandage on the back of her hand. "They wanted me to go into some kind of church work. My major in college was religious studies, to please my parents, but I minored in business and design. I nannied to help pay for the extra classes. I started designing and sewing my designs sophomore year. By the time I graduated, I had several clients.

"Agnes helped set me up in a booth at a crafts warehouse. My shop. She's helped me a lot actually. Sometimes I think it's too much." She rested her fingertips on her collarbone. "Anyway, at graduation, I showed my parents my five-year business plan, my designs, my list of clients. They asked me for the list of churches I planned to send résumés to." She turned to her window and lowered her voice. "Completely discounted my work, my plan." A muscle in her jaw worked. "They're biding their time till I fail."

She'd shared something deeply personal with him. He could either lighten the mood, tease her like he normally did in situations like this, or he could honor the fact she'd trusted him with a personal hurt.

Although he wanted to, he thought better of reaching across the console and holding her hand. Instead, he gentled his voice and smiled. "You're following your dreams. That's a good thing, right?"

"Designing children's clothes doesn't exactly save the world."

"You add beauty to it. You don't ruin it like the people in my line of work."

"I wish my parents could see it that way."

"Thanks for telling me that. You surprised me again."

She leaned back against the headrest. "Since I probably won't see you after today, I guess it doesn't matter if you know or not."

"Yeah. About that." He swiped his jaw. "We need to talk."

The quick wariness that flared in her eyes caught at his gut. The events of yesterday put that wariness in her big green eyes. He wished he had more than nice words to reassure her.

"You ready for a break? I need some caffeine. How about a Starbucks?"

⁊⁊⚃⚃

Grateful for the heat in her hands, Mary Wade cradled the grande cappuccino. Her body had turned to ice at Brett's mention of the word "testify." They'd purchased their caffeinated beverages and hopped back on the road to discuss her involvement in his case.

Brett sipped his black coffee and settled the cup into the holder.

She understood his hesitation to talk in the tiny coffee shop. Not only were the tables within inches of each other, but also, people were interested in him. Heads turned as soon as he entered the doorway. Women noticed him.

Mary Wade understood their interest too. His ponytail emphasized high cheekbones and unusual eyes. His height commanded attention. Dressed in black jeans and a T-shirt, he evoked an intimidating presence. With her reddish-brown hair, pale skin, and freckles, she disappeared beside him.

"Do you understand what testifying means? Nothing's set in stone yet, but I'll answer any questions you have."

She dragged her eyes from his T-shirt and sipped her cooling drink. Yes, she was stalling, but her mind was spinning. She'd be called to testify. She'd miss more days of designing, more days of selling. She'd have to deal with her parents. She'd have to face those terrifying men again, but she'd be part of putting them in prison. A dull ache bloomed in her chest.

"Mary Wade." Brett's soft voice brought her attention back to him. "Like I said, I already texted the pictures of your wrists to my captain. He knows every detail I could provide. The other evidence we have is thorough and tight. Yours would be the icing on the cake, so to speak."

Brett passed a crawling late model sedan. The driver, a little old lady with cotton candy hair, kept her hands at the ten and two o'clock positions on the steering wheel. Where was she going before eight thirty in the morning? A doctor's appointment? A brunch with friends who play Mahjong? Certainly not escaping from kidnappers. With a stranger—

"Earth to Mary Wade. Are you listening?"

She shifted in her seat. "Oh, yeah. When are we talking about? Two weeks? Six months?"

He tipped the cup to finish the coffee. "Don't know for sure. Just about everything is in place to move in and start the arrests, but we want every 'i' dotted and every 't' crossed when we go to trial. Making sure everything's in order usually takes months."

"I guess I don't know enough to ask questions." She raked her teeth over her bottom lip. "I'd have to see Dusty and Skeet again, right?"

"No, not necessarily. The DA could interview you in the judge's chambers with a video relay to the courtroom. You wouldn't have to see them again."

She trailed her finger around the rim of the cup's plastic lid. "Would you be in court?"

He hesitated and glanced in the rearview mirror. "Yes, I'll come to court the day I testify, but we might not be called on the same day."

Nodding, she studied her bandage. "So I probably won't see you at trial."

He rubbed his chin. "Probably not."

Yep. That's what she thought. She checked her watch. Time with Brett was running out. Although she pushed against it sometimes, a lot of times, she liked his strong presence protecting her, helping her, opening doors and windows for her. That butterfly feeling signaling homesickness fluttered in her stomach. Now safely away from the real criminals, she wasn't ready for this interesting adventure to end.

The real criminals? When had she started trusting him, believing in him?

Probably when he hadn't retaliated with a slap after she head butted him yesterday afternoon.

Yesterday afternoon?

That time seemed an age away from the present. In less

than a day, she'd come to rely on a stranger. In less than a couple of hours, she'd probably never see him again. If she did, a quick "hello" in a courthouse hallway might be it.

Robert's rejection may have smarted, but she suspected the absence of Brett in her life might produce a longer lasting regret. She wanted to get to know more about him. She wished they had more to hold them together than a midnight escape and a common goal of imprisoning Dusty and Skeet.

A whole lot more.

Chapter 10

Mary Wade read the road sign: thirty-five miles to Charlotte. She didn't want to think about the possible trial. She wanted to pretend she journeyed in a car with an interesting person, maybe on their way to an interesting place. A concert perhaps. Maybe a play. She wanted to have a normal conversation, not talk about criminals or investigations.

"Tell me about your sister."

His head snapped toward her, then back to the road. "What?"

"You said you have a sister. What's her name? Are you close? What does she do for a living? Is she married?"

Brett rolled his neck, and for a moment, Mary Wade thought he'd tell her to mind her own business. He shrugged, however, and glanced out the window. "Her name's Carly. She's a nurse. She's married to Timmy, a great guy. He's a firefighter. They live in Boone. They have a little girl. Yes, we're close. It was just the two of us for a while. I don't get to see them as often as I'd like to."

She adjusted the volume on the Zac Brown CD. "Wow. I wasn't sure you'd answer me."

"Why?"

"It'd be easy just to say, 'Mind your own business.'"

He raised a pinky from the steering wheel. "I've got some manners."

With a laugh, she grinned at him. "Uh huh. You keep telling me."

He gave her a hurt look. "Hey, I open doors for you."

"Yes, you did. You also use napkins when you eat. Good job." She patted his arm, his firm, solid arm with the black T-shirt stretched tight over his bicep. Mistake. She tucked her hands under her thighs. "How old's your niece?"

"Lilly?" He smiled, softening his angular face. "She's one and a half. Wait. No, almost two. She's got a birthday coming up soon." He raised his eyebrows. "I should get you to make her an outfit or something."

Her heart skipped a beat. "I could do that." Especially if it meant she'd see him again. "Two is such a fun age. She's beginning to have a sense of herself, develop her personality more, have a little more independence."

"I've heard this age described as the terrible twos."

She wagged her index finger at him. "No. No. No. Put a positive spin on it. Haven't you ever heard people rise to the level of expectation, or something like that? The same goes for children."

"And you speak from experience," he glanced at her, "as a mother?"

"Of course not. It's part of my job to know children if I'm designing for them. Plus, I've worked as a nanny since college."

"You still nanny?"

"Strictly on an as-needed basis. Some overnights now and then when the parents travel."

He massaged the back of his neck, kept his eyes on the road. "Do you ever wonder if you'll burn out, not want kids of your own?"

"Absolutely not." An image of a little boy with silver eyes waved at her.

"So you have three jobs? Nanny, designer, business owner?"

"My designs don't pay all the bills. Yet. Periodically, I teach some sewing and handiwork classes too." She combed a wayward tendril from her temple with her fingers. "If you're serious, I'd love to make something for Lilly. I owe you for rescuing me anyway."

He clenched his jaw and shook his head. "You don't owe me anything. I was doing my job. That's all." His voice had an edge to it.

Fun conversation over. Back to all business.

Listen to him, Mary Wade. He's reminding you this car ride isn't going to end at a concert or play. It's going to end with goodbye and going separate ways.

She was a job to him.

Nothing more.

ഇഇഇരുര

Brett read the road sign: seven miles to Charlotte. Why did he tell her about Carly? He'd been loose with all kinds of personal info. What had gotten into him? He knew better. Sharing personal stuff would make things only tougher when it came time to part ways. He should know. He'd lived it.

Mary Wade, however, was easy to talk to, and it felt good talking about Carly. They'd probably get along really well together.

Too bad they'd never have a chance to meet.

"The city limits are just up ahead. Why don't we stop for gas and fill up the tank for you?"

"Sure. What does Lilly like to wear?"

He made a face. "I don't know. I haven't seen her wear much besides pinks and purples. Carly likes to put her in ruffles. Girly stuff, for sure, but it's been a while since I've seen her."

"You don't get to visit often?"

The compassion in her voice intrigued him. He glanced toward her. Mistake. Green eyes with lighter bands outlining the irises centered on him, waiting for an answer. Something twisted in his chest, but he refused to explore it. He'd been down that road before with someone who looked to him as her rescuer. He shrugged. "The nature of the job, Mary Wade."

He flipped the turn signal and glided into the exit lane. "Let's get some gas."

ဆာဆာ၁ၵၒၵၒ

Mary Wade's heart fluttered. A few more miles and this crazy chapter in her life would end. Would she ever see him again? Maybe. For a few minutes in a courtroom. He might smile at her and wave. He might even approach her and say, "How's it going?" But then he'd be off to talk to a colleague or answer a reporter's question. She didn't foresee much interaction beyond a perfunctory assembling of all the characters from this absurd tale.

As they coasted into the station and headed for a gas tank, she scanned the view outside her window for some way to postpone the inevitable. A frozen yogurt shop in the adjoining strip mall caught her attention. Bingo. Maybe goodbye could be pushed a little later into the afternoon.

"Hey, look over there. Do you like frozen yogurt? Why don't we get some?"

Brett's gaze followed the direction of her pointing finger. He rubbed his hand across his cheek and shook his head. "Ahm. Yeah. Frozen yogurt's fine, but I need to get to the office. You need to check on your shop, right? Let's gas up and go." He set the emergency brake and exited the car.

Her stomach seized.

Denied.

Rejected.

Heat flooded her cheeks. He must be counting the minutes until he could be rid of her. Well, she'd help him out.

She climbed over the console to the driver's side, adjusted the seat, and buckled the belt.

ဆာဆာ၁ၵၒၵၒ

Brett peered into the car, opened the door. "What's up?"

"I'm driving. What does it look like?" Her smile didn't quite make it to her eyes.

He cocked his head. "Mary Wade, we covered this."

The emergency brake thunked as she released it. "Get in please. We're wasting time."

"I can—"

She cranked the engine. "Let's go."

He jogged around to the passenger's side, strapped himself in the seat. "Why the driver change?"

"We're in Charlotte now. I'm rested. I can drop you off. It'll be faster. You can be on with your day. No more wasting time."

A definite cold front had moved into the car, and now he understood why.

She pulled away from the tank and merged into traffic. "I'm assuming your office is at the courthouse, right? On Fourth Street, right?"

He faced her, considered how to explain his decision. "Mary Wade, I'm sorry about the frozen yogurt. Look. I know how this goes. You're grateful I got you out of a sticky situation, but you're putting more importance on it than it deserves." He lifted both shoulders. "You're probably getting me mixed up with a knight in shining armor. That kind of thing."

She flattened her lips. "Don't pretend to know what I'm thinking or how I'm feeling after being with me for one day. People have been doing that for as long as I can remember. I hate it. So stop." Her chin rose slightly. "Beyond knowing my name and what I do for a living, you don't know anything about me."

True. And he'd like to know more, a definite red flag. He didn't plan to date someone he'd met on the job again. He tried for levity. "First of all, we've packed a lot in one day. It feels like a lot longer."

She snorted. "Thanks so much." She took the ramp to I-85.

"That's not what I meant. Second, I know you have a soft spot for kittens. I know you like to ride bikes and have pedicures. I know you enjoy what you do so much you defied your parents to do it. I know—"

"Congratulations. You're very observant. You should be a detective or something." She turned up the volume of the CD and strains of *Colder Weather* cut off the conversation.

Chapter 11

The defying-your-parent comment had zinged too close to home. Defy. A ruthless sounding word. She'd never called it that herself, but it was exactly what she'd done.

She needed to end this . . .this crazy detour from her regular life.

He'd repeatedly kept his distance, explained he was doing his job, but she didn't listen. She'd allowed herself to fall under his charm. The conversation about his sister and niece, the sound of his laugh, the touch of his hand on hers.

In a short, few hours, she'd become accustomed to his constant presence. The thought of his absence chilled her, left her feeling empty.

Clearly, he had no qualms about leaving her. In fact, the opposite seemed true. He seemed more than ready to be finished with her. He'd checked his watch three times in the last five minutes. Another rejection in less than two weeks.

She concentrated on the tears multiplying in the corners of her eyes. Stand firm, tears. Do not fall. She'd cried once in front of him. Once was enough. She focused on anger instead of disappointment over an abbreviated friendship and fear of being left on her own. "So is it the courthouse? I'll drop you off there."

"Don't make a special stop." His hand hooked in the seat belt, keeping it off his neck. "I can call a cab from your place."

"No." She glued her gaze to the street in front of her.

"I can help with your bag and boxes of yarn."

She shook her head. "Not necessary. I needed your help yesterday in a huge way." She flicked her gaze toward him. "Thank you. Again. But I don't need your help anymore." She checked her rearview mirror. "I'm going to Fourth Street unless you say something different."

ॐॐॐ

Brett dug his fingers into the back of his neck. He felt like he'd suffered whiplash. Ten minutes ago, she wanted frozen yogurt. Now she was practically pushing him out the door. What happened to change her mind? His nixing the yogurt idea? He liked frozen yogurt as much as the next guy, but stopping for a treat would only prolong the inevitable. This interlude was winding to a close. A quick end would be better all around. Small talk over a frozen treat would make the goodbye more difficult and awkward.

He understood they'd been through something extraordinary together, but those few hours wouldn't sustain a relationship. He felt the prick of disappointment he'd seen flash in her eyes when he declined her suggestion. He wasn't ready to end this thing either. He wished she'd let him come to her house. He'd like to help her get settled. He'd like to see her place, see her house plants, the kind of books she liked, but she was right to refuse. He'd like to explore the what ifs, but he'd been down that road before with another grateful lady.

Not a fun trip.

He'd leave this one alone. Let her heal with friends. Let her try to forget about the kidnapping without being reminded of it every time she looked at him.

"Yeah. Fourth Street."

A few stoplights later, she idled in front of the Mecklenburg County Courthouse.

"I hate leaving you to unload all those boxes in the trunk."

She shrugged. "Don't worry about it. I've done it before.

Plus, I have a roommate. She'll help if she's there." She offered a tight smile.

"Someone will be in touch with you about testifying."

Tensing, she nodded, focused on the steering wheel. "Right."

"Okay, then." He searched for another topic to keep him in the car, keep him with her a little longer. Nothing came to mind. Time was up. "Thanks for the ride." He reached for the door latch.

She twisted toward him and grabbed his forearm. "Brett. Thank you. I mean it. You were an answer to a prayer."

"I—"

"Don't say you were just doing your job. Please. I understand from your perspective you were doing your job. From my perspective, however, you saved me. So thank you."

Sincere, green eyes beckoned him to . . . what? To believe her? To linger in the car? Should he explore this connection he felt with her? Did she feel the pull between them too? Or did gratitude to be home, away from Dusty and Skeet play a part in the message her eyes telegraphed? If he trailed his fingers up over her arm, rubbed his thumb against her mouth, leaned in close, and . . .

Quit. Say goodbye and be done with it.

"You're welcome." He raked his fingers through his hair. The loose lock fell from behind his ear and brushed his cheek again. He snatched a wrinkled receipt and a pen from the console. "Here's my cell if you ever need anything." He handed her the rectangle of paper. "So listen. Be careful. Watch your back and all that." He locked his gaze with hers. "Don't take any wooden nickels."

She squinted. "What does that even mean?"

With the failed attempt at levity, he shook his head. "My grandfather used to say it to me." Again with the confessions. Open the door and exit.

This time when he reached for the door, she kept her hand to herself. He dragged his backpack from the backseat and climbed out, glanced back and waved.

But her focus was already on the traffic, not him.

ℰᏬℰᏬᏨᏚᏨᏚ

Biting the inside of her cheek made smiling feel stilted and forced, but it was the only way Mary Wade could keep herself from crying before he shut the door. She'd never felt so alone. Not when her parents dropped her off for her freshman year at college or at graduation when they left after she explained about her business. Both times she saw the future as a place of positive possibilities. Even when Dusty and Skeet had her, surprise and terror had seized all her emotions, leaving no room for loneliness.

Now the future held nothing but hard choices. Should she expand her business, move out of the craft warehouse and into a real brick and mortar building? Should she take out another mortgage on her home to finance all the new changes? Should she acquire another roommate to help split the bills? Or should she just move the business home, forget about a real storefront and a new roommate, and wait for a better economy?

Hard questions. Questions that gave her a headache. She'd rather go home, take a turn-her-skin-pink bath, and contemplate silver eyes and a cleft in a prominent chin. For a split second, before he'd mentioned wooden nickels, she was sure he considered kissing her.

A goodbye kiss? Or more?

She waited for the McDowell Street light to change to green. A red Jaguar passed through the intersection. Yep. She was back in Charlotte. Back to reality. No kisses, goodbye or otherwise, for her.

Just a trunk full of yarn boxes to unload and a long, long time without Brett.

Chapter 12

"I am sick and tired of rolling this bike up and down every driveway from here to yonder. Like looking for a needle in a haystack, if you ask me." Skeet put the truck into drive and eased onto the road.

Dusty chewed on his thumbnail. "I didn't ask you. We're gonna find out the name of that girl or die trying."

"You maybe. Not me." Skeet shook his head. "She's long gone, and I say good riddance." He flicked his hand toward the dashboard.

"Not on your life. We're gonna find her. I got unfinished business." Dusty grinned. "Then she'll lead us to that dirty double-crosser. He needs to pay for cheatin' us."

It could've been worse if Skeet hadn't known how to hotwire the truck. Leaving with the keys . . .Uh uh. Leaving with the girl and the keys. . .

He couldn't wait to get his hands on both of them.

The older man scratched his nose. "I don't like what Matt did either, but I say cut our losses and get on outta here. I don't like how all this feels."

"We'll find somebody who knows about this bike." Dusty pointed down the road. "Stop at that next house."

Skeet waited in the idling truck while Dusty hefted the bike out of the truck bed, rolled it to the front steps, and flipped the kickstand. Grabbing the concrete steps two at a time, he arrived at the front threshold, rang the bell, then knocked for good measure.

An old woman almost as tall as Dusty cracked the door, peering over the chain. "What do you want? I don't need a bicycle." The door headed back to its closed position.

Dusty tumbled his words out. "Oh, no. No, ma'am. I'm sure you don't. We found this here bike beside the road. We're trying to find the rightful owner. I'd appreciate if you'd take a look. See if it looks familiar?"

She squinted at him first, then the bike. "That's Agnes' purple bicycle. I'd know it anywhere. She rides it up and down this road like she's fifteen again. Wears that funny-looking thing on her head, that helmet. At her age. She's a sight for sure. But she wouldn't of been riding it this week. She's on a cruise." She dragged out "cruise" and made a sour face like she smelled a rotten egg.

Dusty pulled on his earlobe, shot a wide-eyed, questioning look at the woman. "Well, I wonder how it could have wound up beside the road?"

"I'm sure I don't know. Except her goddaughter was supposed to be here all week looking out after her house. She was here at first all right, but then I saw her leave early right after the storm with somebody I don't know. Some man I've never seen before. A man with a ponytail." She crossed her arms. "I saw her clear as anything even though she tried to hide, sneaking her head down below the car window."

"So you think her goddaughter . . ."

"Uh huh. Mary Wade. They hightailed it back to Charlotte, I'm guessing, right after the rain stopped. Left with Agnes' tree leaning over and the front yard full of limbs and leaves. Skipping out on the cleanup. That's what." She clucked her tongue and rolled her eyes heavenward. "I don't know what the world's coming to with these careless young folk."

He nodded. "Mary Wade." He repeated the name to remember it.

"Mary Wade Kimball. I should have known what to expect

when she stayed in Charlotte and didn't move with her parents when they took that church at the beach. It's a shame indeed. Sneaking off before breakfast with some man."

"Okay, ma'am, we'll just leave this bike where it belongs if you tell us where it goes."

She squinted her eyes again. "Just leave it here. I'll see that Agnes gets it."

"We wouldn't want to put you out, ma'am. I'm sure you've got a full plate. Is her house near yours?"

Her eyes left his. He turned to follow her gaze and pointed across the road. "Is that it? Is that Ms. Agnes' house?"

She tightened her lips and nodded.

"Well, thank you, ma'am. We'll get it back to the rightful owner. Don't worry about a thing. You have a good day now."

Dusty grinned all the way to the truck.

ಬಂಬಂಬಂ

Two regulars ambled into the hospital rec room as Mary Wade searched for her crochet hook in the bottom of her yarn bag. It had slipped out of the ball of yarn she'd stuck it in at the last meeting. She waved to her friends.

Goldie, a five-year cancer survivor, never missed a meeting of the crochet support group. One of the founding members, she provided stitch instruction, as well as encouraging words, to other members experiencing the same hard path she'd traversed years earlier.

Louise, another founding member and survivor who staunchly refused to learn anything new at her age, also refused to miss the meetings. Instead of crocheting, she sometimes worked on word puzzle books but mostly listened to the chatter.

Harriet knitted sweaters and donated them to homeless shelters every fall. All these women were well into retirement and widowhood.

Over the eighteen months Mary Wade had coordinated the

group of crocheters, knitters, and puzzle solvers, women of all ages in different stages of cancer had joined the group. Some came for a time, and some became regulars.

Twelve-year-old Katie joined when her leukemia had recurred. She came to her first meeting not knowing a single stitch but in only a few weeks began to create cool hats with the craziest color combinations she could imagine. Lime green and purple. Electric blue, hot pink, and neon yellow. Some had tassels swinging from the top. Others boasted flowers sewn onto the side. All were pure fun.

When Katie succumbed to the cancer within a few months of joining the group, several women refused to return. Goldie called them, demanded they return and help the group make one thousand hats to donate to hospitals and overseas children's orphanages in honor of Katie. They came back and in four months, with help from church groups, neighborhood book clubs, and bridge clubs, had crocheted or knitted twelve hundred and thirty-five hats. Louise participated by donating a bulging box of yarn. A picture of the ladies made the hospital newsletter and local paper.

Goldie backed up to an upholstered chair and let herself drop onto the cushion. "Whew. It feels delicious in here. Summer's grabbed on with a vengeance. All that hurricane rain went east, and, believe me, I surely don't want one of those, but we could use some rain. My dahlias look parched."

"There might be some rain in a few days, so the weatherman says." Louise slid a new workbook out of her satchel handbag. "The almanac disagrees, however."

"What are you working on today, Louise?" Goldie attached a magnifying glass around her neck and adjusted it against her pillowy bosom.

"The first puzzle is all about flowers. Maybe I'll find a dahlia in here somewhere." She squinted at the first page and wiggled into her seat. "What're you crocheting, Goldie?"

"I've got about four more inches to go on this prayer shawl. Sending it to my great niece. She just found out she has multiple sclerosis."

Mary Wade patted the woman's age-spotted hand. "What a shame, Goldie. Sorry to hear that."

Goldie released a sigh. "It's hard on her, being a young mother and all that, but she's got a great support system."

A few others trickled in and began working on various projects.

Mary Wade found the stitch where she left off last time and looped her hook for a half double crochet. "I'm glad all of you showed up today. Does anyone have news to share?"

One of the thirty-something members with a colorful scarf wrapped around her head, culminating in an elaborate bow on the side, volunteered a tidbit. "My sister's expecting her first baby. I need to crochet a baby blanket."

"Sweet." "Wonderful news." "Cool." Everyone shared excitement over the possibility of new life.

"Mary Wade, I have some news too." Goldie commanded the group's attention. "My neighbor leads a Girl Scout troop and hoped you'd teach those girls to crochet."

"Oh, sure. I love to teach children."

"Teach 'em young, then when they're old like me, they'll enjoy a skill." Louise gave her approval as she circled a diagonal line of letters in her book.

Rahzie, a newcomer to the group whose feet swung above the carpet floor as she sat in her chair, worked on a lacy doily with fine crochet thread and a steel hook. "We need to keep the needle arts alive."

Mary Wade fished for her phone. "When does she want to start?"

"Well, that's the thing. She's hoping she could bring them three or four weeks in a row. She thinks the consistency would help them retain skills."

"Absolutely." She checked her phone and scrolled to her calendar. Except for work and sleep, pretty much wide open for anything. Certainly no blocks of time with Brett's name filled in. She ignored the spasm in her stomach associated with thoughts of Brett. "My schedule's not a problem. Give me her contact information, and we'll see what we can come up with."

"You're a dear, so thoughtful and willing to help. Speaking of that . . ." Goldie paused and freed more yarn from the skein in the bag by her feet.

"Speaking of what?"

"When are you and Robert going to make it official?"

Mary Wade's hook slipped from her fingers and clattered against the wooden chair leg. She bent to retrieve it, taking a couple extra seconds to will her heart to slow down. How to fix this awkward situation? "Goldie—"

Louise abandoned her ink pen to her lap. "So glad you asked that. I've wondered myself."

Charge ahead. Smile. Give the news and change the subject as quickly as possible. "Robert is seeing someone else. Does anyone remember how to make a double treble crochet in the front post?"

Silence encased the room. Not even Harriet's needles clacked out their persistent rhythm.

"Oh, Mary Wade." Goldie stretched her mouth wide. "Open mouth. Insert great huge foot. Sorry, honey."

Mary Wade shook her head and leaned forward. "Don't beat yourself up. I'm fine. We weren't exactly heading in any direction." According to him at least. "And I'm so busy with work, I don't have a lot of time to devote to a relationship anyway."

Maybe she could find time if Brett . . .

So not happening.

Chapter 13

"So, Jack, what'd'ya think about the rent increase?" Mary Wade asked her neighbor at the craft warehouse several days later.

Jack Windham, a sixty-something Army veteran, opened a cardboard box and removed wadded up newspaper. He pulled several pairs of carved, wooden work boots from the box and settled them front and center on the main table of his display booth. The boots, carved to look sagging and worn, were replicas of the boots his grandmother wore for as long as he knew her, complete with leather laces threaded through the tiny shoe string holes.

A master carver, Jack fashioned anything he wanted. He offered an eclectic mix of interesting items like a working pair of pliers, a length of chain, and assorted miniatures. He explained his talent by saying he saw the piece in the wood and carved out all the unnecessary wood.

The idea made sense and sounded easy until he loaned her a miniature carving knife and she tried to whittle a lamb out of a two-inch by two-inch block of maple. It resembled a scalloped blob with three protruding sticks. She ran out of wood for what would have been the fourth leg. Returning the knife to its owner, she'd promised to stick with fabric as her creative outlet.

"I don't know." Jack crunched the newspaper and stuffed it into the box, shoving it under the back shelves. "I guess if I want to sell my stuff, I'll have to pay the price."

"But the rent is jumping up forty-three percent. How fair is that?"

"Life isn't fair, Mary Wade. We've talked about that before. This warehouse is in a prime location. People already know I'm here. There's a lot to be said for location and reputation."

"I know, but . . ." Mary Wade rearranged the sundresses on the garment rack.

"But what?"

"This booth isn't a real shop, but it keeps getting more and more expensive to run it."

"You display your designs. You sell your designs. You have regular customers. Why don't you believe what you're doing is valid?" He removed his glasses and polished the lenses. "This thinking sounds like somebody else, not you. And I think you know who I'm talking about."

Of course she did. She sounded exactly like her parents. "Jack, I just want my business to succeed."

"You are succeeding. People can succeed in all different kinds of ways these days. Plenty of businesses are only online. No storefront. No rent. No walk-bys. Don't let your parents make you doubt yourself. You've run this business for five years now. Do you remember the statistics for small-business failure?"

She shook her head. "I know it's a lot."

"Fifty percent. Fifty percent, Mary Wade. You've beat that statistic. Don't sell yourself short."

She smiled at Jack. Always her champion. Always encouraging her. "I don't. You won't let me."

"Don't let your parents undermine what you've worked hard to build. Don't compare yourself with other people either." He donned his glasses. "Remember, we aren't supposed to do that."

"I know. Jesus Christ is our yardstick, right?" She closed her eyes to keep from rolling them. "And I know God's taking care of me. He always has, especially lately. And He always will." She blinked and stared beyond his shoulder, heard a cackling laugh in her mind. Her insides quaked at how close she'd come to being raped.

Jack studied her with his hands in his pockets. "Hey, where'd you go just now? What's happened lately?"

Blinking, she brought her focus back to her friend. Concern and curiosity marked Jack's brow as he reached for a bread bowl, his most sought-after item. Should she tell him about the kidnapping? How do you tell someone that? It already seemed like some crazy, surreal dream to her. She could almost make herself believe it didn't happen except that she still had the receipt with Brett's cell number on it.

She couldn't exactly say, "Guess what happened when I went to Agnes' house? A big galoot grabbed me and . . . If it hadn't been for . . . Then we ran through a hurricane. . ." The scenario sounded farfetched to her, and she lived it.

No, better to leave it alone.

Like Brett's phone number. It was a nice gesture on his part to give her his number, but she knew she'd never use it.

"Mary Wade?" Jack's soft voice pulled her back to the present.

"Sorry. I've just got a lot on my mind, but I've been thinking about our conversations. I see God taking care of me even in scary, dark places. I believe that more than ever."

He encouraged her with a nod. "Great. I'm glad you see Him at work." He grabbed his pipe from the back shelf and bit it between his teeth. "Is there something you're not telling me? Are you okay?"

She stepped around a rack of sun hats and reached into his booth to give him a quick hug. "I'm fine, and you're the best. I've done some soul searching recently. I never doubted God's goodness. Just wondered if He cared about what I was doing. Especially since I didn't take the missionary or minister path like most of my family. I didn't think He was angry or rooting against me. I just thought maybe since I'd said, 'No, thank you,' to full time ministry, maybe He'd sort of left me to my own devices, so to speak."

Jack shook his head. "That's so false, Mary Wade."

"I know. I think I always did, but now I know it for real. I know it from experience."

Salt-and-pepper eyebrows rose, signaling a silent question.

"Maybe I'll explain later. Thank you for being patient with me, for answering my questions even when I sounded like a brat. I've got it now, and I'm grateful God didn't give up on me. He was with me, involved in my life even when I wasn't exactly walking the path I should."

"An important epiphany. I'll be waiting to hear what precipitated it."

"Yeah, well." She lifted a shoulder. "We'll see." Her phone buzzed. "That'll be Daphne. We're supposed to have dinner together. At home." Right on cue, Tess, Mary Wade's teenaged helper, sidled up to the booth.

Rocking a cute pixie cut with her coffee-colored hair spiked in burgundy tips, she wore a cross-country T-shirt belted over a pencil skirt. No matter the outfit, she managed to look funky but stylish all at once. "Perfect timing, Tess. It's been a kinda slow afternoon, but I gotta run now. Call me after closing."

☙☙☣☣

Chopped onions and fresh, minced garlic sizzled in the olive oil. Mary Wade sprinkled in a pinch of red pepper flakes and sautéed all three together. As she poured the can of crushed tomatoes into the mix, Daphne burst through the front door. "Oh, wow. Does it smell delicious in here or what?"

Mary Wade lowered the heat under the tomatoes. "Thank you. The pasta water's heating up. If you can start the salad, that'd be great."

"No problem." Daphne sang the short answer with unusual

enthusiasm. Normally upbeat but calm, she created a great ambiance in the apartment. Her laid-back personality marked only one of many positives of their arrangement. Always organized, Daphne paid her bills on time, enjoyed cheesy romance movies, and sometimes brought home a chocolate pastry to share. Together since their sophomore year in college, they enjoyed a comfortable, easy friendship.

Daphne maneuvered the butcher block table in the middle of the kitchen and stood next to the stove. She stretched her hand in front of Mary Wade's face to open a cabinet door.

"What?" Mary Wade grabbed the hand fluttering inches in front of her eyes. A diamond sparkled on the third finger of Daphne's left hand. "Jeffrey finally asked you?"

"For real."

Mary Wade encircled her with an intense hug, focusing on positive thoughts for her friend rather than the heavy feeling tapping at her heart. "That's great news. I'm thrilled for you."

"We met three years ago today. He popped the question this afternoon when he came by the office." Daphne waved her hand. "We're supposed to go to the Lamp Lighter Saturday night and do the whole dressed-up evening thing, but he couldn't wait." She wiggled her fingers, and the diamond twinkled under the fluorescent kitchen light. "He's so goofy, but this way, I get to wear it sooner."

"He proposed at the office?"

"Yeah. It's more romantic than it sounds. He had three dozen roses delivered to my desk, asked me in front of everybody, then rushed away to the restaurant. He couldn't get off tonight. The roses are still in the car. Can you help bring them in?"

"Sure." She tossed handfuls of frozen spinach into the tomatoes and poured the dried pasta into the rolling water, giving both pans a quick stir. "Let's go. We've got a few minutes before everything's ready."

Jeffrey's a great guy.

I love Daphne.

Mary Wade recited the mantra to the car. On the way back, she changed it to be happy, be happy, be happy as the fresh scent of red roses swirled around her head.

Later during dinner, she dragged a rotini through a puddle of sauce on her plate. "So the wedding's in November? We're talking just months." Enough time to find another roommate? If not, she'd be paying the entire mortgage.

"I know, but we don't want a long engagement." Daphne licked red sauce from the back of her fork and wiggled her ring finger for the umpteenth time. "We can pull everything together between now and then. The ceremony will be small. I'm wearing my mom's dress." She shrugged. "Easy peasy."

"Easy peasy, huh?" Mary Wade arched a brow. "Have you ever planned a wedding?"

"No. But I've watched plenty of people on TV do it. With you, remember? We're getting married in my church. We'll have the reception in the fellowship hall. Small. Intimate. Not fancy schmancy."

"It still takes planning, you know."

She nodded. "And I have a really artistic best friend who'll help me, right?"

ॐॐ∞ॐ

A light pressure settled around Mary Wade's heart, not too heavy but reminiscent of the top sheet she lay under now. The soft caress of the cotton fabric surrounded her body, comforting her. The weight in her chest, however, pressed down and sought attention.

You're a complete heel for sliding into a slump because of Daphne's news. Shame on you. She pushed the sheet off, trying to push off the other weight as well.

God, I'm trying to be happy. I am happy for her. I love her and Jeffrey. They're a great couple. It's just I'm wallowing in the practical side of it. I need another roommate. Maybe two. Show me Your path. Help me trust You with details. A new roommate, money for the maid of honor dress, staying in the warehouse or leaving. My head is spinning. I need peace and calm.

Maid of honor. She smiled at the special request, delighted to be the maid of honor. Naomi, her own sister, hadn't asked her to be in her wedding. In Naomi's defense, she hadn't really started planning a wedding. She and Joshua had been engaged for eight months but seemed content to continue with the status quo.

Engaged for eight months and no wedding in sight. Mary Wade cringed. No, thank you. She didn't like the idea of a long engagement. Brett wouldn't like it either.

Brett?

And engagement?

In the same thought?

Totally inappropriate idea. No Brett and no engagement.

For one thing, he kept irregular hours with his job. No, thank you. If she married, it'd be someone who worked till five o'clock, then came home ready for dinner.

For another, he'd made it abundantly clear that he regarded her as part of his job.

She rolled over to her stomach, punched the pillow under her chest and rested on her elbows. She noted the time on her digital clock. Three o'clock in the morning. About the same time she and Brett made a mad dash through the countryside in a hurricane a few days ago. Seemed like eons ago.

What is he doing now? Starting a new case? Probably tying up loose ends in the Dusty and Skeet case. Did he ever think of her? More than likely not. Since she wasn't around to get in his way, she was out of sight, out of mind.

If she were honest with herself, however, Brett had never treated her like she was in his way. He'd protected her, taken care of her, and held her during the meltdown in the laundry room. When she let herself, she could still feel the strength emanating from his arms around her. Could still feel his rock-solid chest against her cheek.

Leaning into his strength was such a luxury. Jack and Agnes never skipped an opportunity to remind her that her real strength came from God. Both had repeated the phrase from Psalms, "God is the strength of my heart and my portion forever," until it had become her theme song during exams and garment deadlines and scary endeavors like signing leases. Yes, she could stand on her own feet and do hard things, but letting someone else be strong was an alluring temptation, especially when that someone was Brett.

With all his tenderness in caring for her, however, he'd remained professional. Caring, kind, and professional.

That was the problem.

She wanted to be more than a job to him. He intrigued her. She'd never met anyone quite like him. At once he was immense and powerful yet gentle and compassionate. He'd kept Dusty and Skeet at bay with only his words and then used words to calm and reassure her. He enjoyed a quick sense of humor, but he could be sincere also.

Flipping to her back again, she covered her eyes with her forearm. She had to stop thinking about him. More important problems to solve loomed in her future, and, anyway, Brett wasn't a problem.

He was just a memory.

Chapter 14

The fourth-grade Girl Scout giggled as she pulled her hook and yarn through the two loops to make a single crochet. "You know, this is kinda easy. And fun."

Joyce, the leader, moved to the girl's side. "I told you, Megan. That looks great." She surveyed the fellowship hall. "Girls, your moms will be here any minute. Let's start cleaning up."

Good-natured groans floated around the room, but the girls obeyed their leader.

"What do you say to Miss Mary Wade for teaching us today?"

A chorus of preteen girls' voices shouted, "Thank you, Miss Mary Wade."

Mary Wade grinned. "You're welcome. I'm already looking forward to next week." Cheers echoed in the hall.

"I'm glad to hear you say that." Joyce stuffed extra balls of yarn into a canvas bag with Mary Wade's monogram on the front. "So we're on for next Thursday afternoon?"

"Sure. And the next, if we need it. These girls are quick learners."

"True. The lesson went really well. I'm hoping by the fall, we'll have scarves to donate to the homeless shelter."

"Fabulous." Mary Wade slid the straps of the bag onto her shoulder. "And the girls are welcome to check out the crochet group at the hospital. They'd love to have younger members. They'd teach the girls even more cool stitches."

"I'll mention it to the moms. Oh." Joyce's attention turned to wave to women at the threshold. "Speaking of them." Several mothers peeked in the door, then entered, searching for their daughters. "Thanks again. See you next week."

ℰℰℭℛℛ

A contented sigh escaped Mary Wade's lips as she coasted to a stop in her driveway. Another generation discovering the simple enjoyment of crafting, making something by hand. Snaps on a job well done. She mentally patted herself on the back and gathered her bags from the passenger seat. Approaching her house, she noticed the front door.

Open.

Weird.

She double-checked the driveway for Daphne's car even though she knew what she'd find. Nothing. Daphne wasn't home yet. Wouldn't be home till probably after ten o'clock or so. She and Jeffrey were wedding planning tonight.

Her adrenaline kicked in, ramping her heart to a quickstep beat. She blew slow breaths out of her mouth.

Calm down. Think of a rational explanation for the open door.

She always closed and locked the door. Daphne did, too, but her roommate left later today. Maybe with the engagement, she was distracted and forgot about the door. Yes, that made sense. Sort of.

Mary Wade hiked the straps of the bags higher on her shoulder and stepped onto the walkway. *God, this situation is probably nothing, but it looks a little suspect. And I'm a little creeped out right now. Help, please.*

She found her phone and gripped it like a lifeline as she neared the door. Holding her breath, she peered inside and gasped. Her entire den had been trashed. Furniture had been toppled. Books thrown off shelves. The TV sat smashed on the entertainment center. Cracked CD cases littered the floor.

Lifting the phone to her path of vision, she punched 911 with trembling fingers.

"Hello, 911. What is your emergency?"

"I . . .I've . . . been robbed."

ഇഇൟൟ

But, really, she hadn't been robbed. As she moved through the rooms with one of the officers, nothing was gone, just ruined. Someone had broken into her home and created havoc. Unfortunately, the kitchen took the brunt of the vandalism. Milk and orange juice soaked the floor. Smashed egg yolks dripped from the wooden cabinets. Flour coated all other surfaces.

"Ma'am," the officer gestured to her to sit on the couch. He perched on the arm of a wingback chair she'd found at a consignment store downtown. "This looks like the work of a few middle schoolers. You say nothing was taken, so we'll rule out robbery. But just to get all the angles covered, I've got a few more questions. If you don't mind, of course."

If she didn't mind? Did she have a choice? Her head swam with questions of her own. All she wanted to do was lock herself in her bathroom and soak in a steaming tub for at least an hour. Yes, she did mind answering questions.

She sat on half the cushion, keeping her back as straight as the officer's tie. "Sure. Go ahead."

He rubbed his finger against the pencil lead. "Can you think of anyone who might be irritated with you, might want to take out some frustration by upsetting your apple cart, so to speak?"

At her hesitation, the officer leaned toward her. "Ms. Kimball?"

She hugged her purse against her chest. "Not anybody in Charlotte, but . . ." She studied the front window.

"Ma'am?"

"Well, somebody back in Bandon is probably really angry with me."

His pencil hovered over his notepad. "How so?"

"I was kidnapped last week, and I escaped."

His hand stretched flat against the pad. "Kidnapped?"

She wound the purse strap around her hand. "Yes."

The officer arched an eyebrow. "And you escaped?"

"Yes."

"Uh huh." He nodded and tapped his pencil against the pad. "How?"

She moistened her lips. "Brett and I escaped through the window and ran to my godmother's house."

"You and Brett, huh? Brett who?"

"He said his name was Brett Davis." Was that even his real name? "He said he was undercover, a deputy. I took him to the courthouse downtown." She dropped her eyes from the speculation in the officer's gaze, listened to his pencil scratching on the pad.

"I know this sounds unbelievable. I didn't plan on mentioning it, but you asked." She slipped a crinkled receipt from her purse. "Here's his cell number. At least, he said it was."

The officer read the numbers out loud and copied them with the notes. "Did you file a report with local authorities?"

"No, but Brett took pictures of the scrapes on my wrist and my swollen cheek."

"Pictures. Uh huh."

"The hurricane had just barreled through. Police were busy with all that. Plus, we needed to get out of Bandon and away from Dusty and Skeet. They're the people who'd be angry, but there's no way they could find me here. Just disregard everything I said." Why did she mention the kidnapping to this officer? He probably wondered if he should admit her to a mental hospital for observation.

He rose. "Like I said, ma'am. We need to look at all the angles." He stuffed the notepad into his front pocket along with the pencil. "I think we've got everything we need except a set of fingerprints from your roommate and her fiancé. We'll be in touch after we sort through the fingerprints we lifted."

"Sure. Could I start cleaning up now?" The kitchen clock on the far wall read eight thirty-five. Such a long time from the Girl Scout meeting this afternoon.

"Yep. No problem. We'll get outta your hair."

Her heart jumped in her throat. Alone. Again. Couldn't he stay until Daphne got home? "Do you think it's safe to sleep here tonight?"

"Like I said. We're probably dealing with pre-teens, but I'll have a cruiser ride by several times tonight. Make our presence known and all that. Call if you need us."

As she stood at the front door and watched the officers drive away, a shudder rippled through her body. Someone had broken into her home. Violated her safe place. Pressure built behind her eyes.

Disturbing images played in her mind. Dusty's grinning face taunted her. She covered her ears against Skeet's hooting laugh. Surely this vandalism wasn't the work of those criminals. Why drive all the way to Charlotte to vandalize her property? The police officer was right. Preteens broke in and had their idea of fun.

Her phone buzzed in her pocket. Daphne. "Hey."

"Sorry I'm just now calling you back. We've been tasting cakes and all kinds of treats for the past hour and a half. Tough job, but somebody's gotta do it." Jeffrey made approving noises in the background.

"Are you heading home now? I've got some bad news." Despite gripping the phone with both hands, her voice broke.

"What is it, Mary Wade? How are you? Turn here, Jeffrey. We need to get home."

"I'm fine. Physically. Somebody broke in and—"

"What?"

"Nothing was stolen. Just a tremendous mess. The police think middle schoolers are probably to blame."

"Oh, honey. So sorry you're by yourself. We'll be there in thirty minutes. Maybe less. Hang tight, sweetie."

ﭏﭏ

"You can't stay here tonight." Jeffrey planted his feet on the only open spot on the den floor. CDs, sofa pillows, and shattered TV glass covered the rest.

"I can't afford a hotel room." Mary Wade wiped the last bit of egg yolk from the cabinet under the kitchen sink. "I'll double-check the doors, keep on all the lights."

"You're coming home with me. I've got two beds plus a couch. You can stay until we secure this place better. Maybe put in a security system."

"Why, Jeffrey, we can't compromise our reputation," Daphne countered in a fake Southern drawl.

He planted his hands on his hips. "I'm more concerned about your safety than your reputations tonight."

"Thank you for your kind offer, but—"

He shook his head. "It's more than an offer. You're not staying here. I'll pay for a hotel room, or you can bunk with me. That's the choice you have."

"Oh, how I love a man who takes charge." Daphne dumped a dust bin load of orange flour paste into the garbage.

Mary Wade chewed on her cheek. Jeffrey was right, though she didn't like to admit it. She really didn't want to stay here either, but he couldn't afford a hotel room. Not on a sous chef's salary. Bunking with Jeffrey one night could work.

"Why don't we finish the kitchen and call it a night. We'll start bright and early tomorrow morning. I can help for a while, then I have to open for lunch."

Tears tingled for the umpteenth time since she walked in on her trashed home—she checked her watch—five hours ago, but she didn't allow them to fall this time either. She had work to do. She couldn't collapse now.

What was going on with her? She'd lived her life for twenty-seven relatively boring years, and then in the space of a week, her life had been turned topsy-turvy by criminal activity. Was this some sort of message? Pay attention. Life is short. Be careful. Call Brett.

Call Brett?

Should she? She thought about the receipt with his number on it stuffed back inside her purse.

No. She absolutely shouldn't call Brett Davis. He was probably long gone by now anyway. Why on earth had she mentioned his name to that cop?

If she were honest with herself, maybe a tiny part of her wanted him to come over and take charge, lead her through this mess, the literal one, as well as the figurative one.

But he wasn't going to come. She'd have to be her own knight in shining armor. She could do it, too, with friends like Daphne and Jeffrey, not to mention God's sustaining strength. She'd get through this bump in the road.

She grabbed Jeffrey in a bear hug. "You're the best. I love you, Jeffrey." She kissed his cheek. "Are you sure you don't mind roommates?"

Daphne slapped her fist into her palm in mock irritation. "Hey. I'm standing right here. Cool it with my fiancé." Her grin softened the command.

"He's safe with me. Just wanted him to know how much I appreciate not sleeping here tonight."

Not that she thought she'd get much sleep at Jeffrey's apartment either, but at least she wouldn't jump at every creak and bump in the dark till morning.

Chapter 15

Bright and early the next morning didn't happen. By the time they finished the kitchen and arrived at Jeffrey's place, midnight had visited and left. After twisting and turning for several hours, Mary Wade greeted four thirty-two before falling into a fitful nap. No one stirred until nine fifteen.

Jeffrey dropped them off after a quick breakfast and headed to his restaurant. Daphne, apologizing and promising to be home as soon as possible, left for a not-to-be-missed meeting at her office.

Resting a disposable coffee cup against her lips, Mary Wade surveyed the room, gauging the best place to start the family room cleanup. No TV for company today, but she had a CD player in her bedroom the vandals had overlooked. The CDs were strewn all over the variegated throw rug, but, thankfully, none looked completely ruined. She stacked a few as she looked for her favorite Christmas collection. She needed something happy to see her through righting this room. As her fingers lighted on the longed-for disc, banging rattled the front door.

Coffee splashed out of the travel lid and pricked her fingers with dots of fire. She caught her breath, her heart thundering in her chest. Who would be at the door in the middle of the morning? Beating on the door like a life depended on it. Were the vandals back? Did vandals knock?

More banging. "Mary Wade. It's me, Brett. Let me in." Another round of banging.

She set the cup on the floor and rose, licking her smarting fingers. Brett was here. She glanced at her attire. Cutoff jeans and a T-shirt from high school band days. Why hadn't she worn that cute sundress? Put on some makeup? Styled her hair instead of grabbing it into a wild ponytail?

Because she'd planned to clean up her trashed house, not entertain some—

"Mary Wade." A single bang.

Her phone buzzed on the kitchen counter. She ignored it and swept open the door. Brett filled the whole space, one hand on his hip, the other pressing his phone to his ear. He lowered the phone as he searched her face with intense, silver eyes. So. She hadn't dreamed those eyes.

An indefinable look flickered across his face before he blinked and shoved his hands in his pockets. "You can't stay out of trouble, huh?"

She squeezed her arms around herself. "This trouble found me. I didn't go looking for it."

"How're you doing?" Without waiting for an answer, he examined the doorjamb. "I knew I should've come to your place and checked it out. You don't even have a deadbolt."

"I have a chain. And I live in a safe neighborhood, thank you." She didn't acknowledge the irony in her statement. Hoped he wouldn't call her on it.

He raised an eyebrow and stepped over the threshold.

Of course he would call her on it. She let him in, closed the door, and locked it. He nodded his approval.

She tightened her arms in front of her, fingers wadding T-shirt fabric into her fists. "This is a good neighborhood. It isn't the boondocks."

"It isn't Fourth Ward either."

"Fourth Ward isn't as great as it's advertised to be."

"Don't say that in front of the young professionals who

110

shell out two hundred thousand plus for a one-bedroom condo down there." He swiveled to survey the room.

She gasped. "You cut your hair."

He raked his fingers through his cropped locks. "Yeah." His gaze swept the scattered detritus. "What a mess."

"Yes, it is, but to answer your original question, I'm fine. I just need to clean up as you've pointed out. It's nice of you to come, but everything's under control here."

He cocked his head. "Oh, really? Have the cops canvassed the neighborhood? Dusted for fingerprints? Taken inventory of stolen items?"

"Nothing was stolen."

"What?" He glanced at the empty entertainment center.

"Nothing was stolen. They smashed the TV and a few vases, turned over chairs, emptied the bookshelves, poured orange juice and flour all over the kitchen floor. One of the policemen suggested preteen vandals sowing some wild oats."

"You and I both know that's false. Preteens spray paint graffiti or toilet paper a front yard or throw eggs at passing cars. They don't break and enter. All this," he gestured at the chaos in the middle of the floor, "was a message. And I know who sent it."

A cold finger of fear pressed on her chest. "Dusty and Skeet?"

"Of course. According to my sources, they'd already cut and run before midmorning. They took the pickup, so one of them must have hotwired it. Looks like they found where you live."

Phantom zip ties cut into her wrists, and she shivered. "No, I think you're wrong. There's no way they'd know where I live." She couldn't believe they knew her address, not if she continued to live in this house, walk around without a bodyguard.

His eyes narrowed. "You think I'm wrong, huh? Is that why you shivered just now?"

111

She leaned against the arm of the couch, fisted her hands to still the trembling. He noticed too much.

"You walked around town and went in how many stores that afternoon? Remember, I saw you come out of the grocery store myself."

Yes, she remembered how he'd held the door for her as she exited with a bag of groceries. She'd noted his hair, his scruffy beard, and his eyes. Those piercing, silver eyes had swept over her with a glance and as quickly dismissed her. At least, she thought he'd dismissed her.

Today his square jaw was clean-shaven, and his hair was cut just short of military length, emphasizing high cheekbones and those unusual eyes that had struck her the first time she saw him. He wore dark suit pants and a stark white shirt with a dark green paisley tie. The look was enough to make her forget she stood in scattered piles of what used to adorn her shelves.

Enough to make her forget his question.

ℰℭℭℭℛℭℛ

Under her scrutiny, Brett felt warmth rise from the pit of his stomach up the side of his neck. Didn't she have the air conditioner on? He loosened his tie, unbuttoned the top button. "Anywhere else besides the grocery store and the pedicure place?" He dropped his gaze to her feet. Remembered hot pink toes. He rolled the sleeves of his shirt to his elbows.

Her tongue darted to the corner of her mouth. "Ahm, Ellen's shop."

"Where?"

"The yarn shop, but none of the people at these places would tell perfect strangers my contact information. Most don't even know it."

"These strangers aren't perfect, as you well know. They might look idiotic and act it most days, but they're career criminals. They know how to get what they want."

"Why would they want me?"

"You outsmarted them for one thing. For another, you're on the list of witnesses. I think you need to spend a few days away from Charlotte. Go visit your parents."

"Are you kidding me? I can't leave. I have responsibilities. I—" Her phone buzzed from the counter. She tiptoed through the mess and retrieved it. "Hello, Heidi. What's up?"

Giving her some semblance of privacy, Brett knelt and scooped up several CDs, stacked them on an empty shelf. As he reached for another, she sucked in a quick breath. He pivoted toward the sound.

"What?" Every bit of color had seeped from her face. She pressed the phone to her ear with one hand and her stomach with the other. "How is he? Where is he?" Her chin trembled, and she turned away from Brett. "Oh, Heidi, I'm so sorry." She wiped a hand across her cheek. "My shop? Did he say why? What did they look like?"

Brett rose and crossed to her.

"Sure, Heidi. Go. I'll call you later. I'm praying for both of you." She kept her back to him.

He gave her a moment, then stepped closer. "Mary Wade. Tell me." He touched her shoulder, and she flinched. He drew back his hand. "Let me help. What happened?"

"Jack's in the hospital." Staring toward the kitchen window, she wouldn't face him. "Two men beat him up this morning in the craft warehouse. Broke his nose and his wrist. He needs two pins in his arm. He's going into surgery soon."

"Who's Jack?"

She covered her face with her hands, and he stepped to face her. He gently moved her hands and nudged her chin up with his finger, braced himself for the dark green eyes filled with hurt and confusion. Cupping her cheek, he brushed away a tear hesitating on her bottom lash with his thumb. "Tell me all of it."

"Two men came into the warehouse where I have my shop.

113

They were rifling through my things, and Jack saw them. Heidi said he arrived early before opening time. He asked what they were doing, and one of them smacked him in the jaw. When he came to, they were gone. He called 911. She said the police should be coming here soon." She let her gaze wander the room and picked up a CD. "But I have to go to the hospital. I have to be with Heidi and see Jack when he's out of surgery."

"Not happening. Pack a bag. You need to get out of Charlotte for a while."

She jerked her head back to him. "What?"

He pried the CD from her fingers." You heard me. Your place was trashed yesterday. Your shop today. Sounds like Dusty put your friend in the hospital. Go visit your parents until we need you to testify."

"No. I need to see Jack. I have to check on my shop and finish here. I have clients waiting on orders. I can't just leave." She stepped toward her bedroom.

He caught her arm. "These people don't play, Mary Wade. Don't you understand? They tracked you all the way from Bandon. Found your shop."

Troubled eyes searched his. "How'd they do that? How'd they find my shop?"

"Probably found a clue here that led them there."

She slapped her forehead. "The receipts. I'd been going over them and left them on the table. I filed them after the police left. They have the shop's address on them." Her face fell. "Oh, wait. My website."

"Yep. Easy. They're persistent. They'll be back. Go pack a bag for a week."

"A whole week? No. I—" A crack rang out, and the front picture window shattered. Brett threw his body against hers, knocking her to the carpet.

"Get down." He grabbed his phone. On his side, he punched the screen with his thumb. His other hand palmed Mary

Wade's skull. Another pop. A framed watercolor on the back wall splintered and fell to the floor. "Stay." Draping a leg across hers, he rammed his chest against her heaving back. "Shots fired at Stony Creek Way. No. Into the house from the outside. No, not domestic disturbance."

She whimpered. Her body trembled under him. He stroked her hair, mentally kicked himself for wanting to unfasten the elastic confining her soft, chestnut hair. "Hey. I've got you. We're fine. A squad car is almost here."

A distant siren sounded. "See? The good guys are coming." A muffler rumbled and tires squealed. "Dusty. I'd know that muffler anywhere." He scrambled to throw open the front door. He barked a coarse word at the taillights. Returning to Mary Wade, he helped her to stand. Tears streaked her face. Ignoring wise judgment, he gathered her to him.

Quiet sobs grew more forceful. He soothed her back with slow caresses, liked the feel of her in his arms. He nuzzled close to her ear, forgetting the shambles in the room and concentrating on the subtle scent of sunscreen and flowers. "Shhh. We're fine. The police'll be here any minute."

"I'm sorry." Her voice hitched. "I hate crying in front of people."

"You've cried in front of me before and survived."

"Doesn't make me like it." She burrowed her head into his chest. "This is not my life. I design children's clothes. I crochet with cancer victims and Girl Scouts. I play by the rules." Her hands slid around his waist, pressed against his back. "My life is really boring."

He snorted. "Not anymore, but we'll get you back to boring as soon as we can."

A car door slammed outside. He tipped his head back to see her face, hating to loosen his arms. "That'll be the police. Are you up to answering questions?"

"I guess I have to be."

Chapter 16

How did her arms wind up around his waist? Clinging to him. Sobbing into his chest again. Mary Wade frowned and pushed away from his solid strength, hugged herself instead of leaning in for more time in his arms.

A knock yanked her away from futile thoughts.

"Ready?"

She nodded and wiped her face as Brett opened the door.

Two uniformed men entered the den, shook hands with Brett, and tipped their hats to her. Four policemen in her house in the past eighteen hours. Unreal.

"Ma'am, we were on our way here to interview you about your vandalized shop when we got the call about shots fired. We'll get information about that also." One of them retrieved an index-card-sized pad from his front shirt pocket. Just like last time. "You've had some excitement lately."

"My idea of excitement is finding a deal on fabric, not dodging bullets."

Brett moved to stand beside her, and she forced herself not to sway toward him. "And none of it was her fault."

"We didn't say it was. And you are?"

"Brett Davis." He fished his wallet from his back pocket and flashed a badge.

"Mecklenberg deputy."

"Right. Shall we sit?" Brett gestured to the sofa, bent to

clear a path in the strewn CDs. "And I'll fill you in on what's happened."

He really was who he said he was. A deputy. Undercover.

Brett spent the next twenty minutes explaining why Dusty and Skeet would want to harm her, giving detailed description of the two men. He skillfully skirted around irrelevant, nosy questions while one officer scribbled notes and the other took pictures of the bullet holes.

ဢၜၜၨၐ

These guys were competent at their jobs, but they didn't need to know everything about the investigation. Couldn't know everything. He glanced at Mary Wade. Except for her pale face, she put on a stoic front, acted like the trooper she was.

"One of the officers already asked me that question yesterday."

"Humor me, Ms. Kimball. I need a complete report."

"It feels like you're trying to catch me in a lie."

Brett swiped his hand over his face to hide his smile and rose. "Ms. Kimball has had a harrowing two days. You've asked questions and taken pictures. If other questions come up, you can call her or me."

"Well, now—"

"Here's my card. I'll be in touch with Chief Monroe as well." Brett dropped the name of the chief of Charlotte police. "I appreciate how thoroughly you've done your job here." He ushered them to the door. "I'll be sure to mention it to the Chief."

Closing the door, he locked it. Leaning back against it, he considered the scene in front of him. Mary Wade collapsed in the wingback chair perpendicular to the sofa, covering her eyes with her forearm.

He loosened his tie again, re-stuffed his shirt into his waistband. Anything to keep his hands busy. To keep them from scooping her back up into his arms.

She popped from the chair. "Okay. I need to go by the shop. No, first I need to check on Jack." She shook her head. "But I'm supposed to clean up this mess first." She bit her lip. "Sorry. I'm not usually this scatterbrained." She wrapped her hand over her mouth.

"Mary Wade."

She faced him. "Oh, thank you, Brett, for helping with the questions. I appreciate your being here." She pressed her middle finger between her eyebrows, rubbed a straight line over her forehead to her hairline and back. "I think they would've stayed for hours if you hadn't stepped in. Thanks for that too." A pained expression crossed her face. "It's such a mess in here."

"Everything can be fixed."

"Yeah. Well, I'm sure you need to get back to your office or somewhere . . ." She trailed off with a vacant look in her eyes.

"Actually, I don't have any place to be right now." He quirked his eyebrow. "I've got some, ah, vacation time. Free as a bird, as they say. How about you sit for a few minutes. We'll talk about what we're going to do."

"We?" She let him guide her back to the chair.

"Is this yours?" He picked up the forgotten coffee cup on the floor. "Although you probably don't need any more caffeine."

Perching on the edge of the cushion, she accepted the coffee, fiddled with the flap instead of sipping it. "I'm fine."

෨෨෬෬

"You don't look fine. You look like you need a vacation."

Her chest tightened. She probably did look a sight. Her nose felt twice its size. Her eyes were probably swollen. She twisted the cup in the sleeve. "Thanks for the compliment."

"It wasn't one. You'll know when I compliment you." Avoiding a darkening red blotch, he touched her knee, and she gasped. "Sorry. Did you get this when I tackled you?"

His touch, light as an eyelash, shocked Mary Wade, made

her forget about her throbbing knee. Made her want to be back in his arms, forget about Jack and the chaos in her house, in her shop. Of course, she couldn't linger in that fantasy. She had to get to work on righting her life. He had to get back to his.

As grateful as she was to have him beside her during the interrogation, she needed him to leave now. She needed to think about a plan. How to move forward. What to do next.

Tears burned in the back of her eyes. The third time was not the charm. She would not cry in front of him again. Twice was more than enough.

"Yeah. I hit the floor pretty hard. But the alternative would have been worse. Thanks, again, for saving my life. The bruise'll be gone in a few days. See," she held out her wrists, "the other ones have already faded."

He clasped her forearm to inspect the wrist, trailing a finger over diminishing bruises that shivered straight to her heart. "I'm glad." He returned her arm to her lap. "Now about our plan."

"You keep saying, 'we,' and 'our,' but there is no 'we.' I got myself into this mess. I can get out of it."

"How exactly?" He knelt, stacking CDs and stuffing them on the shelves.

She scanned the room. "I'll get a deadbolt for starters. I'll be more careful, more attentive." The deadbolt would have to do for a while. Buying a security system was definitely not in the budget for a while. A long while.

He cocked his head. "Do you seriously think a deadbolt would protect you against those bullets that whipped beside our heads this morning?"

"I said, 'for starters.'"

"You need to pack a bag, go visit your—"

"No. I'm not going to my parents'."

"Fine. Go stay with an old college friend."

"I live with an old college friend."

"She needs to crash somewhere else for a while too. Just

119

in case." He righted a blue vase that had survived colliding with the floor.

"Just in case?" She raked trembling fingers through her hair. "You're freaking me out here."

"Good. Understand this situation is serious. Dusty and Skeet mean business. They are peeved, to put it mildly. That I double crossed them. That you got away."

A quake racked her body. "You don't even look like a criminal anymore."

He raised an eyebrow. "Oh, how does a criminal look?"

"You know what I mean. You cut your hair. You're wearing a suit. You look all . . ."

He smiled. "All what?"

She covered her face with her hands, a shield against those piercing eyes. "You look different from what you did last week. That's all." He looked good. Great, in fact. Very professional. Very swoon-worthy, if she were the swooning type. But she wasn't.

"I'll take that as a compliment."

She shot from the chair. "I have to call Daphne." She grabbed her phone and punched in numbers, left a voicemail and a text.

"Back to your trip." He leaned against the shelving unit, arms crossed, one ankle draped over the other.

"My trip?"

"You can't stay here. My guess is Dusty and Skeet will stay away today, but they'll be back. Count on it." He rubbed his chin. "Yeah. You should go somewhere not connected to you."

She frowned. "What do you mean?"

"Like a hotel room in Greensboro."

"No."

"Just for a few days until we can pick up those two."

"I can't afford a hotel room."

"Don't worry about the cost. We can take care of that. I'll pay for it till I can get it approved."

"Absolutely not."

Her phone buzzed. "Daphne." She read the screen. "No, Agnes." She answered the phone. "Hey. How was your trip?" Her stomach lurched at Agnes' answer. "Oh, no." She moved the phone away from her mouth, addressing Brett. "They trashed her house." He moved closer to her to share the phone, his arm bumping hers.

"I'm fine, but it's a little disconcerting to come home to a mess all over everywhere. Nosy Nan made a beeline over here before I could get out of my car. Thank the good Lord she didn't push her way inside the house. She told me some wild story about two scraggly-looking men and my bicycle."

Mary Wade looked at Brett, realized how close she was to his face and lowered her lids to concentrate on Agnes. "She saw you leave the morning of the hurricane with some man. Mary Wade? Is that true? What's going on?"

She flattened her fingertips against her temple. "Agnes, it's a long story. Are you all right?"

"I'm fine, and I've got nothing but time. Tell me about your young man. It couldn't have been Robert. Was it?"

Mary Wade gritted her teeth, willed the heat creeping up her neck to retreat. "No. Listen. I'll tell you all the details but later. Just know those men are the reason I left early and the ones who trashed your house."

Brett moved away from the phone. "Ask her if she's called the police."

She nodded. "You did call the police, right?"

"No. I wanted to make sure you're fine." Agnes sighed. "I didn't know what to do."

"Call the police. Let them dust for fingerprints. On the bike too."

Brett crossed to the counter, an impressed smile softening his countenance. He jotted something on a scrap piece of paper and handed it to her.

She read the note to Agnes. "Their names are Dusty Parker and Skeet Rushing."

"Mary Wade, tell me what's going on. Are you mixed up in something? I'll help you. Are you okay?"

"No, I'm not mixed up in anything." Not really. "Just call the police. Give them the information. I'm so sorry about your house."

"Something's going on, and I don't like it. I'm going to hang up and pray for you."

"Good." Pray hard. I need all the prayers I can get.

♏♏⤣⤢

Dusty popped his head back and hooted. "Listen to the sirens. Yes, sir. That was close." He strained to see through the rear windshield.

"And stupid." Skeet headed the truck north out of the neighborhood. "We were gonna case her house is all. Why'd you shoot for?"

"Mainly because I wanted to."

Looking left and right, Skeet rolled through an intersection without stopping. "We're gonna have to lay low for a couple days. Somebody might've read off the license plate." Skeet glanced into the side mirror and chewed the side of his cheek.

Dusty smirked. "I put mud on the plate. No problem."

"You're just a genius, huh? They could still give a de-scription of the truck." Skeet sighed. "We'll have to see about changing vehicles."

"Changing vehicles." Dusty showed his crooked teeth. "I know what that means." He glanced down a shaded street. "Turn down here for a minute. Let's listen to the scanner. See what they say about the dustup at Mary Wade's house."

♏♏⤣⤢

"Mary Wade Kimball, victim on Stony Creek Way. Brett Davis with the victim." Skeet slapped his knee. "That scanner works like a charm. You think that was him?"

"I know it was him, even with his new haircut and fancy duds. I saw him when he opened the door, and he saw us. He knows we're coming."

"You think that's his real name?

"Who knows, but we got to find out."

"How we gonna do that?"

"When I was in high school—"

Skeet scratched behind his ear. "You went to high school?"

"Yes. I did. In fact, they liked me so much they asked me to stay in ninth grade twice. I obliged them till my sixteenth birthday."

"So you dropped out."

"I had better things to do. Anyway, one time I had to write a paper—"

"One time?"

"Will you let me get a word in, old man? When I worked on that paper, I learned a few things about looking up people."

"Oh, yeah?"

"I need a computer."

"How we gonna get one o' them?"

Dusty smirked. "Don't need to get one. Just use one. At the library."

"What?"

"Free." Dusty puffed his chest. "Might even get a librarian to help."

Skeet grunted. "You. In a library." He shook his head and stared passed the houses in the neighborhood. "My momma used to take me to the library. Saw a puppet show one time. They used to give out candy in the summertime for every book we read." He swung his gaze back toward Dusty. "Don't mess with the library."

"I ain't gonna mess with it. I'm going to use it. That's what it's for."

"Fine. But clean up some first. No librarian'll talk to you, much less give out any info looking like you do. And we need to dump this truck. Find another ride."

"Sweet. We got a plan."

Chapter 17

Daphne arrived within minutes of Agnes' phone call. Mary Wade grabbed her roommate, clinging to her for a long, centering hug. She broke contact, offering her hand to Brett. "I'm Daphne."

"Brett Davis."

"Police?"

"Deputy."

"Deputy?" Daphne's wide eyes questioned Mary Wade.

"It's a long story."

Daphne dropped her purse onto the floor beside the door. "I'm all ears."

Mary Wade bit her bottom lip. "When I was at Agnes' house last week, I was kidnapped."

Daphne's jaw slackened. "Kidnapped? Are you kidding? Why didn't you tell me before now?"

"It's not exactly something you mention in casual conversation."

Knitting her eyebrows, Daphne dipped her chin. "Don't we merit more than casual conversation?"

"I'm sorry. You were excited about wedding plans. I was trying to forget about it, move on." Mary Wade sucked in a deep breath. "Here's the short version. Two men kidnapped me the first afternoon I was at Agnes'. That's the real reason I came back early."

Daphne dropped her keys into her purse. "You said you were concerned about your booth."

"True. As usual, but I'd planned to stay longer than one night." She rubbed circles across her forehead. "Anyway, Brett was working undercover and helped me escape. We headed west, and I dropped him off downtown." She shrugged. "I thought that'd be the end of it. Except for maybe testifying. Which may or may not happen." She moved her fingers to her temples. "I had other things to worry about. I was trying to forget. To move on."

ဆုၥဆုၥာၐၒၐ

So. To be clear. She wanted to move on. She had other things to occupy her mind. Good to know. Brett stuffed his hands in his pockets.

"You think all this," Daphne waved about the room, "is related to your . . .your kidnapping? It's hard to even say the word, Mary Wade."

He straddled a bar stool. "We know it is. Before they sped away this morning, I got a look at the truck. It's them. They've probably ditched it by now, though. Daphne, Mary Wade is going out of town for a few days. I think it'd be wise for you to come too."

"I haven't agreed—"

"They've trashed your place, Agnes' house, and your shop." He stood and crossed to her. "They shot at you today." He held up two fingers for emphasis. "Twice. What more convincing do you need?"

Daphne glanced wide-eyed at Mary Wade. "The shop?"

She nodded. "They broke Jack's wrist. He's having surgery right now."

Daphne circled her shoulders in a one-armed hug. "I'll sleep on my aunt's couch, but I can't leave Charlotte. I'm lead on my presentation. It's due next Tuesday. If we get this account, it'll be mine. I really should be at work right now. What about the window?"

"I'll call a repairman." He stepped into the kitchen and scrolled through his contacts, called a friend who usually knew a friend. Waiting on hold, he had a few moments to observe the two friends.

Daphne held Mary Wade, smoothing her hair, then loosening the sagging ponytail. Luxurious waves spread over her shoulders, and Daphne murmured into her ear. Brett tamped a ripple of emotion. Jealousy? Better not be jealousy. She'd made her feelings transparent on the subject. He'd enjoy comforting, though. He remembered how she felt in his arms.

The repairman could come first thing tomorrow morning.

Mary Wade gathered her hair into another ponytail. "What about tonight?"

He slid the phone into his front shirt pocket. "Tape some trash bags over it."

"I'll get Jeffrey to spend the night with some buddies. It'll be okay." Daphne rubbed her back. Mary Wade closed her eyes. "Don't worry, roomie. Everything will be okay."

Yeah. Just as soon as Dusty and Skeet got picked up.

A cell buzzed. Daphne checked hers and grunted. "Honey, I hate to leave you, but I've got to get back. It's crucial." She glanced at Brett. "Listen to him, okay?"

He smiled. An ally. "I also suggested visiting her parents."

Daphne's eyebrows flew into her bangs. She moved her head in an almost imperceptible shake.

Right. No parents. "But she declined."

Daphne blinked her eyes in one, slow blink, grabbed Mary Wade into a massive hug, then made for the door. As she opened it, she whipped her head toward him. "Sorry to meet you under these circumstances, Brett Davis, but I'm still glad. I'm getting good vibes from you." And she was gone.

"Thanks." I think.

Mary Wade shut the door behind her. "My roommate. She marches to a different drummer."

"I picked up on that. And she loves you."

"Still observant." She faced him, straightened her spine. "Brett, thank you for all you've done."

"I'm not done. We're leaving in," he checked his watch, "fifteen minutes. Get a bag."

"No."

"Ten."

"I told you. I have—"

"Five minutes."

She huffed and stomped her foot. "I can't leave. My shop—"

He clasped her arm and moved toward the door. "You can call someone from the car. We've already spent too much time here. We'll stop for whatever you need on the way."

She dug in her heels. "I'm not used to having people telling me what to do."

"You're not used to people shooting at you either, are you?"

She wrenched her arm from his hold and ran to her room. "You said I had fifteen minutes. I'm packing a bag."

He grabbed his phone, swiping the screen. "Make it quick. You already used five."

☜☜☞☞

Returning to the den, Mary Wade froze at the sound of something ripping. Brett slapped a final piece of duct tape on the windowsill, securing several trash bags over the open window. "Not perfect, but it'll do till morning."

"Thank you for taking care of it. Daphne texted me. Jeffrey and a buddy will be here as soon as they finish the lunch shift."

"Good. We'll take my car and leave yours in the driveway to look like somebody's home." He did a double take. "What are you doing?" He eyed her bags. "You're not moving. You'll be gone a week. Tops."

128

"I have my clothes in this one. My designs I'm working on and laptop in the backpack. I've got a few pieces of fabric to play around with in this one." She jiggled the mini duffel bag and cinched the top closed. The motion juggled her brain. "Wait a minute. I don't even know where we're going." She palmed her cheek. "What is wrong with me? How can I just up and leave like this?"

"We're going to a safe place."

"Where?"

"I'll fill you in on the way. Come on." He grabbed the duffel bag and carryon bag and pushed her out the door.

He threw the bags into the back seat of his silver SUV and opened the passenger door for her. "Hop in. We shoulda been on the road a while ago." He donned his sunglasses and had the vehicle moving before she could fasten her seat belt.

As they neared an intersection, she pointed toward the windshield. "Turn left up here."

"I know how to go."

She stared at him. "To my shop?"

"We're not going there." He turned right onto Tryon Street.

"I have to go. Dusty and Skeet struck there too. Remember?"

"Do you remember the bullets that flew by us? Mary Wade, we can't go to your shop or the hospital either. I'm sorry you can't see your friend, but we're leaving town."

She chewed her lip and counted crepe myrtles as they passed her window. Anything to keep from crying. And, oh, how she wanted to cry. One of her dearest friends languished in surgery because of her. Her godmother's house was trashed because of her. Her shop was vandalized. No telling how much of her inventory was ruined. How much money she'd lost. Her house was attacked, her roommate displaced.

And here she was running away from it all. Packed like she was heading toward a vacation. How could this be fair? It wasn't fair. "Stop."

"Why?"

She gripped the dashboard. "Turn around. I can't leave all this mess behind. I have to stay and help."

"Mary Wade, we've been over everything. You're going to a safe place for a few days so that you can help in the greater good."

"But what about Jack and Agnes and Daphne? What about my shop that's lying in ruins right now? Along with my house."

Brett checked the rearview mirror. "Jack's in good hands. He wouldn't want you to put yourself in danger."

"I don't even know you, and I'm allowing you to drive me to who knows where. This is all wrong." She stuck her hands between her legs, concentrated on breathing in and out.

Brett slowed to halt at a stoplight. He laid his hand on her knee. "We haven't known each other long, true, but circumstances have sort of ramped up our . . . association."

She looked at him. "That sounds like a business deal."

He arched his eyebrows. "Relationship?"

She shook her head. "Sounds like we're dating."

"Which clearly we're not." The light changed, and he accelerated through the intersection.

She adjusted her seat belt. "Clearly."

"Friendship, then."

"Not exactly. Friendship isn't normally based on escaping kidnappers and dodging bullets."

"So we're not friends?"

"I didn't say that. It's just . . . We've been thrown together for some strange reason." She shrugged. "We don't have a basis for friendship. Think about it. We probably wouldn't have been friends in high school. You know?"

"Why?"

"Different crowds. You'd be out on the football field. I'd be up in choir or the band. Our paths would've never crossed." Cool kids versus nerds.

He glanced at her. "You think I played football?"

She nodded. "Safe bet, I think. You've got the build, for sure." His bicep worked under the white fabric as he turned right. Dark gabardine stretched over his muscled thigh. The back of her legs tingled at the memory of his thigh draped across them during the ambush back at the house. She rearranged the air vent to blow directly at her and studied the scene outside her window again.

"Well, you're right and wrong. I played football for two years, then dropped out."

ಐಐೞ

Brett rubbed his jaw. Why did he admit to that? Why did he let the conversation wander into another topic he normally didn't discuss? Take the lead and go with a new topic. "Hey, we're stopping for lunch in about an hour, but do you want anything before we get onto the interstate?"

"No. I'm fine. Thanks. So you dropped out? You don't like school or what? But wait, you're in a professional job. Don't you need a degree of some sort?"

Of course this stubborn woman wouldn't follow his lead. She walked right through the door he opened.

He sighed. "I dropped out when my grandfather died. Worked construction for a year. Got my G.E.D. Realized I needed an education. Went to college for two years. I didn't know what I wanted to do. My sister did, so it was more important for her to go. I joined the Army. Took a tour in Afghanistan. Realized I liked being close to family. Came back home. Worked construction by day, took online classes and studied at night." He shrugged. "Not an attractive résumé, but I earned a degree in criminal justice. The rest is history."

"You're a kind person."

He whipped his head toward her. "What?"

"And compassionate. You put others first. You put your

sister before your own college career. You put me before your job."

"No . . ."

"It's true. Where are we stopping for lunch?"

Now you want to change the subject? Good. "About that. One of my favorite places. I called for reservations while you packed." He checked his watch. "We'll be there in about an hour. You can take a nap if you want."

"Take a nap? You're seriously suggesting with all that's gone on I take a nap?"

"I see your point, but the adrenaline is going to evaporate. You'll crash sooner or later."

She rested her head against the headrest. "Maybe."

"Not ready for a nap? Call your parents."

Her head snapped to attention. "I need to call Tess." She fished her phone from her purse and placed the call. After several seconds, she left a message. "Hey, Tess. Listen. Call me before you go to the shop today. We've had some . . . Well, just call me before you go, okay? Bye."

Brett set the cruise control. "So what's the deal with your parents?"

She closed her eyes and leaned back again. "I think I'll take that nap now."

Chapter 18

The sound of crunching gravel woke Mary Wade. Where was she? She stretched her toes and touched the floor of a car. A car?

"Good morning. I mean, good afternoon, Sleepy Head." Brett.

She sat in his car. Traveling to who knows where.

With Brett.

She hadn't meant to sleep. She'd only wanted not to discuss her parents, but the fatigue from the night before caught up with her. "Where are we?"

He slowed to a stop in front of a farmhouse. "Time for lunch."

Blue hydrangeas flanked the front steps. She'd seen this house, or at least one very similar, in every dream of her future house. A wide front porch with a swing. Gardenias and butterfly bushes elbowed each other between holly and lilacs. Gerbera daisies and dahlias dotted open spaces. Gladiolas in vibrant pinks, purples, and yellows shored up a fence to the right side of the yard. The owner of this place adored flowers.

She scanned the scene, packed with color. "It's beautiful. Is this a restaurant?"

"Not exactly. It's my grandmother's house."

She sought his gaze. "Your grandmother's?" Her heart drummed in her chest. "Why?"

He pushed his sunglasses to the top of his head. "I had to stop here for the key to the cabin. She cooked lunch for us."

"What cabin?" Before he could answer her, a tall, thin woman dressed in black capri pants and a pink oxford shirt with an upturned collar stepped out the front door and onto the porch. Her silver hair, styled in a fresh, short cut, framed her shining face as she waved to Brett.

"That's your grandmother?" Her heart fluttered. "She looks like…I don't know…a friend of Audrey Hepburn's. She's gorgeous." Mary Wade lifted a silent prayer of thanksgiving that she'd changed clothes before leaving her house. Even still, her jean skirt and knit top were a poor match for the elegant woman greeting them.

Brett smiled and nodded. "Thank you, but don't let her looks fool you. She's more than the outside wrapping. Come on. She's waiting for us."

The grandmother skipped down the steps and darted into Brett's arms. "Yea. I'm so glad you're here. It's been too long, Brett." She rose on dark purple-tipped toes and kissed his cheek. "Love you to pieces."

Hugging his waist, the grandmother turned her attention to Mary Wade with an arched brow. An inquisitive smile hovered on her pink-tinted lips. "Well, Brett?"

"Oh, yeah. Gigi, this is Mary Wade Kimball. Mary Wade, this is my grandmother, Grace Davis."

Grace released Brett and clasped both hands around Mary Wade's. "So nice to meet you, sweetheart. Welcome." She latched onto Brett again. "Come on. Let's eat before everything gets cold."

Inside the house, Mary Wade counted three vases of roses scattered from the entryway into the kitchen. She buried her nose in the bouquet on the side board. "These smell wonderful."

"Thank you. I picked them this morning from my rose garden." With an oven mitt, she retrieved a casserole dish from the stove. "Brett, we need ice in the glasses. I have lemonade, sweet iced tea, and unsweetened too. Mary Wade, could you bring over the biscuit basket, please?" She tsked and shook her head at Brett. "I wish you'd called earlier. I didn't have a lot of time to pull much together."

"You've got five bowls on the table already. That casserole and the biscuits make seven. Are you feeding anybody else today?"

"No, but I wanted to cook some of your favorites. Choices are good. " She smiled. "I'll take a plate up the road to Franklin for supper. He always likes home cooking. Plus, when you said you were bringing a friend, I thought it was another man who'd probably eat like a horse. Like you." She glanced at Mary Wade, curiosity shading her countenance.

Not knowing how to answer that indirect question, Mary Wade moved to the table. "Your china pattern is lovely." She trailed a finger along the tiny pink, yellow, and blue roses bordering a plate.

"Thank you. That china was a great deal at a consignment shop years ago. I still love it."

"I thought it might be your wedding china."

A delighted laugh bubbled up Grace's throat. "The first few years I was married, we were grateful to have the plates I'd collected out of Oxydol laundry detergent boxes."

Not exactly a tale she expected from this woman who could adorn the cover of a magazine.

As they sat at the round table, Grace grabbed their hands and looked pointedly at Brett's free one. He obeyed the silent command and offered his hand to Mary Wade, his grip warm and solid.

Grace prayed a quick, concise, heartfelt prayer, squeezed their hands, and commenced the meal. "So, explain this story. What's going on here? Why exactly do you need the cabin? What's the deal with you two?"

Mary Wade's head swiveled toward the hostess and back

to Brett. He swallowed a bite of the sweet potato biscuit. "I told you when I called I need the cabin for a few days."

"Right. Why?" She glanced at Mary Wade. "Honey, take more of those peas. They're fresh. Picked them myself two days ago."

Brett sighed and related the entire story, beginning with the kidnapping and ending with the shooting.

"Oh, my." Concern furrowed her forehead. "So she's in danger? Why the cabin? Why not some—"

"I don't have time to go through all the regular channels, and, frankly," he ducked his head, "I'm on a little vacation right now."

"What does that mean? You didn't lose your job."

Mary Wade bit her lip. "Helping me escape jeopardized the undercover mission."

"For Heaven's sake. He saved your life. That's his job."

"I didn't lose my job. I just got a few days off while they review everything that went down."

"But that cabin is so remote. There's no phone. It's barely got electricity and running water."

"It was rustic till you got your hands on it and turned it into who knows what. It's a good place for some R and R."

"There're no neighbors for several miles. She can't stay by herself."

"I'm staying with her."

Grace's mouth dropped. Her eyes ping-ponged from Brett to Mary Wade. She pursed her lips.

He snagged another biscuit from under the bread towel. "Gigi, it's not like that."

"Not at all." Mary Wade glared at Brett. "And you never explained this situation to me."

"It's got two bedrooms, remember?" He broke the biscuit in half and chomped on it.

"My husband's been dead for seventeen years, but I'm not

dead yet. I know what can happen between a man and a woman in an isolated, beautiful setting like that. This arrangement isn't exactly kosher, mister."

"Two minutes ago, it was remote and rustic and barely a hovel. Now it's a love shack."

Grace laid her fork on her plate and drew herself up straight. "I certainly did not call it that, young man."

"Romantic hideaway then."

Panic dueled with embarrassment in her chest. How could she get out of this situation? "Mrs. Davis, please believe me. We're not . . . It's not . . . I'm—"

"Honey," Grace patted the younger woman's hand, "this situation has Brett Davis smacked all over it. If I didn't know it already, the color rising in your cheeks screams you had nothing to do with it." She passed her fingers over her chin, similar to Brett's familiar gesture. "Tells me something else also."

Mary Wade sucked in a breath.

"Oh, I'm sorry. I didn't mean—" She shook her head. "He's never brought another woman to that cabin." She cut her eyes to her grandson. "Not that I know of anyway. I meant he has a way of head butting his way through. Asks forgiveness later rather than permission first."

"I'm sitting right here." Brett scooped up the last bite of his baked chicken.

"And please call me Gigi. Just about everybody does." She tapped a finger near Brett's plate. "We need to think this through. She could stay here with me."

"No." Both Mary Wade and Brett spoke at once. Three locations had been trashed because of her. She wouldn't let a fourth be added to the list.

"Good. We agree on something." Brett sipped his lemonade.

കൗകൗരുരു

"And I've already thought it through." Brett pushed his

plate away. "We won't have to worry about fake names and IDs. It'll be for only a few days. A week at the most. There's no way to connect her to the cabin."

"If they connect her to you, they can connect her to the cabin." She rose and retrieved another casserole dish from a trivet on the counter. "Cherry cobbler for dessert."

"With whipped cream?"

"Of course." As she returned to the table, she tapped Mary Wade's shoulder. "That's his favorite."

"Okay."

Gigi plated a hefty portion on a dessert plate and handed it to Brett. He plopped a dollop of whipped cream on top of the warm concoction and set it in front of Mary Wade. Gigi repeated the process one more time but didn't scoop any dessert for herself. "I'm watching my girlish figure."

Mary Wade ran the tip of her fork through the creamy topping and tasted. "This is real whipped cream."

Gigi smiled. "Yes, it is."

"My grandmother makes most of her meals from scratch. She's a great cook."

"Thanks to the diner and a few cooking classes, but thank you, sweetie, for saying so." Gigi squeezed her grandson's hand.

"And PBS cooking shows every Saturday morning." Brett shoveled a huge bite of cherries and golden crust into his mouth.

"The diner?"

"My mother worked at the local diner. I sort of fell into the same work. Learned the basics there, which sufficed through the first few years of marriage. Then I discovered PBS and checked out Julia Child's cookbooks from the library. Years ago, the community college offered some cooking classes that were a hoot."

"This is fabulous." Mary Wade slid her finger along the edge of the saucer, licked the light red cherry gravy from her finger. Brett watched until his grandmother cleared her throat. He drained his glass of lemonade.

"So let's get back to the real conversation. You are both grown. You can make your own decisions, but both of you staying at that cabin, no matter if you're in separate rooms, will not look right. Think about Mary Wade's reputation."

"I'm thinking more about her life and putting criminals where they belong than I'm thinking about her reputation."

Both women looked at him, two sets of eyebrows drawn together.

Mary Wade broke the silence. "Mrs. Davis. Gigi. I appreciate your concern about my reputation. I'm not the kind of girl who takes it lightly." Her mouth flattened into a line. "In this case, however, I'll follow Brett's lead. He's saved my life twice now." She glanced at him. "Although we haven't known each other very long, I trust him."

He blinked and swallowed, nodded. "Okay, then. We'll help clean up and get on our way."

"You don't have—"

Brett's phone jingled in his front pocket. "Sorry. I need to take this." He stepped outside the back door.

Snagging the utensils, Mary Wade stacked Brett's plate on top of hers.

"No. Just leave them. I've got plenty of time to clean this kitchen when you're gone."

"Sorry. Can't do that." She brought her stack to the sink.

Gigi carried the cherry cobbler to the counter. "Are you sure you're all right with . . ." She fluttered her hand.

"Please don't worry about me or your grandson either. We met last week under crazy circumstances. We'll know each other for about another week or so. Then we'll go back to our regular lives."

Gigi narrowed her eyes. "You believe that?"

"Well, depending on the trial—"

"I mean, you think after all this is over, that'll be the end of you and Brett?"

Her heart skipped at the sound of that combination. "There is no me and Brett. After the trial, he'll go back to his job. I'll get my life back." Such as it was. "Thank you for preparing this feast. Everything was delicious." Mary Wade brought two more bowls to the counter. "I apologize for creating all this work for you."

"Fiddlesticks, honey. I love to cook, and my cooking brings Brett around. I'll keep cooking for as long as I can hold a spoon." She retrieved plastic dishes from a bottom cabinet. "Let's pack up these leftovers so you'll have something up at the cabin. You'll find a few things already up there. My garden club and I met at the cabin this past weekend. We left some unopened goodies. Feel free to eat."

Mary Wade liked this woman. In the short time they'd been together, she felt a connection with her. She didn't want Brett's grandmother to have the wrong idea about her. "Look, Gigi. Thank you for being concerned about my reputation and everything. I am too. I'm not the kind of girl who steals away on weekend trips with guys."

"I picked up on that." Gigi squirted blue dish detergent into the sink filling with hot water. Tiny bubbles floated between them.

"Yes, well. You don't have to worry about this situation. It's not ideal, but don't worry about me and your grandson. He's made it clear he's not interested in me." Mary Wade grabbed a dish towel hanging on the oven handle.

Gigi arched a brow. "Oh? How so?"

"He's doing his job. He's determined to salvage his assignment. The assignment includes me. That's all. When this is over," she shrugged, "we'll be over."

Gigi tilted her head. "What about you? How do you feel about my grandson?"

140

"I'm just getting over a breakup. I'm not ready for another relationship."

"You didn't really answer my question, did you?" Gigi lowered water glasses into the suds.

Mary Wade twisted the towel around her hand. "Brett and I don't have anything in common. My father is a minister. His life is the church. Growing up, I hardly saw him. He was always at the church or with a member. Brett's job is important to him. He has wacky hours. I promised myself to fall for someone who worked a normal, eight to five job."

"Uh huh." Gigi rinsed a glass and handed it to her. "What do you do for a living?"

"I design children's clothes and own a boutique." Boutique? Where did that come from? A pathetic attempt to make Gigi think she was a worthy woman.

"Mmm. The way you answer questions, I thought you might be a young politician."

"Actually, my shop is a wannabe boutique. I'm working up to it. Right now I have a booth at a crafts warehouse and an online presence."

Gigi chortled. "No. You're not a politician, for sure. I'm going to be praying for you, honey." She patted Mary Wade's hand. "Count on it."

The door creaked, and Brett filled the opening. "Sorry about that."

"No worries. We had a nice chat. You've got a special person here, Brett."

"Yeah, I plan to keep it that way." He playfully pushed his grandmother away from the sink with his hip. "I'll do those. You should sit down and rest."

"I'll rest when I'm dead. Right now, I'll pack up food I'm sending with you." She pecked him on the cheek again and patted his back before finding aluminum foil in a nearby drawer.

He handed Mary Wade a plate, and she grabbed it with a tea towel, avoiding his fingers.

Washes dishes and dodges bullets. What a combination.

She'd have to take care to avoid him in the next few days as well. She'd need those Gigi prayers.

Chapter 19

Ten minutes into the thirty-minute drive to the cabin, Brett chanced a look to his right. She still stared out her window. Not one word since she'd hugged Gigi goodbye. What was going on in that beautiful head of hers? What was their nice chat all about? And that hug? More than a polite, nice-to-meet-you hug. They'd clung to each other like kindred spirits.

Mary Wade turned, caught him staring. "I like your grandmother."

"My grandfather used to say, 'a woman of substance.' Safe to say she likes you too."

"She doesn't like this arrangement, however."

He flipped down the sun visor. "You're not crazy about it either."

"No, but I know nothing's going on, and I want to be safe. I hate disappointing her, though." She worried a hangnail on her thumb. "I want her to approve of me, not disapprove."

"Why? You just met her. You'll probably never see her again. Why does her opinion matter to you?"

She frowned. "Ouch. That's harsh. But, okay, more than likely true." She smoothed her skirt. "Caring about her opinion, I guess, is lingering echoes of my people-pleasing days."

"They're over, huh?"

"Mostly, yes. Ever since . . ."

He glanced at her. "Don't stop mid-thought. Ever since

what? You refused to do what your parents wanted you to do?"
He checked the rearview mirror.

"Ever since I decided to buck family tradition and go my
own way. Yes."

"My grandmother would applaud that. She's her own
woman. She's a church-going, Bible-believing woman, but she
knows her own mind. Married my grandfather, secretly, when
she was seventeen. The day she graduated from high school."
He adjusted the armrest, draped his forearm over it. "She turned
eighteen two months later and spilled the beans then. Her mom
hit the roof. She'd wanted Gigi to go to college, so she kicked
her out for two days, then got her a job at the diner where she
worked."

"How'd she marry secretly? Didn't she need a parent's
signature?"

"It's her story, but she never refuses to tell it when asked,
so I'll tell you the *Reader's Digest* version. Her dad was the
town drunk. She knew where he stayed, found him, and got him
to sign the license." Mary Wade caught her breath. "Yes, that
beautiful woman back there has overcome a lot. She's a force all
right and has no patience for silly stuff. Notice how small talk
was minimal at lunch? She jumped right to the information she
needed. Sleeping arrangements."

He smiled at the color creeping up her cheeks. "How old
are you anyway? You blush like you're fifteen."

She groaned. "It's this hair and my fair skin. And it's bad
manners to ask my age, FYI."

"And unnecessary. I know how old you are and your birthday too."

"What?"

"Part of the job." He turned onto a dirt road.

"I don't believe that."

"Just so you know, I don't lie."

"Are you kidding me? I met you in an undercover job."

"That's my job."

"And you tell me I'm your job, so . . ."

"No. Wrong logic. Whatever I say to you will be the truth. Bank on it." He slowed the car and turned onto a gravel driveway. "We're here."

ജ്ജ്ജ്

Situated several yards off the road, a cabin peeked through pines, oaks, and azalea bushes. Mary Wade scooted forward in her seat to get a better view. Gigi had definitely written her signature all over the yard. Mountain laurel and rhododendron traded turns in the flower beds framing the porch. Colorful perennials skirted some of the pines.

"This looks like an enchanted forest."

"Gigi would love that description."

"Where are we?" She'd given up trying to keep up with the directions with the many turns Brett had taken to arrive here.

"A few miles on the other side of Hickory." As he set the emergency brake, she exited the car and grabbed her bags from the backseat. "I can get those for you."

But she wasn't listening. She called over her shoulder, "Do you mind if I take a look in the backyard?" Not waiting for an answer, she made her way up the driveway, set the bags on the porch, and continued beyond the side of the cabin.

"Hey, be careful. It slopes off, and the brook—"

"Owww."

He threw his duffel on the porch and jogged to her. Sprawled on the ground, she held her ankle. He knelt beside her. "Did you twist it or—"

"I stepped in a hole."

"Ah. Gigi's been warring with moles since the beginning. Here." He slipped his arm under her knees and one under her arms, lifting her in one swift movement. "Let's get you inside and take a look."

"You don't have to carry me. I can walk."

He tightened his grip around her. "Just relax and let me help you."

She relented but didn't relax.

He ascended the stairs two at a time and stopped at the front door. "You know, you're light as a feather."

"I thought you said you didn't lie."

He chuckled. "Put your arms around my neck and hang on. I'll get the key out of my pocket."

"No. Put me down."

"This is a case of déja vu all over again." He touched her good foot to the porch slats and steadied her as she got her balance. Letting the screened door flap against his back, he inserted the key. "Be warned. This was my grandfather's hunting cabin. In the past few years, my grandmother added some touches, I've heard, to make it homier. She can't bear to part with it, but it's still a cabin. Rustic. No amenities beyond running water and electricity." He widened the door so that she could pass through.

She gasped.

He lurched beside her, eyes searching the room. "What is it?"

She hobbled farther into the cabin. "It's gorgeous."

An overstuffed sofa upholstered in chintz fabric anchored the room. Two wing chairs covered in contrasting stripes and polka dots bordered the fireplace. The rough-hewn walls still told the story of a hunting cabin, but Gigi's touches definitely added a new chapter. She'd left her elegant touch on every detail.

Framed photographs dotted the room. Chessmen waited for a match on a pie crust table in one corner. Books stacked on end tables invited visitors to sit and read. Instead of glossy picture books, a family Bible weighted the coffee table.

Happiness swirled in her chest. Grace Davis' fingerprints lit the entire room. If, as Brett predicted, she'd never see Grace again, she could get to know this interesting woman through her special get-away during the next few days. Living in this idyllic setting could also be the perfect fuel for new design ideas. She pictured herself designing on the back porch, listening to the brook in the morning, at the game table at night.

Goosebumps tingled on her arm.

This could be good.

ᏰᎧᏰᎧᏣᏹᏣᏹ

This could be bad.

Brett scanned the room, not believing his eyes. What had gone down here? Flowery curtains framed the windows. Candles, tall and thin, as well as fat and squat, manned the mantel. A basket of pinecones filled the fireplace. Fancy throw pillows lounged on a flowery couch. When was the last time he'd been here? Five years ago? Seven? Had it been that long?

Gigi had struck and struck hard.

"This looks like a beautiful little bed and breakfast. It's like—" Mary Wade clamped her mouth shut.

He had a fairly good idea of where her thoughts were leading her.

Yep. Bad, for sure.

When Tony had given him some days off for "going rogue" as he'd put it, the cabin popped into his mind. He'd come up here, relax, review what went down in Bandon, keep tabs on developments through his buddy, and exorcise all thoughts of this intriguing woman wobbling beside him. When she'd been shot at, he'd included her in his getaway plan without thinking about all the ramifications. He'd simply wanted her safe.

He guided Mary Wade to an armchair. "Have a seat, and let's look at that ankle. Do you ever wear substantial shoes?" He sat on a needle-pointed foot stool and pulled her ankle onto his lap.

"It's summer. Sandal time."

"Can you move your foot?"

Rotating her ankle, she started and squeezed her eyes shut.

"Sorry. Looks like it's sprained." He rose and gingerly laid her foot on the stool. "Okay. This is what we're going to do. I'll check for an Ace bandage. Granddad always kept a well-stocked first aid kit. That'll help reduce swelling. So will icing it." He opened a kitchen cabinet, found a box, and returned to her.

He took her ankle again and unfurled the bandage. Her white knuckles stood out against the polka dots she gripped on the arm chair. "I'll be gentle, okay? I'm starting just below your toes, and I'll wrap all the way to about mid-calf. I'll make it snug, but tell me if it's too tight. We want it to give support, not cut off your circulation."

She bit her lip and stiffened at his touch, keeping her eyes on the bandage.

"You took off the pink."

She glanced at him. "What?"

"Your pedicure. You took it off."

She blinked. "It was ruined, so I removed the polish. Haven't had a chance to repaint them."

He nodded. "You know, I've had a few sprains myself. You'll be good as new in a few days." He rounded her arch and skipped her heel. Her skin was soft and warm. He had to force himself to concentrate on his task and not on other, more interesting thoughts. "Is it too tight?" Resting her heel on his thigh, he held the end in one hand and slipped a finger under the final round.

She shook her head.

"Good." He placed the clasp to fasten the end. "You need to stay off it for a couple days. Rest it. Our bodies usually do a good job healing an injury like this, if we let them." He continued to hold her leg, caught himself exploring the underside of her calf with his thumb. Checking himself, he wiped his palm along his pants leg.

"Sounds like you know something about medicine. Does

that come with your job?" Her voice sounded strained, a little breathy. Was it the pain or something else?

"Comes with several sprains and some medic training in Afghanistan."

She glanced at him then. "Right. You were in the Army."

He held her gaze a beat longer than necessary, tracked an emotion pass over her eyes. "Yep. A few years." No more Army talk. He set her foot on the stool and snagged two pillows from the couch. He flicked a tassel hanging from one corner and shook his head. "Gigi." He checked the height of her foot. "We need to keep your ankle elevated. Helps the blood get to where it needs to be."

Raking his fingers through his hair, he moved to the front door. "Stay put. I'll bring in our things."

Chapter 20

One patch of night sky sparkled through the branches waving outside Mary Wade's bedroom. Her foot, propped on pillows brought in from the couch, throbbed despite the ibuprofen Brett insisted she take. Instead of sheep, she counted the stars she could see. Twelve. Not enough to make her sleepy. How could she sleep with him in the next room?

After choosing bedrooms, they'd shared a simple meal of cheese, crackers, and fruit, both of them still full from Gigi's feast in mid-afternoon. Her room, modest and cozy, displayed the same Gigi touches as the den. Decorated in blue and yellow, the room held a wooden, regular-sized bed in the far corner, a dresser, an upholstered chair, and a bookshelf filled with more books, sea shells, and picture frames.

Brett's room, dressed in green and mauve, was the more masculine, slightly larger one. A shared bathroom separated the two bedrooms. When he'd seen them, he rubbed his hand over his eyes. "I can't believe what she's done to this cabin. My grandfather . . ." He shook his head.

"She's done an amazing job with it. Every room is beautiful, and so are the grounds, except for the mole holes." She winced and held to the door frame as they surveyed the cabin. "You've got a sweet vacation spot up here."

"Yeah, well, I don't take a lot of vacations. This is the first time I've been up here in years. And I don't remember her taking many vacations either."

Remember that, Mary Wade. He doesn't take many vacations. That means he works a lot. Undercover usually means crazy hours, doesn't it? Wouldn't make for an easy relationship. So next time he wants to check how tight the bandage is wrapped, do it yourself.

She shivered, imagining the zings arcing from the touch of his thumb on her calf. She'd clung to the chair arms with a death grip to keep from pulling his mouth up to hers and . . . She turned onto her side and a sharp zap shot from her ankle. "Ow." She bit off the rest of her reaction.

Footsteps shuffled outside her door. A soft knock. "Mary Wade, are you okay in there?"

"Yes. Thanks. I just moved my foot too fast."

"You can have some more ibuprofen in a couple of hours if you're still awake, but try to sleep if you can."

"I will."

Silence, until an owl hooted from the darkness. She closed her eyes and tried to think of anything besides Brett.

"Night, then."

Mary Wade's eyes flew open, her heartbeat pounding in her ears. He'd been standing outside the door. Waiting? Listening? Could he hear her heartbeat?

"Good night."

So much for putting Brett out of her mind.

ഌഌാ⬩⬩

The scent of lavender mingled with a hint of coffee smells. Mary Wade smiled, stretched, and a knife jabbing her ankle woke her. She groaned, the throbbing reminding her of her surroundings. Brett's cabin. Alone with Brett. Brett, who by the aroma wafting into her room, had already gotten up.

She cringed. Somehow the events of yesterday afternoon embarrassed her more the morning after. The way he'd cradled her foot, caressed her calf, looked deep into her eyes. What did he expect from her up here in this remote cabin? What did he say to her in the first few hours she'd known him? He'd do more with a beautiful woman than watch TV. The cabin didn't even have a TV. What had she gotten herself into?

Wait. He'd told his grandmother—what? He'd said the cabin had two bedrooms. He'd never explained beyond that statement. Heat crept from under the dappled sheet up her throat to her cheeks. She'd have to be resolute if he had plans other than keeping her safe from Dusty and Skeet because if she were honest, she might like to find out what he'd do instead of watching TV.

Brett was different from other guys she'd been involved with, especially Robert. When she thought of Robert now, she wondered why she ever mourned that relationship. Compared with Brett, he faded into the background without a blip. Brett fought for her, protected her and took care of her, clearly loved his grandmother, and even washed dishes. He made quick decisions and followed through with them. No second-guessing.

And of course, he was just plain good-looking with his athlete's body, high cheekbones, and eyes that saw everything. She'd certainly never been around anyone like him for more than a quick hello. She'd have to keep her mind on designing, not on Brett.

She sat on the edge of the bed. Pain flashed from her ankle when she touched the floor with her foot. She'd have to hobble to the bathroom. Brett had helped her last night, holding her waist and making sure she didn't use her foot. She could manage this morning.

A shower would help fortify her, wash away crazy thoughts of Brett. She grabbed a pair of cargo shorts, an amethyst blouse, and her toiletries bag. She hopped to the door and peeked into the den. From the doorway, she saw the empty kitchen and den. The bathroom door was open. The coast was clear. Excellent.

With one hand clutching the wall for support, she limped into the bathroom.

By the time she'd finished showering, her ankle felt twice its size, like it might explode any minute. Her hair would have to air dry. No way could she stand at the mirror for ten more minutes. She gritted her teeth and opened the bathroom door.

"What are you doing?"

౭౦౭౦౦౭౦౭

Brett held the front doorknob in one hand, a walking stick in the other. "You're not supposed to be on your foot." He knew he shouldn't have left her, but she needed a crutch. As much as he enjoyed having his arms around her, he figured giving her a little independence was best. He reached her in four strides and was assaulted by steam and wafts of soap and shampoo, flowery smells that swirled around his senses.

"Give me that, and you take this." Motioning toward the heap of things in her arm, he offered the stick.

She clutched the bundle tighter to her chest. "No. I've got it." With her movement, a corner of soft, gauzy material swayed against her shirt. Her pajamas?

He swiped his chin with his free hand. "Fine. Look. I found a forked stick, perfect for a makeshift crutch. It should work till I can get to Hickory for a real one."

She placed the fork under her arm. "You found it this morning?"

"Yeah. That was the quick part, surprisingly. Whittling off the bark took a little bit longer."

She hobbled past him with hesitant steps. "This works great. Thank you."

"Your arm will get sore at first, but we can cover it with an old towel or something. Hey, you unwrapped your ankle."

One more step, and she crossed her threshold. "Yeah. So it wouldn't get wet."

He followed her. "Sit down, and I'll wrap it again."

"No. Thank you. I . . .I watched you wrap it yesterday. I can do it."

"But—"

She closed the door.

Disappointment settled in his chest.

Stubborn woman.

ℰℰℭℭ

Relief settled in her chest.

Bossy man.

Wrapping an ankle can't be that difficult.

Walking with a sprained ankle and a hand-whittled crutch, however, proved to be difficult and exhausting. She dropped onto the bed and ran her fingers over the bare wood. Brett had searched for the perfect stick and whittled it for her. That act showed a kind and caring person, not a control-hungry, wannabe-boss-of-the-world. She reclined onto the pillows still clutching the stick. She'd have to apologize.

She'd walked all of twenty or so steps, but her body reacted as if she'd climbed a mountain. Standing on one foot was exhausting. Brett's crutch would be a substantial help. She'd be mobile. A positive. She wouldn't have to wait for him to help her. Snuggled up beside him. With his arm around her.

Another positive.

Kind of.

An image of him in the entryway floated in front of her eyes. Pushed-up shirt sleeves revealed muscular arms. A day's worth of whiskers covered his square jaw.

Rugged. Handsome.

Capable. Handsome.

She blew out a cleansing breath. She should rise and meet the rest of the day, not hide in her room all morning.

Pushing drying wisps of hair off her face, she dragged her-

154

self to sitting and reached for the Ace bandage at the foot of the bed. She could do this. Starting with wrapping her own ankle.

Or maybe not.

At first, the wrap was much too tight. Her toes turned pink. She unraveled it and began again. Too loose. It felt like a sock missing its elasticity. How did he wrap it so perfectly? She worked with fabric, understood it. It shouldn't be difficult. The third try worked better, but the result resembled a shabby version of Brett's handiwork.

Her version would have to do. She couldn't let him wrap her ankle again.

She stilled herself on the edge of the bed before facing him. *Please, God, help me. He's out of my league.*

✣✣✣✣✣✣

The scalding mug of coffee warmed Brett's hand. The air had a chill in it left from the night before. Nighttime temperatures probably hit the low fifties. And she's wearing shorts. Did she bring a jacket? Did he suggest bringing one? He couldn't remember. He'd get her one when he went into town.

He sipped his black coffee and heard a muffled sound coming from her bedroom. He rose to go to her, then changed his mind. She can do it herself, as she liked to remind him.

The bedroom door creaked, and she hobbled into the den, heading straight for him.

She smiled. "Good morning, by the way."

He nodded. "Yeah. Good morning. I've got coffee and a few choices for breakfast."

She sat in the chair he held for her. "I'm not all that hungry, but coffee sounds wonderful."

"You need to eat something. Your body needs fuel to help heal itself."

"Okay. Okay. A piece of toast?" She glanced at a saucer holding a few pieces.

"With peanut butter?"

"Fine. Maybe a little."

He set a mug in front of her along with a sugar bowl. "Sugar, right?" He brought over the foot stool and raised her foot, caught a whiff of flowers. "Here. Keep it elevated, remember?" He rejoined her at the table. "I can do that for you."

She'd taken a piece of toast and held a butter knife with a slab of peanut butter in midair. "Brett, thank you for helping me, but I can manage toast."

He grinned. "I guess you're right. You didn't do half bad on the wrap either. Good job." He sipped his coffee. "I could straighten it up some if you want."

"It's good, but thanks."

Silence mushroomed in the little kitchen. He ate a couple bites of blueberry yogurt. "So what're your plans for today?"

Eyebrows shot toward the ceiling. "My plans?" She shook her head. "I have no plans. I thought you had a plan."

"Well, the main plan is to hang out here until Dusty and Skeet are where they belong. I meant what do you want to do here? You brought your design stuff you said. Do you want to work on those?"

She swallowed the last of the toast and licked her lips, dropped her eyes. "Yes. I need to do some work. I also need to make some calls. I want to find out about Jack. "

"Uh. About that. No landline and no cell service either. We have to drive up the mountain a little ways to get some bars on your phone. We'll do that, but you really need to rest that ankle today."

She opened her mouth, probably to protest, but closed it. Does her ankle hurt that much to make her acquiesce so easily?

"Fine. Well, designing is good." Her face lit up. "I could sit on the back porch and do some sketching."

"Did you bring a jacket?"

Her face went blank. "No. It's summer. In North Carolina."

"You're in the North Carolina mountains. Nights and early mornings can be cool." He drained his coffee. "I'll find something for you."

Chapter 21

The rocking chair protested as Brett pushed back on it. He pretended to study case notes but watched Mary in the corner of his eye instead. She lounged in the glider, her right foot suspended on pillows, a sketch pad in her lap.

Completely unaware, she made a fetching sight in his faded UNC-Charlotte sweatshirt. Though it swallowed her, hanging almost to her knees, she had rolled up the sleeves and managed to look too cute for her own good.

Or his.

Lost in her thoughts and designs, she drew long lines, studied the brook for several minutes, drew short lines. Did she even remember that he rocked beside her?

"Are you comfortable?"

"Uh huh." She answered without looking up or stilling her pencil.

"You're not cold, are you? It's a little breezy out here."

"No." She wiggled her shoulders. "It's cozy and comfy. Perfect. Thank you." More strokes and shading.

He gave up. He had work to do as well. He checked his watch. Almost noon. He could concentrate till lunch. He stacked the papers and focused on the first paragraph. Again.

Gravel crunched, signaling a visitor. Or an intruder. Dusty and Skeet?

Brett bolted from the chair. He scooped her from the glider in one smooth movement. "Shhh. Don't say a word." The screened door hit his back, and he let it close silently. "Stay in your room and don't move." He dropped her on the bed, grabbed his nine-millimeter from his room.

He sidled along the wall and angled to peer out the picture window. "Are you kidding me?" He stuffed his gun into the back of his waistband.

"Yoo hoo, Brett. Guess who? I'd open the door, but my hands are full."

Gigi. Of course. Checking on things.

He swung open the door. "Gigi, what are you doing here?" He lifted a wicker basket from her arms.

"I brought provisions. There's more stuff in the car." She gestured with a toss of her head.

He set the basket on the counter and heard Gigi gasp.

Mary Wade hovered in the doorway of her room. The hem of her, no his, sweatshirt hid the hem of her shorts, giving the illusion she wore only the shirt. The Ace bandage had unfurled a couple of rounds, the end hanging loose to her ankle.

Gigi closed her mouth, staring from one to the other.

He could guess her thoughts. The sweatshirt covered what Mary Wade wore to breakfast, but his grandmother had no way of knowing that. "Wait, Gigi. No. Don't jump to wrong conclusions."

"I . . . I haven't said a word. Good morning, Mary Wade."

"Good morning, Gigi." She hobbled into the room. Another round of bandage fell from her calf.

"Stop. Don't move. I'll help you."

As he neared her, she clutched his arm and whispered, "Don't you dare pick me up."

He grabbed her waist instead and helped her to the striped wing chair. "I'll get the stool and your crutch."

"Crutch? Oh, dear, what happened?" Gigi sat in the polka dot version, compassion replacing suspicion in her sharp eyes. "You were fine when you left my house yesterday."

"Mole holes in the backyard," Brett called from the porch.

"Oh, those varmints." Gigi slapped the arm of the chair. "I've tried everything I can find, and they keep ruining my yard. Honey, I'm so sorry you got hurt."

"It's just a little sprain. A few days of rest should make it as good as new."

Brett let the back door slam shut. "If she listens to what I say." He propped the crutch on the mantel and set the stool in front of her.

"That's her crutch?"

"It's the best I could do for the time being." Lifting her foot, he sat on the stool. "Let's rewrap this ankle."

ഇ)ഇ)(രു(രു

His warm hands were doing the job before Mary Wade could protest, not that she really wanted to.

The sweatshirt fabric ballooned around her and insulated the heat swirling in the pit of her stomach. Time to take it off. She pulled it over her head and wiggled out of it. "Brett loaned me his sweatshirt because it's cool on the back porch."

"I see."

"Yeah. I'm good like that." He'd rounded her arch, his fingers brushing the sensitive hollow at her ankle. "It's looking better today. Not as much swelling."

She hugged the sweatshirt to her chest.

He straightened the wrap and continued rolling the bandage up her leg, fingertips skimming across her skin. "So you came with provisions. I already had some stuff. Sure you didn't come to chaperone?"

Gig arched a brow. "Do I need to chaperone, young man?"

He snickered. "No ma'am. Everything's on the up and up, Gigi. You can check out the bedrooms if you want. No hanky-panky going on here."

"Quit being so cheeky, Brett Daniel Davis. You're embarrassing me, as well as Mary Wade."

Evidently, the heat simmering in her midsection had risen to color her neck and face. As soon as he let go of her leg, she'd claim a headache and hide in her bedroom for the rest of the afternoon. Except she didn't want to be rude to Gigi. She'd stick it out for her, endure his hands inciting electrical charges, his sassy comments, and Gigi's questioning gaze. She'd stood up to her parents for years.

She could hold her own with Brett Daniel Davis.

ଈଈଔଔ

As long shadows stretched across the backyard, Gigi rose from her rocking chair.

"I've had such a lovely afternoon, you two, but I really should be getting back. It'll be dark soon. Ugh. I sound like an old woman who won't drive at night." She scowled. "I drive at night. It's just that I don't like driving in the dark up here." She grabbed Mary Wade's hands. "Thank you for sharing your designs with me, honey. You are talented. I'll be praying for God's blessings on your business."

"Thank you for bringing all the goodies. Snickerdoodles and chocolate chip too. Love them both."

The two women hugged like long-lost sorority sisters. An uncomfortable emotion climbed from Brett's midsection and tapped on his heart. "I'll get your basket."

"Great idea. You can take it to the car for me." She turned to Mary Wade. "Here, take my sweater. It fits better than that tired sweatshirt." She shook her head when the younger woman protested. "I insist."

"Come on, Brett. Walk me to my car."

She stopped at the hood, facing him with crossed arms. "Son, how do you see all this," she fluttered her fingers, "ending?"

161

"I see Mary Wade testifying, and criminals going away for a long, long time."

"No." She shook her head. "Not that. What's going to happen with you and Mary Wade?"

"There is no me and Mary Wade."

"I'm not so sure about that." She moved to the driver's door and turned to him. "Brett, she's a good girl. She's not the type—"

"I hear you, Grandmother. I know I'm not the kind of man for her."

"Wrong. That's not what I mean. You're strong and kind and loyal. Exactly the kind of man for any woman."

"Don't forget good-looking." He bobbed his eyebrows.

She punched his shoulder. "And modest. I thought you were smart till you brought her up here."

"I agree." He rubbed the back of his neck. "I didn't think the whole scenario through. Plus, I didn't realize you'd turned Pop's hunting cabin into a magazine photo shoot. What were you thinking?"

She shrugged. "I attended a decorating class at the community college. I redid my house and then started up here."

Brett chuckled. "The college? Have they asked you to be on the board of trustees yet?"

"Actually, someone approached me two weeks ago about that very idea. I'm praying about it. Listen to me, Brett." She grabbed his hand, held it with both of hers. "You have a tendency to leave broken hearts behind you. You don't mean to, but it happens anyway. I've seen it since you were in high school."

"Which couldn't have been many since I dropped out." He scuffed his boot over the gravel.

She pursed her lips. "You've overcome that unfortunate misjudgment."

He kissed her forehead, grateful for her long-suffering love and support. "I'm not going to hurt Mary Wade."

162

She cupped his cheek with her palm. "Honey, I know you don't plan to."

"I promise. She's probably looking for a preacher to settle down with, not some tough lawman. Truth be told, she'll—" He clamped his mouth shut. No sense in continuing this line of conversation. He opened the door for her.

Gigi narrowed her eyes. "Uh huh." She slid inside and rolled down the window. "I remember that girl who didn't treat you right a few years ago."

He worked his jaw. "Enough said."

"You know I pray for you every day, right?"

He leaned inside the window to peck her cheek. "Yes, ma'am. Love you."

"Love you back."

Stuffing his hands in his pockets, he watched her wind down the curved driveway to the road. He remained there long after she blew her horn and waved, wishing he could receive her call when she arrived home safely.

Wishing for other things too.

ᴤᴅᴤᴅᴐᴄᴙᴄᴙ

Although she felt like she intruded on a private family time, Mary Wade couldn't help herself from observing the interaction between grandmother and grandson. Love was clearly evident on both sides.

Brett was different with his grandmother. No longer the no-nonsense, no-humor deputy, he laughed, highlighting the cleft in his chin. He teased Gigi about the abundance of throw pillows in the room. Rolled his eyes like a teenager.

His grandmother helped him relax.

After the first few awkward moments when Gigi gawked at her wearing Brett's sweatshirt, the day had been a gift. The stylish woman had been interested in all the designs in the sketch pad, asked thought-provoking questions, and shared valid advice. Grace Davis was a kindred spirit.

Mary Wade had just settled her foot onto the double pillows on the stool when Brett entered the den. "It's cooling down out there." He rubbed his arms. "I could build a fire if you're chilly."

A fire in the fireplace. Cozy. Warm. Intimate. She should say, "No, thank you," but her rebel streak kicked in. "Sounds good."

He placed the bucket of pinecones beside the hearth and opened the flue. "I'll get a few logs. We won't need many."

With a strike of a match, Brett had logs popping and flames flickering in no time. "Can I get you anything?"

"My sketch book, please?"

"Gigi really enjoyed seeing your designs." He handed her the book and her set of pencils.

"I enjoyed showing them off. She's very encouraging."

He retrieved a medium-sized cotton bag from his room. "You must be really talented the way she oohed and ahhed. She doesn't flatter. She means what she says."

"I picked up on that yesterday at lunch." She glanced toward the bag. "What do you have there?"

He retrieved a pocket knife and a three-inch square block of wood from the pouch. "Thought I'd sit and carve while you sketch."

"What do you carve?"

He pointed to the corner. "See that chess set over there?"

"You carved it?" She arched her neck to see the set better. She'd check it out tomorrow or maybe tonight on the way to bed.

"No. My granddad did, and he taught me. I want to carve my own set." He rose, palmed the king and queen, and handed them to her.

"These are wonderful." She rotated the pieces in her fingers. "They're dogs."

"Yep. The king's a Mastiff. The queen's a St. Bernard. All the pawns are Dachshunds. He copied pictures from a book."

She held a piece toward the light. "The detail is so intricate."

"Yeah. He used a V-tool. He called it his carving pencil."

"But you're using a pocket knife."

"To get the basic form. I started this set when I was a teenager. Thought maybe I'd just try the usual shapes."

Brett started carving and fell silent. Finally, a companionable silence settled with only the sounds in the room of scraping metal against wood and the crackling fire. Mary Wade studied the king and queen and wondered about a man who could create such beautiful pieces. "Your grandfather was very talented."

"He was special all right. Didn't have a lot of patience for small talk. When he did say something, however, you better listen. It'd be good. A lot of people thought of him as stoic and taciturn, but he never seemed like that to me." He stretched out long legs in front of him. "One time a killdeer—do you know what a killdeer is?"

"A bird."

"Yeah. But killdeers build their nests in the ground. Odd, but true. One time, a killdeer built a nest right in the middle of a row of tomatoes. Pop didn't have the heart to ruin it, so every time he plowed his garden, he'd get to that spot," Brett used his hand to emphasize the motion, "raise the plow, roll carefully over the section with the nest, lower the plow, and then keep going."

"He cared about things." She rotated the pieces again. "He liked beauty too."

"Yep." He blew wood dust from the block.

She added another ruffle to a sundress design, decided against it, and erased it. "Could we drive up the mountain tomorrow? I have to check on Jack, and Tess."

"Yeah, I guess so. If you let me help you to and from the car."

"Fine."

"It's not that far. Walking distance, really, but not with a crutch."

She couldn't think of what the sundress needed, but it needed something. Doodling in the corner of the sketch usually jogged ideas. Tonight, nothing. A log popped, and the shooting sparks grabbed her attention. The flames absorbed her thoughts for several moments, the coziness of the room comforting her. She snuggled into her chair, and the fire's hold on her broke. Her gaze bounced to Brett, whose attention zeroed in on her.

Self-conscious, she straightened in her seat. Warmth not associated with the fire in the hearth stole her breath. They were two people, a man and a woman, alone in front of a fire. The companionable silence she'd enjoyed evaporated, leaving her tense and shy. "Well, it's getting late."

Brett checked his watch. "If you're a chicken or born before electricity. Mary Wade, you don't have to be afraid of sitting in front of the fire with me."

She stuck a pencil back in the box. "Don't call me a chicken."

"I meant as in 'going to bed with the chickens.'"

"You said I don't have to be afraid. What makes you think I am?"

"Body language."

She loosened her grip on the pad and box. "I enjoyed sitting here in front of the fire."

"Yeah, until about thirty seconds ago." He tossed the shavings into the fireplace. The fire hissed and flickered.

She closed her sketch pad. "You think you know everything."

"Reading people is part of my job." He replaced the carving and pocketknife in the bag. "Listen, I promised Gigi—"

"Promised her what?"

"I promised her I'd take care of you. That I wouldn't let you get hurt."

"You've already proved you can protect me."

Brett studied her. "We weren't talking about only the kidnapping and the shooting. And I think you know that."

Hot and cold tingles flashed inside her body. She stood and reached for the crutch, but he was there first, holding it for her.

"I can take those for you." He clasped her hand, still holding the chess pieces. Inches separated her face from his chest. A faint hint of soap and spice floated toward her. She remembered the feel of his chest against her as he helped her limp from room to room, as he swooped her up and carried her from the porch this morning. She steered her rebel brain to the constant throbbing in her ankle.

"Mary Wade," he lifted her chin. "We're in an unusual situation here. Emotions run high when people are thrown together like this for several days. You don't have to be uncomfortable around me. Nothing will happen that you don't want to happen."

Ding. Ding. Ding. The problem hit square on its head.

She wanted something to happen. She wanted to get to know this man better, listen to his stories about his grandfather. Find out about his tour in Afghanistan. She wanted to trail her fingers along his arms, trace his biceps. Feel her heart race when his lips touched hers.

Even as these thoughts ricocheted in her brain, calmer thoughts were winning the charge. She should listen to his words and not her heart. He'd just explained this situation was unusual, explained about high emotions. Clearly, she didn't make his heart race. Clearly, he was cautioning her not to fall for him.

She secured the fork of the stick under her arm. "Good to know. Good night." She left him in front of the fire, holding the king and queen. Back in her room, she leaned against the closed door, clutching her sketch book and pencils and taking deep breaths.

A few more days and it'd be over. Brett would begin a new case, and she'd begin the process of forgetting him. Again. Like she had succeeded so well at forgetting him after the kidnapping.

In June, she had the idea in the back of her mind that she'd see him again at trial. When he left this time, however, it'd be for good.

Did you hear that, heart? He'd be off with a new case, someone new to protect. A new woman? One with an exciting career to match his own and no freckles sprinkled across the bridge of her nose?

Lord, take away my interest in this man. Let me be interested in someone who comes home at six o'clock every night and doesn't have the courthouse on speed dial. Help me stop tingling every time Brett touches me. Or looks at me. Or says my name.

She pulled in a ragged breath.

Help me make it through the next few days.

Chapter 22

The SUV still coasted as Mary Wade reached for the door handle.

Brett's long arm corralled her into the seat. "Wait a minute. I'll get your crutch, but you don't have to get out to make a call. Just being up here will get you a working signal."

"I want to see."

He'd brought her to the top of the mountain to make phone calls. The overlook hung above a green valley that stretched for miles. "It's rocky out there. Be careful. Look for a few minutes, then come sit down. Your ankle's still healing, remember?" He met her at the door as she climbed out. "Little steps. Take my arm."

"Look, there's a bench. I can sit over there and make calls."

"Sit sideways with your foot up. Better than when you're in the Tahoe." He propped the crutch in easy reach and nodded to the other side of the clearing. "I'll step over there, and we won't disturb each other."

Grateful for privacy, she pulled out her phone from her pocket. Brett might be a tough guy. Might be comfortable around criminals. Might be used to guns and bullets. But he was more than that. A lot more. He understood little things like giving her space when she needed it.

He hadn't pushed last night when the conversation veered toward topics she didn't want to discuss. Breakfast could have been an awkward time, but he'd served her oatmeal with almonds without any hint of whatever happened between them in front of the fire. He'd given her a chess lesson while he'd described his grandfather's talent.

Yep. A good man.

Several minutes after the last "goodbye," footsteps signaled his return. "Everything okay?" He waited with his hands in his pockets, observing her.

"Jack came home yesterday. He's sore. And his arm hurts too." She shifted to place her foot on the ground, and the crutch clattered off the bench. "He's former Army, and those two guys getting a jump on him rankles his manly pride."

He made a face. "Hey, now. Don't disparage manly pride."

"I'm sure yours is robust and can withstand anything I might say or do."

As he bent to retrieve the crutch, he muttered, "You'd be surprised." He held it steady as she positioned her arm. "And Tess? She's manning the fort?"

"As well as she can. I had to cancel my Girl Scouts." She sighed. "They were doing so well."

"It'll be over soon. Ready to go?" He supported her arm to help her back to the car.

಩಩ఞಚಚ

Against his better judgment, Brett built a fire in the fireplace after another dinner from Gigi's basket. He flopped in the polka dot chair and stretched out his legs, crossing his boots at the ankles.

Mary Wade opened her sketch book. "Thanks for cleaning the ashes and gathering the wood. The fire's a nice treat."

"No problem. I'd forgotten how much I like to sit in front of a fire." He extracted his knife and partially carved chess piece. "How does your foot feel?"

She wiggled her toes peeking out from the bandage. "Even

170

with the excursion today, it feels better. I think the swelling's gone down."

He leaned forward. "I can take a look."

"No." She slid farther back into the chair. To get away from him? "It's fine."

Settling into his chair, he examined the base of the knight piece. "You think you might be up for a trip into Hickory tomorrow?"

"Yes."

"Good. I need to do a few things, plus—now don't get me wrong. I love Gigi's food, but a steak cooked up here has always been the ticket."

"I thought the purpose of a hunting cabin is to eat what you kill."

"Yes, well, nothing I want to eat's in season right now. I could catch some fish, but I can't find even a cane pole. Gigi must've given all the rods away. You up for a steak?"

"Sure." She shaded a portion of the paper with the side of her pencil.

He focused his attention on the ears of the horse head. "So, how are your parents?"

The pencil flipped from her fingers. She fished for it in between the cushion and arm of the chair.

"Sorry I startled you."

"You didn't. I guess they're fine."

"You guess?" He smoothed the line of the horse's snout, resisting the urge to glance at her. No need to make her feel like he was interrogating her. "You didn't call them today?"

"No. I don't call them every day." She clutched the pencil with both hands.

"But you haven't called them in several days, have you?"

She shifted. He held his breath, waiting for her to bolt. Call it a night. Retreat to her room.

Instead, she repositioned her foot. "And that concerns you how?"

Relief surged in his chest. "I apologize for prying."

She dropped the back of her head against the chair. "It's okay. I don't talk about my parents much. I don't call them every day or even regularly because, frankly, I don't like feeling like a failure."

"And they make you feel that way?"

"I don't think they do it on purpose. In fact, I'm pretty sure they don't. I know they love me. It's just that I've disappointed them. Hugely. To them, I'm a rebel or, at the very least, ungrateful."

He arched an eyebrow. "Because of your career choice?"

"Of course. They don't need to know that I'm here and not in Charlotte working. If they knew, their conversation would center on two topics. One—," she raised a finger, "how am I making money to pay my bills. Two—maybe this is God's sign to come back to His will."

"They don't think you're in God's will."

"No. According to them, His will for me is the family business. God's work, which means either hold a position in a church like they do or be a missionary like my sister."

"They don't think Godly people can have jobs outside the church?"

"Oh, yes. They do. Just not our family."

"Sorry for what I'm about to say, but that sounds a little arrogant, don't you think?"

She studied her ankle rested on the footstool. "I never thought of them as arrogant. Just narrow-focused."

"Yeah, but God works through laypeople, not just preachers and missionaries. Thank goodness for my buddy, Joe. I'm not exactly hooked up with a church right now, but he keeps me straight. Helps me figure things out. Prays for me every day."

"Jack and Agnes do the same for me. I'm not sure I'd've

had the confidence to start my business without her support. I was always a parent pleaser." She drew swirls in the upper corner of the page. "Jack's great. Our conversations always turn spiritual, which is good because Tess has had a lot of questions lately.

"And even though I'm hooked up with a church, as you say, Jack and Agnes are the ones I turn to for guidance. That's why all this," she waved the pencil, "frustrates me so. I can't stand people I love suffering because of me."

"Friendship isn't only about fun times."

"True, but my friendships don't normally involve bullets."

"Mine do." He'd meant the reply honestly, but her raised eyebrows lightened the mood. "I'm not talking about Dusty and Skeet."

"Kinda figured that." Her smile kicked his heartbeat up a higher gear. He smiled back, and she dropped her gaze to her sketch pad.

Not willing for the night to end abruptly like the evening before, he didn't respond. Instead, he trimmed a few tiny curls from the neck. He held the carved piece up to inspect it. "Not too shabby."

"That looks exactly like a miniature horse's head."

"Good. That's exactly what a traditional knight piece is supposed to look like."

Chapter 23

With the tip of the crutch resting on the porch slats, Mary Wade hovered above the top step, contemplating maneuvering the steps alone.

"Don't even think about it." The screened door slapped behind Brett.

"I can hold the railing for help."

"You got me for help." He slipped his arm around her waist. "Anybody ever mention how stubborn you are?"

"I wish I had a dollar . . ."

"Yep. Thought so." He slid the crutch into the backseat while she settled into the front, then he slipped something black under his seat.

She craned her neck to peer, but his legs obscured her vision. "Is that a gun?"

"Yes."

Her stomach dropped. A gun. Brett kept a gun under his seat. "Do you always take a gun with you?"

"My job, remember." He turned the car around and crept down the driveway.

"Yes, but you're not working today, are you?"

"I'm not on duty, but I always carry a gun. Be prepared and all that, you know."

At the intersection, he turned left onto the highway and gained speed.

"What kind is it?"

"This one is a nine-millimeter."

"Does it kick when you shoot it?"

"Not really a kick. A recoil." He glanced at her with narrowed eyes. "What do you know about a gun's kick?"

"I fired a shotgun at my grandfather's farm. My shoulder was sore for a week."

"Then you weren't holding it properly." He passed a truck pulling a trailer. "I could teach you to shoot if you want."

She propped her sprained ankle on top of her good one. "Learning to shoot isn't really on my bucket list."

"No problem. I thought you look too girly-girl to shoot."

"Too girly-girl?"

"Yeah, with your fancy sandals and pedicures. You sprain your ankle when you walk in the backyard." He chuckled. "Not much of an outdoorsy person, are you?"

"I stepped in a mole hole. Not my fault. And no reflection on my ability to shoot a gun either." She crossed her arms. "Let's start lessons this afternoon." His opinion shouldn't matter, but she didn't want him to think she wasn't capable.

"No. I feel like I'm pushing you into it."

"You aren't. Teach me. When we get back."

He grinned. "Say, 'please.'"

She snorted. "You were the one who asked me first."

He raised his eyebrows. "And that takes the place of manners? Say, 'please.'"

She gritted her teeth. "Please."

"With sugar and a cherry on top."

She hit him in the arm. Her fist bounced off his bicep.

He flexed his arm. "Can't hurt steel."

The muscle swelled under the fabric of his sleeve, stealing her attention and any reply.

"Do you have your sketch pad?"

"What? Oh. Yeah." She patted her backpack. "Never leave home without it. Why?"

"I need to see someone while we're in Hickory" He checked his rearview mirror. "Thought you could sketch while I do that."

"Sure." She studied his profile. High cheekbones. Straight nose. Strong chin. All angles. No softness. "Who do you have to see?"

His jaw worked. "Nobody you know."

A secret? "Well, since I know your grandmother, and Dusty and Skeet, if you count criminals, I didn't exactly expect to know this person."

He counted off his fingers. "Stubborn, sarcastic, . . ."

"Funny." She swatted his hand from her side of the car. "You don't have to tell me. I wasn't trying to be nosy. Just making conversation."

"You're content with quiet. You don't usually make conversation, so I'm wondering, why now?"

Because. "Someone" summoned images of a woman which resulted in a little, tiny blip of jealousy flaring in her chest. Completely ridiculous but true nonetheless. She swallowed it back to where it came from.

"I've never been to Hickory. What's there?"

"And she's changing conversations. Or are you trying a new tactic to find out what I'm doing in town?"

She angled toward her window. "Could you not be a detective for five minutes?"

He laughed. "Sorry. It's innate."

"The scenery is gorgeous."

"Okay. We can change the subject. Never been here before?"

"I've been to Boone and Asheville a couple of times."

"Did you see the Biltmore House?"

"No."

"Too bad. It's really something. Did you ride Tweetsie Railroad?"

176

"No."

"Climb Grandfather Mountain?"

"No."

"Explore Linville Caverns?"

"No, no, and no. We went on mission trips." She flipped down the sun visor.

"Ah. With your church or your family."

"My church was my family. Literally. My father is a preacher, remember?"

"I remember. But preachers take vacations."

"Not my father. Any long weekend, any week off was always centered around a mission trip. I don't remember him ever taking an afternoon off. He came home late, missed dinners and piano recitals. A classic example of a workaholic."

"It's a wonder he didn't sour you on church altogether."

"That's where Agnes and Jack come in. They helped me see that humans, even preachers, aren't perfect. Churches are made up of imperfect people."

He nodded. "A lesson for all of us."

"My dad's heart's in the right place. He just has his own opinions that, unfortunately, he thinks everyone should follow."

"How about your mom?"

She shrugged. "She follows his lead."

"So clearly you don't take after her."

"Right. I don't agree with him."

He adjusted the side vent. "No. I mean you have a hard time following my lead too."

"You're a funny man. I consider it thinking for myself."

"Which is usually a good thing."

She folded her arms in front of her. "Are you saying thinking for myself sometimes isn't a good thing?"

"Not when bullets are flying over your head."

ഇള ⊙ ⊙ രു റ

Brett tossed the cellophaned sirloin tip into the grocery cart along with the basket of mushrooms, salad kit, and potatoes. A manly kind of dinner, but since he was cooking, he could choose. He'd planned to shop with Mary Wade, choose all the fixings together. Find out more about what she liked and didn't like. After the visit with his dad, however, he needed to decompress, shake off the ill-sitting humor.

He cherished his dad. He just hated seeing him in the state he'd been in for the past twenty-plus years. A stroke during surgery had robbed his speech and paralyzed him except for his right index finger.

Clint Davis enjoyed his son's stories, and Brett always liked to share. Communication was slow at best. Sometimes awkward. It was easier to keep talking than wait for his dad to spell words on a keyboard. Now, at least, with the changes in technology, his dad could carry on a decent conversation.

Seeing him bound to a chair and talking only with the help of a computer still frustrated Brett. A vibrant man reduced to being trapped inside a useless body in the prime of his life. Brett shook his head.

He had to get it together before he saw Mary Wade. His dad was happy, as much as possible, that is. Gigi visited every other day. Focus on dinner. Meat, salad, starch. Check. Need dessert. Ice cream?

The display case offered dozens of varieties. What kind would she like? He considered one of his own favorites, Java Chocolate Chip. She liked coffee. She liked chocolate chip cookies judging by the number of Gigi's she ate yesterday afternoon.

Yep. Java Chocolate Chip would be the ticket.

ഽ൧ഽ൧ിരൂരൂ

A breeze fluttered the sheet of paper against the concrete table. Mary Wade smoothed it back in place, and something caught her eye. Brett. Striding toward her clutching grocery bags, a little grin on his handsome face. Her breath hitched. A surge of excitement beat in her heart. This guy with the broad shoulders. With the muscle-y arms. With the to-die-for eyes. Yes, that guy walked toward her, the geeky girl with the bum ankle.

"So you're still here with your foot propped on the other stool." He set the bags on the table and sat near her foot. "You didn't go exploring and hurt yourself again."

"I sketched here on the town square like the obedient girl I am. Followed your instructions to enjoy the day to the letter. You set me up before you left. Put the towel from your trunk under my foot. Left a water bottle for me." Her words dripped with sweet innocence. "Why would I want to disobey you?"

He narrowed his eyes. "Sounds suspect to me."

She grinned. Why should she tell him she'd explored a couple of the antique shops lining Main Street? Walking with the real crutches Brett purchased at the medical supply store first thing this morning proved much easier than hobbling with the forked stick, but the crutches didn't have as much charm as Brett's homemade one. "You'll never know. How was your appointment?"

"It went well. Thank you." He leaned his elbow on the table. "I picked up everything we need, including dessert."

"Ooh. Dessert. What is it?"

"A secret."

She craned toward the bags, but he tied the handles closed, obscuring her view. "Don't look. You'll know soon enough."

"More intrigue. Your job doesn't afford you enough? You make more?"

He swatted away a yellow jacket. "Maybe it's not intrigue. Maybe it's as simple as I don't know if you'll like it."

"Me? Not like dessert? Don't see that happening."

"I'm going to remind you of those words." He scanned the square. "Ready to go home?"

Home.

Nice.

ఐలఐలయలయల

From a parked Chevy pickup on the other side of the square, Dusty and Skeet watched their ex-partner exit the grocery store. "Yep. I told you the library was the ticket."

"Yeah. The search sent us to Hickory, and I don't know how many hours of waiting and looking. I thought we had a needle in a haystack. You just said 'Hickory,' nothing else. Not a real address anyway."

"All that finally paid off. He came out of that nursing home back yonder and then took his time in Harris Teeter. You shoulda let me go in after him. I'm going now." Dusty reached for the door handle.

Skeet held Dusty's arm. "And do what?" He spit a wad of tobacco juice into a Bojangles' soda cup. "Make a big ruckus in a public place?" Skeet wiped his mouth with his thumb.

"He's a half a football field in front of me, looking like somebody's daddy with the grocery bags." Dusty slid his sunglasses over his eyes.

Skeet tightened his grip. "Settle down. We ain't gonna do nothin' yet. Let's see what else we can find out. I suwanee. For somebody who knows about libraries—Hey." He pointed out the windshield. "Well, well, well. Look who he's meetin' up with." He slapped the steering wheel.

Dusty peered out the window and strained against Skeet's hold. "Pay dirt times two. Let me go. I got business with them."

"Are you really that stupid?"

"I can take him."

"Yes, sir. Then Hickory's finest will take you. Let 'em chat, then we'll see what they do next. All we have to do is follow where he leads. Then, if you're serious about…"

Dusty cracked his knuckles. "We waited long enough. It's time to make him pay."

"We will." Skeet turned the key. "Look. They're leaving. Let's see which car is theirs and where they go."

Chapter 24

Brett swept the parking lot with a final long look. He dropped into the driver's seat, catching Mary Wade with her hand on one of the bags. "Hey, quit. It's a surprise."

"Fine. I don't need to know. I can wait."

"Sure you can. Waiting's not your strong suit, huh?"

"I can wait."

"Like you didn't wait to go bike riding until after you put away all the groceries at Agnes' house. Like you couldn't wait to check out the backyard and sprained your ankle. Like you're having a hard time waiting for your business to take off so that you can prove to your parents—"

"Hey." She frowned. "I thought we were teasing. I didn't realize you were analyzing my personality."

His gaze skimmed the side mirror. "Not at all. Just proving my point."

"You don't like to lose."

"Bingo."

"Well, guess what? Neither do I."

"That sounds like a challenge." A fun one he'd enjoy exploring. He glanced in the rearview mirror and squinted.

"What do you see?"

He threw a quick look her way.

"You see something. You've looked in the side mirror and the rearview one. You're gripping the steering wheel like there's no tomorrow." She turned around in her seat. "What's back there?"

"A car followed us out of town. Even though I took an extra turn. Now it's following us on the highway. A truck's between us, but it's still there."

"You think—"

"I don't know, but I'm gonna find out. Hang on." He accelerated and searched for a turnoff point. The first left turned into a subdivision. No good. He gunned the gas again.

Mary Wade watched the road behind them. "He's passing the truck."

Brett ground his molars.

A green road sign signaled the next right. A side road. Better. He whipped the steering wheel to the right, crutches clanked in the backseat. Her face slid into his arm. She scrambled away from him. They passed a house and a little corral. Next, corn stalks flashed by. At the end of the field, a path with trees on either side opened. He checked the rearview mirror before slinging the car to the right again. His car jumped and bounced on the rough path, but he kept control of it.

He fishtailed left into a grassy path between the trees and drove deeper into the woods. Another path to the right appeared, and he swerved onto it. He hadn't seen the car in several minutes. Maybe he'd lost them. He coasted to a stop behind a scraggily bank of briars.

Letting the engine idle, he glued his gaze to the path, praying for it to remain empty. He stayed that way, like a hunting dog trained on a scent, for ten, twelve, fifteen minutes? A movement beside him captured his attention.

For the first time since she'd slammed into him on the first turn, he noticed Mary Wade. Her breathing still came quick and shallow. With whitened knuckles, she clutched the edge of the seat and the armrest in death grips.

Forgetting his promise to himself to stay away from her, he

unbuckled both seat belts and gathered her to him. "Come here. We're okay." He stroked her hair, inhaled flowers and sunshine. "How'd you like that fancy driving?"

Her trembling fingers fisted his shirt sleeve into a tight ball.

The adrenaline seeped from his body, leaving a weakness he didn't like.

Her heart slammed against her chest. "If you lost whoever was following us, great, I guess." Her head nestled into the crook of his neck. "Kidnappings, shoot-outs, car chases. You really know how to show a girl a good time."

"Whoa. I wasn't responsible for the kidnapping or the bullets. In fact, I rescued you, remember?"

She released his shirt sleeve and slid her hand up and over his shoulder, settling her fingers on the side of his throat. "Yeah. I was there, remember?"

He steeled himself against the light touch of her fingertips. "What do we do now?"

He tightened his arms around her. "Sit for a few more minutes. Let them give up looking."

"If they don't? If they come down this path?"

He stretched and retrieved the nine-millimeter with one hand, sticking it between the seat and the console. "I'll deal with it."

ಬಂಬಂರ್ಣರ್ಣ

Sighing, Mary Wade leaned into him, closing her eyes against the image of the gun, the car chasing them. Brett said he'd deal with it. He would, too, but she didn't want to think about what he might have to deal with. She wanted to think about other things. Her thumb traced an arc on the warm, smooth skin of his throat. Even the cords of his neck were taut and tough. Inhaling a breath of his spicy scent, she felt safe with his arms wrapped around her.

His arms wrapped around her?

She pushed against his shoulder blade.

He released her but wrapped a fist over her wrist. "What's the matter?"

"Nothing. I'm fine."

He swiped his jaw with his palm. "You don't seem fine. Your pulse is racing double time."

She pulled her arm from his hand and dragged her fingers through her hair. "We were in a car chase, remember?"

"Yeah, but I thought you were calming down."

"I was. I am. I mean, I'm fine." She settled back in her seat. She had been calming down and had been enjoying the process until she realized where exactly she was. Realized his hand cradled her head, caressed her face. His touch had revived the fading adrenaline, had brought her back to her senses too.

He extended his arm along the back of the seat. "Mary Wade, I wasn't going to—"

She nodded. "Ahm, you did a great job getting away from them. Do you have to practice driving like that?" She could hear his fingers scratching the cloth of the seat just behind her shoulder.

He tipped his head. "Comes with the job. And instinct takes over." He glanced into the backseat. "Our groceries look like fruit salad all over the floor."

She turned to look.

"Ah, ah, ah. Don't. You'll spoil the dessert surprise."

"Even after all that," she waved toward the window, "you're not telling me the dessert?"

"Not till the unveiling time." He covered his heart and pinned her with his silver eyes. "I'm a man of my word."

And a decent man. He let her go when she pushed away from him, didn't try to persuade her with words or actions. He let her change the subject without a macho attitude. A gentleman.

ഇ൬ഇ൬ര൩ര൩

Dusty pounded the dashboard. "I knew I shoulda drove. You drive like a old woman. You let 'em get away."

"I didn't let 'em get away. He turned down one of these paths off the main road."

"We've been down them. He ain't here, man."

"He musta figured a way out I can't see."

Dusty picked at a scab on his arm. "He's like Houdini or somebody, escaping out windows in the middle of the night."

Skeet scratched his nose. "Didn't look like he went in the corn field. So he had to turn left into the woods." He shook his head.

"How we gonna find out where he stays now, huh?"

"Let's think for a minute. Who might know something in Hickory?"

Dusty slapped his fist into the palm of his hand. "The nursing home. He visited somebody, right?"

"Right. You sweet-talked a librarian. Think you could sweet-talk a nurse?"

"I know I could. Right after we get something to eat. Let's get back to civilization. I'm starving."

"What happened to that Bojangles' biscuit you ate not more than two hours ago?"

"Gone, man. Gone, gone, gone."

Chapter 25

The coffee can sat on the top shelf, just beyond reach of Mary Wade's fingertips. Why did Brett have to put it so far up? The bottom shelf had plenty of room for a coffee can. But, no, he had to put it way, way out of her reach.

Determined to make coffee for him since he prepared the whole, delicious dinner last night, she dragged a chair from the table to the cabinet. She'd heard the door click when he left twenty minutes earlier. Did he go for a run? His SUV was still parked in the driveway.

Balancing with a crutch in one hand and leaning on the countertop with the other, she hoisted herself, very carefully, onto the chair. Keeping the injured foot raised, she leaned the crutch against the counter and reached for the coffee. Success.

She resisted the urge to clap for herself and set the can down. Bending her knee, she flattened one palm against the counter and gripped the back of the chair with her other hand, readying herself to hop off the chair. As she studied the floor and her healthy foot, Brett burst through the front door, shimmering with sweat.

With his arms outstretched, he bounded toward her like a momma bear in protection mode. "What the heck are you doing?"

Dropping to sit, she held her hand in the stop position. "No need to get all huffy. I'm good."

He leaned over her, his hands on his hips. "Do you realize how dangerous standing on a chair is? And with a gimpy foot?"

187

"More dangerous than bullets and car chases?"

"You love bringing that up." He shoved the can with his knuckles. "You needed coffee so bad you couldn't wait ten minutes for me to get back?"

"You've been gone longer than ten minutes." If he'd back out of her personal space, she'd be able to stand, not feel like he was bearing down on top of her. Sweat trails trickled from his sideburns as he stared down at her. "You're dripping."

Lifting the bottom of his T-shirt, he wiped his face, giving her a peek of his flat abdomen. "Sorry. I ran six miles."

He scooped her up and deposited her on the wing chair by the fireplace, placing her foot on the stool. "If you don't stay off that foot, you're gonna feel it the rest of your life."

She crossed her arms in front of her. "I hope I feel my foot the rest of my life."

He snorted. "I meant feel the effects of the sprain, Miss Literal." He turned back to the kitchen. "I'll have the coffee ready in three minutes."

"I wanted to make it."

He whipped around. "You don't like my coffee?"

"No. I wanted to make it for you. You keep serving me. You wouldn't let me do anything last night, after all you did yesterday. And stop yelling at me."

His expression softened. He rubbed his jaw. Shyness gripped her as he returned and knelt beside the stool.

"Mary Wade, I'm sorry I raised my voice. Seeing you on top of the chair surprised me. I don't like being surprised. You're injured, and I don't want you to hurt yourself more. I don't mind doing what I'm doing. Cooking for two is as easy as one." He clasped her foot, heat seeping through the bandage. "Take care of it, okay?"

Tears burning in the back of her throat robbed her voice. She nodded.

He rose. "Right, then. I'll start the coffee, shower six miles of grit off me, then we'll have breakfast. Do me a favor, please? Sit there and wait." He grabbed some magazines from the side table, dropping them in her lap as he headed into the kitchen. "Look at Gigi's magazines. Meditate. Just don't get up. We'll have the coffee cake she broke in and left yesterday."

"She didn't break in. She has a key. It's her cabin." She thumbed the edges of the magazines.

He spooned the grounds into the filter. "It felt a little creepy knowing someone had been in here while we were away though."

"Speaking from firsthand experience, finding a homemade coffee cake is nothing similar to having someone break in your house."

"I concede your point." He disappeared into his bedroom.

"Wow."

He peeked around the threshold, arching his brow. "Don't get used to it."

ॐॐ☙☙

As Brett promised, coffee dripped into the carafe within minutes. Mary Wade rested her head against the chair and concentrated on the aroma of coffee drifting from the kitchen instead of the sounds of splashing water coming from the bathroom.

Brett.

In the shower.

Don't go there.

Read the magazine instead. Turn it right side up first. Read the captions. Flip the pages. An ad for soap.

Brett.

In the shower.

She slammed the magazine shut. Think about the coffee cake.

Finding Gigi's offering in the middle of the counter when they'd returned yesterday had been a little disconcerting to both of them. The attached note, "Sweets for the sweet," had assuaged his attitude a tad. "She must be talking about you because she's never called me sweet before." He'd tossed the note onto the counter. "You know what this means, don't you? She's visiting us every day we're here. At least every other. Her way of keeping her presence in the room." He shook his head. "She's a card."

"She should be dealt with?"

He'd smiled then at her finishing the old line. "Yeah. By me."

Despite Mary Wade's suggestion to eat light and save the special dinner for another night, Brett cooked a delicious meal. "I'm not tired," he'd said. "Cooking will help me relax."

So they'd spent the evening in the kitchen, Brett chopping vegetables, sautéing the mushrooms, checking on the grill. Mary Wade camped at the table with her foot resting on another chair. He allowed her to help with one part, setting the table. Her stubborn streak flared, and she fashioned the napkins into swans, a trick she'd learned at a summer camp.

"Swans? Really? You couldn't just fold over the napkin?" Brett twirled the paper swan by its beak.

"You made a fancy dinner." She shrugged. "I wanted to make special napkins."

"Competitive too. Note taken." He grinned. "Nice job."

The sound of water stopped.

Brett.

In the shower.

Toweling off.

Think of something else. She closed her eyes. Dessert.

Last night's dessert. Java Chocolate Chip ice cream.

"What do you mean you've never tried coffee ice cream, never wanted to? You like coffee. You like chocolate chips. It's a match made in heaven." The disbelief on his face had made her laugh.

"I like drinking coffee. I like strawberry ice cream."

"Just plain strawberry?"

"Uh huh."

"How about strawberry cheesecake or strawberry swirl or strawberry and kiwi?"

"Just plain. It's a classic."

"I can see your knowledge of ice cream choices needs expanding."

She'd look forward to trying new flavors if Brett introduced them to her. The coffee ice cream tasted delicious. Would he have other yummy suggestions?

"Good. You haven't moved."

She jumped in the chair.

"Oh, sorry. I didn't realize you were asleep."

Steam poured out around Brett, his wet hair still tousled from the shower. "That felt fantastic." He padded with bare feet into the kitchen. "Okay. Time for coffee and coffee cake."

Chapter 26

"So you ready?"

Mary Wade lifted her gaze from her crochet hook. Like the other days before, they sat on the back porch after breakfast, Brett reading and she sketching. Today, however, she'd set aside her pad and worked on the front panel of a cotton cardigan.

She wiggled the hook into the ball of yarn for safe keeping. "Are we going somewhere?"

"I thought you wanted to learn to shoot."

"Well, I—"

"Already changing your mind?"

"No. It's just. . . Okay. Sure. I'm game." She folded the panel and tucked it into her yarn bag. "You're going to let me stand long enough to shoot?"

"You've been good this morning with resting it. I'll take a chair with us. You can rest between rounds. If you're up for it, I'll go set up the targets."

"Where?"

"Shoot right here in the backyard. Gigi owns the land on both sides of us and about three hundred yards beyond the creek. Let me get started."

He grinned and bounded down the back steps, headed for the shed at the end of the driveway. A minute or so later, he emerged carrying two sawhorses. Calling from the shed, he lifted them to show her. "Thankfully, Gigi didn't get rid of these."

He placed them a few feet apart near the stream, returned to the shed and emerged with a sheet of plywood.

As he collected and placed targets, reality tiptoed into Mary Wade's mind. She was here because of bullets, because of people who wanted to harm her. Not because she was on a holiday with an attractive man who played havoc with her breathing whenever he looked her way. He was here as an extension of his job. How many times had he reminded her about his job?

Too soon she'd be back in Charlotte up to her ears in debt, unfilled orders, and decisions to make.

She'd do well to remember her reality, not dwell on the fiction she wanted.

Pleased with the makeshift target area, he brushed off his hands and flashed a thumbs-up. Grinning the whole way back from the creek, he stopped with his foot on the bottom step. "It's not perfect, but it'll do for our purposes."

She tugged the edges of Gigi's cardigan close to her heart, hoping to slow its beating. "A bucket, two paint cans, and a block of wood. Those are my targets? You sure you want me to ruin your bucket?"

"Confidence. I like that. It's an old, aluminum bucket. Go ahead. Bust it up. If you can." He pounded up the steps. "I'll get my pistol and the stool from the kitchen. Your sunglasses in the car?"

She nodded.

"Good. Be right back."

ဆၣဆၣၣ�%ၣ%

Brett planted the stool several yards from the targets. "Have a seat for a minute."

"This is close."

"We start short. After you try it about three yards away, we'll move back." He laid the crutches on the ground beside her. "Here. Get a feel for it first."

She grabbed the gun, her hand dropping a few inches. "It's kinda heavy."

"Yep."

Turning the gun over in her palm, she studied it with a frown.

Something was going on in her brain. "What?"

"Just thinking." She shrugged. "This is a relatively little thing, but it can do a lot of harm. It's sobering to hold it."

"You're right, Mary Wade. That's why it deserves to be handled correctly. It deserves respect. I don't take owning guns or using them lightly."

She raised her eyes to his. "I know."

Way down deep in his chest, something swirled and rose and gripped him with a force that wrecked his oxygen intake. He scrubbed his hand over his jaw. "Ready to try it?"

"I guess so."

"Put these on." He handed her sunglasses. "I don't have safety ones."

"Is it going to be loud?"

"Not bad." He pulled a small package of earplugs out of his pocket. "In fact, you can use these."

He offered his arm to help her stand. "Line up your shoulders with your feet. I usually say distribute your weight evenly between both feet, but today just do the best you can with your ankle." He pulled the magazine clip from his pocket and inserted it into the magazine well. "Here." He handed her the pistol. "Fit the web of your hand up against the backstrap. Get a solid grip." He moved her finger. "We're not ready for the trigger yet."

"Okay."

"Put your other hand on top of the slide. Like this." He placed her hand on top of the pistol. "Now slide it back. Yes, that's it. Did you hear that click? It's ready."

She nodded.

"Will it kick?"

"It's not a shotgun. It won't throw your shoulder out. You'll feel some recoil, but it won't hurt you." He positioned her left hand on the pistol. "This is your support hand. Point both thumbs toward the target."

She bit her lip and closed one eye.

"Nope. Keep both eyes open." He pushed the gun up. "Aim it toward the bucket. Line up the front sight here," He pointed to the end of the pistol. "With the rear sights here. See? Focus on the front sight."

"Bend your elbows a bit." He touched her elbow. A lock of chestnut hair blew into his face, carrying the scent of sunscreen and her flowery shampoo. He brushed it away.

"I feel like I'm too close."

"Take a step back then, babe." Babe? Where did that come from? He cleared his throat. "Whatever works for you, Mary Wade."

She stepped back and aimed the pistol.

"You want the full pad of your finger on the trigger. Slowly pull back on it. A nice, easy squeeze."

She pulled the trigger, shot, and missed. The recoil raised her arm several inches but she kept the gun pointing straight ahead. Determined. Cool.

"Good try."

She aimed again and hit the bucket, pushing it backwards a few inches on the two-by-four stretched across the sawhorses. She aimed a third time and missed. The fourth try hit the bucket again. Part of the bottom hung over the edge of the wood. She lowered the pistol.

"Fifty percent. You've done this before." He held out his palm for his pistol, removed the magazine clip, depositing it in his pocket, the gun in the back of his waistband.

"Not with that kind of gun."

"The shotgun?"

"No. My sister had a BB gun. We practiced in the backyard."

His mouth dropped opened. "A BB gun?"

She wiggled her hands. "Oh, my arm feels wobbly."

He rubbed her arm. "I'm impressed."

She looked up at him, her cheeks flushed, her green eyes flashing delight. "That's fun. I thought it'd be a little scary. When you think about what a gun can do, it's intimidating." Laughing, she grinned. "But when you hit the target, wow. That's cool."

He zeroed in on another, more interesting target. Waiting a beat, he gave her a chance to step away, to break the spell her elation had helped create, but she didn't move. Was she waiting for him? The promise he'd made to Gigi warred with his desire for this woman.

She placed her hand on his chest. An invitation?

He slid his palm to the small of her back and pulled her toward him, lowering his mouth.

Tires crunched from the driveway.

She stiffened.

A door slammed. "Yoo hoo. Anybody home?"

Gigi.

Mary Wade backed out of his embrace, but before she moved away from him, something passed over her eyes.

Was it regret? Disappointment? Relief?

He picked up the crutches for her and headed toward the cabin and his grandmother without a sound.

ಬಜಿಂದ

Shoving the crutches under her arms with more force than usual, Mary Wade chafed at the soreness. Good. Think about that instead of how close Brett's mouth was to yours. How close you were to being foolish.

"I hope I didn't interrupt anything. I made a double batch of chicken casserole this morning. One for the seniors group at church and," she lifted a dish toward Brett, "this one's for you two." He grabbed it and bent to receive Gigi's peck on his cheek.

196

"Hey, what are those storm clouds doing hovering across your brow? Mary Wade, has he been in a grouchy mood all morning?"

Mary Wade concentrated on Gigi, kept her eyes off Brett. "He was teaching me to shoot. I must've been a poor student."

"Teaching her to shoot?" Gigi glanced at Brett.

"She scored fifty percent at the first lesson. I don't think she needs a teacher. But she does need to get off that foot. Let's get in the house."

"Well, excellent, honey. Every woman should know how to take care of herself. I remember when I got my concealed carry permit."

"You have a concealed carry? You know how to shoot a gun?" Mary Wade considered the polished woman walking beside her. Dressed in white capris and a blue and white tunic, lapis jewelry at her ears and wrists, Gigi evoked a summer luncheon, not a gun show.

Gigi bustled up the stairs first to stretch the door open, the canvas bag she carried knocking into her hip. "Absolutely. I've lived alone for a long time. My .38 special is under the front seat of my car right now. What do they say? Never leave home without it. Right, Brett?"

From behind them, he chuckled, and the storm clouds cleared. "Yep. My pistol packin' granny. That's her." He moved around them to set the casserole on the counter, motioning to Mary Wade to sit. "Did you remember to take some ibuprofen this morning? You walked more than normal yesterday and now today . . ."

"Did he take you hiking yesterday?"

Mary Wade sank onto the couch, grateful at its proximity. "We drove into Hickory. Brett had an appointment."

Gigi's eyes flew to Brett. He didn't acknowledge her, busying himself with filling a glass with water. "Anybody thirsty?"

"That's where I'm headed when I leave here."

He downed the glass. "I'm going up to the clearing, check messages while you ladies visit. I'll be back in a while."

"Take my car. I'm parked behind you."

"I'll walk. On the path. It's not far." With a nod to no one in particular, he left, leaving an odd sense of disappointment in his wake.

Gigi shook her head. "That boy. He's always been moody. Stubborn." She sat beside Mary Wade and plopped the bag on the coffee table.

That boy? There was nothing boyish about Brett. No doubt about it, he was a man. Mary Wade rubbed her palm along her olive cargo capris to erase the feel of his rock-hard thighs against them.

"Are you okay, sweetie? Both of you seemed a little . . . off when I got here." Concern wrinkled Gigi's forehead.

Should she confess? She hadn't had time to process the almost-kiss herself. Should she discuss it with his grandmother? Was a non-event discussion worthy?

"I think he was about to kiss me right before you drove up." Too late she remembered his promise. "But he told me about his promise to you, so probably it was my imagination. We were both excited about my shots hitting the targets. It was probably that. I think I probably misunderstood. In fact, I'm sure I did."

"Oh, honey." Gigi rubbed her chin. Just like Brett. "I made him promise not to hurt you. I didn't exactly make him promise not to kiss you." She pushed back a tendril of Mary Wade's hair. "Such a lovely chestnut color." She folded her hands in her lap. "My grandson is a good-looking man."

Yes, definitely. On that they could agree.

"Women like him, and I know he enjoys women too."

Of course. And why are we talking about his love life?

"But he doesn't exactly have the best track record. He doesn't get close. He shies away from long-term involvements."

Good to know. Listen, heart. Listen, foolish heart.

"A few years ago, there was a girl that didn't treat him right." Gigi twisted her watch face to the underside of her wrist. "I didn't get the whole story. Not much of the story at all, really, but he met her on a case. She...it didn't end well." She shook her head, tightening her lips.

"You seem like a real deal kind of a girl. I liked you from the first afternoon he brought you to the house. That's why I made him promise not to hurt you. I thought if he made a conscious effort not to, you'd be spared. I don't think he realizes."

"No need to worry. He's been nothing but a gentleman to me. He helps with this," she raised her bandaged foot, "cooks for me. He's really wonderful."

Gigi narrowed her eyes. "I'll tell you something, not all of it, but the beginning anyway. It's his story, but I'm involved in it. His mother, Shelly, left him when he was only nine years old. His sister was seven. I helped raise them, so I have more insights into him than I might otherwise. He has confidence up to here." She tapped the top of her throat.

"But sometimes I wonder about that little boy and if there's just a bit of him knocking around inside Brett." She regarded Mary Wade. "Then I wonder if someone like you could come in and . . . I've watched the way he looks at you."

Zings coursed through her body. "Wait, Gigi. It's not like that. At all. If he's looking at me, it's because he expects I'll do something stupid like blow out a flip-flop or sprain my ankle again."

"I'm not sure."

Mary Wade patted her hand. She couldn't afford to let this line of conversation continue. She had enough daydreams keeping her awake at night. "What's in your bag?"

Chapter 27

Brett closed the refrigerator door. Gigi's leftovers could supply them for the next four or five days easy. Then with what she'd probably bring tomorrow, they could add another two days to the mix. Mary Wade would never agree to five or six more days from her business.

After checking messages, he found them chatting about her shop, poring over the vintage fabric Gigi had brought her. She itched to get home to Charlotte, but it wasn't over yet. According to the captain, Dusty and Skeet, or men matching their description, had been seen in Hickory.

So, they had been the ones in the car chase.

How could they have found out about Hickory? He shook off an unsettling feeling. Even if they had been in Hickory, those two had no way of connecting him to this cabin.

Mary Wade rested on the couch, her foot propped on the footstool. She examined the fabric, gasping with oohs and ahs, just short of cooing. He'd have to decide soon about taking her back.

"This is fabulous fabric. I can't believe Gigi gave it to me." She smoothed her hand over a crease. "She wondered if it would work for children's clothes, but I'm already thinking of designs for it. Washing will take out the creases."

Sipping his after-dinner decaf, he joined her on the couch. "It'll please her if you can use it. She likes you, you know. That's one of the reasons she keeps coming up here. Checking on us, yes, but she wants to get to know you better."

"I like her too. She's so interesting and elegant. Spiritually mature." She smiled, and his stomach flipped. "I want to be like her when I grow up."

Think about the conversation, not her lips. "Spiritual things matter to you?"

"Of course."

Got it. "My grandmother hasn't had the easiest life."

"Yeah. She mentioned some of it." Mary Wade bit her lip. "She explained about your mom."

Surprise kicked his gut, not the mention of his mother but that Gigi would share the story with Mary Wade. He set his mug on the side table, threaded his fingers at his waist. "What did she tell you?"

"Just that your mother left when you were nine. That's it. I hope you aren't upset. She said it was your story to tell."

"I'm not, but why'd she tell you? How did the topic come up?" He angled on the couch toward her, his arm stretched along the back cushions. "I thought you talked about fabric and children's clothes."

"She asked how we were doing." A blush crept up Mary Wade's neck, and she fiddled with the edge of the fabric.

Should he push it and ask about that blush? Not if he wanted her to stay on the couch for a while.

"And?"

"She's concerned about you, like a good grandmother. She mentioned your mom's leaving in context with her concern. She didn't give details. We weren't gossiping. I mentioned it now because I felt weird knowing something like that."

"Don't feel weird. And Gigi doesn't need to be concerned. I don't have abandonment issues, if that's what she thinks. I got over it a long time ago. Shelly turned out to be MIA, but other people stepped up to fill that hole. I've had a lot of love. Support out the wazoo, as they say."

She traced a swirly pattern on the fabric. "I envy you that."

201

"Your parents love you."

"But it's always felt a tad conditional. I felt love when I earned all A's or a scholarship to college. When I decided to choose a different path than the one they envisioned for me, not so much."

He hooked his hands behind his head, leaning into the cushions. "They'll come 'round."

"It's been five years." She stacked fabric on the coffee table. "I'm not exactly living up to my namesake."

"How's that?"

"My parents named me Mary for my great aunt Mary who was a missionary to China her whole life. I met her once, I think. She remained there after retiring. Died there too." She absently stroked the last length of fabric in her lap. "The Wade part comes from my brother who died as an infant from the flu."

"Wade is a missionary name?"

"My brother was Paul Wade. You know, Paul, missionary to the Gentiles?"

"I've heard of him. Read some of his letters."

"My mom couldn't bear to name another child Paul, but she didn't have a problem with Wade. The missionary association, however, has always been there."

"I guess your parents want you to marry a missionary or a preacher too, huh?"

"Exactly." She added the last piece of fabric to the stacked pile. "But that won't happen as long as I have anything to say about it."

"Why? You don't want to marry a godly man?"

She cut her eyes toward him. "Didn't say that, of course, but I'm not planning to marry a preacher. In my experience, they make lousy family men."

"That's an interesting thought." He dropped his arms to his chest. "And maybe heartless."

"It's true though. My dad was never home. Someone was

always dead, or sick, or in trouble, or needing counseling. Or there was a meeting at church, and he was always an ex officio member of all the committees. If I ever get married, the guy will have an eight to five job. And no weekends."

"Like Robert."

"No."

He raised his eyebrows. "No?"

"I mean, Robert's job was fine. But," she shook her head. "Not Robert."

"Interesting. Because I thought you and Robert---"

"No."

"I thought you were brokenhearted."

೮೨೮೨ೞೞ

"No. Agnes thought so too." But after meeting Brett, Robert's memory faded like a piece of cotton fabric in the sun. "But, no, not Robert."

Brett extended his legs beside the coffee table, his arm along the top of the couch behind her again. He looked relaxed, perfectly at home on his grandmother's floral sofa. His eyes told a different story, however. Sharp, noticed every detail. She ducked her head to thwart his scrutiny. To keep her hands busy, she pulled a blue paisley from the tidy stack.

"So, every time someone speaks your name, they're evoking the memory of your dead missionary aunt and your dead baby brother." He squeezed her shoulder. "That's a lot of weight to carry in a name."

"Ya think?"

"Then change it." He released her shoulder, rubbed the ends of a lock of her hair through his fingers.

Focus on the conversation, not on what his fingers were doing. "Change my name. Just like that. At my age."

"Why not? Chop off the Wade part. Go by just Mary."

"Hmm. Maybe. Kinda plain, though, don't you agree?"

"Plain, huh? Then change up the whole idea. What about Mary Way?" He poked her arm.

"What?"

"Mary Wa Wa." He poked her again.

She frowned. "That's silly."

"Mary Woo." Poke. "Mary Lou." Poke. "Mary Yoo Hoo." Poke. Poke.

Laughing and swiping at his hand, she shook her head. "You're completely crazy."

He captured her hand in his. "Uh huh. 'Cause I want to kiss you."

The laughter evaporated as their gazes collided. Curiosity and intense emotion flamed in his eyes. Her breath caught in her throat, heartbeats drummed in her ears.

"I promised my grandmother I wouldn't hurt you. I didn't promise not to kiss you." He slipped his fingers underneath her hair, found the delicate spot along her collarbone. "Do you think a kiss would hurt you?"

She dropped her eyes to his lips. "I don't think so."

He leaned in, brushed a whisper of a kiss against her cheek. "Was that okay?"

She nodded, breathing in his spicy scent.

He tucked her hair behind her ear and touched his lips to the sensitive place at her ear lobe. Heat stirred in the pit of her stomach. "And that?"

She swallowed, strangled the corner of a throw pillow in a tight fist.

He kissed the hollow at the base of her throat. "Still fine?"

"Yes." Her voice, a raspy sigh, betrayed her longing for his touch. She crushed the pillow to her lap.

Brett cradled her head. "Good." His lips met hers with the lightness of a flower petal. The exquisite torture of the trail of his kisses summoned a little craziness of her own. Thoughts couldn't pass the tingles zinging through her body. As he withdrew after the latest butterfly touch, she hooked her hand around his neck and pulled him back to her.

Her simple invitation sparked the electricity simmering between them from the beginning. His mouth settled onto hers with a tenderness that captured her. His lips teased her, asking questions as they moved over hers. She answered back honestly from her heart. Tunneling his fingers through her hair, he intensified the pressure of the kiss. She wrapped her arms around him and floated toward a place where fairy tale dreams come true. A soft, low moan rumbled between them. His or hers?

As he shifted her onto his lap, her foot slid off the stool, bumping against the couch. She whimpered and stiffened. He drew back, his breathing as shallow as a sprinter's at the end of a 100-meter dash. "What?"

"My foot. It hit the couch." She covered her mouth with trembling fingers, took deep breaths to slow her own breathing.

He kept his arm around her, fingers splayed against the back of her neck, and slid her foot onto a pillow. "Sorry." He leaned his head against the couch cushion, resting his hand on her knee. "I guess I broke my promise to my grandmother."

"It wasn't your . . . I should have . . ." What? Thought about something besides how his kisses were turning her insides to jelly? No. Before that. How about not pulling him in for a real kiss when those feathery pecks kept driving her crazy. She cringed remembering how she'd—" I'm fine. Really." Lie. Lie. Lie.

She wasn't fine. She probably wouldn't be fine again, not with her heart split open like it was, laid bare for him to trample all over. How to get out of this humiliating situation?

First, get out of his lap. She pushed his hand from her knee and slid to the cushion. "My ankle's fine. It was just a shock." Almost as shocking as his kiss. What did he think of her?

"Mary Wade. Let's talk a minute."

Not a minute. Not a second. If she gave that much, he

could talk her into anything, or more to the point, kiss her into anything. His kisses had the power to lead her right into a broken heart. Hers. No, thanks.

She smoothed her hair behind her ear. Remembered when he'd hooked a lock around it. "Brett." She peeked at him. Another mistake. His eyes had darkened to a deep gray. She focused on the floor, searching for the crutches. "It's been a long day. I think I'll call it a night." She scooted to the edge of the couch.

He leaned forward, his forearms on his thighs. "Don't you think we need to talk about what just happened?"

"Brett, we shared a kiss. That's what happened. We're two adults thrown together in a close situation. Something like that was bound to happen. Right?" She'd stand up soon, as soon as she trusted her legs.

"You speaking from experience? You think a kiss like that happens whenever two adults are thrown together, as you put it?"

"No, but it's the nature of your job, your line of work."

He frowned. "My line of work? You make me sound like—"

"That's not what I meant. Your undercover stuff." She massaged her temples. "You're twisting my words. It goes along with the whole knight-in-shining-armor idea that you brought up yourself, remember?" She couldn't explain how the two ideas meshed, but they did. Her lips still felt swollen from his kiss. Maybe her brain was swollen too. She couldn't think straight so close to him.

He sighed. "Fine. Let me help you." He reached for the crutches.

"No need. But thanks." She grabbed them first and hopped up. "Goodnight." She hobbled into her room trying to ignore the feel of his eyes boring into her back.

Chapter 28

His phone rang as he deleted his last message. An unfamiliar number. "Brett Davis."

"Mr. Davis, this is Tammy. Your dad's nurse up at the care facility. He's had a . . .a setback this morning, and we think you should come in as soon as you can."

His stomach clenched. He pressed the phone against his ear. "What's wrong?"

"Ah, we'd rather not go into that over the phone. He's stable now, but when do you think we can expect you?"

"Tammy, why isn't his doctor calling me?"

Silence. She cleared her throat. "He was called for an emergency right after your dad was stabilized."

"Is my grandmother on the way?"

"Ah. No. We called you first."

"All right. Do me a favor. You say he's stable, right?"

"Yes, sir."

"Then don't call her yet. I'll call her when I get there."

"No problem. Can we expect you in the next hour?"

"Forty-five minutes."

"I'll see you when you get here." The nurse hung up without waiting for goodbye.

Brett slid his phone into his gym shorts pocket. He jogged back to the cabin, making plans to shower and leave within fifteen minutes. Questions about the conversation jiggled in his mind, but he pushed them back. He'd think about them on the drive to Hickory.

First, he needed to formulate a plan about facing Mary Wade again. He'd thought about her and last night's kiss during his whole six-mile run this morning. Enjoyed replaying the scene in his mind multiple times. The way she closed her eyes and leaned into him as he planted kisses along sensitive spots. And definitely the way she hooked her hand around his neck and pulled him to her.

Like she was ready for a real kiss.

Like she wanted to kiss him as desperately as he wanted to kiss her.

He stopped at the base of the porch steps, crossed his ankles and touched his fingers to the ground. He'd played with fire last night and got burned. He knew he shouldn't kiss her, not while he was on duty. And even though he wasn't technically still on the case, her safety rested on him. He'd never compromised a professional relationship before, yet last night, he blew right over that line.

And although part of him wished he could rewind last night, erase his lapse in judgment, another part of him relished the memory.

He dragged in a deep breath. They should've talked last night. Now he had to walk in there and what? Play it cool like nothing happened? Did she really believe nothing happened?

Something happened, all right, and he felt it all the way to his toes. But that didn't have to mean anything. He'd enjoyed kisses before. Plenty of them. Something about Mary Wade's, though, something felt different this time.

He rolled his neck.

Stop thinking of that kiss and focus on Dad.

ෂ⬭ෂ⬭ෂ⬭

Three more steps, and Mary Wade would've been back

inside her room, but the door flew open with Brett standing in silhouette.

The air crackled with the tension between them.

"Good morning." He moved into the room. Today he wore a black T-shirt and black running shorts.

Imposing.

"Good morning."

He rubbed his jaw. "I just got a call at the clearing. I've got to go back to Hickory. Need to be out of here in about fifteen minutes, so I'll hop in the shower."

"Is this something to do with the case?"

"No."

She startled at the bark in his voice. "I'm sorry. It's none of my . . ." He'd left her, standing in the den talking to herself. He rummaged in his room for thirty seconds before slamming the bathroom door. She gathered her things for the Hickory trip, glad she'd charged her phone last night.

Last night. She'd refolded her clothes, read or pretended to read three days' worth of devotions, and sketched four horrible outfits for two-year-old girls. Anything to keep her mind from dwelling on Brett and his kiss. The activities helped somewhat, but her stubborn mind kept circling back to his lips and the feel of his arms around her.

So. Going to Hickory would be good. She needed to call people. Find out about Jack. Talk with Tess. The ride up there might not be great, but she'd make it work. She'd pushed through worse things before.

Brett burst out of the bathroom and charged back into his room. She grabbed her backpack and waited by the front door.

He secured his watch as he entered the den.

"You've got a nick on your chin." Right beside the cleft.

He licked his thumb then rubbed it against the red spot. "It'll be okay." His gaze hit on her backpack. "Ah, how about if you stay here this time? Gigi will probably arrive in a little bit. You two can keep each other company."

Stay here? He didn't want her to go. Why? To keep Gigi company? Really? Or was there another reason? Could it be a woman? Could he kiss her like he did last night, then see another woman this morning?

"Well, I need to make some phone calls. I haven't checked on things in two days."

"I'll take you up to the clearing when I get back." He moved by her to the door. "Okay?"

Not okay. She was packed and ready to go. She wouldn't bother him. He could meet his girlfriend in peace. She'd make her calls, make sure she still had a business.

He stopped at the threshold. "About last night." He swiped his jaw. "It shouldn't have happened. I apologize." He glanced out the door. "It's a half hour drive, so there's an hour in travel. Not sure how long it'll take beyond that."

Thanks for telling me how you really feel.

Good to know.

A mistake. Something he had to apologize for. "Be careful."

He was really going to leave her alone in this cabin. Butterflies flitted in her stomach, reminding her of being dropped off at college.

For the first time since he burst through the front door after his run, his face softened. "I'll try not to take long, but I have to go. I . . . You'll be fine." He turned and bolted outside, his gun peeking out the back of his waistband.

She certainly would be fine. As soon as she had her own life back—away from him.

Checking her watch, she calculated with the hour travel time and another hour to take care of his appointment, Brett wouldn't be back before eleven o'clock probably. When Gigi had visited in the mornings, she'd usually arrive about the same time. So Mary Wade had maybe two hours to call Jack and Tess.

Her foot felt well-rested today. She rotated her ankle, satisfied with the diminished twinge. Better than yesterday. The swelling had subsided enough to wear her tennis shoes. She could walk with the crutches to the clearing herself. She didn't have to wait for him to come back.

And she wouldn't.

ഇരുജ

Brett hit the main highway before he let himself think about Mary Wade. He hated leaving her like that, looking like she'd lost her last friend. No explanation about his appointment. Just a lame promise to take her to the clearing when he got back. What must she think?

He halfway expected a little pushback from her. He couldn't remember too many times when she accepted he said at face value with no "why" or "why not" to push his buttons. Interesting. He'd come back to that. Now, focus on getting to his dad.

That nurse. What was her name? Tammy. She'd sounded young, not exactly sure of herself. CNAs could be as young as late teens, so a young nurse didn't really raise a red flag. But would a CNA make a call to the family?

He grabbed his phone and hit the recent calls, touched the screen. Quick rings, then, "The number you've dialed is no longer in service."

No longer in service? His pulse ratcheted up a notch.

He searched for the skilled nursing facility's number. "Good morning. Greenwood Care. How may I direct your call?"

"Michael Benson, Clint Davis' doctor." He checked the rearview mirror.

"Dr. Benson's making rounds now. Could you call back in about an hour?"

Brett worked his jaw. "So he's finished with his emergency call?"

"I'm not aware of an emergency call this morning."

He gripped the steering wheel. "What about Mr. Davis' nurse, Tammy. I'll speak with her."

"Sir, Mr. Davis' nurses are Glynda, Sylvia, and Heather, not Tammy."

He swallowed anger and panic, enunciating every word. "Does a Tammy work anywhere in your facility?"

"Doesn't ring a bell, but let me check." Seconds felt like hours. "No, sir. No Tammy in the directory."

"Okay." He skidded into an abandoned mechanic's lot to turn around. "Give me one of Clint Davis' nurses."

He didn't wait for Glynda or Sylvia or Heather to confirm his suspicions that his dad was fine. Brett had already eaten up three miles by the time Glynda explained that his dad had a great night and enjoyed all of his breakfast.

The steering wheel vibrated when his hand cracked down on it. Dusty and Skeet. He knew something was off with that phone call, but his mind had been muddled with thoughts of Mary Wade. Rookie mistake. One he wouldn't make again.

If traffic remained clear, he could be back to the cabin in about fifteen minutes. That would give Dusty and Skeet only about thirty minutes to move. Not a lot of time, but lots of stuff could happen in thirty minutes. He'd seen situations go south in less than five.

Brett envisioned Mary Wade with the crutches. Gigi with another basket of—Gigi.

Gigi would be involved this time.

His accelerator foot pressed closer to the floor.

෨෨෨෨෨

Mary Wade reclined on a boulder at the edge of the clearing, the scent of pine soothing her. She arched her back and stretched her arms over her head to work out the kinks of the trek through the woods. Her underarms ached with the effort of maneuvering over the uneven path.

She lifted her face toward the warm sun. Even with her daily dose of sunscreen, she'd probably pay for this outing with a couple new freckles. At this point, she didn't care. The sun felt delicious on her cheeks, and Brett was on his way to meet some tall, blond with a golden tan.

Probably.

Thank goodness Jack was recovering and back manning his shop. He sounded strong and lighthearted. Did his best to absolve her of any guilt from the attack. She missed him, needed to talk with him face to face.

About Brett.

Stop thinking about him.

Tess was a different story. Orders had fallen off. She didn't make one sale in the last three days. Mary Wade had tried to absolve her of guilt. "Dropping sales aren't your fault, Tess. People need to forget about what happened. They'll be back."

"When will you be back? I need a frozen yogurt run."

Code for Tess needed to talk. "Soon. I promise."

And she would be too. That'd be the first topic of conversation when Brett Davis returned from his rendezvous. She'd put her life on hold long enough. If Dusty and Skeet hadn't been arrested by now, they were probably long gone. She needed to pick up the pieces of her life and move forward before her business completely tanked.

She checked the time on her phone before sliding it into her backpack. Her arms protested at the thought of the return trip to the cabin, the thought actually hurting worse than her ankle, which was holding up very well. She tugged her sketch pad from the backpack. Gigi wasn't due for at least another half hour or so. She should've left a note in case the older woman arrived early. Although, if she missed Gigi, would that be such a bad idea?

That woman had a way of loosening her tongue, and Mary Wade wasn't ready to talk about last night's kiss yet, if ever. She wanted to hold on to it by herself, keep it special. She wanted to lock the memory away for a time when she'd need a knock-your-socks-off kind of memory.

She certainly didn't want to see Gigi's sad eyes warn her again about getting her heart broken by her grandson. She was well aware of all his charms without Gigi's warnings. She'd swayed against him during his onslaught of teasing kisses, dragged him to her mouth when she couldn't take one more second of waiting for his lips to touch hers. She cringed. He must be enjoying the idea of such a willing, easy conquest.

Or not.

He seemed embarrassed. Couldn't wait to leave, in fact, but made time to apologize for his mistake. When would people stop associating her with mistakes?

Tapping her fingers on her forehead, she spoke out loud. "Stop thinking about Brett Davis." He left this morning without much more than a greeting and an apology. A vision of him with a brunette on his arm flitted across her mind. A voluptuous brunette. With dark brown eyes and perfectly tanned skin.

"Stop. Think about something else."

Anything else.

Not in the mood to design clothes, she focused her fragile attention on the wildflowers dotting the landscape surrounding the clearing. Fishing around the bottom of her backpack, she found the box of watercolor pencils. Maybe she could use the color combinations or petal shapes in future designs.

Brushing broad strokes with a cornflower blue pencil, she battled Brett out of her mind and concentrated on capturing the curve of a flower holding its own in a crevice between two stones.

One brave little flower surviving despite its surroundings.

She'd take a lesson.

Chapter 29

"Well, the plan worked until we got here and nobody." Dusty propped his filthy boot on the footstool in front of the polka dot chair.

"So she ain't here now. She rode with Doc to the emergency." Skeet fashioned air quotation marks with his fingers. "They'll be back. And then what? I don't like how this feels." He picked his teeth with a toothpick he'd had since breakfast. "I can't believe you dragged me here. I can't believe you got that girl to call him for twenty dollars."

Dusty smirked. "I got charm. What can I say?"

"Yeah, right. Say she knows how to keep her mouth shut."

"She won't say nothing. I put the fear a God in her when I broke that phone right before her wide eyes."

"I don't like it." Skeet shook his head. "This could be bad."

"Nope. It's gonna be good."

Tires churned rocks in the driveway.

"Hush. They're here." Dusty knelt beside the end table. "Get down so they won't see us yet."

Footsteps skipped up the stairs and stopped in front of the door. A key clicked in the lock.

"Yoo hoo. Anybody here?"

ෂ෧ෂ෧ඎ෫ඎ෫

Brett skidded to a stop behind Gigi's car. Everything looked normal from the driveway, but he grabbed his nine-mil-

215

limeter from under the seat anyway. No need to underestimate Dusty and Skeet again. He'd formulated a plan on the wild drive back. Grab Gigi and Mary Wade. Send them packing to Valley Hills Mall. Wait for Dusty and Skeet to show up.

Maybe he should have called for backup. But back up to what? He'd been working on intuition and hunches since finding out Tammy was a fake nurse. He bounded up the stairs and burst through the door. Gigi sat on the couch, her arms stretched funny behind her back.

Like they were tied behind her.

"Brett, look out."

His world went black.

ℒℒℂℛ

"That's not for you." A slap sounded from far away, then a whimper.

Brett tried to open his eyes but moaned instead.

"Honey, wake up. Brett, are you all right?"

"Put a rag in her mouth so she will. Shut. Up. I'm tired of her jabbering. Hmm, but she sure can cook."

This was a crazy, horrible dream. His jaw ached, and he tasted blood. The tangy aroma of oregano, basil, and tomatoes swirled around his nose. He wasn't hungry. Why was he dreaming of Gigi's lasagna?

"You shouldn't have slapped her. Not a woman like her. We already had her tied up. What's she gonna do?"

"Talk me to death. That's what." The words sounded lumpy and crowded together. Talking with a mouthful of food? "I don't wanna hear about Jesus. I don't wanna hear about the Bible. I just want her to shut up unless she can tell us where Mary Wade is."

Mary Wade. Brett almost smiled, but the knife-like pain in his jaw prevented him from it. Mary Wade. That's who he wanted to dream about. Not Gigi's lasagna. His pillow felt like

216

a rock. He moved his arm to plump it but couldn't bring his arm where he wanted it. He pulled his eyelids open to a slit but squeezed them closed again, the light searing his brain.

"Hey, he's coming 'round. Set him up and let's find out where she went."

Brett eased his eyes open again and squinted through the fog and pain in his head. Hands brought him to sitting, leaned him against something. Still couldn't move his arms. Something hard cuffed him in his side. Hands righted him before he toppled over.

"Quit. Let him wake up first."

"Hey, Matt. Or Brett. Or whoever you are. Guess who come to dinner?"

Crazy, bad dream. That voice sounded like—He forced his eyes to focus on the face inches from his own. Dusty.

Dusty was in the cabin, but where was Mary Wade?

ഇ൭ഇ൭ഭ൰ഭ൰

Mary Wade's armpits vacillated between numbness and stinging. What made her think she'd be able to walk to the clearing and back? Less than a mile in reality, the trek felt more like fifteen or twenty miles with crutches stuffed under her arms. A couple more steps and she'd be back in the yard.

As she cleared the woods, she stopped to regroup before finishing the journey. Two cars in the driveway. Gigi's and Brett's. Brett was already back from Hickory? She checked her watch. He'd been gone for barely an hour. How was that possible? He'd be so peeved with her for walking to the clearing. For not following his directions and waiting for him. For being stubborn.

Too bad.

She hiked her backpack straps higher on her shoulders. Maybe Gigi would take her side. "Okay, Brett. Here I come." She plopped the tip of her crutches near a clump of pine straw, but before she could move her foot forward, a gleam from the backyard caught her eye. A rear bumper of a pickup stuck out from behind the shed.

A creepy sensation crawled up the back of her neck. Why was a truck parked behind the cabin? She stepped back into the trees. Something wasn't right. She glanced toward the cars. Gigi's was first. Then Brett's came behind hers, but the angle looked funny. His SUV wasn't lined up behind Gigi's like a regular parking job. Instead, it had fishtailed into the driveway, gravel sprayed along the grass.

Like Brett had been in a hurry.

Her heartbeat thumped harder. She pulled in breaths through her nose, coaching herself to calm down. She watched the cabin, feeling helpless.

God, what am I supposed to do here? Is something wrong or am I just conjuring up stuff from my wild imagination? I need help here, please. I need wisdom. Courage too.

Should she call the police? But what to tell them? She thought something was wrong? She'd have to walk all the way back to the clearing. Maybe she'd get a couple of bars before walking the entire trek. But would that take too long? She didn't know the address. She groaned and bit her lip.

A screened door slammed. Someone left the cabin from the back door, heading toward the shed. A man. Not Brett. It looked like. . . Her heart dropped to her stomach.

Skeet.

Dusty and Skeet had Brett and Gigi. She had to do something. Think, brain, think.

Her words to Tess came back to her.

You are big, God. Bigger than all of this. And smart. I'm not. Clearly, or I wouldn't keep getting into these crazy situations. Help me figure out what to do. And how to do it.

Gigi's gun. She always traveled with it under her seat. Brett might have left his under his seat, too, if he was in a hurry.

A truck door slammed, and Skeet strolled back to the cabin, a cigarette dangling from his mouth.

Would he come back out? Would Dusty come with him? She counted off seconds, watching for any movement from the house.

Nothing.

Crouching, she laid the crutches alongside a butterfly bush, shucked off her backpack.

God, I don't know what I'm doing. Help me.

She scooted to an oak tree between the woods and the driveway, crouching on her hands and feet. Held her breath and peeked around the trunk. She swallowed a surge of panic and scooted to the bumper of Brett's SUV. Waddling to the passenger side door, she bit her lip and ignored the pangs in her ankle. She tried the handle. Locked. She leaned her forehead against the door panel.

God, protect my ankle and keep it mobile. I still need some wisdom down here. Keep them safe.

She waddled around the grill, checked the front of the cabin again, and made it to the driver's door. The handle unlatched.

Thank You, God.

She ran her hand under the seat. Nothing. She growled then checked herself. She pressed the door to the frame and waddled to Gigi's car.

The faint scent of Italian food warred with her churning stomach. Determination spurred her to her goal. When her hand closed around the cool metal of Gigi's gun, she wanted to yell a victory shout. Her triumph lasted as long as the time it took for reality to settle on top of her shoulders.

What was she supposed to do now?

ℝℝ℞℞

Drums beat between Brett's temples. His jaw throbbed every time he tried to speak. Blood trickled from his nose. Most likely broken. He'd been clocked but good. Gigi's ashen face registered fear and confusion.

"Be decent. Take the gag out. She won't scream." The words struggled out of his bloodied mouth.

"Are you sayin' I ain't decent? Good. Because I ain't, and when your girlfriend gets back here, I'll show you how indecent I can be."

Brett gritted his teeth and counted to ten. Do not lose your temper now. Calm and collected always wins. Calm and collected would save Gigi and Mary Wade.

Mary Wade. They obviously didn't have her, but where was she? *God, please keep her safe.*

A prayer? From him? It'd been a long time, but it felt right. His eyes flashed to his grandmother. His own prayer had surprised him, but he knew Gigi prayed even as she sat, tied and gagged on her flowery couch. He strained his wrists again, but the rope didn't give an inch.

Keep them talking. Maybe he'd come up with a plan.

"Mary Wade's not coming back."

"You're lying. Just like you did before. Which reminds me." Dusty bent in front of him and slapped the side of his face. Gigi's gag muffled a scream. He closed his eyes against the daggers stabbing all over his head. Fresh blood tickled his upper lip. He sucked in painful streams of air through clenched teeth.

"That make you feel better?"

"No, Mr. Double Crosser. But maybe this will." A boot toe crashed into his rib cage, knocking him sideways to the floor. Pain seized the length of him, demanding attention. Blackness threatened again, but he fought to remain conscious. He had to save Gigi and Mary Wade.

"That's enough, Dusty. Set him up."

"Maybe I don't agree with you."

"If you keep beatin' him, he'll keep groanin', and she'll

keep cryin'. You want Mary Wade to hear all this and hightail it the other way?"

Dusty grunted. "All right. He makes me mad." He yanked Brett upright, shook him hard before letting go. "He did us wrong, Skeet."

"Yeah. I know. He'll get what's coming."

Chapter 30

The little revolver banged against Mary Wade's lower thigh. It fit perfectly in the pocket of her cargo shorts as she clomped across the yard to the cabin. Her knotted blouse rode high above her midriff, and her hair swished across her cheeks with every stride of the crutches. She'd found a lint-covered tube of tinted lip balm in the front pouch of her backpack and smeared on several layers.

She hoped she could pull off the crazy plan that bloomed in her mind while she knelt by Gigi's car.

Maybe if Dusty and Skeet kept their eyes on her waist up, they wouldn't notice the lumpy pocket.

At the top of the steps, she tousled her hair again, pinched her cheeks, and bit her lips to darken them.

Here I go, God. Give me courage to do this. Help me help Gigi and Brett.

As her trembling hand hovered over the doorknob, her racing heart swelled and crowded her lungs. Hard to breathe. Hard to think. How could she pull this off?

The door flew open. "Well, look who's here. Come right on in, darlin'. We been waitin' especially for you."

Dusty.

She licked her lips, tasting the cherry Chapstick. "You came for me. Finally."

ಓಓಅಃಅ

His head whipped toward the sound of Mary Wade's voice, ignoring the searing pain in his jaw. What had happened to her? Her hair had been in a ponytail this morning. Her blouse had been buttoned up and fluttering around her waistband, for sure not revealing her flat stomach. The only time she'd worn lipstick was the morning they'd driven over to Hickory. What was she doing?

"Get in the house." Dusty dragged her through the doorway. "And say what you just said again."

"You came for me. I knew you would. I've been waiting for you."

"What? I ain't stupid. You're lying like your rat fink boyfriend."

"He isn't my boyfriend." The tip of her tongue showed at the corner of her mouth. "I don't have a boyfriend."

"Mary Wade." Brett pushed with his foot to straighten himself.

Dusty pointed the nine-millimeter to Brett. "Shut up, or I'll shut you up." He focused on Mary Wade again. "You want me to believe you been waitin' for me?"

"You came for me in Charlotte, right? You came to my house and to my shop, right?"

Dusty grinned. "I certainly did." He glanced at Skeet. "Wadda you think, partner?"

"I don't know. She's sure singin' a different tune than she did in Bandon."

"Yeah. You weren't too friendly then." Dusty tilted his head. "You left in the middle of the night."

"He thought he was saving me from you, but I didn't want to be saved."

Brett clenched his fists. How could he make her stop? "Mary Wade, don't—"

Dusty cocked the pistol. "This is your second warning."

"I knew if I waited long enough, you'd find me. And you did. It just took so long."

"We were in Hickory the other day. Saw you sittin' at that table."

"That was you? It felt like someone was watching me." She tossed her hair over her shoulder. "I was hoping it was you." She set her crutches against the wall and dropped her backpack. She cocked her head. "Did you follow us out of town?" She fiddled with the collar of her blouse with one hand, emphasizing how far it was unbuttoned. Her right hand dangled at her side.

Brett strained against the rope. His face contorted with fresh pain. What kind of game was she playing? Don't do this, Mary Wade. Give me more time. I can get us out of this.

Help me, God, get us out of this.

Gigi had closed her eyes. Pray hard, Gigi. Pray hard. If God doesn't listen to me, I know He listens to you. Look at me, Mary Wade. Look at me and stop this craziness.

"Yeah, we followed you, but Mr. Double Crosser put the slip on us. You didn't today, though, did you?"

"Don't be mad at him, Dusty. He thought he was doing the right thing again. He wanted to protect me." She stuck her hands in her back pockets and arched her back. "But I don't need to be protected from you, do I?"

A low, throaty snigger rumbled in Dusty's throat. He stepped within inches of her. She stood firm. "Well," he snuggled his lips against her neck. "I'll let you be the judge of that." He slid his arm around her, shoved his other hand up under her blouse.

She pushed at his hand. "Wait."

He tightened his grip on her back. "Oh, no. You can't just stop now."

"Not in here."

Another vile laugh. "We're gonna do it here, there, and everywhere, darlin'."

"I'd rather start in my bedroom. My bed's so comfy, and I . . . I have . . .some fun things in there."

"Why do I think you're tryin' to pull something over on me?"

She pouted. "Just because I want some privacy? She's a nice lady, but she's crying, and I know she's over there praying. Not exactly the best ambiance . . . for what I want to do."

"The best what?"

"Atmosphere. I don't think I'd be able to . . ." She tugged at the pocket on his T-shirt. "You know, make you as happy out here as I could in there." She nodded to her room.

Dusty narrowed his eyes. "You know how to talk, woman. Let's find out if you can back up what you say." He grabbed a hank of hair, snapped her head back, and seized her lips with his open mouth. Skeet hooted from the side chair.

If this crazy scene lasted much longer, Brett's head would explode. His wrists were raw from fighting the restraints.

God, do something.

An eternity passed before Dusty lifted his head but continued his grip on her hair. She fisted a wad of her shorts. To keep from wiping her mouth?

Don't do this, Mary Wade.

"Well, all right then." He released her and trailed his hand over her exposed back. "Let's go."

"First," she cleared her throat, "could you do a favor for me?"

"You're getting' ready to do me several, so spill it. Then I'll decide."

"Could you, please, take the gag out of her mouth?" She cut her eyes to Gigi. "She's been so kind to me. She won't bother us. With the door closed."

"Skeet, take out the gag." He shoved her toward her bedroom. "Get in there, darlin'." He peeled off his T-shirt before the door slammed shut.

ဢ)ဢ)ᏸᏸ

Dear God, what am I doing?

Mary Wade trembled on her bed and faced a shirtless Dusty. A thick roll of hairy fat hung over his belt, the belt he unbuckled as he strode toward her, grinning. She forced herself not to shudder, not to relive his mouth swallowing hers. She removed a shoe. He slid his belt out of the loops and slung it across the room.

"Hey, what's the rush, Dusty. They're not going to bother us now. Let's take our time." She dropped another shoe as he pushed her back on the bed.

"We'll go fast this time. Slow the next." He crawled on top of her, straddling her midsection and laying his gun beside her head. "Then maybe something in the middle."

"I just don't like to be rushed."

He ripped her blouse open to the knot. Buttons popped and scattered on the floor. He tugged against the knot. "This time's about what I like. Got it?"

"Let me help you." She loosened the knot with icy fingers. Tried to breathe. Swallowed bile rising from her stomach. "There. That's better, don't you think?"

"I ain't thinking right now, woman." He slid his legs down alongside hers, prostrate against her, his weight crushing the breath from her lungs. He ran his mouth over her collarbone.

Gulping air to stem the revulsion, she arched her back, angling her leg to her hand. Fumbling with shorts, she found the pocket and slid her fingers around Gigi's pistol.

Thank You, God.

Moaning, he pushed her blouse and bra strap from her shoulder. "I've been waitin' for this."

"So have I." She rammed the barrel into his fleshy side.

"Hey. Ow." Dusty reared back to investigate. "What—"

"Get off me. Now." Capitalizing on his momentary confusion, she kneed him in his groin. He cried out as he rolled onto the floor.

Skeet hooted from the den. "Take it easy in there."

Mary Wade scrambled off the bed. "Tell him to mind his own business, but don't say another word or I'll shoot."

Curled in a fetal position, he lay mute with his hand between his legs. His lips clamped together. She cocked the gun.

He glared at her. "Mind your own business."

She slid out the bottom drawer of the dresser and found what she needed. Holding the gun steady, she tossed the camouflage print scarf to him. "Put your legs around the bedpost. One foot on one side and the other on the far side. Take the scarf and tie up your ankles with the post in the middle."

"I ain't takin' orders from you." His voice sounded more strained than defiant.

She leveled the gun at his head. "Then how about taking them from this?"

He swallowed. "You wouldn't dare."

"Don't bet on it. You've already given me more than enough reasons. Tie. Up. Your. Feet."

He scooted to the corner of the bed, slid one foot underneath. "If you shoot me, you still got Skeet to worry about."

"Wrap the scarf around your ankles. Again. Now knot it. Pull it tight. Again." His feet looked secure, but what about his hands? "What do you care what happens after I shoot you?"

"Yeah. You talk big, but I see you shaking. You probably ain't never shot a gun in your life."

"I hit a bucket from five yards yesterday. You're a wider target, and I'm three feet from you. Kinda like my odds. Yours, on the other hand?" She shrugged. Her arms begged to sag with the weight of the gun. Sweat made it slippery in her hands.

What now?

�☜☞☜☞☞☞

Okay, God, I'm completely helpless. Do something, please.

I'm desperate. I can't stand this. I can't stand it. She's in there. I need You to help me. Now.

Two prayers in one day. No answer. Brett scanned the room for the fiftieth time. Nothing.

"It's gonna be a while." Skeet grinned. "Think I'll go stretch my legs. Don't try anything funny." He let the back door slam behind him.

Brett scooched over to Gigi. "Untie me." He swung a leg underneath him, pushed himself to kneeling, and wiggled onto the couch beside her. The pain in his side stole his breath. He angled his back to her. "Here."

"Oh, Brett, your arms."

"Just scratches. Quick. Turn your back to me. Can you feel the knot?"

"My arms are numb. I don't know if I can work my fingers."

"Let me try yours." He felt the knot and wiggled his fingers.

Please, God, let this come loose.

One tiny give budged in the knot.

Thank You, God. Thank You.

His arms screamed. Fire streaked from his ribcage, but he compelled his fingers to pull against the rope until she was free.

Gigi's arms sagged. "Ow." She rolled her shoulders and flexed her hands. "Let me try to free you."

"So sorry."

"Hush. I'm built out of solid stock. So are you. Oh, Brett. My fingers won't work right."

"Slow and steady. You'll get it."

Help her, God. Get this rope off me.

Gigi sniffed. "We've got to get her out. What was she—"

He gritted his teeth. Pain flashed from his jaw. He'd have to work hard to delete her vamp show from his mind. What was she thinking? "We will." Absolutely. "Keep trying. Not much time."

Chapter 31

Mary Wade heard a door slam. Did Skeet leave? What was going on out there? What was she supposed to do in here? She couldn't tie up his arms without setting down the gun. She couldn't make him tie up his own arms.

She tossed him the tassel cap. "Put the ball in your mouth and tie the strings around your head."

"What?"

"You heard what I said. Put that yarn ball on the top of the hat in your mouth. Tie the strings behind your head. Tight."

"No. I'll choke."

"I didn't get to protest when you gagged me. Neither did Gigi. Do it. Now."

To her surprise, he obeyed her order.

Don't get too confident, girl. He's trying to think his way out of this room just as much as you are.

"Lie with your arms beside you."

A frown.

"Do it." She backed up to the overstuffed chair in the corner, squeezed behind it with the gun zeroed in on the man lying flat on the floor. Grunting, she pushed it toward him, bumped the front legs into his side.

Muted words she couldn't understand jumbled in the woven yarn.

She stepped around the chair and pointed the gun direct-

229

ly in the center of his chest. "Hush and be still." He stopped squirming, but if looks could kill . . .

Her options were slim. She couldn't shoot him. The noise would alert Skeet. She could try to clonk him over the head, but she probably wouldn't hit him hard enough to do anything but enrage him more than he already was. The only thing left. . .

This was a ridiculous idea. She didn't have a better one, unfortunately.

She blew straggly pieces of hair from her face.

"Lay your left hand palm up."

Again, he obeyed her. Carefully keeping the nose of the gun pointed at Dusty, she pushed and lifted with her hip, her knee, anything that would move the chair, then wedged one front leg on top of his palm. "There."

What was happening in the other room? Silence. Did Skeet really go outside? Was he still out there?

Fury streamed from the cap. He moved to push it off with his other hand.

"Stop. Put your right hand beside the bed frame." Keeping her sights on Dusty, she dragged his belt closer to her with her foot. "Hold it up. Close your eyes."

He opened them wider.

"Close your eyes. Why do you make me repeat everything I say to you? That infuriates me."

He closed his eyes, muttering into the cap.

"Hold your arm beside the bed frame." She wound the belt around the frame piece and his wrist, cinched it, looped the end through a couple of times, and pulled again as tight as she could. Maybe this would keep him for a few minutes.

She grabbed his gun from the bed, moved to the door, and listened. Nothing. She peeked under the door. The bottom of the back of the couch. Nothing. If she could catch Skeet off guard, maybe she could. . .

Carefully, she laid his gun on the dresser and slowly turned the knob, opened the door a crack. The striped chair was empty. She widened it another inch. Gigi and Brett sat on the couch with Brett turned away from her. Gigi worked at his back. Where was Skeet? Outside? She grabbed Dusty's gun and surveyed the room before bolting toward the couch.

Gigi sucked in a gasp. Brett's face lost all color. "Oh, honey, you're safe. Thank God. But. Your blouse."

Mary Wade glanced at her disheveled clothes. She'd forgotten her state of almost undress. She laid the guns in Gigi's lap and fumbled for missing buttons. She gathered the ends and knotted them.

Brett blew out a breath and started giving orders. "Untie me. Skeet'll be back. Untie me." His words were clipped, strained through gritted teeth.

His blood mingled with the rope fibers, making untying the knot even more difficult. Mary Wade chewed the inside of her cheek to keep her eyes clear of blinding tears. His efforts to free himself from the rope had gnawed gouges around his wrists.

Footsteps scuffed on the back steps.

Gigi thrust the bigger gun to Mary Wade. "Hide."

Brett growled. "Wait. One more pull."

Gigi shook her head at her grandson. "No time." She moved to her original position, her hands gripping her gun behind her back. Her heart drumming triple time, Mary Wade crouched beside the sofa, eyes pinned on the back door.

Skeet burst through the doorway and snorted. "Things quieted down in there yet?" He opened the refrigerator and checked the contents. Mary Wade noted a black handle peeking from his waistband. "Ya'll ain't got nothing but milk and juice?" He grabbed the orange juice and unscrewed the top. Leaning against the counter, he guzzled the contents.

Brett whispered out of the side of his mouth. "Be patient."

Tossing the empty jug into the trash, Skeet wiped his mouth with the back of his hand. "This sure is a pretty place you got up here. Nice and secluded. I just saw a buck across the brook." He pushed away from the counter and headed for the den area. "Too bad it ain't deer season." He snorted again as he sank into the wing chair, stretching out his brogans and crossing his ankles. "Too bad I ain't got my shotgun." A muffled thump sounded from the bedroom. He glanced toward the bedroom door left ajar, frowned and pushed himself upright. "Hey."

Gigi dragged her arms from behind her back and anchored her fists, wrapped around the gun, on top of her knees. The gun pointed squarely at Skeet's chest. "Too bad for you I've got my .38 Special."

Skeet slapped his hand against the arms of the chair. "What the—"

Mary Wade rose from her hiding place, leveling her pistol at Skeet. "Don't move. Gigi, we need to get his gun. Do you want to or me?"

"You do it. I'll shoot him if he tries anything." She glared at Skeet. "Put your hands straight up and lean forward."

Skeet's eyes skittered between both women. His mouth gaped open like a caught fish.

"Do it." Gigi's voice dripped steel and demanded obedience.

Skeet skewered Gigi with a fierce look but followed her order. Mary Wade lifted the gun from his waistband and moved back to Brett. "Have you still got him? I'll untie Brett." She laid Brett's gun beside him, Skeet's on the end table, and worked on the knot restraining Brett.

"Easiest target I've ever had in my sights."

"What've you done with Dusty?" He jutted his jaw over his shoulder. "Dusty?"

Scuffling came from the bedroom.

Gigi cocked her gun. "I told you not to move, old man."

More thumps.

"This knot is so stubborn. Stop moving. Every time you move, it tightens back up."

Brett huffed out a whooshing stream of air. "You can do it. How'd you get out?"

"I hid Gigi's gun in my side pocket. When he . . . When he was distracted, I got it out and made him tie his feet to the bedpost. Oh, this knot." Trembling to the point of uselessness, her fingers struggled with commands to free the knot. Her chest tightened. She wiggled a thumb into a loop.

"You're getting it. It's loosening."

"One hand is tied to the bed with his belt. One has—ooh, there it is."

ℰↃℰↃℭℛℭℛ

Brett's wrists separated before Mary Wade's pronouncement. Holding his breath against the pain shooting from his ribs, he limped into the bedroom with his pistol drawn, stopped short at the sight greeting him.

Dusty, flat on the floor, legs tied to the bedpost, one arm tied to the bed with his belt and the other arm? How did she get him? If the situation was less dire, the sight of Dusty spread out and captured by an overstuffed bedroom chair would be laughable.

"Ready to get up?"

A grunt from the floor. For the first time, Brett realized why the usually talkative Dusty was silent. A tassel cap? Are you kidding? The bed rested several inches away from the wall. He'd tried like a trooper to free himself, but the restraints held, although his belted arm was more twisted now than tied.

What a piece of work Mary Wade Kimball turned out to be. Dusty grunted again, drawing Brett's attention to his shirtless chest this time. The tangled bedcovers caught his eye next. An image of Mary Wade and Dusty burst in his brain.

He swallowed the nausea threatening to rise.

Thank You, God.

"You're comfortable enough. I'll check on your partner."

He returned to the den to find Gigi commandeering the couch, still aiming for Skeet. Mary Wade sat on the floor at his feet, wrapping the rope that had bound his wrists only moments earlier around the older man's ankles.

Had he slipped into a parallel universe?

Mary Wade glanced from her work. "Did he get loose? I knew the scarf and belt wouldn't hold long."

"And the chair." Humor laced his words.

She flushed and dipped her head. "It worked, didn't it?"

A chuckle died before it blossomed, strangled with a biting stab from his side. "Yep. I've got handcuffs in the car. I'll be back. Skeet, don't try anything."

Skeet scowled at him.

"Oh, handcuffs. Why didn't I think to look for those?"

Brett grunted. "You thought of enough. Believe me."

Another flush.

"Brett, honey, tell me where they are. I'll get them. I need some fresh air." Gigi sounded weary, exhausted. She pointed the gun with it resting on her knee. "Mary Wade, you did great with my gun a while ago. Why don't you take over for me now that his feet are secured?"

Mary Wade rose and shuffled to the couch.

In the fracas, he'd forgotten about her ankle. He'd forgotten most everything except his inability to help these two women and the sight of Mary Wade vamping herself into the cabin, all the way to the bedroom. With Dusty.

"You need to sit down. Hold this." He handed Mary Wade Skeet's gun. "I'll get handcuffs."

"But—"

"But nothing. Grandmother. You're off duty." He laid her gun on the coffee table, his wrists and side screaming with every movement. "It's here if you need it." He glowered at Skeet. "She better not need it."

Within fifteen minutes and with liberal help from the women, Brett had both men handcuffed and sitting in the wing chairs. "I'll drive up to the clearing to call the sheriff's department."

Mary Wade and Gigi sat on the couch with their arms around each other, whispering, patting their backs. He could use a hug, too, but his work wasn't quite finished.

Chapter 32

The soft scent of White Linen perfume drifted from Gigi's collar. Hugging her more tightly, Mary Wade drank it in, trying to erase the smell of Dusty's sweat and her fear. It was over.

Thank You. Thank You. Thank You, God.

"Are you okay? Really okay, Mary Wade?" Gigi pulled the edges of an afghan around her. "He didn't . . .He didn't—"

"No. He didn't. Thank God, I could reach my pocket. I had your gun out and jabbed in his side before . . . before—" Mary Wade shuddered and buried her head into the crook of Gigi's neck.

"Shh. Don't think about it. I shouldn't have brought it up, but we were going crazy out here. You saw Brett's wrists. You were in there by yourself." She rubbed Mary Wade's back. "Maybe it's better Brett couldn't get free. I don't think that boy would be alive now if . . . I'm just so thankful you're free. We all are." Her voice caught. "Why don't you go change now? We're finished with everything."

The deputies had taken all their statements, locked Dusty and Skeet into the back of their cruiser, and chatted with Brett in the front yard.

"Good idea." She craned her neck to the room and swallowed. "I don't know if I can go back in there yet."

"I know what you mean. I'm calling Bill Dunlap first thing and putting this place up for sale."

"Oh, no. Don't do anything yet. You love this place. You've owned it for years."

"I did love it, but those nasty men came in here and trampled all over those memories. They ruined it. You were almost—we were almost . . ."

"Almost. That's the key word. We beat them, Gigi. Evil didn't win today."

Gigi raked her teeth across her bottom lip. "I see your point, but I don't know."

"Don't do anything right away. Wait a bit."

The door opened, and Brett leaned against the doorjamb. The cruiser rumbled behind him and crept down the driveway. He looked haggard. His left eye was almost swollen shut, matching his swollen jaw. "Why don't you have your foot up?"

Her sprained ankle was the last thing on Mary Wade's mind, but she lifted it to the coffee table.

"Brett, honey, why didn't you call for an ambulance when you called the sheriff's department? You should have let them call for one when they saw your face."

He moved into the room, hissing a breath between his teeth. "I'm fine."

Gigi gripped her knees, white knuckles highlighted on dark capris, "You don't look fine."

"Some ice and three or four ibuprofens will do the job." He scanned the room like a caged animal. Something was bothering him. But what? Dusty and Skeet were in custody. They should be celebrating.

"You might have a concussion."

He ignored that suggestion. "I'm going to get you ladies home now. I'll come back and clean up, get your car to you tomorrow. You're in no condition to drive."

"I could say the same thing to you, Brett Davis."

"Grandmother, I don't feel like arguing right now." He pinned Mary Wade with a scowl, dropped his gaze to her blouse. Favoring his left side, he limped into her room.

Gigi squeezed her hand. "He's upset."

Mary Wade's mouth twitched. "I picked up on that."

"And hurt."

Brett returned and tossed a pink T-shirt onto her lap. "Change in the bathroom. I'll pack up your stuff. You don't have to go back in there." He moved her crutches to the couch. "Don't forget these."

Gigi patted Mary Wade's knee and stood. "Brett, sit down before you fall down."

He crossed his arms over his chest and drew in a breath. "Grandmother—"

"That's right. I'm still your grandmother, and I'm playing that card right now. Sit down."

He glared at her, breathing short, shallow breaths. Several seconds ticked by before he lowered himself onto the couch beside Mary Wade, beads of sweat evident above his upper lip.

Gigi smiled, though her eyes were still sad. "Good boy. Now relax while I get ice and ibuprofen, and I'll tell you what we're going to do."

Brett opened his mouth, but Gigi stopped him with her raised index finger. "Ah, ah, ah. Now is the time for me to talk and you to listen."

ಬಂಬಂಬಬ

Knife blades sliced into Brett's ribcage with every breath. His temple and jaw ached with a brutality he hadn't felt since his Army days. Why not just lean back and let Gigi take over? She excelled at it anyway. Mary Wade collected the crutches and headed for the bathroom with the T-shirt.

Mary Wade. The reason he couldn't just roll over and slide into a pain-induced coma. She'd seen him at his worst, helpless, humiliated, beaten by bumbling yahoos. He'd have to work hard to erase that mental picture. Yep. He'd rest just a few minutes, then get the ladies out of here, away from the memories of Dusty and Skeet. Finish his job.

Dusty and Skeet.

How could he let this happen? He gritted his teeth and cringed at the fire in his jaw. How could he be ambushed by those two? Another rookie mistake rushing into the cabin without a plan. Without scanning the area first. If he'd done that one thing, he'd have seen the truck in the back. He could've surprised them instead of ending up needing Mary Wade and his grandmother to save him.

How did they plan it? How did they find him? They didn't have much of an IQ between them. Followers, not leaders, they'd never had an original idea in their life, wouldn't know one if it hit them in the face.

Fortunately, he had a plan and could execute it. Get these two women back to their safe, stable lives. Remind Mary Wade he was a competent law man.

He pushed to rise from the couch, but searing pain cemented him to his seat. Dropping back against the cushions, he closed his eyes, wiped sweat from his upper lip. Concentrated on blowing the pain from his body.

"Adrenaline kept you going when you had to be tough a while ago."

He opened his good eye. Gigi perched on the coffee table in front of him.

"Here." She handed him a plastic bag of ice cubes. "Now that everything's over, the adrenaline is running off, leaving nothing but fatigue and pain. Am I right?" She unscrewed the bottle of ibuprofen, shook out four tablets.

Gigi was right, though he refused to acknowledge it. Pain warred with fatigue inside his body, and he wasn't much interested in which one would win. He simply wanted to sink into this couch and thank God these two special women were safe.

Special women? Gigi, of course. Mary Wade?

Yes. He admitted it.

Mary Wade was special.

She'd surprised him in many ways during the past few days. These few days with her had shown him multiple sides to her personality. She was funny. She didn't complain, wanted to carry her own weight. Thwarted criminals with gumption and an upholstered chair.

No, he didn't want to think about that.

"Sweetheart, I'm going to put some Neosporin on your wrists. He kicked you so hard in your side." Gigi's voice cracked. "You probably have a broken rib or two. You might have a concussion. Your jaw and nose are swollen. Your nose looks broken."

He touched tentative fingertips to the bridge of his nose. Swollen. Was it broken? More than likely. His eyes would turn black, already were probably. He'd be a sight for sure.

"We're going to let you rest for a bit, then we're driving to Hickory to Dr. Jones' office."

Brett squinted his eye. Mary Wade had joined Gigi on the coffee table. She'd changed into the pink T-shirt. *Thank You.* But he could still see snippets in his mind's eye of the lacy bra concealed now under the fabric. Nope. Nothing but trouble contemplating that image.

"The ibuprofen—"

"Will dull the pain at best. It won't fix what may be wrong with you."

"Broken ribs don't get casted. I can tape my nose myself."

"Stubborn boy." Gigi fisted a hand at her mouth. "You may have internal bleeding. Humor me and get checked out. Please."

Her pleading eyes cut into him. When he'd dropped out of high school, she'd told him he was making a mistake. When he'd enlisted in the Army, she promised to pray for him. Both times she'd observed him with sad eyes but never begged him to change his mind.

Brett glanced at Mary Wade who sat mute watching the exchange. He arched a brow. That movement hurt too.

"You need to get checked out. For your grandmother if you won't do it for yourself."

Two against one.

He surrendered.

ℬℬℭℛℛ

Unzipping her suitcase conjured a flashback of packing the bag. Returning to her cabin bedroom had been hard, not as hard as with Dusty, but entering the room had ignited all the sights and smells of the episode she wanted to forget. "Just grab your clothes," Gigi had directed. "Don't touch another thing. I'll get somebody to come clean. Sometime."

Mary Wade had obeyed, stuffing her clothes in wads, piling in her sandals and toiletries. Keeping her eyes focused, she avoided looking at the bed or the chair still sitting askew in the middle of the room.

A soft knock brought her back to the present, in Brett's former room at Gigi's house.

Gigi eased onto the edge of the bed looking years older than the first time Mary Wade visited her house. "Are you okay?"

"I will be. Is Brett settled?"

Gigi nodded. "I can't believe Dr. Jones didn't wrap his chest."

"Impedes breathing he said."

"Okay, it restricts breathing, but I think the broken ribs also do that. Seems like the wrap would help support the ribs. Also, I think he should've had to stay in the hospital. What in the world are they thinking?" Her face crumpled. "They're not. That's what."

"If he'd broken five ribs, the doctor would've made him stay. With three, he could come home."

"Yes, but with the broken nose and the slight concussion. You'd think . . ."

"Gigi, Brett was adamant about going home. You were

241

lucky to talk him to coming here instead of driving him to his place."

"You're right." She sighed. "Maybe the medicine Dr. Jones gave him will knock him out." She sighed. "At least he's resting. Stubborn boy. He's stopped growling orders too. For the time being."

"I discovered where he got that stubborn streak and the giving orders thing." Mary Wade grinned. She witnessed a struggle of wills between grandmother and grandson from medical ministrations to driving back to Gigi's house. In the end, Gigi had won the battle. She drove her car followed by Mary Wade at the wheel of Brett's with him silent in the passenger side.

Gigi lifted her chin. "Guilty." She sighed again and scanned the room. "I left his room mostly the way he had it in high school. Carly's room I turned into my sewing room complete with a daybed so I wouldn't have to go all the way downstairs to my room when I needed a nap from sewing."

"I'm glad he didn't have to climb stairs. Every time he moves, his face goes whiter. If that's possible."

"Maybe I can talk him into staying with me while he lets those broken ribs heal."

"Good luck with that."

"Oh, don't I know it." Her mouth moved, reminiscent of a smile. "A grandmother can dream, can't she?"

Mary Wade set her makeup case on the dresser. "So they lived with you after their mom left?"

"That's part of the story. Brett talked with you about his mother?"

"I told him you'd mentioned her leaving. He confirmed it. That's about it."

"He doesn't share about that time."

Mary Wade fingered an elementary picture on a shelf. "He has lots of trophies and awards through tenth grade, when he dropped out."

Gigi cocked her head. "He told you about that, huh?" She studied the floor. "His grandfather died the summer before eleventh grade. Brett took it hard. They were very close."

"I sense there's more to the story."

"Yes."

"He told me some of it." Mary Wade hugged her arms around her sides. "He has a lot of stories."

"Yes, and he'll have to tell you them. I hope he will. I probably shouldn't have told you about his mom, but I wanted you to understand."

"I understand he's a complicated man."

"Not so complicated, Mary Wade. He loves deeply and strongly. He's loyal and committed to family. He has a strong sense of right and wrong. He could have been damaged in so many ways when his mom left the family, but . . ." She rubbed her forearms as if she were cold, "he persevered. He let us love him. He loved us back. He's a good man."

Mary Wade settled beside Gigi and slid her arm around her shoulder. "I know he is. I've seen him in action."

Gigi stared toward the window and blinked back tears.

Mary Wade squeezed her shoulder. "Don't think about it, Gigi. We're safe. God protected us and brought us through."

Gig touched her cheek. "I was praying so hard. When you appeared in that doorway, looking like . . ."

"I know. I couldn't think of anything else. I knew I couldn't go charging in there like the cavalry. I thought if I could separate them, distract Dusty . . ." She clamped her mouth shut. Didn't want to talk about it anymore. Didn't want to think about it.

"Enough." Gigi patted her knee. "I'm still stuffed from the cheeseburger this afternoon. I can't believe I ordered one of those things. But let me get you something. What would you like? I have some sandwich fixings. That's about it. I guess throwing out that lasagna wasn't so smart, but after he . . ."

"Shh. Not gonna think about him, right?" The cheeseburger she'd split with Gigi after Brett's appointment weighted her stomach like a lead anchor.

"Right. How about some peanut butter crackers?"

"No, thank you. I'm taking a long, hot shower and calling it a day."

"We'll call this one a doozy of a day."

Chapter 33

The face contorted into a goblin-like smile emitted a warped laugh. Mary Wade's eyes flew open, and the goblin face morphed into the full moon shining through the transom. She gripped the soft top sheet, willing her breathing to slow to normal. The creepy face produced a hammering in her chest. Her heartbeat clanged in her ears. She rolled to her side and considered her surroundings illuminated by the moon. A frown creased her brow. Not the little cabin's bedroom. A different one.

Brett's.

Memories from the day flooded her mind. No wonder she'd had that nightmare. Wide awake, she sat up and fluffed her pillow behind her. Her stomach growled. The half cheeseburger was long gone. She checked the clock on the bedside table. Two o'clock. A long time till breakfast. Maybe a glass of milk would soothe her stomach and her insides.

She threw on one of Gigi's cardigans and opened her door. Listened. Nothing. She descended the stairs guided by moon rays streaming through the bay windows in the family room below. At the bottom, she got her bearings and headed for Gigi's kitchen. As she reached through the doorway for the light switch, a disembodied voice from behind her chastised, "Where are your crutches?"

Her hand flew to her mouth too late to muffle the scream. She turned toward the stairs, listening for Gigi's call.

"She didn't hear you. Hearing aid, remember?"

"Are you trying to scare me to death? Why didn't you say something?" The late-night trip was supposed to soothe her, not give her apoplexy.

"I did."

"I walked all the way from the stairs."

"And you didn't see me?"

She pulled the cardigan closed. "And you didn't say anything?"

"Anything I said would've startled you."

He had a point.

"Startle is an understatement."

"I apologize for scaring you."

And for kissing me.

Don't think about kissing in the middle of the night. "That's okay." Turn the light on. Erase some of the intimacy. She blinked against the chandelier's cheerful brightness. "I thought you were sleeping in Gigi's room tonight."

He squinted with the light flowing from the kitchen. "The recliner works better."

"I came for a glass of milk. Would you like something?"

"For my ribs to stop screaming, but I hear that'll be a few days or more."

She buttoned a couple of buttons. "I could make some tea."

"Thank you, no. What might help is upstairs with my grandmother. Didn't trust me with the Jack Daniels she keeps for her recipes. Didn't want me mixing meds and the Tennessee whiskey." He shifted in the recliner and sucked in a breath. "Why don't you get your milk and sit for a while?"

Sit with him. The last time she'd sat with him in a cozy den, they'd ended up . . . She padded into the kitchen and jerked open the refrigerator. Stop those thoughts right now. He'd already explained his view of last night.

Last night? More like night before last, but it seemed like two months ago. Milk sloshed over the juice glass. She licked off her index finger and wiped up the white puddle. She could sit with him for a few minutes. Forget about the kiss and concentrate on how he'd taken care of her sprained ankle.

When she returned to the family room, he'd lit the short reading lamp beside his chair and angled the shade away from him. Instead of brightening the room, the soft lighting created an intimate atmosphere. Mary Wade chose the farthest end of the couch from Brett, clutched the milk with both hands. She curled her legs underneath her despite the ankle's pang.

"You never answered me. Where're your crutches?" He held himself straight, still. His only movement his silver eyes as they flicked over her.

She flushed and sipped the milk. "I'm giving my arms a break."

"You still need to stay off it as much as possible. Hasn't completely healed." He closed his eyes. White medical tape crisscrossed his broken nose. Even in the low light, blotchy skin showed around his eyes and over his jaw. If only she could help ease some of his pain, help him like he'd helped her.

"Can I get you something? Is it time for more medicine?"

"Not yet time for ibuprofen. The muscle relaxant makes me feel loopy. Not planning to take any more of that."

"But if it helps?"

"I like to have a clear head. I—" He reached for his water glass, and every bit of color in his face drained. The discolored splotches faded.

Before she thought it through, she jumped to her feet and handed the glass to him. "Maybe take the muscle relaxant just to get some sleep tonight."

He grabbed her hand, lowered his lids. "No. I'll be fine." He breathed several slow breaths out of his mouth. He opened his eyes. "Sit closer to me. Let's talk about last night."

She twisted her hand carefully from his. "You explained it

this morning. I'd rather talk about tomorrow. It's time for me to go home."

"Oh. Your foot's better, so you leave me all busted up?" His lip twitched a tiny bit.

"More like Dusty and Skeet are in custody, so the danger's gone. I have to get back to my business. Something's going on with Tess. Gigi's a great nurse. You'll be fine."

An emotion flickered across his brow. "Gigi is wonderful, but I'd rather have a nurse with green eyes and chestnut hair."

She pulled her gaze from his. Refused to get caught in his web of emotionally-charged words. "That medicine really is doing a job on you."

"I know exactly what I'm saying."

"But will you remember it in the morning?"

"It's already morning."

She drained the rest of the milk. "Back to the other conversation."

"I like my conversation better."

"Of course you do." She licked the milk from her upper lip. "But I'm leaving in the morning. I texted Daphne. Jeffrey doesn't work till dinner shift, so he's coming to pick me up."

"Remind me who Jeffrey and Tess are."

"She's my teenaged helper at the shop. He's my room-mate's fiancé."

"He doesn't need to come. I can drive you back."

"You're taking some powerful meds. You won't be driving for a couple of days."

He rolled his head from one side to the other. "No more loopy stuff. I'll drive you."

She smiled. "I appreciate your offer, but you can barely move without going white as a sheet. You need to give your body a chance to heal. Let Gigi love on you with all her special food. She adores caring for you."

"I'm not hungry for Gigi's food."

The temperature in the room rose several degrees. Was it from the heat rising up her neck or the fire smoldering in his eyes? If last night's kiss was a mistake, then why was he talking like Don Juan on steroids?

The medicine. Despite his insistence that he'd remember this conversation, he was still in a lot of pain, still taking potent painkillers, and exhausted from the whole day. She should end this little tête à tête before he completely shredded her heart. Ignore his words. Ignore the question in his eyes. Leave with her dignity still in place.

"Well, don't tell her that. She's already writing up a legal pad's worth of dishes to make for you." She rose.

He moved, too, but stopped short, grunted and exhaled a long, slow breath. "Wait. I can't move without pain. You're in no danger from me. Stay."

His invitation tugged at her heart, but she strengthened her resolve. "You've just made my point about driving. We're both exhausted. It's been quite a day. You need to rest. So do I."

"Please stay. I promise to be good. I'd cross my heart, but I don't want to cry in front of you."

She smiled. Indecision gnawed at her. He oozed charm, even foggy with pain and hepped up on medicine.

Against her better judgment, she sank back onto the couch.

ဢဢဢ

Brett let his eyelids flutter closed. She stayed. Her struggle showed clear as day on her expressive face, but she stayed.

Thank You, God.

Now maybe something beyond the relentless pain in his side and nose and jaw could pass through his mind. A rustle on the couch stirred him from his thoughts. "I'm not asleep."

"Didn't think you were." She set the glass on the end table and repositioned her foot on the couch.

"It's bothering you?"

"Probably not as much as your injuries." She leaned her head against the back of the couch.

"I'm fine."

"You keep saying that, and maybe in a few months, or several, according to the doctor, you will be." She reached for the medicine bottles on the table beside him.

"Harping on it doesn't help, FYI." He moved his hand to swipe his jaw but thought better of it.

"Why don't you take some of your painkillers and let them start to work while we talk? Here."

She shook a capsule into his palm and offered the glass of water from the side table. Close to a minute later, he swallowed the pill and some water and sagged against the recliner. Last time he was going to move in a while.

Don't talk about the pain. Forget about it. Talk about something, anything else. "So you're up in my old room, huh?"

"Gigi thought I'd be more comfortable in there than on the daybed in Carly's. I think she wanted to brag on all your accomplishments too."

He muttered, "You saw the trophies."

"Yep. All of them through tenth grade."

Was she fishing for more sordid details than bare facts he'd already shared? So what? He knew about her business woes, about clashes with her family. If it made her stay with him a little while longer, what did it matter? He'd be laying himself bare, wide open, but, strangely, he wanted her to know.

"When I dropped out of high school."

She nodded.

No raised eyebrows. No smirk.

"Because my grandfather died."

Another nod. "It must have been a rough time."

"Made worse by being an idiot."

"People have regrets, but your story has a happy ending."

"Does it?" A happy ending would be great. What would that look like?

"You have a loving relationship with your family. You're a respected deputy."

Extended family, yes. No one special to help chase away the darkness. To sit and talk about the day. "A wide gap from high school to here. Lots more struggles in between."

"Do you want to talk about those?"

"Do you want to listen?"

"I'll listen to whatever you want to tell me." She pulled a throw pillow into her lap and clasped her hands in front, like she was content to sit with him. Not demanding the story but willing to wait for whatever he wanted to share.

"To understand it, you need to know why we lived with Gigi and Pop. After Shelly left, we had peace in the house. Always the pot stirrer. Drama happened every day with her." He closed his eyes and took a few breaths. "In a way, we were better off without her. At school, a different story. I had plenty of fights defending my family, especially Carly. Until she made me stop. Said she could fight for herself." He laughed and immediately regretted the quick movement.

"She sounds feisty."

"Yep."

"So you have a close relationship with your dad."

A tingle in his chest signaled a rusty topic. Peel one layer back and underneath lies another. "I do, but it's different." He'd started this conversation, invited her. No. Almost pleaded with her to stay to hear it. He focused his attention on the empty fireplace. "When I was about twelve, my dad fell off a roof helping a neighbor lay shingles. Had a stroke in the ER. He's in a care facility in Hickory."

A gasp brought his gaze back to her. "That was your appointment in Hickory?"

"Yeah."

"I thought . . ."

"What?"

"Nothing. So the call yesterday morning was about your dad?"

"A ruse. Got me out of the cabin." Clamped his teeth before his aching jaw reminded him not to. "Should've followed my gut. I knew something was off, but . . ." No need bringing up why his instincts were off that morning.

"You thought your dad was in trouble?"

He nodded. "Figured it out too late. Dusty and Skeet already had Gigi."

"I shouldn't have stayed at the clearing as long as I did."

"Hey. Don't go there. It's over."

"I could say the same to you."

"What do you mean?"

"Sounds like you're kicking yourself for not figuring out the ruse, but you couldn't know Dusty and Skeet would find your cabin, kidnap us again."

"That's what I can't figure out. They aren't smart enough to figure out tomorrow's lunch much less find out where my dad stays or the cabin's address. I don't talk about either of those two things."

Her eyes met his, then skittered toward her lap. "You must have told somebody or else how would they find out? You used a false name with them, right?"

"Yeah. Makes the mystery more puzzling."

"Lots of information is available online now. How many people knew you were undercover? Could they get your real name from one of those people?"

"No. I trust them with my life. Have to undercover." His brain was spinning with the who and why and how, but his eyelids weighed heavier every second. Medicine must be kicking in. He'd just rest his eyes for a minute, then think about Dusty and Skeet some more.

A whoosh sounded. Somebody moved on Gigi's couch. Mary Wade. He peeked through leaden eyelids. She was leaving. He grabbed her nearest hand and grunted with the effort.

"Thank you for staying with me. And for making me take the meds. It's helping." He rubbed his thumb over her wrist, the only movement that didn't hurt him.

"You're welcome. Can I get you anything before I go upstairs?"

Besides a hug so that I can lose myself in the scent of sunscreen or another kiss to block the incessant pain or how about just keep staying here with me? "Yes. One question. How did you think to put that chair leg on Dusty's hand?" The side of his mouth tipped up.

She snatched her hand back. His hand landed on the arm with a soft thud. "Are you teasing me about the way I got us out of that situation?"

"Uh uh. Best criminal-nabbing idea ever. If there's a list of those ideas, I'll submit it."

"Very funny. I just prayed like crazy. I didn't know what to do. I was shaking so hard, Dusty even mentioned it."

"And yet he obeyed you."

She crossed her arms. "He's a follower."

Brett closed his eyes. "You're a piece of work."

"I hope that's a good thing."

"It's a good thing." A real good thing.

"Get some rest."

"I'd rest better if you stayed."

She paused at the bottom of the stairs. "Wouldn't Gigi love finding us asleep in the morning? I'll sleep upstairs."

In my bed.

Chapter 34

A multicolored butterfly flitted around the arm of the purple chair in front of the frozen yogurt shop. Mary Wade checked her watch. Tess was fifteen minutes late. As she fished her phone from her purse to text the teenager, she spotted the girl's hand-me-down sedan zip into a parking place near the end of the row.

Her body language as she sauntered up the parking lot indicated the conversation might be a difficult one, especially considering the topic Mary Wade had to broach with her. "Hey, girl. Ready for a treat?"

She shrugged. "I guess."

Mary Wade pulled Tess in for a hug, but the teen remained stiff and unresponsive. "I haven't had frozen yogurt in ages. My cup will probably weigh the most."

"Yeah, well. I'm not hungry."

"Since when do you have to be hungry to eat frozen yogurt? Come on. Let's go." With one arm around the younger girl's shoulder, Mary Wade pulled her through the doorway. Ten minutes later, she licked strawberry frozen yogurt sprinkled with sliced almonds and kiwi slices from her electric blue spoon. Tess sat with her purple spoon stuck in the middle of a minute dollop of cotton candy flavored yogurt.

"Okay, Miss Tess. Give it up. What's going on? As much as you love coming here, you refused at first. Now, you're here with about a tablespoonful in your cup. You haven't even had the first taste. Spill."

Tess twitched one side of her mouth, dragged the spoon through the yogurt, then through her teeth, and glared at her boss. Mary Wade slid a napkin toward the teen. "You're being deliberately snarky tonight which isn't like you at all. And I haven't even mentioned the shop. Tell me what's the matter."

"You said God would always help. You said God would never give you more than you could handle."

Oh, no. A spiritual conversation. For several months, Tess had asked questions, probed her answers, and asked more questions. Just before the trip to Bandon, she'd seemed more willing to listen, more open to accepting the truths she read in the Bible Mary Wade had given her at Easter. Something had happened. Something enormous had rocked her searching faith.

Dear God, I need some help here. Wisdom, please.

Mary Wade pushed the cup of yogurt to the side of the table. "Right."

"Well, that's a crock."

"So what happened?"

For several seconds, Tess worked her jaw. Contemplating keeping the secret? She raised her dark brown eyes in a defiant gaze. "Remember the car accident last April?"

"Of course." The accident had claimed the life of one of the sax players in the high school band. The brand new driver, a sixteen-year-old drummer, had survived, along with another student. All of them had been active in their church youth group.

"Randall killed himself."

Mary Wade's heart lurched. The driver.

"So I guess God did give him more than he could handle. Or he'd still be living."

"Tess," Mary Wade closed her hand over the fist curled around a napkin. "Let's pray."

Tess snatched her hand away. "I don't want to pray. I want to hear what you have to say now."

"I don't have anything to say. It's a horrible story."

"Oh, so you don't have any more platitudes about what God can do?" Tears shimmered in Tess's eyes.

"They aren't platitudes to me. I believe what I've said to you because I've experienced God's help first hand. I've never been in Randall's shoes. I can't image what he felt like, nor do I want to. But I know from my life, when I pray, God hears me and helps me." The reality of what she'd just said hit her square in the head.

Had she prayed about her finances? Completely surrendered them to God?

"You really believe everything you've said to me?" One lone tear escaped her eyelash. She flicked it away with a black-tipped finger.

"I really do. I don't know why these horrible things happened, but I do know that God will help us if we allow Him to."

Tess cocked her head. "We have control over God?"

"Of course not, but we have free will. We can ask God into a situation, or we can leave Him out."

"So you're saying it's Randall's fault because he didn't ask God into his situation?"

"Don't put words into my mouth, Tess. I didn't know Randall at all. What I do know is God's bigger than any problem I face. He's the creator of the universe. The God who measured the waters of the earth in the palm of His hand. The God who held the dust of the earth in a basket. He can take anything I throw at Him."

Tess shook her head. "All these words sound so easy."

"You're right. Speaking words is easy. Living them is much harder, but these words are backed up with truth. Don't just listen to me. Keep reading your Bible. You'll find out for yourself."

Another tear. "Why does it have to be so hard?" She wiped her fingers under her nose.

"We're not in heaven yet, Tess. We're going to have hard times, but Christians have a Helper."

She pushed away from the table. "You always have a comeback."

Mary Wade pressed her lips together. "I don't mean my words to sound like empty comebacks. Everything I tell you is the truth. I want you to believe it. Whether you want me to or not, I'm going to keep praying for you and for Randall's family and friends too."

"But you don't even know them."

"God does."

ഇഇഇ

Mary Wade stretched the tape across the box of toddler dresses, set it on top of the one marked "accessories." She swiped a tear before it had a chance to wet her cheek.

"Are you sure you have to close up shop?" Jack half sat, half leaned against the wooden stool in the middle of his booth at the craft warehouse. A sling of camouflage fabric supported his arm.

"The tale was written in the receipts I memorized before the break-in. If I had any doubt, the last few days would seal the deal. Tess sold two pieces during the time I was away, including a five-dollar headband. I haven't done much better." She opened another empty box. "My lease is up at the end of the month. The rent goes up forty-three percent. How is that even legal? It's highway robbery."

"Mary Wade, you've been under a lot of stress lately. Do you think you should make an important decision right now?" He shaved a rectangle of mahogany to match a piece of cherry wood, the pieces forming part of a three-by-four-inch wooden box.

She packed smocking plates into the box. "I don't have a choice. I can't afford the increase."

"Maybe we could talk to the owner. Ask for reprieve, a grace period. I'd go with you."

Love for this man squeezed her insides. Always positive. Always for her. "He has a business to run too. Maybe I should take a break from this shop and focus on my online business."

"Sounds like a smart plan, but I'll miss you."

"Me too. We'll still grab a coffee every now and then so you can give me sage Christian counsel, right?"

He nodded. "Speaking of Christian counsel, have you heard from Brett? How's he doing?" He blew dust off the block of wood strips he held, slid his finger over the edge.

Caught off guard by the new topic, she ducked her head to regroup. "I haven't heard directly from him and don't expect to unless I'm needed to testify. I'm not sure if he'd call or if I'd get the message from a court representative. No other reason to hear from him."

Jack raised his eyebrow. "Oh?" He opened his mouth to speak, hesitated, then closed it again.

She ignored him. "But I text with Gigi almost every day and talk on the phone. She's an unexpected blessing out of all of this. She says Brett's doing okay. He's back to work, tying up loose ends."

"From all you've told me, he's a determined man. He'll knot 'em but good."

"Aloha, sweetheart! Hello, Jack."

She whipped toward the greeting. Agnes. Clothed in a bold skirt fashioned in Hawaiian fabric and a lime green flowing blouse, her godmother wrapped her in a cocooning hug. An exotic scent sharpened her senses.

Peace descended on Mary Wade. "You smell good."

"Like it? It's called Island Dreams. I mixed it myself at a perfume factory on my spectacular trip. I especially love the notes of spice and rose blossoms."

"Mmm. It's wonderful."

"Great because I also mixed a bottle for you."

"Thank you. You look fabulous as always, but I told you,

you didn't have to come. Poor Ellen. Did you find a replacement for you at her yarn shop?"

Agnes made a face and waved her hand. "She's got plenty of help. She lets me hang around the store because I can knit and crochet. Plus, she thinks it keeps my mind off losing my dear Henry." She leaned close to share a secret. "I love the shop, but I think about Henry every day. Fifty-four years of memories don't evaporate with beautiful yarns and patterns."

Mary Wade nodded. "Got it. I'm fine. Really."

"Of course you are. You'll be better than ever, too, once you have a dose of me. Just wait."

Mary Wade laughed and surrendered to another hug. A dose of her godmother was exactly the ticket. Agnes had always championed her, encouraged and supported her dreams. Agnes loved her unconditionally.

Surveying the booth, Agnes planted her hands on her hips. "What do we need to do first?"

Mary Wade's phone buzzed on the counter. She read the screen. Brett. Electric flashes zipped up and down her body. Two weeks with no word and now a call. Must be something to do with the case.

"Who is it? You look like you've seen a ghost."

Not a ghost. "Brett."

"Well answer it, girl." Agnes swiped the screen and held the phone toward Mary Wade's ear.

"Hello." She pressed her lips together, frustrated with the breathlessness surrounding that one word. Agnes moved to Jack's booth, picked up a miniature old-fashioned boot. He said something to her, and they both laughed.

"How ya doin'?"

"Fine. How are your ribs?" How are your ribs? That's all she could think of?

"Better. I can breathe now without wanting to break something else."

"Well, that's good. I think."

Silence. Why did he call? What else could she talk about?

"Gigi sends her love."

"I talked with her yesterday. She sounds like she's recovered from the ordeal."

"She's resilient. Once she realized I didn't need a full-time nurse, she got right back into her volunteer stuff." He drew a breath. "How 'bout you? You recovered?"

"Daphne's still trying to talk me out of taking a concealed carry class."

Laughter bounced into her ear. "Ow. That still hurts."

"Sorry."

"You want to get a gun? For real?"

"I didn't say that, but Gigi's sure came in handy. Knowing how to use one might be good."

"Yeah."

More silence.

"Hey, well. I gotta go. Just wanted to check on you. Take care."

Her stomach twisted. That's it? "You too."

The call ended, leaving her with a shining screen and deflated hopes. Sadness enveloped her. He didn't call because he missed her. He wanted to check on her. He felt responsible for her.

Agnes moved back into the almost-empty booth, scrutinizing her face. "What's up, sweetie?"

"Nothing. Brett just checked on me."

"When're you telling me more about this Brett fellow?"

She shook her head. "Nothing to tell." She swept the booth with clear eyes. "The rest of those outfits can fit in the last two boxes. Let's fill those and go home. Everything will be finished here."

Like whatever had been between her and Brett.

Twenty minutes later, a wayward garment tag fluttered to

the concrete floor before Mary Wade could catch it. She bent to retrieve it, and tears rushed to the front of her eyes. She held the bent position a couple of extra seconds to get control of her emotions. "Well, I think that's it." She stuck the tag in her pocket, hugged Jack, and headed for the door without looking back.

Chapter 35

As every signpost flashed on her way to Gigi's house, Mary Wade counted her blessings.

Catawba County line. She counted Agnes. Three days with Agnes equaled an enormous blessing. Besides bringing several gifts for her from the cruise, Agnes also came armed with chocolate peanut M&M's, Reese's cups, and Snickers bars. She'd stopped for strawberry and chocolate almond ice cream, the full fat kind, on the way home from the craft booth.

She'd allowed Mary Wade to cry about the closed shop. When the original reason for tears morphed into missing Brett tears, Agnes opened a new box of tissues and grabbed another handful of M&M's. A true friend.

"You know," Agnes crunched a chocolate peanut and swallowed, "I don't think you were this upset when you and Robert broke up." She made air quotations around "broke up."

Mary Wade wiped her nose that felt twice its size. "Why did you put fake quotation marks around 'broke up?'"

"Because I never saw you and Robert as a couple to begin with. I think you kept company with each other, but I never felt any kind of passion from you when you talked about him. But with this Brett fellow . . ."

"I haven't said a word."

"You've said plenty, dear. You've described his magnificent physique so that I even got a little hot and bothered. You've related most of the conversations you had with him. Did you forget you shared how you felt when he wrapped your sprained ankle?"

"Okay. Okay." Mary Wade tossed the soggy tissue into a wicker garbage basket. "Please remember I'm under duress. I just closed up shop. Take everything I'm saying with a grain of salt."

"I know, honey. But you need to be honest with yourself. You seem to be mourning more than the shop." She picked up the empty ice cream bowls. "Maybe you don't have to mourn over Brett."

Another road sign passed. Another blessing to count. She counted Agnes again. The eternal optimist. Always looked for the best. Always kept hope alive.

But the truth remained. Brett had called once in three weeks. To check on her. Not to ask to see her again.

Two miles to Valleymore and spending the day with Gigi. Another blessing. When they'd talked earlier in the week, Gigi suggested attending the arts and crafts fair in Asheville. She'd pack a lunch, and they'd make a day of strolling through the fair. Gigi insisted on an overnight visit so she could attend church with her the next morning.

When she pulled into the driveway, Gigi waved to her from the front porch. "Keep going around back into the garage. We can pack the picnic basket from there."

Mary Wade followed the driveway and inched into the empty bay beside a red Passat. Gigi appeared at the back door, her fingers pressing a control pad. The garage door rolled down behind her. At Mary Wade's questioning gaze, Gigi shrugged. "Silly me. Habit, I guess."

"Come in. Come in." Gigi enveloped her into a tight hug. "You look beautiful as usual. What a great day this is going to be. The weather is perfect for a picnic. Did you eat breakfast? Because we don't need to leave right away. In fact, let's sit and chat a few minutes."

The older woman's barrage of words amused Mary Wade. "How much coffee have you had this morning? Taking a few minutes before we go might be prudent." She peeked into the basket waiting on the counter.

"One cup, same as always. I used my handy dandy mini coffee maker Brett gave me a couple of years ago." She cocked her head. "Speaking of Brett, have you heard from him lately?" She glanced at the gold watch encircling her wrist.

Mary Wade paused in checking the basket's contents and studied Gigi. "I thought we were talking about how fidgety you are this morning. But, yes, he called last week to check on me."

"Oh, how nice. He's a nice boy. Calls to check on me too. Wasn't that nice of him to call you?"

"Yes, Gigi." Mary Wade arched a brow. "Are you okay?"

"Well, actually, I think I'll sit for a minute." She glanced out the side window before sinking into a kitchen table chair. "I do feel a bit woozy."

"Can I get you something?"

"No, just sit with me. I'm sure I'll feel better soon."

Mary Wade slid back the opposite chair and sat. "We don't have to go to Asheville today. Let's visit here."

"I don't want you to miss the fair." She tipped her head. "How's your ankle, by the way?"

"Much better. I hardly notice it, but I still keep it wrapped. I'll probably have to take breaks today."

"No problem, honey."

The doorbell rang. Gigi's eyebrows jumped above her blue eyes. "Ooh. A visitor. On a Saturday morning." Smiling, she headed toward the kitchen door. "I'll be right back."

A deep voice mingled with Gigi's high-pitched, agitated one.

Brett. A tingling skipped up her neck. A puzzle piece fell into place.

Matchmaking.

She rose, pushing the chair behind her. Slow down, heart. Breathe in. Breathe out.

Her feeble admonitions to her body failed to prepare herself to see him again. His wide eyes proved he hadn't known she'd be in his grandmother's kitchen.

"Gigi." Her lone word sounded like a plea.

Why are you doing this? Brett is not interested. Couldn't have made it plainer. A vise seized her insides from her stomach to her breastbone.

"Look who's here, Mary Wade." Gigi tugged him into the kitchen by his arm. "What a great turn of events."

Brett's head whipped to his grandmother. "What are you talking about?"

"Mary Wade and I are supposed to go to Asheville for the crafts fair today. See, I've got a picnic basket ready for lunch." Gigi reclaimed her kitchen chair and rubbed her forehead with one hand. "But I don't really feel up to it today." She fanned her face with the other.

He scrubbed his jaw. He'd removed the medical tape from across his nose, and the swelling had receded, but a few patches of slightly darker skin told the tale of the broken nose. "I thought we were supposed to go over your living will."

Gigi touched her cheek with her hand. "Did we schedule that for this morning?"

Brett crossed his arms in front of his chest. "You called me last night to confirm."

"Silly me." She shrugged. "Well, it's a good thing you're here. You can take Mary Wade to Asheville, and she won't miss the fair." She reached for her friend and pulled her close. "I'll stay here and get over whatever it is that's grabbed hold of me. Please do me this favor. I'll be embarrassed to death if she misses all the fun on my account."

"Gigi, this isn't—"

"Grandmother, I'm not—"

Their words tumbled over each other.

Mary Wade smoothed the shoulder seam of Gigi's blouse, struggling to keep her hands off the meddling woman's neck. "We can plan another outing when you're feeling better." If only the floor would open and accept her as a sacrifice to all the grandmothers who ever tried to fix up their bachelor grandsons with single females. "We planned today for us." She sought his eyes. That's code for I didn't know about this setup either. "I'm sure Brett has other plans after he helps you with the will." She hoped Gigi heard the determination in her voice.

He opened his mouth to speak, but Gigi beat him to it. "He's fine. I invited him to lunch, so I know he's free through about one o'clock. Surely you didn't schedule anything else today. We didn't know how long the will would take right, Brett?"

"No, but—"

There's the but. He has plans.

"Wonderful." Gigi clasped her hands. "I have the basket all packed. We'll put the cold food in the cooler, and you'll be set to have a marvelous day."

Brett sighed, raked his hand through his hair. "Cooler still out in the utility room?"

"Sure thing. Aren't you a dear to retrieve it without being asked?"

Mary Wade waited until the back door clicked closed before pouncing on Gigi. "Why in the world did you do this, Gigi? Surely you couldn't miss how much he's dreading this outing."

"You two need a day without bullets flying or guns waving or broken bones. You need just a fun day."

Mary Wade pressed her temples. "It won't be fun for him. It's a crafts fair. Today will be a fiasco. He'll be bored out of his mind." Think. Think of some way to get out of this train wreck.

Gigi waved away her protests. "Don't judge a book by its cover. He's a skilled wood carver. They'll be plenty of booths with other crafts besides yarn and needle work."

"I know he's talented. I've seen the chess set he's carving, but—"

Gigi clutched her arm. "He showed you those pieces?" One corner of her mouth tipped up.

"Sometimes he'd carve while I sketched or crocheted."

"Uh huh."

Mary Wade scowled. "What does that—"

The back door swung open. "It was under a box of canned tomatoes. I thought you weren't canning this year."

"Home canned tomatoes are the best. Now, let's pack the food, so you can take off."

ℬℬⱰⱰ

Silence reigned in his car. A faint hint of sunscreen floated from his passenger, made him smile. Brett chanced a peek at her. Staring straight ahead. Clamped jaw. Tension vibrated across the console. At this rate, today would be a disaster. Make some conversation or the car ride would be miserable.

"You think you're up for walking through a craft fair?"

"I have a walking brace and substantial shoes." A subtle dig at his comments about her flip-flops and sandals? "But I'll probably have to take some breaks." She drew in a breath. "Look. I get that you don't want to do this, so what about dropping me off, then picking me up later."

He merged onto the highway. "And suffer the wrath of my grandmother? No can do."

A blush bloomed in her cheeks, and she dropped her gaze.

"Wait. I didn't mean it the way that sounded." Way to make her feel worse. "That'd be like lying to my grandmother. Can't do that."

She chewed on her bottom lip.

"FYI. I didn't know about today. I believed Gigi when she invited me."

He set the cruise control. "We've both been bamboozled by

my grandmother. I get that you're not thrilled about the change in plans."

She widened her eyes. "I never said that."

"You didn't have to. Body language, remember?"

"That's not it. I'm looking forward to Asheville. You, on the other hand, probably have ten other things you'd rather be doing today."

He checked the mirrors and relaxed in his seat. "Not true. I'm open to new adventures. I don't like being blindsided like what Gigi just did, but if she'd asked me straight out like a regular person, I'd've said yes."

"Really?"

He nodded. "Why didn't you mention it the other day when we spoke?"

"Honestly?"

"Always."

"Your call caught me off guard. I couldn't think of anything to say beyond finding out about your injuries."

"Why'd it catch you off guard? You didn't think I'd call you?"

"It'd been two weeks. So . . ."

Brett adjusted his grip on the steering wheel. "You didn't call either."

"I don't usually pursue men, especially ones who think of me as a mistake."

He glanced at her, but the passing scenes outside her window consumed her attention. Crimson patches crept up the side of her neck. "Mistake?"

No answer.

"And anyway, who said anything about pursuing anybody. How 'bout just calling to see how I'm doing?"

"Gigi enjoyed keeping me informed about how well you followed doctor's orders, and you strike me as someone who might not appreciate being called by a woman."

"You don't think men like being called by women?"

"You like to be in charge. Your ego might be stroked by a phone call from a woman, but you probably wouldn't take her seriously."

"Is that why you didn't call?" He grinned. "So that I'd take you seriously?"

She huffed. "We're talking about you, not me. And, I said, Gigi kept me updated."

"Hmm. Wouldn't call just to hear my voice, huh?"

"Look, you arrogant—" She turned to him, ready for the skirmish.

He burst out laughing, then checked himself. "Sorry, but that was too easy. I promise I won't do it again. It still hurts to laugh."

"Good."

Chapter 36

"Oh, no. I left my hat." Mary Wade shut the car door behind her and fished through her tiny strap purse for the travel tube of sunscreen.

"No problem. We'll get one."

Her budget had no line item for an extra hat when a perfect one waited back in her car. In Gigi's garage. "I'll be fine. I'll just put on more sunscreen." She craned her neck as she tried to see her reflection in the window. "Any smudges not rubbed in?"

Brett touched her shoulder. "Let me see." He tipped her chin with his knuckles. "Yep. You missed a spot." He ran his fingers along the side of her cheek, met her gaze, and smiled. "Got it. You're good to go."

No. First, her breath had to return to normal. A terrible sign. Less than an hour into the day, and she already tingled at his touch. Already wanted to read more into this outing than reality supported.

Being with her wasn't his idea. He was here to satisfy his grandmother. If she repeated that mantra all day long, maybe she'd arrive back at Gigi's with her heart unscathed.

He grabbed her hand and pulled her toward the square packed with tents. "Come on. Let's get this party started."

She fell into step beside him. Why did he grab her hand? What did that mean? Something? Nothing? "Sounds like you're trying to convince yourself to have fun."

Grinning, he squeezed her hand. "No need. We're gonna have fun."

They crossed a street and strolled by three booths. Still his hand surrounded hers. "Bingo." He pointed ahead to a booth with straw bags and straw hats. "Just what we wanted." He stepped up his pace until they found a tent with all shapes and sizes of straw hats hanging around the perimeter. "Ta da. I knew we'd find a hat for you. Which one do you like?"

Which one? All the hats were beautiful works of art. Of course. Hats at a craft fair. How to explain that they'd be too expensive for her budget without embarrassing herself?

"Brett, these hats are handmade. Beautiful, but expensive. I have a perfectly good one languishing on my back seat. I can't justify buying another one."

"Note to self, she's thrifty with money."

Thrifty out of necessity.

"This hat will be my treat."

"No."

"Here try this one." He chose a dark stained, tightly woven style with a thin, brown band. Not exactly a match to her outfit.

The hat settled and covered her eyes. "This one's more your speed."

He lifted the brim and peeked underneath. "Are you saying I have a big head?"

"If the hat fits." Her mouth twitched.

"Funny girl." He placed it on his head. "Yeah, I admit you're right. Much better fit." He studied the mirror hanging at the corner. "Not half bad. Which one do you like?"

"I can't let you buy me a hat."

"You're not letting me. I know how you feel about your freckles, even though I happen to like them. You need more protection than sunscreen." He turned his attention back to the hats and rubbed his chin. "If you don't choose, I'll have to, and we saw the result of my choice."

271

Her eyes rested on a honey-colored lace weave hat with a black ribbon circling the crown. The black would go with her slate skort and lavender and slate top. He intercepted her gaze and unclipped it from the edge of the tent. "Let's try this one."

As she reached for the price tag, he held it away from her. "Uh uh. Try it on without the price influencing your decision." He set it on her head. "Wait." He hooked her hair behind her ears, his hand lingering on the base of her neck, sending heat to the pit of her stomach. "Nice." He held eye contact. "It looks great to me." He lowered his eyes to her mouth. "How does it feel?"

"Brett? Brett Davis. That is you." A voice snatched her out of the fuzzy state she'd slipped into. His hand fell to his side.

Two women, probably late thirties to mid-forties, strolled toward them from across the street. Dressed in similar black capris and embellished sandals, each carried canvas shopping bags. One with a loose, dark brown braid hanging in front of her shoulder grinned broadly and waved. The other clutched the bag's straps and hosted a blank expression on her round, pale face framed with limp, beige hair.

"Fancy meeting you here, huh?" The friendly one with the braid cuffed him on his shoulder. The other one focused on Mary Wade, giving her a once-over from the straw hat to the tips of her tennis shoes and back again. The corners of her lips moved a millimeter. A smile? If so, the woman's eyes didn't receive the message. The hair on the back of Mary Wade's neck rose. She removed the hat.

Brett stuck his hands in his pockets. "Yeah."

The friendly woman smiled at Mary Wade, glanced back at Brett, again at Mary Wade. She huffed and stuck out her hand. "Hello, I'm Sandy Owens. This is Gwen Fraiser. We work with this guy." She hooked her thumb toward him.

"I'm—"

"This is Mary Wade Kimball." No explanation. No label. At least he didn't say, "A friend of my grandmother's."

272

"Nice to meet you both. Looks like you've found some treasures." She nodded to the bulging bags.

"Yes, we have, and Gwen didn't even want to come today. I had to drag her here with the promise of a visit to the home-made ice cream shop on Laurel Street."

Mary Wade liked this engaging woman. The silent, brooding one? Not exactly. "That sounds like a good idea." She glanced at Brett with a smile.

The silent one stepped forward, eyes zeroed in on Brett. "How're you feeling?"

"Fine, thanks. Still a little tender." He touched his chest.

"Take it easy today. Don't overexert yourself." She glanced at Mary Wade with narrowed eyes.

"Neither of us is up for much exercise today, Gwen, but thanks." He gestured to the ankle brace on Mary Wade's foot. "We'll definitely take it easy."

Gwen clamped her mouth shut. Sandy transferred her bag to the other shoulder. "We'll leave you to it then. We've got a few more stops before ice cream."

Something akin to relief filled Mary Wade as the two women ambled down the street. Opposites attract definitely ruled that friendship.

ഇഉ൝ᑭᑭ

Mary Wade burped the lid of the plastic bowl of chicken salad and returned it to the cooler. "Small world, huh? To meet some of your co-workers here."

"Yeah, how 'bout that?" Brett crunched on a potato chip.

She snagged a branch of grapes. "Sandy seems like a lot of fun. Very positive."

He brushed the crumbs from his hands. "They're both nice people."

Mary Wade popped a grape in her mouth to avoid responding. "Mmm."

Brett arched his eyebrows. "You don't agree?"

"It was interesting meeting them."

"Kind of evading my question?" He shrugged. "Gwen seemed off today, but she's fine. Always nice to me in the office."

"And she was definitely nice to you today. Just didn't engage in the rest of the conversation."

He grinned. "Jealous?"

How to respond to that question? Ignore it. Ignore the flutter in her chest too. She adjusted the new hat, lighthearted at owning such a sweet work of art. Guilt over the price followed immediately after.

"Your hat looks fantastic, by the way. Especially with your hair like that. I'm glad you left it down. You wore it in a ponytail a lot at the cabin."

Another compliment. If only he'd stop acting as if they were on a real date and not something engineered by Gigi's shenanigans.

"Hey. Let's text Gigi a picture of us. She'll love it." He moved to her side of the picnic table they'd secured near his car when Brett had nixed Gigi's picnic-on-a-blanket idea. "If I could get down to the ground, I'm sure I couldn't get back up. We'd have to call for help." He'd left the blanket in the trunk.

She reached for his phone. "Let me take one of you."

"What fun would that be?" Stretching his arm in front of them, he slid closer to her, close enough to smell a faint scent of aftershave. "Smile, Mary Wade. We're having fun, remember?"

Yes, because Gigi tricked them both into the day trip, but they didn't have to pretend to be a couple. She pushed his arm to his lap. "Let's don't do this."

"Why not?"

"Because I don't feel like doing that to Gigi."

"Doing what? She'd love to see a picture of us."

"Stop saying 'us'."

274

He slid his arm along the top of the weathered picnic table. "Mary Wade, what's up?"

A little boy of about five years old scampered by with a golden retriever, the dad jogging behind. She followed their chase to the swing set at the edge of the park. Brett gently tugged her chin back to him. "Talk to me."

She sighed. "I appreciate the way you appeased your grandmother and brought me here but, please. Let's stop the charade."

Grooves marred his brow. "What charade?"

"The handholding, the compliments, the buying me presents. If you take a picture of us all huddled up together like a real couple, you'll just fan the flames of her schemes."

"And that's a negative thing?"

"Yes, because it's a lie. She needs to know the truth. I've tried, but she won't listen."

"What if I like the compliments and the handholding? What if I want to do it some more?" Capturing her hand, he shifted closer to her. "What if I like being all cuddled up together with you?"

Keep focused. Don't melt into him. Don't fall under his spell.

She wiggled out of his clasp. "No. You called once in three weeks. The only reason you're here today is because Gigi tricked you or guilted you into bringing me. And don't forget…" She pressed her lips together.

"Don't forget what?"

"Nothing." She shook her head. "If we leave now, Gigi won't be disappointed we cut the day short." She reached for the bag of grapes.

He stilled her arm. "Wait. You've brought a lot of charges against me. Give me a chance to answer them, even the one you haven't spoken yet."

She opened her mouth, but he pressed his finger against

it. "Shh. As Gigi says, now is the time for me to speak and you to listen. First, you're right. I should've called. I'm sorry. I was slammed at work, and I'm still trying to find out the connection between Dusty and Skeet and how they knew about my dad, the cabin."

He shrugged. "I admit. Flimsy excuses." He let out a long breath. "I hesitated to call because I had to get over myself not being able to save you and Gigi. Being helpless is kind of sobering. Also, relationships between law enforcement and civilians aren't usually successful. Stressful job and all that. Plus, I didn't know how you'd receive a call. You were kinda in a hurry to get away during our late night talk at Gigi's."

"I—"

He shook his head. "Still my turn. Gigi didn't trick me into coming today. I could have refused. I have a ton of stuff to do at my place, but the thing is, I wanted to come." He locked eyes with her. "I missed you, Mary Wade. I missed sitting by the fire while you sketched and I carved. I missed talking on the back porch." He brushed tendrils from her forehead.

"I was afraid you'd cut and run this morning. I'm glad you didn't." He swiped his thumb across the back of her hand. "Then you didn't snatch your hand out of mine earlier. You let me hold it. And you blush whenever I get close." He inched toward her. "Like now."

Heat crept up her neck. Cursed pale skin. He was close enough to kiss her.

If only he would.

"What was the other problem?"

Another problem? Not kissing her? His thumb, a pendulum across her hand, radiated tingles up her arm. Her brow knitted.

"Please tell me. Let's get everything out in the open. You said, 'And don't forget.'"

She closed her eyes, the humiliation flooding back. "The last night in the cabin. The kiss. You said it—"

"Was a mistake." He nodded. "It was."

Blood rushed in her ears. She pulled her hand from his, scanned the park for an escape route. Where was a sinkhole when you needed one? She could call Daphne to come pick her up. She pushed against the bench, but Brett wrapped his arm around her shoulders, planted his other hand on her knee.

"Wait, please. Hear me out. It was a mistake because even though you weren't officially under my protection, I was responsible for you. Besides being completely unprofessional, kissing you was a bad idea. It muddled my thinking. Case in point, running into that cabin without a plan, without checking the perimeter of the property. What was I thinking?" He wiped his palm over his jaw. "I wasn't. If I'd been clear-headed, I'd've seen the truck. I'd've called for backup. I wouldn't have been blindsided."

"But everything worked out fine."

"If by fine you mean you and Gigi terrorized, a few broken ribs, a busted nose—"

She touched his forearm. "All of us got out safely. And the way I see it, I'm closer to evening the score."

Furrows lined his forehead. "What score?"

"You've saved my life twice. I've saved yours once."

"Ah. Thank you, by the way."

"Now maybe you don't have to worry I'm in danger of falling for my rescuer slash hero slash knight in shining armor. Because if you play that card with me, I'll have to play it also." She arched a brow.

A slow grin stretched across his face. "Okay. Got it." He threaded his fingers through hers, palm matching palm. "How's your ankle holding up? You ready to shop some more?"

She didn't care what they did as long as they spent the afternoon together. She flexed her foot, felt a familiar twinge. "What about you? You can't be looking forward to more walking."

"I'm looking forward to this afternoon with you." His frank interest in her made her stomach flip.

"Wow. Silver eyes. Silver tongue. I'll have to be careful around you."

"No, you don't. I told you. I mean what I say."

"Why don't we skip the walking part and drive the Blue Ridge Parkway for a while? It's beautiful in any season."

"Sounds good to me. You and Gigi won't be disappointed?"

"She's thrilled we're spending the day together. I wasn't planning to buy anything today anyway."

"You want to get some of that famous ice cream first?"

And chance running into Miss Congeniality again? No, thank you. "We've got Gigi's chocolate chip cookies and grapes. I'm fine if you are." She turned toward the picnic basket.

"Hey, wait a minute. Just so we're clear." He swooped his head toward her, captured her lips in a quick kiss. "That wasn't a mistake." He slid off her hat and tipped her chin back, combing his fingers through her hair and cradling her head. His silver eyes had darkened to a stormy gray. "I'm not making a mistake now either." As he lowered his mouth, she swayed toward him.

෨෨෨෪෪

Moving slowly and tenderly, Brett pressed his lips against Mary Wade's. Take it easy. Treat her special. Let her know right here with her was where he wanted to be.

Her fingertips skimmed the stubble on his cheek, slid around his neck under the collar of his golf shirt. Her touch sent a thrill through him, making him heady, reminding him of his drinking days. She leaned into him, sighing somewhere down in her throat. The pleasure gripped him with a force that shocked him.

Relishing the feel of her in his arms, Brett spread his hand at the small of her back, wanted her closer, urged her toward him, but the bench wasn't yielding. The bench. They sat at a picnic table. In a park. In full view of children and teens and grandparents. He dragged his mouth from hers and twisted away.

Wrong move. A knife sliced into his side. He sucked in a breath as she shrank out of his embrace.

She watched him with wide eyes, her chest heaving with ragged breathing. She pressed her fingers against her mouth. "Looks like that kiss was a mistake too."

"Not. On your. Life." He winced his way through the words. "Moving away from you. That's what did it." He braced his arm on the table, concentrating on blowing the pain away. "Give me a minute?"

She glanced away, fidgeting with her blouse. She was retreating. He could feel it. He ground his teeth and reached for her. "I'm fine really. The pain grabs me sometimes when I move too quick. It still surprises me." He found the soft space behind her ear. "But I'm getting better now. Much better." Especially if now included the beautiful woman sitting beside him, still affected by his kisses. He brushed his thumb across her lips.

"You went as white as a sheet just now. That's some kind of pain if it can still drain the color from your face." She covered his hand with hers. "What if I drive us back to Gigi's, and you can call out orders from her recliner the rest of the afternoon."

He barked a laugh, then grimaced. "Not happening. I'm spending the afternoon with you. Alone. Not with Gigi hovering and sighing."

She smiled then, wide and happy, turned her mouth to his palm and kissed it. The zing from that kiss skittered to the pit of his stomach. Chased away the lingering pain. Did she know what her touch did to him?

He pushed off from the bench. "Let's go. Got more fun coming, right?"

She nodded and grabbed the basket.

He caught her arm. "Wait." Cupping her cheek, he kissed her again. "No mistake. Remember that."

Chapter 37

The elevator seemed unnecessarily slow descending from the fourth-floor rec room. Mary Wade tapped her toe as the doors opened on every floor. She amused herself by daydreaming of Brett and anticipating their upcoming date.

She couldn't hide her happiness from the crochet ladies, but she wasn't ready to talk about it yet. It was too new. They'd tried to wrangle it out of her, but she resisted. She'd tell them later and enjoy it. But right now, the idea of Brett was hers alone.

She smiled at how he'd asked her out. They'd played it cool with Gigi, admitted they'd had a fun day but didn't reveal how much, how their relationship had changed from friends with an interesting background to something more. Before he left his grandmother's, they'd lingered on the front porch, his hands on her shoulders. Although they'd spent the day together, her nerves jangled like a fifteen-year-old's on a first date.

He trailed a finger along her collar bone. "I had fun today."

"Me too."

"I want to see you again, not because you need to be protected and not because Gigi finagled us into it. I want to ask you out on a real date. Pick you up and get to know you better. Without craziness or other people around." He shoved his hands in his pockets. "What do you think?"

"I think I'd like that."

He smiled and stepped closer to her, slid his arms around

her waist. "Are you free Monday night? I could get reservations at the Lamplighter. I've heard it's a great restaurant."

"One of the best in Charlotte."

"Great. I want our first official date to be special." He kissed her temple. "So I'll call you with the details. Okay?" And he'd sealed the deal with a scorching kiss that heated her cheeks even now.

As she approached her Honda, a white flier fluttered under her windshield wiper. Another coupon for pizzas? She snatched it free and unfolded it with one hand, unlocking the car with the other. Images on the page jumbled like dancing cartoon bubbles. No pizza coupon. She blinked and focused. Cut-out magazine letters formed the words, BACK OFF. The keys fell to the asphalt as she spun in a circle, surveying the parking lot. Was this a joke?

She checked other windshields, hoping this message might be the beginning of a new marketing blitz for some new something. Empty windshields. Hers was the only one to receive this message. Back off from what? She scrambled for her keys, concentrated on sliding the shaking key into the lock. Safe behind the locked doors, she gripped the steering wheel, searched the parking lot.

Nothing looked out of place. Must be some sort of game with teenagers. They'd seen a note made of magazine letters on TV and wanted to try it. The words weren't really a threat like BACK OFF or what? We'll kidnap you?

This was a joke. Unfortunately, teens had chosen her car, but it had nothing to do with Dusty and Skeet. They were in jail.

She tossed the hateful page into the backseat. Out of sight. Out of mind.

A few hours later, as she shared a chocolate mousse with Brett, an image of the flier floated through her mind, but she banished it back to her car. Again. Nothing was going to ruin her perfect first date. It was a silly piece of paper. She'd throw it away. Never give it a second thought.

She'd focus on the cleft in Brett's chin, on his eyes reflecting the same kind of excitement fluttering in her chest, on anticipating another date with him.

❧❧❦❦

A pen popped against his knuckles. "Earth to Brett. Are you here, buddy?"

Brett blinked. Tony's office. Not the Lamplighter. Focusing on Tony, he erased the silly grin that had found a permanent home on his face for the past two days. Ever since their first real date. Ever since Mary Wade had agreed to another one. This lightness inside him felt new. Different, but not in a negative way. Different in a way that made him want to grab it and hold tight.

"I don't know who she is, but she must be something. Haven't seen you smile much, much less grin like a school boy." Tony raised his eyebrows. "Care to fill me in?"

Brett swiped his jaw. "Respectfully, no."

"Ha ha. Got it." Tony straightened and rolled the chair under his desk. "Everything looks kosher. Glad to have you back. Any updates on how those guys found you?"

"They both claim getting information from the Internet at the library." Brett shook his head. "The library. From there they connected dots and asked questions at the right places. I can't see them opening a book much less a library door, but they're sticking to the story."

"Right. Hey, do me a favor as you walk out. Take this down to Sandy." Tony slid a folder across his desk. "Thanks. And try to cheer up, okay?" He grinned. "I'm looking forward to meeting her."

Brett caught himself humming the Willie Nelson tune playing when he drove Mary Wade home the other night. He'd never live this down if he didn't rein in his emotions. He bit the inside of his cheek to quell another smile as he neared the administration office.

Sandy's head popped up from her computer screen when he entered the office. "Good morning, Mr. Sunshine." She stood, stretching her back. "What brings you down here with that enormous smile plastered all over your handsome face?"

Note to self. Biting-the-cheek trick doesn't work. "It's a beautiful day." He handed her the folder. "From Tony."

She accepted the folder without removing her gaze from Brett. "Uh huh. And did you enjoy the rest of the craft fair last weekend? With Mary Wade, right?"

Despite himself, the corners of his mouth tipped up again. "Yeah. It was all right."

"Just all right, huh? And have you seen her since then?"

He fingered a silver-framed photograph of her husband and children. "No comment."

"The twinkle in your eye tells me you have."

He grinned. "You angling for a detective spot?"

Shattering glass demanded their attention at the back of the room. Gwen, color flushing her cheeks, stood in the middle of glass shards and spilled coffee. "It slipped." She gestured to the broken carafe at her feet.

Gwen's color intensified. She'd either start crying or explode. Brett moved to her. "Hey. Accidents happen. Let's make sure you don't have any shards on your feet." He knelt in front of her sandals. "Looks good." He offered his hand. "Step over here."

Sandy hung up her phone. "Maintenance is on the way."

Brett reached for the glass. "I can get the biggest pieces."

"Stop." Gwen's loud shriek startled both Brett and Sandy. "You'll cut yourself."

"Too late. It got me." He brandished his index finger, a trail of blood beginning its trek to the knuckle.

"I have Band-Aids." Gwen pulled him to her desk. "Sit down. I'll fix it." She held onto his wrist as she rummaged through her top drawer.

"Really. I'm fine." Brett tugged his hand backward, but she kept her grip firm.

"I feel responsible." She laid his hand on her desk. "Sit still while I apply a dab of this antibacterial cream."

"You got everything you need, huh?"

"I'm always prepared." She pressed the dot of cream to the Band-Aid and applied the dressing to the wound, examining the bandage, the tip of this finger, the back of his hand.

Sandy joined them. "Need some help?"

Gwen laid her palm over Brett's, a protective shield. "No."

Brett raised his eyebrows to Sandy and glanced back at Gwen. "It's just a nick. I think I'm good." Once again, he pulled for his hand. She wouldn't let go.

Sandy crossed her arms in front of her. "I can't believe how that thing shattered. I thought coffee pots used tough glass."

Gwen's head whipped to her. She stiffened in her chair. "I didn't break it on purpose."

"Of course, you didn't. Must have been defective or something." Sandy swiveled to the door. "Here's maintenance."

Brett narrowed his eyes, patting her hand with his uninjured one. "Thanks a lot, Gwen. I'm good to go now." He extricated his captured hand from her grip. "See you ladies soon."

He left the office, an unsettled feeling cloaking him. Was it his stinging finger or the memory of Gwen's clinging hand that dimmed his morning? He shook off the negative weight.

Pushed his thoughts back to Mary Wade and smiled.

Chapter 38

The spicy scent of Hibachi shrimp filled her car as Mary Wade eased up her driveway. Her stomach growled again. Ten minutes till dinner. Be patient.

Glancing in the rearview mirror, she gathered her purse and dinner. Tess parked right behind her. Perfect timing. The teen seemed much better today than the last time they'd spoken. At least she'd agreed to come to the house for her favorite, crab roll.

As Tess climbed out of her car, Mary Wade raised the plastic box for her to see. "Got your favorite. Just like you ordered."

"Sweet." She gave Mary Wade a one-armed hug. "I'll even share." She squeezed Mary Wade's shoulder. "That's the kind of friend I am."

"No, thank you. Raw veggies? Sure. Raw fish? Not happening." They moved toward the stoop.

Tess laughed. "You don't know what you're missing." She pointed at the house. "Hey, look. You got a delivery."

A long, white box rested on the concrete stoop. Flowers from Brett? Mary Wade's heart picked up speed.

Tess reached for the food. "Here. Give me the goodies, and you get the box."

"Ooh. It's heavier than I expected." Mary Wade crooked her arm over the box and unlocked the front door. When Brett brought her home after the Lamplighter, he'd asked her to a movie on Friday night which had seemed forever away. Flowers would be a welcome mid-week treat and a great excuse to call him. A grin curved into her cheeks.

"Come on. Open it. Let's see what kind of flower man this Brett dude is."

Mary Wade cocked her head. "How do you know they're from Brett?" She lobbed her keys onto an end table.

"Oh. So you have another admirer, huh?"

"I'll never tell." Mary Wade lifted the top, and an odd odor wafted from the box. She pulled back the tissue paper, screamed, and dropped the box. Frogs, fat ones and little ones, jumped and climbed over each other. The entire bottom of the box moved with damp, green frogs. Two giant ones jumped over the edge onto the area rug.

"What the—?" Tess caught the escaped frogs, threw them back with the others, and slammed the lid shut.

Bile rose in Mary Wade's throat. She covered her mouth with her hand and squeezed her eyelids together. Mistake. Frogs squirmed in her mind's eye. She'd hated frogs since a doomed science project in eleventh grade. A shudder rolled through her body. Who could have played such a horrible joke?

Tess scooped up the box. "I'm taking it outside."

Mary Wade nodded. "I think I should call Brett."

"Good idea. Are you okay? Sit down while I get your phone."

She flexed her fingers to calm the trembling before scrolling for Brett's number. She passed by his name twice, once going forward, then backward, before she managed the tremors enough to start the call.

Brett answered on the first ring. "Hey. This is a nice surprise. What's up?" His voice sounded so good, tears pricked behind her eyes.

She bit her lip. "Sorry to bother you." Her voice caught.

"What's wrong?"

"Ahm, Dusty and Skeet are still in jail, right?"

"Mary Wade, where are you? Talk to me." Authority laced his words.

Tess grabbed the phone from her. "Brett? This is Tess, a friend. We're at Mary Wade's. There was a box on her stoop when we got here."

"What kind of box? Is she okay? Put her back on the phone."

"She's shaken up. The flower box was filled with frogs."

"Call the police. I'm on my way."

སཽ⊗⊗⊗⊗

"Why would someone send frogs to you?"

Brett itched to take Mary Wade into his arms, but he settled for sitting beside her, holding her hand while one cop dusted for fingerprints, the other interviewed Mary Wade.

"Good question. She hates them."

All heads whipped to Tess, observing from the Bentwood rocker.

The cop scribbled in his notebook. "That common knowledge?"

The teenager fiddled with the hem of her polka dot skirt. "It's mentioned in the About section of her website." She raised her eyebrows and glanced at Mary Wade. "Remember when we wrote the blurb for it? You thought it was silly to list your likes and dislikes. I thought including them made your site more personal."

"So you mean a disgruntled customer?" Mary Wade shook her head. "But I offer a money-back guarantee."

The cop twirled his pen. "Have you had any returns lately? Some people might want their money and revenge?"

"No. I don't remember a return. Tess?"

The young girl shook her head. "No returns for a while now."

"Well, Ms.—" he checked his pad, "Ms. Kimball, we'll take all this information."

The other cop joined them in the den. "Hey. I found a note in the tissue paper."

Brett bounded off the couch toward the cop. "What does it say?"

"Stay away."

Mary Wade gasped. "There's something else."

Brett swiveled back to her. "What?"

"Someone left a note on my car Monday."

"What kind of note?"

"It said 'Back off.'"

He planted his hands on his hips. "And you're just mentioning this now?"

"It didn't seem important, maybe a little creepy, but I reasoned through it. Dusty and Skeet were locked up. I didn't feel threatened." A tiny bit of color bloomed on her cheeks. "I wanted to think about other things that afternoon."

The tension in his body relaxed at her reference to their date. "Do you still have it?"

Please still have it.

"I threw it into the backseat of my car."

Brett made for the door, but the fingerprinting cop beat him to it. "I'll go. I've got gloves."

"I wanted to be done with all the craziness. I decided it was a sick joke. I'd parked in the wrong space."

He sat beside her, slid his arm around her shoulders. Didn't care what the cop thought. "The craziness is going to be done. We'll get to the bottom of this."

"Ms. Kimball, just a few more questions. These warnings, 'back off' and 'stay away,' may indicate a new endeavor. Have you started something new lately?"

She shook her head. "In fact, I closed my booth at the crafts warehouse." Her lips flattened.

"Well, then, how about old boyfriends? Any of those got a sick sense of humor?"

Brett squeezed his jaw with his fist. "Two threatening notes and a box of frogs don't constitute humor."

"There is one new thing." Tess rocked the chair with the toe of her purple sneakers.

"What?"

She cocked her head to Brett but kept her eyes on Mary Wade. "Him."

The cop raised an eyebrow as his gaze swung from Brett to Mary Wade. "So you two are an item. What about jealous old girlfriends?"

"We're not . . . We've just . . ." Mary Wade sought Brett for help.

Awkward. "What Ms. Kimball is trying to say is that our relationship is new." Did two dates and a promise for another make up a relationship?

"How long is new, and who knows about it?"

Brett cleared his throat. "We've been together twice. We haven't exactly posted it on social media."

The cop scratched more in his pad. "Try to think of people you've mentioned your situation to. We'll check them out as possible suspects."

"My grandmother's over the moon about the arrangement. No need to question her."

The cop pointed to Tess. "This young lady knew about the relationship."

"I knew someone named Brett made Mary Wade grin like crazy. No details." She glanced over to the abandoned takeout bags. "I was hoping to get the scoop over sushi."

Brett's spirits rose at Tess's description of Mary Wade grinning like crazy. Nice. He stole a look at her, but she kept her gaze averted, light color staining her cheeks.

"You live alone here, Ms. Kimball?"

"My roommate is with her fiancé, working on wedding plans."

"Okay then." He closed his pad. "We'll question the neighbors. See if they saw anyone drop off the box." He rose to leave, extending his card. "Let me know if you think of anything else."

ℰℐℰℐℭℛℭℛ

The policeman stuffed his pad into his front pocket, shook hands with Brett, and left. Relieved, Mary Wade sank back into the couch cushions.

Tess considered Brett, planted in the middle of the room, and leaned forward. "I know we were supposed to have dinner, but I sorta feel like a fifth wheel. I'll take a rain check."

"Don't feel uncomfortable on my account."

Mary Wade reached for the teen. "Stay. Eat your sushi. Brett can have my shrimp. I don't want to eat."

"Thanks, but you two should discuss possible suspects. I need to study calc. Unfortunately. Text me if you need anything."

"You already were a great help. I'd completely forgotten about the website information. Maybe we should rethink what I've allowed in that About section."

Brett rested his arm along the mantle. "Good idea."

Tess gathered close to Mary Wade for a hug, tempered her voice for her ears alone. "This guy seems solid. Can't wait to hear about him. And thanks for the other day. Sorry I was such a snot."

Mary Wade made a face. "You know I hate that word."

"Yeah, I do. Didn't make it onto the website, but it got a rise out of you. Sorry about the scare, but you'll be fine. Especially with him around, right?" Tess grinned and wiggled her eyebrows.

"Funny girl. Did you say something about having to study? We'll talk soon, okay?"

Tess nodded, pulled away from Mary Wade, and extended her hand to Brett. "Nice to meet you."

"I'm glad you were here tonight. Thanks for your help."

As she closed the door behind her, the sushi bag in her hand, Brett moved to the couch. "She's right. We do need to talk, but let's take a break first. Did you say shrimp?" He brushed a wisp of hair behind her ear.

"Yes, but I can't swallow a thing. I keep smelling frog musk. Frogs keep jumping in front of my eyes. Big ones. Little ones." She groaned.

He pulled her onto his lap, nestled her head under his chin. "Hey. For the record, frogs creep me out too."

She leaned into him, careful of his tender ribs. "No, they don't."

"Truth. The bulging eyes. The slimy, bumpy skin." He wiggled his shoulders. "No, thanks."

"You're making fun of me."

He captured her face, locking eyes with her. "I never make fun of people's fears. I know what they can do."

She touched his bicep, trailed her hand to his palm. "A capable, powerful guy like you knows about fear?"

"Of course. My mom left. That's scary to a little kid. My dad . . . And former Army, remember? I've stared at the wrong end of a gun barrel." His hand traced lazy patterns on her back. "Knowing someone is targeting you with a sick sense of humor, or worse, scares me. Makes me determined to find him."

He slid his hand up to the nape of her neck. The heat in his touch worked to dispel the tension coiling inside her body. He tugged at the end of her ponytail. "Can we . . .?"

She nodded, and he released the catch on the barrette. "Nice." He combed his fingers through the locks tumbling free.

Tingles zipped along her spine, raised goose bumps on the back of her arms.

"So. You didn't tell anybody about us?"

"Obviously Tess knows something. We were going to talk tonight."

"She knows more than she lets on. She's smart."

"Uh huh."

"It'd been fine if she stayed, but I'm glad she left." He rubbed his thumb over her ear. "Okay. What about Jack? Daphne, at least?"

"Jack knows about you but not the date. Daphne knew about the date, but we haven't had a chance for all the details yet."

"All the details?" His eyes widened. "Sounds promising. But I didn't come up in any more conversations?" The corners of his mouth drooped, but his eyes twinkled. "I'm hurt."

"We've had one date. I wasn't sure one date equaled us status."

Another pout. "You've forgotten so soon? Two dates."

"The craft fair doesn't count. Your grandmother wrangled you into it."

"I think that steamy kiss we shared warrants that day a date."

"Well, if you go by kisses, then the night—" She caught herself, stopping the words out of her mouth but not the blush flashing in her cheeks.

Grinning, he dropped his hand to the small of her back. "Ooh, you're right. The last night at the cabin. Now, that was a kiss."

Emotions from the kiss that had shaken her core were too fresh for teasing. She grabbed the arm of the couch to leverage herself off his lap.

"Wait. Hold up. Look at me." He kept her from rising. When she relaxed, he loosened his arms.

Mary Wade chanced a quick peek. All trace of laughter and teasing had vanished, replaced with a fervent emotion shining in his silver eyes. "We've had an unusual beginning to whatever this is. I know more about you than if we'd just had one or two dates. When you think about it, that's what dates are, right? Times to get to know each other. So by my calculations, we've had a lot of dates. Do you agree or not?"

She nodded.

"So a lot of dates could equal us, don't you think?"

One corner of her mouth tipped up. "Yes." Her eyes lowered to his mouth. "I like those calculations."

ജ്ഞ

She liked those calculations.

Brett's heartbeat kicked up a notch. Until her admission, he hadn't been completely sure of her thoughts. She enjoyed their kisses. She laughed at his jokes, but she didn't gush like most women he'd known. She observed more than talked. His grandpa called it keeping her cards close to her vest. He thought he could read her, then she'd pull something like vamping Dusty to get the best of him.

She was different than any other woman he'd known. That's why she intrigued him. That's why he wanted to hang around, get to know her more. That's why he'd take it slow, follow her lead.

And right now her gaze zeroed in on his mouth, inviting him to kiss her again?

He craned his neck inches toward her and waited. She framed his face and brushed her lips against his. As much as he wanted to take control of the kiss, he let her lead. Unfortunately, she broke contact and moved back.

"Thank you for coming tonight. I was a total mess as you heard on the phone." She fiddled with the point of his collar. "Thank Heaven for Tess."

"Of course, I'd come. I'll stay till Daphne gets here." He looked at her. "She'll come home, right?"

"Yes." She swallowed. "Brett, all this," she fluttered her hand, "is kind of new to me." She shook her head. "It's really new to me. Robert and I—I get it—we were . . .we were just . . . Because now I . . .You . . ." She pulled in a breath. "I'm babbling." She covered her face with her hands. "I don't move very fast, and you . . ."

"Will pace myself to your speed." He tugged her hands down. "Okay?"

"Okay."

"How about that shrimp?"

Chapter 39

As she left the group of giggling Girl Scouts for the last time, a persistent ringing pulled Mary Wade out of her dreamy musings about Brett. She retrieved the phone from the cup holder and checked the screen. Her parents. Not the interruption she'd hoped for.

"Hi, Mom. Dad. What's up? I'm driving, so you're on speaker." Make it quick, please. Brett daydreams are calling.

"Great news, honey. We're coming to a retreat in Charlotte. This weekend."

Her stomach sank with something akin to dread. "What?"

"I knew you'd be excited. A church member gave us the whole package, including the hotel room. They can't use it, so he's gifting us. Aren't we blessed?"

"Yeah, sure." Her head spun with the significance of this announcement. She hadn't planned to share the news of the shop's closing until later. Much later. Like maybe not until she could start up again. And Brett. She wasn't ready to share him with the family yet. How would she maneuver this weekend?

"What's up, sweetie? Is something wrong?"

"No. Where're you staying? What's your schedule? Maybe we could have lunch?"

"We'll be over near the airport. Instead of lunch, what about dinner Saturday night?"

⁋⁋❧❧

"Why do you have to cancel for Saturday night?" Disappointment pooled in Brett's chest. An undercurrent laced Mary Wade's announcement, but he couldn't label it yet. He wasn't ready to give up seeing her this weekend. "Maybe we can change the time."

"No, something's come up for the whole night."

A secret? Maybe he could use his interviewing skills to ferret out the problem. "So you don't want to see me Saturday."

"I didn't say that." A sigh filled the phone. "My parents are here for a retreat. They want to have dinner Saturday night."

"Ah. And you don't want me to meet them."

"Well, when you put it like that . . .but, no. I don't want the three of you together yet."

He straightened a stack of papers on his desk. "You know, if I didn't have such a hardy constitution, I might be crushed by not being invited to the family dinner."

"I'm doing you a favor. Believe me."

"You've met my grandmother."

"Gigi's cool and not judgmental and supportive of you and loves you unconditionally."

"But from my perspective, she's nosy, can be manipulative—remember Asheville—and even stubborn at times. I'm sure your parents are nice people, but if you're ashamed of our relationship . . ." He let the words trail off, waiting.

She growled. "You know it's not that, and who's being manipulative now?"

He laughed. "Guilty. I'd like to meet your parents. I could help deflect any uncomfortable topics of conversation. I could regale them with law enforcement tales, but if you'd rather take this one solo, I understand, and call dibs for Sunday."

"Having dinner with them sounds so easy the way you describe it."

Silence. He toyed with his pen, biding his time.

"They'll pepper you with questions. You think Gigi's nosy? They'll make you spill things you've forgotten about."

"Have you forgotten I've worked undercover? I know how to handle people. What time do I pick you up?"

"Don't forget I warned you."

"What time?"

"If we do Saturday night, do we still get Sunday?"

Success. He smiled into the phone. "Count on it."

ഇന്ദ്രൻ

Keeping her shoulder still and hoping her parents in the back seat wouldn't notice, Mary Wade sneaked her hand over the console to capture Brett's free hand as he drove back to her house after dinner. He squeezed her fingers and grinned as he kept his focus on the street. Gratitude for this man, this special gift, pricked her heart. True to his word, he'd answered every question, deflected every unflattering statement, complimented her creativity and hard work. He'd been her champion.

When the news of the booth's closing came to light, Brett allowed the discussion to last for only a few minutes, enough to give the details, then changed the subject. Every time her father mentioned the booth, Brett steered the conversation to a positive light. No rent, growing Internet sales, the pros of working from home. He shielded every negative, and she let him while she licked her spoon clean of her chocolate torte.

Why had she tried to keep him from the dinner? Letting someone else fight for her was an intoxicating sensation. Especially someone so capable, so strong, so emphatically on her side.

And gorgeous. Don't forget gorgeous.

She squeezed his hand back. Two more stoplights, two hugs and "good nights," then she and Brett could spend some time together until Daphne arrived home.

"What time do you leave tomorrow, Mom?"

"The retreat is over at noon. We plan to have the car packed and leave immediately. That way we'll be able to share about our experiences at the evening service tomorrow night."

"You won't be too exhausted after the drive back?"

"Oh, no. We'll be excited to talk about the weekend."

Brett slowed to a stop by her driveway and parked on the cul-de-sac. As the men shook hands near her parents' car, her father nodded to Mary Wade's. "Hey, looks like a flat tire, girl."

Mary Wade shifted from her mom's hug to investigate. "Ooh, it is flat. No worries. I know how to change it, and I have a spare."

"The other one's flat too." Her mom bent toward the other side of the car.

Brett peered at both tires and retrieved his cell phone from his pocket. He leaned close to her. "They've been slashed. I'm calling it in."

She clutched at his sleeve. "Wait. Not yet. Let them leave first."

"Mary Wade, these tires've been cut. This is deliberate. I thought you lived in a safe neighborhood." Her dad made his way to the front of the car.

Brett shook his head. "Too late. We need to get the boys here."

"They left the front two alone, but the others are definitely cut. On purpose." Her father fastened his hands to his hips. "Mary Wade, you're coming with us. You're not staying here another night. All your business is online now? Good. You don't need to live here. You can come home with us."

"This house is my home. I am safe. I have a life here, and I'm not picking up and running home." Tears clogged her throat, forbidding more arguments. Brett gathered her to him, and his solid presence calmed her.

His fingers found the back of her neck. "Mr. Kimball, I realize your concern, but I'm calling in more surveillance on the neighborhood and, in particular, her house."

"More surveillance?"

She stiffened and shook her head against his chest.

"I meant more presence, more cop cars cruising through, more eyes on her house."

Her mother stepped closer to the couple. "Honey, please think about this. Stay with us tonight at the hotel at least. We can think better in the morning."

"No, Mom. I'll be fine. This is a nuisance. Another bill to whack at my budget, but I'm fine."

"I can stay the night for added protection."

Two heads with wide open mouths shot toward Brett. Mary Wade suppressed a giggle.

"On the couch, of course."

"Daphne will be home in a while, Dad."

Peter Kimball loosened his tie. "I'm not simpleminded. You've got three cars in this driveway, and your car, the one in the middle, is the only one to be hit. Seems like there's more to this story."

"Mr. Kimball—"

"Dad." The word sounded like a pleading sigh. How could she defuse this situation without lying or totally ignoring her dad's question? "This neighborhood is safe, but I've experience a couple of things lately that've been a little creepy."

"What do you mean exactly?"

"A note on my windshield, a box of frogs on the front stoop. Kinda like the opposite of a secret admirer." No one appreciated her attempt at humor. "So the neighborhood has nothing to do with what's happening."

"We're investigating the situation." Again, Brett defended. "We'll get to the bottom of it."

"Situation? Don't you mean crime?" Her father reached for her forearm. "I insist you come with us."

How long would she have to butt heads with her father? She respected him, but they viewed almost everything from different perspectives. She turned out of Brett's arms and faced him. "Daddy, I appreciate that you love me and want to protect me." He did love her, but on his terms, without considering her thoughts and desires. "You can insist, but as an adult, I'm declining to leave my house tonight."

A squad car eased to a stop, leaving the driveway unblocked, and two patrol officers exited.

"Hello again, Ms. Kimball."

Great. Just what she needed in front of her parents. Remembered by a policeman.

xxxx

On Sunday morning, the coffeemaker dripped java as slowly as cool molasses. Mary Wade turned from her vigil in front of the carafe and peered through the front window, passed a sleeping Jeffrey jackknifed on the couch. Her stubborn parents had remained planted in her front yard until Brett bid them all good night, but Jeffrey stretched out, with his legs hanging over the arm, on the couch. Sweet Jeffrey.

A glint from the streetlight caught her eye. She focused through the dim early dawn light and gasped. Brett's SUV manned the front of her driveway like a sentry. Did he sleep in his car?

She grabbed two mugs from the cabinet and the carafe from the still-sputtering machine. She dosed one mug with sugar and left the other black. Tiptoeing by her sleeping guest, she prayed a quick "thank you" prayer for Brett and Jeffrey.

Brett startled upright at her knock.

"Good morning."

He unlocked the doors and swiped his face. "Finally. Kinda felt like daybreak was only a rumor." He accepted the mug with a salute. "You bringing me this is a great way to start the day. Thank you."

"Thank you for staying here all night. I can't believe you

did. You didn't have to. I saw a police car circle through a couple of times before we turned in. And Jeffrey stayed on the couch."

"I know. He texted me." He sipped the coffee. "I'd made up my mind to stay before your parents left."

"Sorry about them. They—"

"They're being parents. They have a right to be concerned about you."

"But he doesn't have a right to dictate, especially when I—"

"When you what?"

"I'm one payment away from paying him back for every cent of tuition he paid for me."

"That's the cause of your tight budget?"

"And the sluggish economy. And a couple of surprises with home ownership. And now the necessity of two new tires."

He tilted his head. "That's quite an accomplishment. Among others. Good job."

"Thank you."

"Listen." He cleared his throat. "I'm going to have to ask for a rain check this afternoon. I'm not really on the case since your house is technically in police jurisdiction, but I can't afford to have impaired thinking while I'm doing my own investigation of your stalker. Being with you is too distracting."

Her heart fluttered, not in a good way. "But an investigation could take months." She tightened her hands around her mug. "We don't have any leads at all."

Brett grinned. "Your impatience is a good incentive to solve the mystery sooner than later." He covered her knee with his hand, warm from his coffee mug, and positioned his face for complete eye contact. "But until then, I need to be sharp, one hundred percent. Not thinking about what we did last night or what we're gonna do tomorrow."

Was this a brush-off? Something akin to a let's-just-be-friends talk? Were her parents too direct and hardnosed last night?

Was being with her simply too exhausting with kidnappers and bullets and crazy people leaving frogs on her doorstep? Was he just being kind last night when he directed the conversation clear of her parents' negativity?

He was a kind man. Did kindness propel him to sleep twisted like a pretzel in his car or was that just his protector personality kicking in?

No, no, no. Stop thinking negative thoughts. He's still interested, smiling across the console.

"Mary Wade, where'd you go? What's going on up there?" He tapped her temple.

"You haven't decided this," she twirled her finger between the two of them, "is too much? Maybe too hard or too crazy?"

He captured her hand and set his mug on the dashboard. "You can't be asking me that question. I just slept in my car in front of your house. Maybe if my back could talk it'd convince you. Or my feet, which, by the way, are still asleep." He rotated both ankles and then shifted to face her.

Cradling her face in his hands, he waited for her full attention. "Mary Wade, I'm not intimidated by hard things. You're worth it. We're gonna get through this, but I'm not jeopardizing the investigation by being stupid. I'm pulling back, not because I don't want to see you but because it's the thing to do." He dropped his gaze and rubbed his thumb over her lips. "Do you understand?"

"Yes."

"Also," he tucked her hair behind both ears and retrieved his mug, "you might see more cruisers and unmarked cars through here for the next few days. I called in a few favors. Wish I could get a guard to set up camp here, but the department doesn't have the manpower or the budget right now." He finished the coffee. "Thanks again for the good morning visit. Best part of my day, for sure." He handed her the mug. "You need to get back inside, and I need to get the creaks out of this back." He stretched, flattening his hands against the roof.

As she reached for the door handle, he stopped her. "Call me if anything comes up. And I mean anything. I'll talk to you later, okay?"

She nodded and concentrating on stifling the missing-him feeling growing in her chest.

Chapter 40

Mary Wade headed for the craft warehouse. Three days of Brett's self-imposed exile from her wore on her emotions. The almost constant parade of police vehicles, unmarked or not, in the cul-de-sac reminded her of possible danger. Part of her was grateful for the extra protection, but another part chafed. She'd postponed the crochet ladies' weekly meeting. Cabin fever reigned. She needed a quick break.

Straying from the set schedule once wouldn't upset protocol, would it? For a visit with Jack? She hadn't seen him in weeks.

As she parked in her favorite spot at the warehouse, guilt brushed against her shoulder. The security measures had been put in place to protect her from the crazy person who wanted to harm her, but she needed to see Jack. She'd just go in for five minutes.

Guilt tapped again. She pulled out her phone and texted Daphne her location and possible ETA back home. Good. She'd be home before her favorite TV show began.

🙤🙤🙦🙦

Brett didn't recognize the number on his cell. "Davis here."

"Thank God, Brett. This is Daphne. Mary Wade should've been home a half hour ago. She texted me she was visiting Jack at the warehouse, but she's not here yet, and she's not answering her phone."

"She went—?" Brett bit off a word he'd apologize for later. "Okay. I'm on it. Let me know if you hear from her." He made a U-turn and headed for Mary Wade.

God, keep her safe. Let this be a false alarm.

As he spun into the warehouse parking lot, he spotted her car along with two others. He parked beside hers and grabbed his nine-millimeter. Instead of rushing into the building, he forced himself to think. He'd rushed into the cabin and headlong into an ambush.

Father in Heaven, give me wisdom. Help me to think quick and straight. If Mary Wade's in trouble, help me save her.

Jack's booth was located near the front of the warehouse.

Please let the back door be unlocked.

At a side door, he fingered his pistol and slowly turned the knob. The first answered prayer.

Thank you, God.

Holding his breath, he slipped into the massive space cut up with partitions. A maze of craft items and walkways. His stomach clenched. Plenty of places for someone to hide. He closed the door without a sound and waited, listening. An urgent voice, angry but controlled, carried over the gauzy wreaths, knitted scarves, and homemade soaps. Another voice, softer and calm, answered, joined by a deeper one. Mary Wade and Jack.

Brett crept closer to the voices.

"I'm sorry, Gwen. I didn't know about your relationship with Brett. He never said—"

"Of course, you didn't give him the chance to tell you. You wiled him with your green eyes and your sprained foot. He loves to help people. I know. When Mr. Jeepers died, he brought me a box of chocolate turtles, my favorite. That's when I knew for sure he returned my feelings."

"So you started going out with him after Mr. Jeepers, was he a . . . a neighbor? You started going out with him after Mr. Jeepers died?"

"No and no. Mr. Jeepers was my cat." The last word ended on a sob. "Had been for seventeen years. Seventeen years."

Brett edged behind the partition across from Jack's booth, willed him to look across the aisle and make eye contact. Bingo. Gwen faced Jack and Mary Wade, wearing a gray cape. The folds of the garment hid her hands. Not good. Did she have a gun?

"So after your cat died, Brett asked you out?"

"No, I said. Because he went undercover. But I knew he'd be back, and then everything'd be great." Gwen turned to Jack. "But she showed up and ruined everything. He broke his cover for her."

"But, Gwen, that just shows how professional and kind he is. He broke his cover to save someone. Those men were really going to hurt me. Brett didn't let them do that."

Gwen snorted. "Yeah, Brett is kind and good and smart. And you are the exact opposite. You couldn't figure out a clue if it hit you in the face. If you'd heeded my note on your windshield, you wouldn't have got the frogs. If you'd heeded the frogs, you wouldn't have to buy two new tires."

"I didn't know you wanted me to stop seeing him."

"Because you're so stupid."

"I'm not seeing him now."

"You're lying because you think that's what I want to hear."

"It's true. He said he needed to pull back for a while. I know what that means, Gwen. Believe me, I've heard different versions of the same song. 'Let's be friends,' or 'Let's slow down.' They all mean the same thing. See ya later. I haven't seen him since this weekend." Mary Wade crossed her heart. "I promise I haven't seen him."

Gwen shook her head.

"So are you here to tell Mary Wade to back off in person? And how did you know you'd find her here?" Jack leaned against a stool, his hands clasped loosely in front of him but his eyes sharp.

Another snort. "She's so stupid. I put a tracker device on her back fender when I slashed her tires. I followed her here."

"You're right. I don't know anything about law enforcement. Probably one of the reasons Brett decided to cool things." Mary Wade extended her hand to Gwen. "I'm so sorry I hurt you. I'm really not the kind of girl who steals someone's sweetheart."

What was she doing? Gwen could pull out a gun from her pocket. Brett strained to see her face, but her back was to him.

"He really is a sweetheart, isn't he?" Gwen's voice softened, a husky quality exchanged the anger.

"Yes, he is. He saved my life, Gwen, and I'm so thankful for him." Mary Wade stepped forward a half step. Brett's heart rate accelerated. What was she doing? "But I don't want to hurt you. Please, please accept my apology."

Brett raised his gun. Jack moved his head slightly to the left, then back to the right. No gun? Frustration boiled in his gut. *Help me out here, God. What do I do?*

Trust Jack. He's got eyes on her.

He lowered his hand. Jack's chin declined, then raised.

"I've got water bottles in the kitchen." Jack smiled at Gwen and raised his eyebrows. "Would you like one?"

Her shoulders drooped and began to shake. "Why are you being nice to me? I wasn't nice to you." Her voice was thick and whiny.

Mary Wade took another step toward the crumbling woman. "No, you weren't. But we all make mistakes, Gwen. Like I did with you." Another step. "I'm sorry. Can we start over?" She touched Gwen's forearm.

Brett moved from behind the partition, inched slowly and silently toward Gwen's back.

Mary Wade slid her arm around the sobbing woman. "I forgive you for not being nice. Can you forgive me, please?"

The woman sobbed harder, her forehead pressing into Mary Wade.

Mary Wade's eyes widened when she spotted Brett a few yards away in the middle of the aisle. "It's okay, Gwen. We're going to be fine, right?"

Jack nodded to Brett. "I'll get some water, ladies." As he passed Brett, Jack whispered, "Call an ambulance. Pysch evaluation." Jack continued to the kitchen. Brett kept his eyes on Gwen's back but grabbed his phone.

A shot exploded the silence of the warehouse.

Brett scrambled for Mary Wade. Gwen sprawled on the floor at Mary Wade's feet. Jack raced back to them and knelt beside Gwen, looking for a pulse. "What happened?"

Mary Wade mumbled against Brett's chest. "She moved her arm. I thought—to give me a hug. She just dropped to the floor."

"She's alive. It's faint, but I feel it."

"Thank God."

Yes. Thank God. Brett crushed Mary Wade to him.

Jack pushed back the folds of the cape. "The bullet wound's in her chest. Must've just missed her heart."

Mary Wade trembled in his arms, quiet. The tears would come later.

Epilogue

"Okay, so we're not going by Gigi's beforehand, but how about after we check out the cabin?" Mary Wade jiggled Brett's hand in hers. He'd been distracted all morning. "Hey, is everything all right? I don't think you're even here."

Brett swung his gaze from the windshield. "Oh, I'm here. For sure." He extricated his hand and swiped his jaw. "Just thinking about spending the rest of the day with you." He directed his most lethal grin her way and stretched his arm along her shoulders, massaged the base of her neck. "How did I get so lucky?"

She was the lucky one. Or really blessed was a more accurate adjective. Four months of being with Brett with nothing more stressful than deciding between Italian or Thai or Southern Fusion when they went out certainly qualified as blessed. To some eyes, their dates of sketching and whittling or board games or a classic movie at home might appear boring, but to her, they were blissfully peaceful with just enough spice to rev her heart and melt her bones.

"I'm getting distinct vibes your mind is elsewhere, although I like what your fingers are doing." A shiver tripped though her insides as he stroked her collarbone. "Something up with the case?"

"No. Everything's fine. Once Dusty and Skeet understood the enormity of their situation, they started singing all kinds of songs. The prosecutor is going through the case, making sure every 't' is crossed, every 'i' is dotted, but it looks pretty solid for a slam dunk."

"Great."

"How's Gwen? You know, you don't have to keep visiting her."

"I know, but I want to in a weird sort of way. She's better. She's smiled at me a couple of times. Losing her favorite aunt, her next-door neighbor, and her cat in the space of three months just pushed her over the edge. Your chocolate gift was a lifeline she clung to while she manufactured the relationship between you two."

"The whole thing is still a little creepy. Good for you for rising above." He slowed and turned into the driveway. Reds and golds of autumn replaced the pinks and purples of last summer. "Here we are. Wait. I'll get that door for you."

He wiped his hands on his khakis as she climbed out of his SUV, fallen leaves crinkling under their feet. "How do you feel about coming back here?" They rounded the hood of the SUV and headed for the cabin.

She pulled the front edges of her jacket together. "I'm not sure. I'm glad Gigi hasn't moved forward with selling. This place is so special to your family. Maybe it can be special again."

Brett sighed. "I hope so. She hasn't been here since . . . since—you know. I checked on it a couple of times, but I promised we'd come up today and—"

She grabbed his hand, unusually chilled, and leaned into his side. "I'm fine. You and Gigi experienced most of the hurt. If she needs to sell it to move forward, it's her right. I just didn't want her to do something rash immediately afterward."

"Gigi's never rash. She knows her own mind." At the top of the steps, he dropped to the porch and tugged her hand. "Let's sit for a minute." When she sat beside him, he pushed off and knelt on the steps in front of her.

He displayed a fabric box on his palm.

310

Nerve endings flashed on high alert. She met his gaze.

"Gigi wasn't sure about this plan." He shook his head. "Not the plan exactly. The location." He cleared his throat. "But I'm hoping we can erase the horrible memories here. Start to make good ones."

"We have some pretty good memories here already." Her voice sounded light, breathy, like her insides felt.

He smiled.

The relief and love shining up at her somersaulted her heart. "Yeah, we do."

She pressed her fingertips to her knees, waiting for him to continue.

He covered both her hands with his free one. "Mary Wade, ours hasn't been a conventional relationship to say the least. What started out as an epic disaster and kinda continued that way for months has turned into the best thing." He took a deep breath. "I like who I am when I'm with you. Your sweet example has led me back to a right relationship with God." He cleared his throat. "I love sitting and carving while you sketch. I love that you surprise me." He grinned at her. "I love kissing you."

Heat began a slow rise up her neck.

"I want to keep doing those things with you and more." He opened the box to reveal a vintage silver solitaire. Delicate scroll work on either side showcased a brilliant cut diamond twinkling against a bed of navy blue velvet.

She gasped. "Brett, it's gorgeous."

"I hope you'll accept it and wear it as my friend, my partner, my confidant, my wife. For the rest of my life, Mary Wade. I love you. Please marry me?"

She bypassed the exquisite piece of jewelry and grabbed his collar, pulling him to her and locking her lips on his.

He rose to standing with her. Laughter rumbled from somewhere deep inside him. "Can I take that as a yes?"

The difference in the steps put her eye to eye with him. "Yes." She pulled him back to her.

Brett stopped short. "Wait. Much as I hate to stop you, let's put this where it belongs, okay?"

She held her hand, fingers splayed to accept the treasure. "It's beautiful."

He slipped it over her knuckle and centered it on her finger. "It was Gigi's. She's so excited for you to have it."

"That makes it even more special."

"Here's something else." He reached behind him and extracted an envelope. "It's a note from your father."

She shook her head. "Later." She leaned toward him again.

He brushed her lips in a quick appeasement. "No. It might be important. When I called to ask permission—"

"You called for permission?"

"Yeah, I wanted to ask in person, but I couldn't take time from work. When he gave me permission, he asked me to give you a letter he'd send. He wanted you to have it at the proposal." He handed it to her.

She frowned. She didn't want to spoil this special moment. She wanted Brett to herself to think about their future, not hear disapproval from her parents.

"Go ahead and open it."

She found two pieces of paper inside. A note with her dad's distinctive handwriting and another slip. She read the few lines, bit her lip, then blinked back tears.

"Mary Wade?"

She showed him the smaller paper. "It's a deposit slip. It's all the tuition money. He put every payment in an account for me. He says I can use it for a down payment on a shop. Or a house. Or for whatever I want. He says he's proud of me." A lone tear tracked down her cheek. "I can't believe it. Mom and Dad both signed it." Another tear chased the first.

Brett smoothed away the trail with his thumb. "Hey. No tears. This is a happy time."

She nodded and heard an engine. A car, Gigi's car, coasted to a stop at the top of the driveway. Mary Wade chuckled.

He groaned.

Gigi strained to peer through the window and waved at them with both hands.

He swiped his jaw and shook his head. "I can't believe she's here."

"You can't? I can."

"You're right. If I could have done this without her knowing, I would have, but seeing as how she had the ring . . ."

"A very beautiful ring." She fluttered her fingers.

"So you like it?"

"I love it." She slid her hand up his chest, the diamond sparkling in the sunlight.

Brett cupped her cheek. "You know she loves you, right?"

"Good. Because I love her grandson."

"About time you said it out loud." And he lowered his head to her in front of Gigi, God, and everybody.

About time indeed.

Conversation Questions

1. Describe Mary Wade's personality. Would you characterize her as courageous, reserved, spontaneous, strong-willed? How does her personality affect the story? Brett thinks Mary Wade is a little ditzy at the beginning of the story—not locking the house door, riding her bike with flip flops. Is his characterization of her valid? Why or why not?

2. How does Mary Wade's personality change through the story?

3. Describe Brett's personality. What's his best characteristic? His worst?

4. Gun control is a hot topic. How did you feel about guns in this story? Were you surprised that Gigi has her concealed carry permit and drives with a gun under her seat?

5. Both Mary Wade and Brett enjoy creating with their hands. Talk about the importance of hobbies to a rich life.

6. Discuss Mary Wade and Tess's relationship. Did it feel authentic?

7. Gigi loves through food. What kinds of food do you eat when you want to feel loved? Do you know someone like Gigi?

8. Information from Mary Wade's website is used to hurt her. Discuss the ease of obtaining on-line information. Have you ever Googled yourself? Were your findings surprising, correct, or incorrect? How did seeing your personal information available for public viewing make you feel?

9. Mary Wade took a risk by opening her own business. What kind of risks have you taken, and what were the results?

10. Family is important throughout the novel. How did family affect both Mary Wade and Brett? How has your own family influenced your life?

11. Mary Wade struggles with parental expectations even though she's in her mid-twenties. Do you find the struggle to be real? Can you share a time when you disregarded your parents' wishes to go your own way? What were the results?

12. How did humor play a part in the story? Which funny scene was your favorite? Why? How do humor and drama showcase the characters?

13. What is the theme that runs throughout *Rescued Hearts*?

14. What is the tone of the story?

Other Books by
Hope Toler Doughterty

Irish Encounter

After almost three years of living under a fog of grief, Ellen Shepherd is ready for the next chapter in her life. Perhaps she'll find adventure during a visit to Galway. Her idea of excitement consists of exploring Ireland for yarn to feature in her shop back home, but the adventure awaiting her includes an edgy stranger who disrupts her tea time, challenges her belief system, and stirs up feelings she thought she'd buried with her husband.

After years of ignoring God, nursing anger, and stifling his grief, Payne Anderson isn't ready for the feelings a chance encounter with an enchanting stranger evokes. Though avoiding women and small talk has been his pattern, something about Ellen makes him want to seek her—and God again.

Can Ellen accept a new life different than the one she planned? Can Payne release his guilt and accept the peace he's longed for? Can they surrender their past pain and embrace healing together, or will fear and doubt ruin their second chance at happiness?

Mars ... With Venus Rising

A meddling horse, paper bag floors and a flying saucer on the town square. The little town of Mars has it all—including a brand new resident who might spell heartache for one of its own. Twenty-something Penn Davenport yearns for an exciting life in the big city and wants to shed the label of orphan that she's worn for years. To achieve that dream, she must pass the CPA exam then move away from the two aunts who reared her after her parents died in a plane crash. When John Townsend—full of life and the joy of living—moves to town, he rattles Penn's view of herself, her life, and her dreams... which isn't such a bad thing until she falls for him and discovers he's a pilot.